EDITED BY

MARY
OLSEN
KELLY

A FIRESIDE BOOK

Published by Simon & Schuster Inc.

New York   London   Toronto   Sydney

Tokyo   Singapore

THE
FIRESIDE
TREASURY
OF
LIGHT

Fireside
Simon & Schuster Building
Rockefeller Center
1230 Avenue of the Americas
New York, New York 10020

Introduction & Compilation Copyright © 1990 by
Mary Olsen Kelly

Designed by Black Angus Design Group
Manufactured in the United States of America

Library of Congress Cataloging in Publication Data
The Fireside treasury of light / edited by Mary Olsen Kelly.
    p.   cm.
"A Fireside book."
Includes bibliographical references.
1. New Age movement.   I. Kelly, Mary Olsen.
     BP605.N48F57   1990
  081—dc20   90—40629
               CIP
     ISBN 0-671-68505-8

BOMC offers recordings and compact discs, cassettes
and records. For information and catalog write to
BOMR, Camp Hill, PA 17012.

ACKNOWLEDGMENTS

Most of all, I want to thank my husband and everlasting love, Don Kelly, for his complete support and love, and for teaching me the meaning of true partnership. Thanks to Barbara Gess, the most wonderful dream editor. Profound gratitude to Diana and Paul von Welenetz for creating *The Inside Edge* so that I could hear the top authors, leaders, and visionaries speak about the New Age with passion and inspiration. And a deep thank you to Tim Piering, whose advice, teachings, and guidance I have treasured. And to Dorothy La for her spiritual and secretarial support.

At publishing companies all over the country, there are wonderful people working in the permissions departments who made this book a reality. I would like to especially thank Bea Hurwitz at Simon & Schuster, Joe Aiosa at Bantam, Carol Christiansen at Doubleday, Peter J. Wolverton at St. Martin's Press, Gerald Clow at Bear and Co., and Jose Arroyo at the Putnam Berkley Group, and all the other people who worked so hard. Their superhuman efforts helped me to arrange the permissions and legal contracts for these excerpts.

And thank you to the wonderful authors who wrote these books and gave their blessings to this anthology.

TABLE OF CONTENTS

INTRODUCTION

The Fireside Treasury of Light contains excerpts from the most important and meaningful books in the New Age—books that have changed people's lives, books that have profoundly affected our society, books that have set the courses of our thinking in new and exciting directions. Writers, thinkers, poets, spiritual masters, humanistic psychologists, revolutionaries, and shamans join here to give an indication of the diverse and varied elements of New Age thinking.

So if you want to know what this new type of "healing" is that you have heard about, the works of best-selling authors Bernie Siegel and Louise Hay are here to tell you. If you've wondered about the sudden interest in Southwestern design imagery, primitive artifacts, and folk art and music, Lynn Andrews, Michael Harner, and Sun Bear share their insights gained during adventures into shamanic worlds.

The leading thinkers in almost every area of this wide-ranging field are here to give you an easily accessible, entertaining introduction to this exciting new world view that has been labeled "The New Age."

More than just an anthology of the best writing in the field, this book is a collection of ideas and concepts that represent positive life-affirming values, intellectual breakthroughs, important topics, and passionate attitudes and concerns. This book has emerged as a transformative journey in itself, and one I think you will enjoy.

At the beginning of each of the eleven sections I've written a few introductory pages to set the stage and help you bring the diverse ideas into focus so you can see how they might apply in your own life. Of course, it was impossible to include excerpts from every important New Age book, so I have assembled a list of suggested reading to further whet your appetite. I hope the words of these revolutionary thinkers will set the wheels of your own mind turning, as they have mine.

Happy reading!

Mary Olsen Kelly.

SECTION ONE:

FOUNDATIONS OF THE NEW AGE

There is nothing new about the New Age. The principles and truths shared here are the same as those found in all of the great world religions and the words of saints, mystics, and philosophers throughout the ages. Truth is truth and the various paths portrayed in this book lead ultimately to the same destination: spiritual awakening, personal growth, enlightenment, or a sense of discovery of one's true self.

The New Age is really about people; people with a wide range of spiritual practices, disciplines, and interests. New Age practices and ideas draw from areas as diverse as transformative psychology, esoteric religion, holistic healing, Eastern philosophy, divination, crystals and gems, leading-edge science and physics, alternative medical practices, American transcendentalism, spiritual guides, channels and entities, world peace, and global, environmental change.

The term New Age has been used interchangeably with other terms, such as the Age of Aquarius, the Aquarian Conspiracy, the Golden Age, the Millennium, or the Promised Land. It is a label for a shift in consciousness that is taking place in millions of people worldwide.

There are many theories that attempt to explain the phenomenon. It is believed that the shift is taking place as a direct result of the need for it. Evolution is often preceded by crises, and takes place in response to a survival instinct. The state of our planet would certainly be considered a severe crisis. The widespread feeling is that there is a need for a new paradigm, a new way of viewing life and our planet, a new type of understanding, and new forms of action. As we face unprecedented environmental crises, such as the greenhouse effect and global warming, the deterioration of the ozone layer, and the devastation of the great rain forests (to name just a few), perhaps the human race will make an evolutionary jump into a new age of consciousness and transformation of the species.

The major themes of this new age of consciousness are such worthy concepts as personal and social transformation, self-improvement, and leading a quality life. New Age authors write about the importance of the link between mind and body, and about the value of addressing all areas of the human experience, including mental, physical, emotional, and spiritual. They acknowledge the profound inner peace that can be gained by developing a spiritual connection with one's "Higher Self."

Most people find the theories interesting but not nearly as relevant as questions that directly affect their own lives. How can metaphysics, new psychology, alternative medicine, leading-edge science, and new forms of ancient oracular traditions and practices improve the quality of our lives today? In the following sections, we will take a look at the writings of authors who are grappling with these questions.

The New Age is not an organized movement or group. It is average everyday people looking for ways to improve the quality of their own lives and, perhaps, make a difference in the world. It is natural for a community feeling to evolve whenever people share interests, and a loosely flowing world community has been evolving. But to think of the New Age as a political or organized movement or collective is incorrect.

The New Age embraces all religions and spiritual disciplines. There are many paths to God, and each person has the right to find the one that is appropriate for him or her. It is not necessary to abandon the beliefs or the religion one was raised in. To the contrary, people who have questioned and actively searched for a personal spiritual connection are often more appreciative of the efforts of organized religion.

People who are attracted to New Age ideas are average, successful, industrious types from all walks of life. Celebrities and grandmothers, scientists and doctors, television producers and schoolteachers alike are drawn toward the new discoveries, open-mindedness, and healing capabilities of many of the disciplines, systems, and technologies of the New Age. Perhaps these people have had a brush with death, loss, or tragedy that woke them up to the awareness that there is more to life than meets the naked eye.

Often, people who are seeking spiritual inspiration and connection have achieved a level of material success only to discover that they were left feeling empty and unfulfilled. These people continue to lead successful lives while launching a personal quest for God, Goddess, Universal Energy, Life Force, or some form of authentic spiritual contact with themselves and others.

Unlike the Beats of the fifties, or the Hippies of the sixties, New Age seekers are virtually unrecognizable by any outward appearance. In the early years, the wearing of a crystal or some type of ancient symbol as a pendant might have distinguished a person with New Age persuasions, but now those items have become fashionable as jewelry and are worn by the models on the pages of *Vogue* magazine and other high-fashion periodicals.

In his inspirational letter to the book review editor of the *Los Angeles*

Times, book publisher Jeremy Tarcher maintains that the New Age "offers reason to hope in a time of widespread fear." He adds:

> No one speaks for the entire New Age community. Within the movement there is no unanimity as to how to define it or even that it is sufficiently cohesive to be called a movement. However, I believe that the following statements would satisfy a very large portion of the people who associate themselves with it.
>
> First of all, don't think of the words *New Age* as representing a specific period of time. It is not the Ice Age, or the Renaissance. Rather, it is a metaphor for a process of striving for personal growth through which millions of people are trying to become more fully awake to their inherent capabilities.
>
> Like every other movement, whether religious, political, or economic, the New Age is ultimately based upon a group of assumptions about a place of humanity in the cosmos. At the heart of the New Age thought is the idea that humans have many levels of consciousness and that with the exception of a limited number of spiritual geniuses throughout history, we essentially live in a walking sleep that keeps us from a well-balanced, harmonious and direct relationship with God (however you understand that concept) nature, each other, and ourselves.
>
> Broadly stated, the world view is that:
>
> 1. The everyday world and our personal consciousness is a manifestation of a larger divine reality,
>
> 2. humans have a suppressed or hidden higher self that reflects or is connected to the divine element of the universe,
>
> 3. this Higher Self can be awakened and take a central part in the everyday life of the individual,
>
> 4. this awakening is the purpose or goal of human life.
>
> This set of ideas, which Aldous Huxley called "the Perennial Philosophy" is perhaps the oldest underlying spiritual perspective of humanity and is inherent, though often buried, in the practice of traditional religion. In this sense, the New Age is not new, it is ancient. (Jeremy P. Tarcher, *Los Angeles Times Book Review,* 2/7/88)

A quick glance at the previous century sheds some light on the changes in attitudes and world events that have helped pollinate the current flowering of New Age ideas and lifestyles. An entire encyclopedia could be written tracing the intellectual evolution of the current New Age movement. It is fascinating to research, and a brief overview of the major social and philosophical stirrings of the past century, including the inspirational work of early psychologists, philosophers, and spiritual leaders such as Madame Blavatsky, Gurdjieff, Paramahansa Yogananda, Carl Jung, and Krishnamurti, can shed some light on the phenomenon.

Theosophy was a spiritual organization formed in 1875, based on the Eastern influences of Hinduism and inspired by channeled messages from ascended masters. It was the creation of Madame Helena Petrovna Blavatsky (1831–1891), whose successors included Annie Besant and Alice Bailey. It is possible that Alice Bailey first coined the term "New Age," though she used it to refer to a messianic vision of the coming of a new prophet.

Gurdjieff was a Russian spiritual teacher who led a small group of disciples to France in 1922. There he started "The Institute of the Harmonious Development of Man." He taught about evolution and consciousness, wrote three books himself, and was the subject of many books by followers such as P. D. Ouspensky. Gurdjieff's teaching was timeless and universal, and groups that study "The Work" continue to thrive all over the world.

In the early part of the century, there was an influx of Eastern yogis and teachers to the United States. These swamis had a powerful effect on the minds of spiritual seekers of the time, and many created ashrams and educational centers in the West.

J. Krishnamurti was supposed to be the messiah, the reincarnation of Buddha. He was "discovered" in 1908, when he was thirteen, by founders of the Theosophical movement C. W. Leadbeater and Annie Besant. He was groomed by that organization to become the world savior. He resigned in 1929 and admonished his followers to be free and to look within for their own answers. Krishnamurti was the author of many excellent books that continue to be extremely popular.

Paramahansa Yogananda, the founder of the Self Realization Fellowship and author of *Autobiography of a Yogi*, first arrived in the United States in 1920. Meher-Baba, the silent avatar, arrived in the 1930s. Both of these men had a tremendous effect in the United States, drawing large audiences for their public speaking engagements and convincing those who were searching for a sense of the divine in their lives to meditate, look within, and develop states of inner peace.

There was a great interest in psychic phenomena in the thirties, and many instances of seances, table-tipping, and ouija board use and experimentation were reported.

In the forties the Western mind was filled by World War II and its horrors. At the end of the war, most Westerners just wanted to settle down in the suburbs and quietly raise a family. From a spiritual and cultural point of view, the fifties were important because of the artists and poets of that decade. The writing of the Beats, such as Jack Kerouac, Allen Ginsberg, and Gary Snyder, along with the profound insights and prolific writings of Alan Watts and other philosophers, fired up their generation. Many of the Beats were fascinated by Zen Buddhism. Thousands of young people were infused with a passion for adventure and the desire to explore new lifestyles. World War II had ended. New attitudes in the areas of art, literature, and alternative lifestyles set the stage for the powerful changes of the following decades.

The sixties had an enormous influence on the evolution of what is currently seen as New Age thought. Many leaders in the New Age arena were in their formative early twenties during the sixties and were deeply affected by the tremendous growth and turmoil of that decade. War, revolution, and death became the concerns of teenagers who were being drafted to fight in Vietnam while their friends back home marched for peace.

The sixties brought extreme confrontation with social, cultural, political, and personal values. This inspired an insatiable curiosity to learn more about one's inner life, and to satisfy some of the longing and need for spiritual connection that traditional religion hadn't been able to fill. Pioneers such as Timothy Leary, Ram Dass, and Ken Kesey stirred the waters of consciousness and rode the waves of enormous social, cultural, and political change. The transformative effects of the use of LSD and other psychedelic drugs, the music of the Beatles, and the chaos of the Vietnam War swirled in the wake of spiritual influences of the Woodstock Nation.

Alternative lifestyles and communes were pioneered by groups such as the Diggers, the Hog Farm, Stephen Gaskin's Monday Night Class, Ken Kesey's Merry Pranksters, Esalen, and Findhorn. Haight-Ashbury, Peace, Love, and Flower Power all led to the current movement of the nineties.

The fascination with new therapy techniques gave birth to new forms of psychology such as Fritz Perls's "Gestalt" at the Esalen Institute in Big Sur, California, and Abraham Maslow's "Self-actualization."

The seventies brought forth the women's movement, the consciousness movement, and the human potential movement. Often called the "Me Decade," the seventies were influenced by authors and thinkers such as Werner Erhard, a major contemporary American philosopher and the creator of the EST training and Stuart Emery, the inventor of Actualizations training and author of an eponymous book.

The seventies heralded the emergence of such prophets and psychics as Seth, Edgar Cayce, and Ruth Montgomery. The field of parapsychology was full of exciting discoveries, such as telekinesis, human auras, and healing energies that could actually be scientifically charted. While testing psychic healer Rosylyn Breuer, scientist and skeptic Dr. Valerie Hunt of UCLA made discoveries about fields of energy that she termed "mind fields." Uri Geller attracted media attention with his widely publicized telekinetic abilities. Suddenly, millions of Americans knew about spoon-bending and other psychic abilities.

The eighties turned this cultural and psychological tide toward issues of spiritual evolution, global change, and healing the planet while we heal ourselves. The eighties became known by various descriptions, ranging from the "Greed Decade" to the "We Decade." The latter reflected the growing participation in charitable activities such as the rock stars' "We Are the World" attempt at ending hunger in Ethiopia.

The eighties also brought an explosion of new ideas in books such as Marilyn Ferguson's *The Aquarian Conspiracy* and Jean Houston's *The Possible Human*. These powerful books asked questions and proposed new theories about human consciousness that fired the imaginations of readers all over the country. These authors and many others inspired readers to conduct in-depth programs of self-exploration.

The field of medicine was waking up to discoveries in a new area: psycho-neuro-immunology, pioneered by medical experts such as Dr. Carl Simonton, Dr. Bernie Siegel, and writer/healer Norman Cousins. Meanwhile, mounting concern for the planet and the environment brought new attention to global issues. The AIDS epidemic and cancer research studies gave many people an opportunity to explore new concepts in self-healing introduced by authors such as Louise Hay.

The national obsession with personal transformation spawned forms of new psychology and state-of-the-art technologies such as Neuro Linguistic Programming (NLP), discovered by John Grinder and Richard Bandler while they studied the inspired counseling work of Dr. Milton Erikson.

Lifespring, Insight, and other transformational seminars continued to teach personal responsibility and integrity to thousands of participants. Dr. Leo Buscaglia became a best-selling author specializing in the psychology of *love*. Dr. David Viscott used his "Viscott Method" of psychology on National Talk radio, helping millions of listeners to understand their feelings and handle their lives.

Books were selling in record numbers on such topics as "Sacred Sexuality," "Channeling," "Crystals," and "Death and Dying." Suddenly masses of people were interested in new ideas about their bodies and the connections between mental and physical fitness.

The theories of Jose Arguelles on the Mayan calendar created a national phenomenon in August 1987 called the Harmonic Convergence. In "power spots" such as Taos, Mount Shasta, South America, and Hawaii, thousands gathered to meditate, chant, and lend their energy to planetary healing. As more and more people became aware of their personal growth, they began to seek more tools and technologies for change. The adventure of growth and self-knowledge proved exhilarating to thousands who avidly supported the books, workshops, and products associated with the positive changes they observed in themselves.

An entire industry was spawned with big trade shows and expos such as the famous "Whole Life Expo" held in Los Angeles, San Francisco, and New York every year. Mind, body, and spirit festivals have become very popular and are an excellent place to purchase crystals, oracular devices, and musical instruments ranging from imported "Tibetan Temple Bells" to "Crystal Singing Bowls." New Age consumers practice the art of, in the words of Ram Dass, "Spiritual Materialism," to a high degree.

The media have landed on this aspect of the New Age with astonishing fury. And there is no doubt that some merchants in spirituality are exploiting a "good thing," just as in any other area of American business. But many New Age businesses are providing quality materials designed to heal and awaken others. And many have altruistic mission statements like "Making a difference in the world," "Promoting world peace," or "Helping to save the Amazon rain forest." They seek ultimately to end the tide of war and destruction that threatens all of our lives.

The books included in this section have helped to pioneer this new world view and build or support the foundations of the New Age. As a result of many of these works, the New Age has become part of our daily lives. The concepts have become integrated into mainstream health and medicine, psychology and relationships, and even business and finance. The works of New Age authors have become popular best-sellers as the principles cross over into all areas of our culture. The New Age has provided powerful ideas that get people thinking in new ways and open doors to positive change.

LIVING IN THE LIGHT

By
SHAKTI GAWAIN

A NEW WAY OF LIFE

We are living in a very exciting and powerful time. On the deepest level of consciousness, a radical spiritual transformation is taking place. I believe that, on a worldwide level, we are being challenged to let go of our present way of life and create an entirely new one. We are, in fact, in the process of destroying our old world and building a new world in its place.

The old world was based on an external focus—having lost our fundamental spiritual connection, we have believed that the material world was the only reality. Thus, feeling essentially lost, empty, and alone, we have continually attempted to find happiness and fulfillment through external "things"—money, material possessions, relationships, work, fame, good deeds, food or drugs.

The new world is being built as we open to the higher power of the universe within us and consciously allow that creative energy to move through us. As each of us connects with our inner spiritual awareness, we learn that the creative power of the universe is within us. We also learn that we can create our own reality and take responsibility for doing so. The change begins within each individual, but as more and more individuals are transformed, the mass consciousness is increasingly affected.

My observation that a profound transformation of consciousness is taking place in our world at this time is based on the changes I see within myself, those around me, and in our society. It is affirmed by feedback I receive from thousands of people I work with all over the world.

Living in the Light is about this transformation of consciousness within each individual and in the world. My use of the terms "old world" and "new world" throughout the book refer to the old way of life that we are leaving behind and the new one that we are creating.

For many people, this time may be distressing, because the world situation and/or our personal lives may seem to be going from bad to worse. It's as if many things that used to work are not working any more. I believe things *are* falling apart and will continue to do so with even greater intensity, but I do not feel this is negative. It will only be upsetting to the degree that we are emotionally attached to our *old way of living* and steadfastly follow old patterns, rather than trying to open our eyes to the profound changes that are occurring.

Paradoxical as it may seem, these changes are the most credible blessing that any of us could possibly imagine. The simple truth is that the old way of life that we have been following for centuries does not work. It has never brought us the deep fulfillment, satisfaction, and joy that we have always sought. Of course some people have led relatively happy lives (although far more, I'm afraid, have led relatively disillusioned, painful, and unfulfilling lives). Even the happiest of lives in the old world cannot compare to the depth of fulness and bliss that will be possible at the higher level of consciousness available in the new world.

It's as if we've been in school for our entire lives, receiving an education that teaches the exact opposite of the way the university actually functions. We try to make things work as we've been taught, and we may even enjoy some degree of success, but for the most of us things never seem to work out as well as we had hoped. That perfect relationship never materializes, or if it does, it soon sours or fades away. Or it may seem as though there is never quite enough money; we never feel truly secure or abundant. Perhaps we don't get the appreciation, recognition, or success that we want. Even if we do achieve some of these things, we still may suffer from a vague sense that there must be something more, some deeper meaning.

THE AQUARIAN CONSPIRACY

By
MARILYN FERGUSON

THE CONSPIRACY

A leaderless but powerful network is working to bring about radical change in the United States. Its members have broken with certain key elements of Western thought, and they may even have broken continuity with history.

This network is the Aquarian Conspiracy. It is a conspiracy without a political doctrine. Without a manifesto. With conspirators who seek power only to disperse it, and whose strategies are pragmatic, even scientific, but whose perspective sounds so mystical that they hesitate to discuss it. Activists asking different kinds of questions, challenging the establishment from within.

Broader than reform, deeper than revolution, this benign conspiracy for a new human agenda has triggered the most rapid cultural realignment in history. The great shuddering, irrevocable shift overtaking us is not a new political, religious, or philosophical system. It is a new mind—the ascendance of a startling worldview that gathers into its framework breakthrough science and insights from earliest recorded thought.

The Aquarian Conspirators range across all levels of income and education, from humblest to the highest. There are schoolteachers and office workers, famous scientists, government officials and lawmakers, artists and millionaires, taxi drivers and celebrities, leaders in medicine, education, law, psychology. Some are open in their advocacy, and their names may be familiar. Others are more quiet about their involvement, believing they can be more effective if they are not identified with ideas that have all too often been misunderstood.

There are legions of conspirators. They are in corporations, universities and hospitals, on the faculties of public schools, in factories and doctors' offices, in state and federal agencies, on city councils and the White House staff, in state legislatures, in volunteer organizations, in virtually all arenas of policy-making in the country.

Whatever their station or sophistication, the conspirators are linked, made kindred by their inner discoveries and earthquakes. You can break through old limits, past inertia and fear, to levels of fulfillment that once seemed impossible ... to richness of choice, freedom, human closeness. You can be more productive, confident, comfortable with insecurity. Problems can be experienced as challenges, a chance for renewal, rather than stress. Habitual defensiveness and worry can fall away. *It can all be otherwise.*

In the beginning, certainly most did not set out to change society. In that sense, it is an unlikely kind of conspiracy. But they found that their *lives* had become revolutions. Once a personal change began in earnest, they found themselves rethinking everything, examining old assumptions, looking anew at their work and relationships, health, political power and "experts," goals and values.

They have coalesced into small groups in every town and institution. They have formed what one called "national non-organizations." Some conspirators are keenly aware of the national, even international, scope of the movement and are active in linking others. They are at once antennae and transmitters, both listening and communicating. They amplify the activities of the conspiracy by networking and pamphleteering, articulating the new options through books, lectures, school curricula, even Congressional hearings and the national media.

Others have centered their activity within their specialty, forming groups within existing organizations and institutions, exposing their co-workers to new ideas, often calling on the larger network for support, feedback, back-up information.

And there are millions of others who have never thought of themselves as part of a conspiracy but sense that their experiences and their struggle are part of something bigger, a larger social transformation that is increasingly visible if you know where to look. They are typically unaware of the national networks and their influence in high places; they may have found only one or two kindred spirits in their workplace, neighborhood or circle of friends. Yet even in small groups—twos and threes, eights and tens—they are having their impact.

You will look in vain for affiliations in traditional forms: political parties, ideological groups, clubs, or fraternal organizations. You find instead little clusters and loose networks. There are tens of thousands of entry points to this conspiracy. Wherever people share experiences, they connect sooner or later with each other and eventually with larger circles. Each day their number grows.

NEW MIND, NEW WORLD

Not even the Renaissance has promised such a radical renewal; as we have seen, we are linked by our travels and technology, increasingly aware of each other, open to each other. In growing numbers we are finding how people can enrich and empower one another, we are more sensitive to our place in nature, we are learning how the brain transforms pain and conflict, and we have more respect for the wholeness of the self, as the matrix of health. From science and from the spiritual experience of millions, we are discovering our capacity for endless awakenings in a universe of endless surprises.

At first glance, it may seem hopelessly utopian to imagine that the world can resolve its desperate problems. Each year fifteen million die in starvation and many more live in unrelenting hunger; every ninety seconds the nations of the world spend one million dollars on armaments; every peace is an uneasy peace; the planet has been plundered of many of its nonrenewable resources. Yet there have been remarkable advances as well. Just since the end of World War II, thirty-two countries with 40 percent of the world's population have overcome their problems of food scarcity; China is becoming essentially self-sufficient and has controlled its once-overwhelming population growth; there is a net gain in world literacy and in populist governments; concern for human rights has become a stubborn international issue.

We have had a profound paradigm shift about the Whole Earth. We know it now as a jewel in space, a fragile water planet. And we have seen that it has no natural borders. It is not the globe of our school days with its many colored nations.

We have discovered our interdependence in other ways, too. An insurrection or crop failure in a distant country can signal change in our daily lives. The old ways are untenable. All countries are economically and ecologically involved with each other, politically enmeshed. The old gods of isolationism and nationalism are tumbling, artifacts like the stone dieties of Easter Island.

We are learning to approach problems differently, knowing that most of the world's crises grew out of the old paradigm—the forms, structures, and beliefs of an obsolete understanding of reality. Now we can seek answers outside the old frameworks, ask new questions, synthesize, and imagine. Science has given us insights into wholes and systems, stress and transformation. We are learning to read tendencies, to recognize the early signs of another, more promising, paradigm.

We create alternative scenarios of the future. We communicate about the failures of old systems, forcing new frameworks for problem-solving in every area. Sensitive to our ecological crisis, we are cooperating across oceans and borders. Awake and alarmed, we are looking to each other for answers.

And this may be the most important paradigm shift of all. *Individuals are learning to trust—and to communicate their change of mind*. Our most viable hope for a new world lies in asking whether a new world is possible. Our very question, our anxiety, says that we care. If we care, we can infer that others care, too.

THE SEAT OF THE SOUL

By
GARY ZUKAV

We are evolving from five-sensory humans into multisensory humans. Our five senses together form a single sensory system that is designed to perceive physical reality. The perceptions of a multisensory human extend beyond physical reality to the larger dynamical system of which our physical reality is a part. The multisensory human is able to perceive and to appreciate the role that the physical reality plays in a larger picture of evolution, and the dynamics by which our physical reality is created and sustained. This realm is invisible to the five-sensory human.

It is in this invisible realm that the origins of our deepest values are found. From the perspective of this invisible realm, the motivations of those who sacrifice their lives for higher purposes make sense, the power of Gandhi is explicable, and the compassionate acts of the Christ are comprehensible in a fullness that is not accessible to the five-sensory human.

All of our great teachers have been, or are, multisensory humans. They have spoken to us and acted in accordance with the perceptions and values that reflect the larger perspective of the multisensory being, and therefore their words and actions awaken within us the recognition of truths.

From the perception of the five-sensory human we are alone in a universe that is physical. From the perception of the multisensory human, we are never alone and the Universe is alive, conscious, compassionate and intelligent. From the perception of the five-sensory human the physical world is an unaccountable given in which we unaccountably find ourselves, and we strive to dominate it so that we can survive. From the perception of the multisensory human the physical world is a learning environment that is created jointly by the souls that share it, and everything that occurs within it serves their learning. From the perception of the five-sensory human, intentions have no effects, the effects of actions are physical, and not all actions affect us or others. From the perception of a multisensory human, the intention behind the action determines its effects, every intention affects both us and others, and the effects of intentions extend far beyond the physical world.

What does it mean to say an "invisible" realm exists in which the origins of our deeper understanding are located? What are the implications of considering an existence of a realm that is not detectable through the five senses, but that can be known and understood by other human faculties?

When a question is asked that cannot be answered within the common frame of reference, it can be classified as nonsensical, or it can be dismissed as a question that is not appropriate, or the person who is asking the question can expand to encompass a frame of reference from which the question can be answered. The first two options are the easy way out of confrontation with a question that appears to be nonsensical or inappropriate, but the seeker, the true scientist will allow himself or herself to expand into a frame of ref-erence from which the answers he or she is seeking can be under-stood.

DANCING IN THE LIGHT

By

SHIRLEY MACLAINE

I needed affirmations which would help reduce body pain. So I would affirm to myself (sometimes silently and sometimes audibly, depending on whether I would disturb someone else) a resolution such as: I am God in action. Or, I am God in health. Or, I am God with ease. Whatever came to my mind dictated my creative requirement. Sometimes if I was not feeling as full of fun as I wanted to feel, I would say, I am God in fun. Or, I am God in humor.

What happened was remarkable. I wouldn't have believed it had I not experienced the results myself.

Call it concentration, or call it *believing*, it makes no difference. *I felt no pain.* My perception, and therefore my truth, was altered if I uttered *I am God in happiness* to myself. The result was a feeling that was real. I uttered each affirmation three times. The vedas claim that three times designates mind, body, and spirit. In the middle of the grueling dance number when I wondered, after double days of two shows a day, whether I could finish, I would chant to myself along with the music, *I am God in stamina* and all the pain melted away. One has to try it to believe it. During workout classes when the "burn" was nearly intolerable, I chanted under my breath three times, *I am God in coolness.* The burn was less. Then I would go on to chant gently, *I am God in strength*, or *I am God in light.* The effect is stunning.

If, as happened, there were days when I had either not had enough sleep the night before, or something occurred to jangle my mood, or just the pressure of performing itself caused me to be out of my own center, I would, as soon as I opened my eyes in the morning, begin my affirmations and in five minutes or so I felt better.

Before performing, I always did them during the overture and continued right on through my entrance. I felt the alignment occur all through me and I went on to perform with the God Source as my support system.

I began to use this technique in other ways too.

There were many times, over the course of my life, when I was asked to be a public speaker. Either to accept an award or to be a keynote speaker at a political rally. Public speaking terrified me. I always felt the need to have a prepared text to refer to. Either I would write the speech or a professional speech writer would do it for me. I couldn't feel comfortable doing it spontaneously. This discomfort began to ebb away too. I began to work only with an outlined idea in my head. If I carried notes with me, I found that little by little I didn't bother referring to them. I realized that it was what I was feeling that communicated to the audience more than the words anyway. The words, frankly, got in the way if I was in sync with my feelings. A pause or a decision-making moment was infinitely more effective than the studied intellectual twist of a well-planned phrase. Again, I was learning to trust in the moment and with my affirmation. My higher self was my guide.

This process was so self-enlightening that at times I wanted very much to share it, attempting to light a candle for someone rather than tolerate their cursing of the darkness.

I quickly learned that this is where karma comes in. While pursuing my own awakening, *if* I was working with balanced principles, I was aware at all times that everyone else was pursuing their own path, consciously or unconsciously. They had their own perceptions, their own truth, their own pace, and their own version of enlightenment. It was not possible to judge another's truth. I had to simply proceed along my own path, continually reminding myself of the true meaning of "Judge not, that ye be not judged."

The process of self-realization (or even the theories of reincarnation and karma) does not lend itself to proselytization. It is highly personal, ultimately self-responsible. All one can say, really, is: this happened to me. This is how it feels. It if interests someone else, they must do their own learning, their own reading, their own searching.

THE ROAD LESS TRAVELED

By

M. SCOTT PECK

Discipline, it has been suggested, is the means of human spiritual evolution. This section will examine what lies in back of discipline — what provides the motive, the energy for discipline. This force I believe to be love. I am very conscious of the fact that in attempting to examine love we will be beginning to toy with mystery. In a very real sense we will be attempting to examine the unexaminable and to know the unknowable. Love is too large, too deep ever to be truly understood or measured or limited within the framework of words. I would not write this if I did not believe the attempt to have value, but no matter how valuable, I begin with the certain knowledge that the attempt will be in some ways inadequate.

One result of the mysterious nature of love is that no one has ever, to my knowledge, arrived at a truly satisfactory definition of love. In an effort to explain it, therefore, love has been divided into various categories: eros, philia, agape; perfect love and imperfect love, and so on. I am presuming, however, to give a single definition of love, again with the awareness that it is likely to be in some way or ways inadequate. I define love thus: The will to extend one's self for the purpose of nurturing one's own or another's spiritual growth.

At the outset I would like to comment briefly on this definition before proceeding to a more thorough elaboration. First, it may be noticed that it is a teleological definition; the behavior is defined in terms of the goal or purpose it seems to serve — in this case, spiritual growth. Scientists tend to hold teleological definitions suspect, and perhaps they will this one. I did not arrive at it, however, through a cleverly teleological process of thinking. Instead I arrived at it through observation in my clinical practice of psychiatry (which includes self-observation), in which the definition of love is a matter of considerable import. This is because patients are generally very confused as to the nature of love. For instance, a timid young man reported to me: "My mother loved me so much she wouldn't let me take the school bus to school until my senior year in high school. Even then I had to beg her to let me go. I guess she was afraid that I would get hurt, so she drove me to and from school every day, which was very hard on her. She really loved me." In the treatment of this individual's timidity it was necessary, as it is in many other cases, to teach him that his mother might have been motivated by something other than love, and that what seems to be love is often not love at all. It has been out of such experience that I accumulated a body of examples of what seemed to be acts of love and what seemed not to be love. One of the major distinguishing features between the two seemed to be the conscious or unconscious purpose in the mind of the lover or nonlover.

Second, it may be noticed that, as defined, love is a strangely circular process. For the process of extending one's self is an evolutionary process. When one has successfully extended one's limits, one has then grown into a larger state of being. Thus the act of loving is an act of self-evolution even when the purpose of the act is someone else's growth. It is through reaching toward evolution that we evolve.

Third, this unitary definition of love includes self-love with love for the other. Since I am human and you are human, to love humans means to love myself as well as you. To be dedicated to human spiritual development is to be dedicated to the race of which we are a part, and this therefore means dedication to our own development as well as "theirs." Indeed, as has been pointed out, we are incapable of loving another unless we love ourselves, just as we are incapable of teaching our children self-discipline unless we ourselves are self-disciplined. It is actually impossible to forsake our own spiritual development in favor of someone else's. We cannot forsake self-discipline and at the same time be disciplined in our care for another.

We cannot be a source of strength unless we nurture our own strength. As we proceed in our exploration of the nature of love, I believe it will become clear that not only do self-love and love of others go hand in hand but that ultimately they are indistinguishable.

Fourth, the act of extending one's limits implies effort. One extends one's limits only by exceeding them, and exceeding limits requires effort. When we love someone our love becomes demonstrable or real only through our exertion—through the fact that for someone (or for ourself) we take an extra step or walk an extra mile. Love is not effortless. To the contrary, love is effortful.

Finally, by use of the word "will" I have attempted to transcend the distinction between desire and action. Desire is not necessarily translated into action. Will is desire of sufficient intensity that it is translated into action. The difference between the two is equal to the difference between saying "I would like to go swimming tonight" and "I will go swimming tonight." Everyone in our culture desires to some extent to be loving, yet many are not in fact loving. I therefore conclude that the desire to love is not itself love. Love is as love does. Love is an act of will—namely, both an intention and an action. Will also implies choice. We do not have to love. We choose to love. No matter how much we may think we are loving, if we are in fact not loving, it is because we have chosen not to love and therefore do not love despite our good intentions. On the other hand, whenever we do actually exert ourselves in the cause of spiritual growth, it is because we have chosen to do so. The choice to love has been made.

HOW TO HAVE MORE IN A HAVE-NOT WORLD

By

TERRY COLE-WHITTIKER

LIVING YOUR VISION

This book is about living your vision. What is a vision? I call a vision that which inspires you, motivates you, and turns you on to life. Your vision is your special way, the way in which you want to express yourself and contribute to the quality of other people's lives at the same time. What is it that you've always wanted to do? Where is it that you know you could make a contribution to others' lives? What is of great importance to you? *That is your vision. Do that.*

I have discovered that everyone has a deep commitment and burning desire to give to others, to assist others, and to make this world be the heaven that it can be. For some that vision is clear and they are living it, step by step. They have a purpose and a commitment that is greater than themselves.

To draw upon your greatness, you must have a great and worthwhile purpose. Otherwise you stay small, petty, and painfully boring. Unless you unlock your greatness, the only people around you will be those who seem to have an undying commitment to the trivia of their latest ailment, their relationship problems, and their victim stories in the form of "I said, and she said, and I said, and then she said," along with a generous sprinkling of "Isn't it awful?" "When is somebody going to do something?" and the "Things are getting worse, woe is me" blues.

Your life depends on this. Living your vision is rediscovering (if you haven't already) what it is you've always wanted to do. When you take your natural talents, which may not seem like much to you, and combine them with a commitment to use those talents to enrich, inspire, empower, and transform other people's lives and the quality of all life, you have the key to paradise. What could be greater than loving and being loved and doing work, whether as a volunteer or a professional, that is your dream? All you've ever wanted to do is give, contribute, and help people. If you've failed or been shut down in some way, even ridiculed and laughed at, you may have deeply hidden your vision beneath the hurt and pain, swearing never again to let it be known. Your life depends on your finding your vision again.

THE LAZY MAN'S GUIDE TO ENLIGHTENMENT

By
THADDEUS GOLAS

HOW TO FEEL GOOD

It's all right to have a good time. That's one of the most important messages of enlightenment.

We should try to comprehend the highest pleasure level, the pleasure of God, so to speak, in all that we perceive. No one in higher consciousness wants any of us to have a miserable time on earth.

There is a paradise in and around you right now, and to be there you don't even have to make a move, not even lifting your eyes from this page. You can open yourself to the diamondlike perfection of everything you see and feel. If you don't think it can happen that easily, just be loving, moment by moment, and trust that it will come to you.

No one on the space level ever put barriers or tests in the way of someone who is trying to raise his spiritual level. Hindsight may make it look as though you were being tested, but in truth you are always being allowed to decide for yourself, to define the universe that is real to you.

Higher beings are only too happy when you show yourself loving enough to rise. You will be given every help and chance when you ask for it, whether you ask by taking LSD or any other way, be it simple prayer or writing a letter to Santa Claus. You are never asked to torment or frustrate yourself. You don't have to prove anything. You *can't* prove anything: your vibrations always speak true, you can't lie about them.

And it is easy to rise on the wings of love. No matter how convincing any perception of any level of reality, no matter how overwhelming, intricate and complex, you are still seeing only a fragment within our true reality: being just us, unresisting, unattached, loving all.

It is also all right to have a good time in sexual relations. In truth, a satisfying orgasm is a spiritual realization more than a technical accomplishment. The flesh is not apart from the spirit. The body is an ecstatic creation of many beings vibrating on other levels of consciousness. A deep orgasm is a realization of love on many levels, including those which many of us now think of as "animal." Love, getting into the same space or on the same vibration with others, is the ground of our being, and takes an infinity of forms. As in all other experiences, we always have the sexual experiences we deserve, depending on our loving kindness toward ourselves and others.

UNKNOWN MAN

By

YATRI

The ending of our century has more than its fair share of predictions and omens. No other century has had such a wealth of apocalyptic prophecies surroundings its closing years. And yet interwoven throughout the visions of a cataclysmic end to our dark warring age is one very particular thread of light—the supposed appearance of a totally new being who heralds a new age of consciousness.

Our collective consciousness is abundantly saturated with such archetypes and the fascination of a popular superman image is all the more likely to appear at the end of the century. The final years of any century are notorious for wacky ideas which sweep across the planet and coming "golden ages" are the perfect stuff for the end of our seventh millennium. One of the prime requirements of our dreams of golden ages is that they never happen now. Such glorious epochs are invariably reserved for the distant past or the far future. The Hindu golden age is safely ten thousand years old while John's Christian vision of Revelation sets the coming age of Light and Peace two thousand years into his future.

But, like that apocalyptic vision, other prophecies are also coming home to roost. And most of them firmly place the golden egg on our present doorstep.

Gurus, psychics, mediums and channelers, all add their voice to the gathering mystery of the forthcoming age, each with his favorite hero of higher consciousness. The golden boy has become a commodity to be sold in the New Age market place even before he has left the womb.

EVERY AGE HAS HAD ITS FUTURE AND ITS DREAM

The dreams of the thirties now seem sinister and totalitarian — fascists dreaming neo-romans and Soviets dreaming over-life-sized comrades in superstates. Even as early as the 1920s, Carl Gustav Jung prophesied that a blond monster would arise in Germany. He had been shocked to find this archetype in so many of his patients' dreams. It took another fifteen years for the Nazi Aryan ideal to come into being. But all these supermen proved to be inhuman monsters, horrendous parodies of the collective mirage.

With such tragic failures so fresh in the memory just how realistic is the new dream? Is this unconscious collective vision of a new magical hero destined to end up in the same dark grave as his monstrous brothers of the thirties?

Supposing we were to assume that a new changeling is a possible reality. At this stage it doesn't matter whether he or she has arisen in the collective mind, awaiting actualization, or that somewhere deep within us is a global precognition of an event which will send our species into oblivion. The simple question is, how might we go about looking for him or her?

Clearly, as investigators, we are at a considerable disadvantage right from the start. These new entities are, by definition, unknown. There is no description of what or who they might be like. There are no photo albums, passports and forwarding addresses.

Testimony of their existence is, to say the least, questionable, being totally confined to such vague announcements as the "dawning of the new man" or the coming "herald of the new age." And it certainly does not help that most of the prime "witnesses" have been dead for centuries. So we must now look further afield than either the prophets or their prophecies if we are to satisfy our curiosity concerned with such predictions.

We might start the inquiry by asking whether there are any pre-requisite conditions in the environment for such a profound evolutionary change. There are many conflicting evolutionary theories, but there is only fact that does emerge, which seems to be shared by most biologists. Available evidence points to the fact that any major evolutionary jump is preceded by some kind of crisis within the environment of the organism. This usually happens when there is an imbalance or extreme in the natural habitat which triggers powerful adaptive, evolutionary responses.

Never before has humankind faced so many crises all together at one time. We stumble over critical threshold after critical threshold in a long chain of events running parallel to one another which are destined to clash simultaneously any moment. Any one of these thresholds of pollution, population explosion, destruction of the ozone shield or the dramatic climatic changes brought about by the greenhouse effect is, even by itself, sufficient to detonate an evolutionary bomb which could totally change the direction of our species.

However, if we then add the new technological thresholds which we overstep daily in atomic physics, communications, artificial intelligence, space technology, genetic engineering, solar energy and the revolutionary new conceptual models of science, we have the most volatile mixture ever concocted in our little solar system. From the sheer number and magnitude of these accelerating lines of change all converging at the one crossroads in the last years of this century, something quite shattering is about to happen. On close examination the choice does not seem to be whether it will happen, but whether we manage to destroy ourselves before it happens.

If, for the moment, we assume that by some miracle we do survive the chaos of the next decade what would then be the most likely coming scenario?

Before we can even begin to envision such a happening, some plausible context, some background must be created. So as a prelude to the event let us take a good look at the crossroads upon which we stand at the present moment. Only by carefully surveying the landscape can we hope to discover whether the claim, that we are about to walk across an evolutionary minefield, is reasonably justified.

Most of the issues are so well-known and popularized that it is necessary to enumerate them in detail. However, the main point to be made is that, despite the sheer weight of evidence, we still overlook the magnitude and range of changes we are living through.

CHOP WOOD, CARRY WATER

By the editors of
NEW AGE JOURNAL

PEAK EXPERIENCE

Frequently the experience that sets people on the spiritual path seems to come "out of the blue." It is an experience of intense happiness or joy, or unity or love that has much in common with the "mystical" visions described in traditional literature.

The psychologist Abraham Maslow called these experiences "peak-experiences." Maslow was the founder, in many ways, of what we now call Humanistic Psychology. He discovered the importance of peak-experiences when he took the unusual task of studying people who were healthy. "I picked out the finest, healthiest people, the best specimens of mankind I could find," he wrote in *The Journal of Humanistic Psychology* in 1962, "and studied them to see what they were like."

Maslow discovered that these people "tended to report having had something like mystic experiences, moments of great awe, moments of the most intense happiness or even rapture, ecstasy or bliss (because the word happiness can be too weak to describe this experience). . . .

"These moments," said Maslow, "were of pure, positive happiness when all doubts, all fears, all inhibitions, all tensions, all weaknesses, were left behind. Now self-consciousness was lost. All separateness and distance from the world disappeared as if they felt one with the world, fused with it, really belonging in it and to it, instead of being outside looking in. (One subject said, for instance, I felt like a member of a family not like an orphan.)"

Maslow noted that these peak-experiences "had mostly nothing to do with religion—at least in the ordinary supernaturalistic sense."

> They came from great moments of love and sex, from the great esthetic moments (particularly of music), from the bursts of creativeness and the creative furor (the great inspiration), from great moments of insight and of discovery, from women giving natural birth to babies— or just from loving them, from moments of fusion with nature (in a forest, on a seashore, mountains, etc.), from certain athletic experiences, e.g. skindiving, from dancing, etc.

Maslow then found that these peak-experiences were "far more common than I had ever expected. As a matter of fact, I now suspect they occur in practically everybody although without being recognized or accepted for what they are."

THE FIRST NOBLE TRUTH

For some people, the spiritual journey begins with what may first seem to be a "negative" experience. The Buddha, for example, began his spiritual search in earnest when he realized that all beings were subject to old age, sickness and death. The First Noble Truth of the Buddha is the truth of suffering or unsatisfactoriness. It was only after he had faced this truth in deep meditation that he was led to the discovery of the three other Noble Truths—the origin of suffering, the cessation of suffering, and the path leading to the cessation of suffering.

This sort of entry point may range from a nagging sense of discomfort and boredom—the feeling that *there must be something more*—to the feeling that St. John of the Cross described as "the dark night of the soul." In any case, the negative entry point results from a feeling that something is lacking, and though it may seem to be the opposite of the kind of positive peak-experiences described by

Maslow, it can have the same effect—it propels us through the entry point of our spiritual journey.

Or the search may "begin with a restless feeling, as if one were being watched," Peter Mattheissen writes in *The Snow Leopard*. "One turns in all directions and sees nothing. Yet one senses that there is a source for this deep restlessness; and the path that leads there is not a path to a strange place, but a path home . . ."

P. D. Ouspensky, a teacher of the G. I. Gurdjieff system and author of *In Search of the Miraculous*, reports receiving the following advice from Gurdjieff: "It can be said that there is one general rule for everybody. In order to approach this system seriously, people must be disappointed, first of all in themselves, that is to say in their powers, and secondly in all the old ways . . ."

Chogyan Trungpa Rinpoche, a Tibetan Buddhist teacher, says in a similar vein: "Disappointment is the best chariot to use on the path of the Dharma."

PERSEVERE

The wiser and more honest spiritual teachers warn that the first flush of enthusiasm so characteristic of the new spiritual seeker may be a kind of false dawn. At this stage the whole world is suddenly alight with new knowledge and it seems that all the problems of the world can be explained or understood and resolved according to a certain experience or system of belief.

Before too long, however, a certain disillusionment or uncertainty may appear. "Times of growth," the *I Ching* tells us in the hexagram called Difficulty at the Beginning, "are beset with difficulties. They resemble a first birth. But these difficulties arise from the very profusion of all that is struggling to attain form. Everything is in motion: therefore if one perseveres there is a prospect of great success."

Here it is important to follow the advice of the *I Ching:* persevere, again and again.

THE DRAGON DOESN'T LIVE HERE ANYMORE

By
ALAN COHEN

To think positive is to think with God. This must be true because God is positive and God can do anything. When we think with God, we can do anything.

The key to success in life is to know without a doubt that God is our Mother/Father who wants only the best for us. All failure stems from the mistaken thought that we do not deserve the best that life has to offer. We are Divine Children of God. We were created to be great.

I have grown to have such a faith, such a belief, and such a confidence in the never-failing power of positive thinking that I believe it to be an absolute prerequisite for all success in life. We've all got to believe in ourselves. We've got to believe in our families, our friends, and our businesses. We've got to know the rightness of our hopes, our aspirations, and our dreams. God is desperately looking for people who will trust in the dreams He gives to us. There are so few people who are willing to take the inspiration that God breathes into them and hold tenaciously to it until the possibility becomes a reality. The world is numb to imagination, to creativity, to life. The neon lights of the cities block our view of the stars. The world has settled for second best, and in the bargaining has settled for nothing.

There is a story of a man who comes to the outskirts of an ancient city. There he finds a gatekeeper sitting quietly. The traveler tells the gatekeeper that he has just left his old city, and that he is thinking of moving here. "What's this city like?" asks the traveler.

"What was it like in the city you came from?" returns the gatekeeper.

"It was a rotten place. People were unfriendly, there were no jobs, and the government was crooked."

"Well, that's pretty much what you'll find here," explains the gatekeeper, and the traveler moves on in search of a better city.

A few hours later, along comes another man with a suitcase, also seeking a new home.

"What was it like in your old town?" asked the gatekeeper.

"Oh, it was quite a nice place," tells this second traveler; "lovely people, nicely kept; a shame I have to relocate on account of my job."

"Well, that's pretty much what you'll find here," reports the gatekeeper, and the man happily enters the city.

How we use our mind is crucial to our finding and getting what we want out of life, and giving what we want to it. Success, love, and abundance are not given to a privileged few by the whim of a capricious God. Those who enjoy happiness do so because they have earned it with their thoughts. They have the faith that God is working for their good, and that every moment of life is a precious gift. By so thinking, they open the door to goodness and success.

The foundation of positive thinking is this truth:

To think is to create.

If we want to make it in life, we need to start with our goals clearly in mind; we need to decide what it is that we want, and then get a sharp mental picture of it. Then we must hold steadfast to our goal until it is realized. Refuse to be distracted by thoughts of failure; the Beatles were turned down by several recording companies before they were accepted by one. We've got to believe that if God gave us an idea to do something, He'll find a way for us to get it done.

We cannot allow temporary setbacks to be a cause of disappointment. God often has a bigger plan for us than we have for our little selves. Recently I was working on making a tape for deep relaxation exercises for my classes. I had the hardest time getting it down. First the microphone didn't work, and then the recorder short-circuited, and it seemed that one thing after another went haywire. A project that I expected to take no more than a few hours turned out to take weeks. I did not understand it, but I persevered. Finally the tape was finished, and I eagerly sat down to listen to the final product. It didn't turn out! All that I had recorded had mysteriously disappeared from the tape! I really couldn't figure that one out.

In desperation, I telephoned an electronic engineer friend of mine to ask his advice. "Why don't you come to my house and use my equipment," he offered; "I'll be glad to help you with it." I was delighted! There he gave me use of very expensive and sophisticated recording equipment, plus his expertise in pushing all the right buttons at just the right time, the sum total of which produced a recording far superior to any that I could ever have done by myself. While God was saying a temporary "No" to me in my earlier attempts, He was actually saying "Yes!" to a much bigger idea.

"Yes!" is the most dynamic word in the English language. It is the symbol of affirmation, acceptance and positivity. It makes me feel happy and strong just to look at the word.

When I went to visit a beautiful, Christ-like teacher named "Freedom," he asked me, "Do you want to be happy?"

"I sure do."

"Then say 'Yes!' " he advised me, with much love in his voice. "Say 'Yes!' to God, say 'Yes!' to life, say 'Yes!' to Love, say 'Yes!' to your Self. Then you will be happy."

Too often we miss opportunities because we do not live in the expectation of goodness. We believe that something is too good to be true, when in fact, blessings are the only things good enough to be true.

Norman Vincent Peale, one of the most dynamic and enthusiastic people there has ever been, tells of two salesmen at an outdoor sports exposition, selling motorboats in booths adjacent to one another. Sales were slow and customers few. An Asiatic gentleman with sunglasses approached one of the booths and, after a few pleasantries, told the salesman, "I would like to purchase one million dollars worth of your boats."

The salesman was annoyed. "Listen, friend," he grumbled, "it's been a bad enough day without a comedian . . . Come back some other time when I'm in a mood for a laugh."

"Very well, sir," the customer replied, "Good day."

The man with the dark glasses went on to the next booth, and told the salesman, "I would like to buy one million dollars worth of your boats."

This salesman did not bat an eyelash. "Yes, sir!" he smiled, "Which models would you like?" and he began to fill out an order form. To the astonishment of the first salesman, the customer took out his checkbook, wrote a deposit check for $100,000.00, shook the hand of the salesman, and went on his way. The buyer was a wealthy Arab executive, and the salesman received his standard 10% commission—in this case $100,000!

Understood on a more subtle level, abundance is not something that we create, but that we accept. The second salesman made the deal only because he was willing to accept it. We can look at God, consciousness, and man through the symbol of the hourglass. God's infinite abundance is above us, waiting to flow down, and we have the space to hold it all. At the meeting point, at that skinny little juncture of the upper and lower vessels, is our mind. It regulates how much can come through. If our mind is small, tight, and fearful, a few meager grains will flow through. If the mind is open, free, and expansive, all of God's riches can pour through. We receive as much as we let in.

Ernest Holmes gives a good illustration of this principle. He asks us to imagine three people praying for jobs. In his last job, A earned $100 a week, B earned $200, and C, $500. All of them use the same prayer or affirmation, and all of them get new jobs. The results: A's new job pays him $100, B's job, $200, and C's, $500. Each of them put positive thinking to work, but each one was rewarded only to the level of his expectation. There is no reason for this confinement, except in the subconscious thought of limitation held by each person.

Real positive thinking means learning to look at all of life from a positive viewpoint. It does not mean just making money, gaining health, and finding the right spouse (although these are all valuable demonstrations). Real positivity means seeing the blessedness in everything. It requires a complete revision of the way we look at life. It means tearing down our judgments and opinions of what is good and what is bad, what is right and what is wrong. It means owning up to the truth that God is and lives in everything, and there is not one thing that exists, or one event that occurs, that is not blessed by the Light of God. Simply, it means being willing to give up our mortal limited opinions.

When we let go of these binding concepts, we are initiated into a new level of evolution; the realm of God consciousness. This simply means that we see all as God and all as Good.

Learning to see God in all requires effort, creativity, courage, and love. Our old thought patterns of lack and failure will kick and scream, and they will find the subtlest and craftiest ways to retain their hold on our consciousness, for, in truth, their very life is being threatened. And that is the very best thing that could happen to us, for their life is founded on erroneous thinking and illusion. To break out of this old way of thinking, we must at first make a determined effort to deny the ranting and raving of our old mind which tells us that something is wrong. When negative thoughts assert themselves, we must challenge them with the light of Love, and dare to live the truth of goodness. Many people believe that it is courageous to live through a negative life. I believe that to live a life dedicated to happiness, freedom and forgiveness is the most courageous of all.

Overcoming negation with love is a matter of attunement. We must concentrate on that which is Good, Beautiful, and True. If there seem to be 999 negative attributes of a situation, and one positive aspect, we must seize on that one thing, bless it, hold to it with determination, meditate on it, be grateful for it, exaggerate it, and glorify it. We will find that our tiny trickle of goodness has opened unto a rushing stream, and then into a mighty river which pours into the ocean of God's storehouse abundant.

Life is showering its gifts upon us at this very moment. There is a source of love and light that is streaming, rushing, pouring toward us from all angles at all times. All we have to do is to let it in. Blessings are being offered to all of us without condition or limit. It's all already given to us. The keys to the Kingdom are ours whenever we are willing to accept them. What we have to lose is fear, lack, limitation, and sorrow. What we have to gain is peace of mind, success, health, and love. We do not need to become anything that we are not already. We need only to say "Yes!" to what the universe would just love to give us. We need to think with God.

THE POSSIBLE HUMAN

By

JEAN HOUSTON

AWAKENING THE BRAIN

We have entered upon one of the greatest explorations of all time as
we begin to probe the mystery of the brain. This small organ weighs
less than three pounds and, in the mature adult, comprises less than
8.5 percent of our weight, and yet it is complex beyond our wildest
imaginings. Here is encoded the wisdom of the millennia and the
dreams of tomorrow, the capacity to decode the abstract symbols of
this page and the desire for communion and community. Language,
memory, and the great achievements of civilization emerge from the
complex interaction of billions of neurons. Recent brain research has
underlined the extraordinary complexity of the brain and provided a
rationale for an extraordinary education. We know now that many of
the dualistic ways of thinking historically attributed to the human—
spatial and temporal, analogical and digital, intuitive and rational,
divergent and convergent, subjective and objective—may be linked
to the two very different ways of processing information in the two
hemispheres of the neocortex; that by taking thought we may control
the firing of a single muscle cell; that different states of consciousness
are correlated with different patterns of brain waves; that we respond to subliminal perceptions; and much more.

Here I want to suggest that it is possible to "speak" directly to the
brain, to exercise it, if you will, just as you might use calisthenics to
exercise your body when you get up in the morning. Such an idea is

not new in itself. Over a century ago Oliver Wendell Holmes suggested that we could increase our brain use by thinking ten "impossible thoughts" before breakfast. And I have been known to begin seminars by asking people to tell each other three outrageous lies! The resistance that some people experience to such a suggestion may be indicative of the extremely literal mind-set that results from an acculturation that worships "the fact" and logical proof. This kind of brain exercise is designed to increase the capacity of the brain to consider multiple possibilities, however outrageous, without the premature interference of The Judge in each of us who is well trained to slam down the gavel and declare "Impossible! Won't work! Case dismissed!" before the trial has even begun.

Cross-cultural studies hint at the dormant possibilities, as do the studies of the "exceptional" person. Feats of prodigious memory are now well documented, as is the deliberate use of dreams to elicit healing and great conceptual insights.

For our purposes here, the primary findings to be underlined are that this process we have called "thinking" is much more complicated than any purely rational model would suggest. Further, relying on such a model limits and inhibits our understanding of much that is actually going on, and what we think deeply influences who we are and how we behave.

THE PROCESS OF IMAGERY

The present state of brain research suggests that thinking in images may involve areas of the brain where the thought process is more passive and receptive, and also more susceptible to patterns, symbolic processes and constellational constructs. In verbal-linear thinking, for example, the thinking process tends to go 1–2–3–4–5 or a–b–c–d, one specific thing following another. So your sequential verbalizer knows that "the ankle bone's connected to the shin bone, the shin bone's connected to the knee bone, the knee bone's connected to the thigh bone," and *hears* the *word* of the Lord. Your imagizer will *see* the *way* of the Lord, and so perceive and conceive of the skeletal frame as a connected functional whole.

Thus, in imagistic thinking the pattern is more often 1 through 5, 5 through 20, a through m, m through z—a patterning of ideas and images gathered up in a simultaneous constellation. And because the brain can process millions of images in microseconds, and images seem to have their own subjective time not related to serial clock time, a great deal can be experienced in imagistic thinking in shorter times and in ways that evidently cannot occur in verbal thinking. It is also important to note that whereas verbal thinking is largely bound to left-hemispheric processing and therefore to the left brain's time-specific nature, visual thinking is chiefly a right-hemispheric function, and the right hemisphere is not timebound. For all these reasons—in the dynamic inherent in coded symbolic imagery—more information is likely to be condensed in short time frames. The so-called "creative breakthrough" might then be seen as the manipulation of larger patterns of information that are part of the imaginal, symbolic process. When we look at the phenomenology of high-level creativity, we often note minds engaged in imagistic thinking, racing over many alternatives, picking, choosing, discarding, synthesizing, sometimes doing the work of several months in a few minutes.

Many children are natural visualizers; indeed, some are much more geared to visual thinking than to verbal thinking. Many of these children are cut off from their visualizing capacity by the verbal-linear processes imposed on them by the educational system. Such children may subsequently do poorly in school and suffer a sense of inferiority. Bright and talented as they may naturally be, they quickly lose a sense for their own capacities and intelligence, not only in school and among their peers but throughout their lives. The strong emphasis on verbal-linear processes appears to have grown out of the medieval scholastic system of educating clerics in such a way as to seek out the high-sensory types from the more austere students given to conceptual, verbal thought (who would be less trouble in the monastery). This was fine for medieval Catholicism, but its long arm is still felt in modern education to the detriment of the many natural nonverbal thinkers.

ZEN AND THE ART OF MOTORCYCLE MAINTENANCE

By

ROBERT M. PIRSIG

The desert road winds through rocky gorges and hills. This is the driest country yet.

I want to talk now about truth traps and muscle traps and then stop this Chautauqua for today.

Truth traps are concerned with data that are apprehended and are within the boxcars of the train. For the most part these data are properly handled by conventional dualistic logic and the scientific method talked about earlier, back just after Miles City. But there's one trap that isn't—the truth trap of yes-no logic.

Yes and no . . . this or that . . . one or zero. On the basis of this elementary two-term discrimination, all human knowledge is built up. The demonstration of this is the computer memory which stores all its knowledge in the form of binary information. It contains ones and zeros, that's all.

Because we're unaccustomed to it, we don't usually see that there's a third possible logical term equal to yes and no which is capable of expanding our understanding in an unrecognized direction. We don't even have a term for it, so I'll have to use the Japanese *mu*.

Mu means "no thing." Like "Quality" it points outside the process of dualistic discrimination. *Mu* simply says, "No class; not one, not zero, not yes, not no." It states that the context of the question is such that a yes or no answer is in error and should not be given. "Unask the question" is what it says.

Mu becomes appropriate when the context of the question becomes too small for the truth of the answer. When the Zen monk Joshu was asked whether a dog had a Buddha nature he said *"Mu,"* meaning that if he answered either way he was answering incorrectly. The Buddha nature cannot be captured by yes or no questions.

That *Mu* exists in the natural world investigated by science is evident. It's just that, as usual, we're trained not to see it by our heritage. For example, it's stated over and over again that computer circuits exhibit only two states, a voltage for "one" and a voltage for "zero." That's silly!

Any computer-electronics technician knows otherwise. Try to find a voltage representing one or zero when the power is off! The circuits are in a *mu* state. They aren't at one, they aren't at zero, they're in an indeterminate state that has no meaning in terms of ones or zeros. Reading of the voltmeter will show, in many cases, "floating ground" characteristics, in which the technician isn't reading characteristics of the voltmeter itself. What's happened is that the power-off condition is part of a context larger than the context in which the one-zero states are considered universal. The question of one or zero has been "unasked." And there are plenty of other computer conditions besides a power-off condition in which *mu* answers are found because of larger contexts than the one-zero universality.

The dualistic mind tends to think of *mu* occurrences in nature as a kind of contextual cheating, or irrelevance, but *mu* is found through all scientific investigation, and nature doesn't cheat, and nature's answers are never irrelevant. It's a great mistake, a kind of dishonesty, to sweep nature's *mu* answers under the carpet. Recognition and evaluation of these answers would do a lot to bring logical theory closer to experimental practice. Every laboratory scientist knows that very often his experimental results provide *mu* answers to the yes-no questions the experiments were designed for. In these cases he considers the experiment poorly designed, chides himself for stupidity and at best considers the "wasted" experiment which has provided the *mu* answer to be a kind of wheel-spinning which might help prevent mistakes in the design of future yes-no experiments.

This low evaluation of the experiment which provided the *mu* answer isn't justified. The *mu* answer is an important one. It's told the scientist that the context of his question is too small for nature's answer and that he must enlarge the context of the question. That is a very *important* answer! His understanding of nature is tremendously improved by it, which was the purpose of the experiment in the first place. A very strong case can be made for the statement that science grows by its *mu* answers *more* than by its yes or no answers. Yes or no confirms or denies a hypothesis. *Mu* says the answer is *beyond* the hypothesis. *Mu* is the "phenomenon" that inspires scientific inquiry in the first place! There's nothing mysterious or esoteric about it. It's just that our culture has warped us to make a low value judgment of it.

In the motorcycle maintenance the *mu* answer given by the machine to many of the diagnostic questions put to it is a major cause of gumption loss. It shouldn't be! When your answer to a test is indeterminate it means one of two things: that your test procedures aren't doing what you think they are or that your understanding of the context of the question needs to be enlarged. Check your tests and restudy the question. Don't throw away those *mu* answers! They're every bit as vital as the yes or no answers. They're *more* vital. They're the ones you *grow* on!

REMEMBER BE HERE NOW

By

RICHARD ALPERT, PH.D.,
INTO BABA RAM DASS

So I left to go to India, and I took a bottle of LSD with me, with the idea that I'd meet holy men along the way, and I'd give them LSD and they'd tell me what LSD is. Maybe I'd learn the missing clue.

We started out from Teheran, and for the next three months we had lovely guides and a most beautiful time and we scored great hashish in Afghanistan, and at the end of three months, I had seen the inside of the Land Rover, I had 1300 slides, many tape recordings of Indian music; I had drunk much bottled water, eaten many canned goods: I was a westerner traveling in India. That's what was happening to me when I got to Nepal.

We had done it all. We had gone to see the Dalai Lama, and we had gone on horseback up to Amanath Cave up in Kashmir; we had visited Benares, and finally we ended up in Katmandu, Nepal. I started to get extremely, extremely depressed. I'm sure part of it was due to the hashish. But also, part of it was because I didn't see what to do next.

I had done everything I thought I could do, and nothing new had happened. It was turning out to be just another trip. The despair got very heavy. We didn't know enough and I couldn't figure out how to socialize this thing about the new states of consciousness. And I didn't know what to do next. It wasn't like I didn't have LSD. I had plenty of LSD, but why take it. I knew what it was going to do, what it was going to tell me. It was going to show me that garden again and then I was going to be cast out and that was it. And I never could quite stay. I was addicted to the experience at first, and then I even got tired of that. And the despair was extremely intense at that point.

We were sitting in a hippie restaurant, called the Blue Tibetan, and I was talking to some French hippies . . .

I had given LSD to a number of pundits around India and some reasonably pure men:

An old Buddhist Lama said, "It gave me a headache."

Somebody else said, "It's good, but not as good as meditation."

Somebody else said, "Where can I get some more?"

And I got the same range of responses I'd get in America. I didn't get any great pearl of wisdom which would make me exclaim, "Oh, that's what it is — I was waiting for something that was going to do that thing!"

So I finally figured, "Well, it's not going to happen." We were about to go on to Japan and I was pretty depressed because we were starting the return now, and what was I returning to? What should I do now?

And I met this guy and there was no doubt in my mind. It was just like meeting a rock. It was just solid, all the way through. Everywhere I pressed, there he was!

We were staying in a hotel owned by the King or the Prince, or something, because we were going first class, so we spirited this fellow up to our suite in the Sewalti Hotel and for five days we had a continuing seminar. We had this extraordinarily beautiful Indian sculptor, Harish Johari, who was our guide and friend. Harish, this fellow, Bhagwan Dass and David and I sat there and for five days high on Peach Melbas and Hashish and Mescaline, we had a seminar with Alexandra David Neehl's books and Sir John Woodroffe's Serpent Power, and so on. At the end of five days, I was still absolutely staggered by this guy. He had started to teach me some mantras and working with beads. When it came time to leave, to go to Japan, I had the choice of going on to Japan on my first class route, or going off with this guy, back into India on a temple pilgrimage. He had no money and I had no money and it was going to change my style of life considerably. I thought. "Well, look, I came to India to find something and I still think this guy knows—I'm going to follow him."

But there was also the counter thought, "How absurd—who's writing this bizarre script. Here I am—I've come half-way around the world and I'm going to follow, through India, a 23 year old guy from Laguna Beach, California.

I said to Harish and to David, "Do you think I'm making a mistake?" And Harish said, "No, he is a very high guy." And so I started to follow him—literally follow him.

Now I'm suddenly barefoot. He has said, "You're not going to wear shoes, are you?" That sort of thing. And I've got a shoulder bag and my dhoti and blisters on my feet and dysentery, the likes of which you can't imagine, and all he says is, "Well, fast for a few days."

He's very compassionate, but no pity.

And we're sleeping on the ground, or on these wooden tables that you get when you stop at monasteries, and my hip bones ache. I go through an extraordinary physical breakdown, become very child-like and he takes care of me. And we start to travel through temples—to Baneshwar and Konarak and so on.

I see that he's very powerful, so extraordinarily powerful—he's got an ectara, a one-stringed instrument, and I've got a little Tibetan drum, and we go around to the villages and people rush out and they touch our feet because we're holy men, which is embarrassing to me because I'm not a holy man—I'm obviously who I am—a sort of overage hippie, western explorer, and I feel very embarrassed when they do that they give us food. And he plays and sings and the Hindu people love him and revere him. And he's giving away all my money . . .

But I'm clinging tight to my passport and my return ticket to America, and a traveler's check that I'll need to get me to Delhi. Those things I'm going to hold on to. And my bottle of LSD, in case I should find something interesting.

And during these travels he's starting to train me in a most interesting way. We'd be sitting somewhere and I'd say,

"Did I ever tell you about the time that Tim and I . . ."

And he'd say, "Don't think about the past. Just be here now."

Silence.

And I'd say, "How long do you think we're going to be on this trip?"

And he'd say, "Don't think about the future. Just be here now."

I'd say, "You know, I really feel crumby, my hips are hurting . . ."

"Emotions are like waves. Watch them disappear in the distance on the vast calm ocean."

He had just sort of wiped out my whole game. That was it—that was my whole trip—emotions, and past experiences, and future plans. I was, after all, a great story teller.

So we were silent. There was nothing to say.

He'd say, "You eat this," or, "Now you sleep here." And all the rest of the time we sang holy songs. That was all there was to do.

Or he would teach me Asanas—Hatha Yoga postures.

But there was no conversation. I didn't know anything about his life. He didn't know anything about my life. He wasn't the least bit interested in all of the extraordinary dramas that I had collected . . . He was the first person I couldn't seduce into being interested in all this. He just didn't care.

AUTOBIOGRAPHY OF A YOGI

By

PARAMAHANSA YOGANANDA

"Sir, I am meditating," I shouted protestingly.

"I know how you are meditating," my guru called out, "with your mind disturbed like leaves in the storm! Come here to me."

Thwarted and exposed, I made my way sadly to his side.

"Poor boy, mountains cannot give you what you want." Master spoke caressingly, comfortingly. His calm gaze was unfathomable. "Your heart's desire shall be fulfilled."

Sri Yukteswar seldom indulged in riddles; I was bewildered. He struck gently on my chest above the heart.

My body became immovably rooted, breath was drawn out of my lungs as if by some huge magnet. Soul and mind instantly lost their physical bondage and streamed out like a fluid piercing light from my every pore. The flesh was as though dead; yet in my intense awareness I knew that never before had I been fully alive. My sense of identity was no longer narrowly confined to a body but embraced the circumambient atoms. People on distant streets seemed to be moving gently over my own remote periphery. The roots of plants and trees appeared through a dim transparence of the soil; I discerned the inward flow of their sap.

The whole vicinity lay bare before me. My ordinary frontal vision was now changed to a vast spherical sight, simultaneously all-perceptive. Through the back of my head I saw men strolling far down Rai Ghat Lane, and noticed also a white cow that was leisurely approaching. When she reached the open ashram gate, I observed her as though with my two physical eyes. After she had passed through the brick wall to the courtyard, I saw her clearly still.

All objects within my panoramic gaze trembled and vibrated like quick motion pictures. My body, Master's, the pillar courtyard, the furniture and floor, the trees and sunshine, occasionally became violently agitated until all melted into a luminescent sea; even as sugar crystals thrown into a glass of water dissolve after being shaken. The unifying light alternated with materializations of form, the metamorphoses revealing the law of cause and effect in creation.

An oceanic joy broke upon the calm endless shores of my soul. The spirit of God, I realized, is exhaustless Bliss; His body is countless tissues of light. A swelling glory within me began to envelop towns, continents, the Earth, solar and stellar systems, tenuous nebulae, and floating universes. The entire cosmos, gently luminous, like a city seen afar at night, glimmered within the infinitude of my being. The dazzling light beyond the sharply edged global outlines faded slightly at the farthest edges; there I saw a mellow radiance, ever undiminished. It was indescribably subtle; the planetary pictures were formed of a gossamer light.

The divine dispersion of rays poured from an eternal Source, blazing into galaxies, transfigured with ineffable auras. Again and again I saw the creative beams condense into constellations, then resolve into sheets of transparent flame. By rhythmic reversions, sextillion worlds passed into diaphanous luster, then fire became firmament . . .

. . . Suddenly the breath was returned to my lungs. With a disappointment almost unbearable, I realized that my infinite immensity was lost. Once more I was limited to the humiliating cage of a body, not easily accommodative to the Spirit. Like a prodigal child, I had run away from my macrocosmic home and had imprisoned myself in a narrow microcosm.

My guru was standing motionless before me; I started to prostrate myself at his holy feet in gratitude for his having bestowed on me the experience in cosmic consciousness I had long passionately sought. He held me upright and said quietly:

"You must not get overdrunk with ecstasy. Much work yet remains for you in the world. Come let us sweep the balcony floor; then we shall walk by the Ganges."

I fetched a broom; Master, I knew, was teaching me the secret of balanced living. The soul must stretch over the cosmogonic abysses, while the body performs its daily duties.

JOURNEY OF AWAKENING

By

BABA RAM DASS

A good traveler leaves no track.
—Lao Tse, *Tao te Ching*

EXPERIENCE

As your mind quiets more and more in meditation your consciousness may shift radically. With quietness can come waves of bliss and rapture. You may feel the presence of astral beings; you may feel yourself leaving your body and rising into realms above your head; you may feel energy pouring up your spine. You may have visions, burning sensations, a sharp pain in your heart, deep stillness, stiffening of your body. You may hear voices or inner sounds such as the flute of Krishna, a waterfall, thunder, or a bell. You may smell strange scents or your mouth may be filled with strange tastes. Your body may tingle or shake. As you go deeper you may enter what the southern Buddhists call jhanas, trance states marked by ecstasy, rapture, bliss, and clarity of perception. You may have visions of distant places or find you somehow know things though you can't explain how.

These experiences may seduce you. If you cling to them, fascinated—whether the fascination be out of attraction or repulsion—you invest them with undue importance. When you've had this kind of seductive experience, its memory can be an obstacle to meditation, especially if you try to recreate the experience. To keep going in meditation, you've got to give up your attachment to these states and go beyond. If these experiences come spontaneously, fine. But don't seek them.

I remember taking a fifteen-day insight meditation course. On the twelfth day I experienced a peace that I had never known in my life. It was so deep that I rushed to my teacher and said, "This peace is what I have always wanted all my life. Everything else I was doing was just to find this peace." Yet a month later I was off pursuing other spiritual practices. That experience of peace wasn't enough. It was limited. Any experiential state, anything we can label, isn't it.

My intense experiences with psychedelics led to very powerful attachments to the memories of those trips. I tried to recreate them through yogic practices. It took some years before I stopped comparing meditative spaces with those of my psychedelic days. Only when I stopped clinging to those past experiences did I see that the present ones had a fullness, immediacy, and richness that was enough—I didn't need the memories. Later, during intensive study of pranayama and kundalini, my breath stopped and I felt moments of great rapture. Once again, the intensity of the experience hooked me and I was held back for a time by my attempts to recreate those moments. When I saw that I was closest to God in the moment itself, these past experiences stopped having such a great pull. Again I saw my clinging to memories as an obstacle.

You come to see through your attachment to such experiences and find yourself less interested in striving for them. The despair and frustration that come from desiring a fascinating state and not getting it becomes grist for the mill of insight. It's an irritating process, in a way. You may see things clearly or have a breakthrough into another state for a second or so. But like psychedelics, it leaves you starving. You can grasp it for a moment, but you can't eat the fruit of the garden.

◦   ◦   ◦

Meditation is not a matter of trying to achieve ecstasy, spiritual bliss or tranquility, nor is it attempting to become a better person. It is simply the creation of a space in which we are able to expose and undo our neurotic games, our self-deceptions, our hidden fears and hopes.

HANDBOOK OF HIGHER CONSCIOUSNESS

By
KEN KEYES

Why do we have lives filled with turmoil, desperation, and anxiety? Why are we always pushing ourselves and others? Why do we have only small dribbles of peace, love, and happiness? Why is it that human beings are characterized by bickering and turmoil that makes animals' relationships with their own species seem peaceful in comparison? The answer is so simple—but it is sometimes difficult for us to really understand because almost every way we were taught to work toward happiness only reinforces the feelings and activities that make us unhappy.

This is a central point that must be understood. The ways we were taught to be happy can't possibly work. Unless we see this point clearly, we cannot progress to higher consciousness. Here's why.

Most of us assume that our desires (backed up by our emotional feelings) are the true guides to doing the things that will make us happy. But no one has yet found happiness by using emotion-backed desires as guides. Flashes of pleasure, yes; happiness, no.

Our wants and desires are so seductive. . . . They masquerade as "needs" that must be satisfied so we can be happy at last. They lead us from one illusion of happiness to another. Some of us tell ourselves, "If I can just get to be president of this corporation, I will be happy." But have you ever seen a really happy president? His outside drama may feature beautiful yachts, Cadillacs, Playboy bunnies—but is he really happy inside? Has his ulcer gone away yet?

We constantly tell ourselves such things as, "If I could just go back to school and acquire more knowledge—perhaps get a Master's degree—then I will be happy." But are people with Master's degrees or Ph.D.'s any happier than the rest of us? It is beautiful to acquire knowledge but it is misleading to expect it to bring us peace, love, and happiness. We tell ourselves, "If I could only find the right person to love, then I would be happy." So we search for someone who our addictions tell us is the right person—and we experience some pleasurable moments. But since we don't know how to love, the relationship gradually deteriorates. Then we decide we didn't have the right person after all! As we grow into higher consciousness, we discover that it is more important to be the right person than to find the right person.

We must deeply understand why all of our negative emotions are misleading guides to effective action in life situations. Our negative emotions are simply the result of an extensive pattern of scars and wounds that we have experienced. And these emotional wounds lead us to perceive differences that make us uptight instead of similarities that enable us to understand and love. The present programming of our emotions makes us perceive other people (and the conditions of the world around us) as threats—potentially dangerous to our well-being. We then respond with adrenaline, faster heart beat, increased blood sugar, and other jungle survival responses that prepare us for fight or flight. We are trapped in our ways of perceiving the world around us.

But no one (or no situation) need be felt as an emotional threat and danger when we see things with the clearer perceptions of higher consciousness. Think of the most threatening situation you have felt in the last day or two. Are you about to lose your job? Is the person for whom you feel the most love paying more attention to someone else than to you? Do you have unpaid bills that you cannot take care of? Do you have a pain that could be cancer? Now, these problems either have solutions—or they don't. Either you can do something about them here and now—or you can't. If you can do something here and now about them, then do it—even if it's just a first step. It saps your energy to be worried or anxious about a problem. Do what you can do—but don't be addicted to the results or you will create more worry for yourself. If you can't do anything about a problem here and now, then why make yourself uncomfortable and drain your energy by worrying about it? It is part of the here and nowness of your life. That's what it is—here and now. Worry, anxiety, or other unpleasant emotions are absolutely unnecessary—and simply lower your insight and the effectiveness of your actions.

You must absolutely convince yourself of the lack of utility of these draining emotions. You must see your unnecessary worrying as depriving you of the flowing effectiveness and joyousness that you should have in your life. As long as you think that these negative emotions have any function whatsoever, you will retard your growth into higher consciousness. If you do not hassle yourself emotionally when the outside world does not conform with your inside programming (your desires, expectations, demands, or models of how the world should treat you), you will have so much energy that you probably will sleep fifty percent less. You will be joyous and loving, and really appreciate each moment of your life—no matter what's happening in the world of people and situations outside you.

Where and how did we get this emotional programming? Almost all of it was acquired in the first few years of life. For example, when we were very young, we had the experience of mother forcefully taking a perfume bottle from our tiny fingers and at the same time sending out bad vibrations based on her desire not to have her perfume bottle broken. We cried. Through being painfully pushed around, dominated, told what to do, and controlled when we were babies, we developed our emotionally intense security, sensation, and power programs. Many of our emotion-backed programs came from repeated moral directives or statements about how things "should" be. We developed a "self" consciousness with robot-like responses to protect the "survival" of this separate self.

So we become emotionally programmed to feel that we must have power to control and manipulate people in order to be happy. We eventually become very finely attuned to the actions or vibrations or any person or situation that even remotely threatens our power addictions—our ability to manipulate and control people and things around us.

As we reach our physical maturity and our biocomputer (or brain) is able to function more perceptively, we have all the power we need. But our biocomputer (backed up by the full repertory of our emotions) is still programmed to compensate for the power deficiency we experienced when we were infants and young children. We now need to learn to flow with the people and things around us. But our power addiction keeps us from loving people because we perceive them as objects that may threaten our power, prestige, or pecking order. If we want to love or be loved, we can't be addicted to power—or to anything else.

As conscious beings the only thing we need to find happiness in life is to perceive clearly who we are (we are pure consciousness and not the social roles we are acting out), and exactly what are the real conditions, here and now, of our lives. How basically simple is our problem! But to achieve this clear perception of ourselves and the world around us takes constant inner work. And this means developing the habit of emotionally accepting whatever is here and now in our lives. For only an emotionally calm biocomputer can see clearly and wisely, and come up with effective ways to interact with people and situations.

ECSTASY IS A NEW FREQUENCY

By

CHRIS GRISCOM

Emotions are in the gut, which is the seat of the emotional body, and emotions are being triggered from there. If you just keep focusing, you'll see what the differences are. What does hunger feel like in the physical when your stomach is growling, and what does it feel like when it's not physical hunger? See if you can identify the difference between emotional hunger—when you need something—or when you're having physical hunger. Begin to palpate for yourself all those aspects of your solar plexus, and then notice what happens when you walk into a shopping center or into a bank.

The emotional body does not want to let go of a condition; it doesn't want to let go of its pain, contraction, or fear. As we begin to conceptualize the emotional body in the solar plexus, see what that fear means physically. See what hunger or tightness or looseness feels like emotionally. Just begin to recognize there's something there that can be palpated in the solar plexus, because we need to be palpating that to learn about the emotional body. "This is hard or this is soft. We can do the same palpation on an emotional level. "This is anger," or "this is love." Or we can do it on a higher level: "This is radiating" or "it's not moving." You can palpate it and get all kinds of data from it by simply focusing in on intention. You can use your fingers as the extension of intention. And you can use your heart. We need to learn how to play these bodies together so that we're not isolated in one body, creating an imbalance.

We only isolate into one body for protection. For example, we can live in our mental bodies while avoiding feelings around us. You might isolate into your mental body to protect yourself against your emotional body. That's the way we sabotage ourselves, and we all have this fascinating way of sabotaging ourselves or identifying ourselves, but there's always a kickback. Even when the mind says, "Oh, no, I'm not going to go through my pulling out my hair and getting emotional," you're going to do it anyway because you're getting something out of it. It's the essence of our work at the institute. We're not going to take away the desires of the astral body; we're just going to quicken it; we're going to raise it to a higher octave.

The gateway to all our multi-dimensions, to all these variable bodies of which we are composed, is through perception. Perception is the latticework of reality. It is the design of reality. It is that structure which defines the limits, the form, the pulse, the color, the texture of reality. As each soul creates a reality, the decision as to whether that reality is an experience of love, light, and God—or whether that reality is an experience of fear, anger, and dying—depends on the capacity of that being to perceive and to recognize choice, and handle the discernment. The enlightened choice creates a reality that promotes, speaks of, and manifests the urge of the soul.

SECTION TWO:

NEW PSYCHOLOGY, CONSCIOUSNESS, TRANSFORMATION

Consciousness and Transformation are areas of fascination for many people. The concept of personal transformation or deep psychological and behavioral change is a form of modern alchemy: the changing of oneself into someone else. This metamorphosis toward a more evolved, spiritual, loving, and conscious human being is also considered by many of today's leading thinkers to be the direction that humanity is moving. Personal growth becomes community evolution and, finally, planetary change.

The New Age, psychological, and therapeutic fields overlap and intertwine in many ways. But, because we have defined the New Age movement by a particular set of principles, only the areas of psychology that address themselves to some form of spiritual awareness and practice have been included in this book.

Jungian psychology embraces spirituality as a component of the mental health of a balanced human being. Many therapists working in this field would trace their therapeutic roots to Carl G. Jung (1875–1961), and the impact of Jungian psychology on New Age thinking has been enormous. Based on the premise that normal human personality includes religious thought and mystical experience, Jungian psychology promoted the existence of a "collective unconscious," a reservoir of psychological images and forces that can be tapped and shared by all people.

Jungian concepts that have gained favor are the "collective unconscious" and the uncovering and acceptance of one's own dark side or "shadow."

Jung also defined a concept he called "synchronicity" as "the simultaneous occurrence of two meaningfully but not casually connected events." Synchronicity is a word that is often used to explain a sequence of events in one's personal growth process. For example, say that you are feeling drawn to visit the ancient temples of Egypt. Suddenly you meet someone who has just returned from a trip to the pyramids, and when you arrive home that day, a magazine has arrived in the mail that features a cover story about the Nile River. You find yourself dreaming that you are an Egyptian priestess and the next day as you are walking through a shopping mall you see a dress displayed that bears a striking similarity to the one you wore in the dream. This series of images and events could be an example of synchronicity in your own life. Perhaps they are simply accidents or coincidences, but they happened with enough regularity in the lives of Carl Jung's patients that he invented the word synchronicity to describe them.

Carl Jung was an incredibly prolific writer. There are thousands of books inspired by, and dedicated to, the interpretation of his work. The excerpt included in this anthology is taken from *Man and His Symbols.*

Aside from Jungian influences, many of today's excellent psychologists and psychiatrists credit their background to a study of the gestalt style, encounter group therapies, transactional analysis, and humanistic psychology pioneered by thinkers and psychologists of the seventies such as Abraham Maslow, Carl Rogers, Fritz Perls, and B. F. Skinner.

Abraham Maslow, best known for his concept of self-actualization, is often considered the father of the human potential movement of the late sixties and early seventies. Maslow felt that the inner nature of human beings was basically good, and that it was best to encourage rather than suppress the growth of this innately positive inner self. He believed that humans are good by nature and that human potential is unlimited. This theory inspired many therapists and psychologists in their counseling practices, and the human potential movement became very popular. Carl Rogers proposed a "client-centered" form of therapy, one in which the analyst did not make a diagnosis. Clients were allowed to achieve self-realization by becoming responsible to their own feelings.

The personal growth movement was in full flower by the end of the seventies. Psychology books were selling like never before, and personal growth seminars such as EST, Actualizations, and Lifespring were full to bursting capacity. All over the country people were on a quest for self-knowledge.

Werner Erhard created EST, the Erhard Seminar Training, in October 1971 after having a revelatory experience while driving across the Golden Gate Bridge. EST taught the concept of personal responsibility, the idea that you create the state of affairs that you find yourself in, that you ultimately create your own reality. Personal responsibility is one of the major premises of the New Age, and it found some of its earliest roots in EST.

During the late seventies and early eighties, the study of "consciousness" and "the Consciousness movement" became the primary topic of conversation for many people who began to "work on themselves." "Consciousness" is a word that was used by humanistic psychologists and motivational seminar leaders, coaches, and trainers to describe a state of awareness wherein one became awakened from the sleep-walk of one's programmed belief systems and free to make new choices. Transformation refers to profound states of inner growth that take place in such quantum leaps that one is deeply and fundamentally changed.

The New Age abounds with stories of personal transformation. Many authors are moved to share tales of their own journey in the hope it will benefit others. These stories appear in this anthology in the section that is appropriate to the type of search or journey. For example, Lynn Andrews can be found in the section on Shamanism and Native Traditions because her personal transformative quest took her into the wilds of Canada to learn from a Manitoba Indian medicine woman.

In his best-selling books *The Road Less Traveled* and *The Different Drum,* M. Scott Peck shares thoughts on community, health, personal therapy, and the search for God within. Nathaniel Branden is the author of many books, including *The Disowned Self.*

Neuro Linguistic Programming, or NLP, is a very powerful therapeutic technique pioneered by Richard Bandler and John Grinder. In their seminal book *Frogs into Princes* they share the results of research directed at achieving states of genius by learning flexibility in the application of new systems and strategies in your life.

One of the true masters in the field of NLP, Anthony Robbins, is most famous for his amazing fire-walking seminars in which hundreds of participants demonstrate the power of "mind over matter" as they walk across burning coals. Robbins shares excellent principles for achieving success and personal power in his book *Unlimited Power.*

These authors, and more, speak of the rewards of the endlessly fascinating journey of self-discovery. They advise that we should never stop learning and growing, never stop working on ourselves. Life can be a dream come true once we have removed all the blocks and resistance to happiness. Come and join these powerful authors as they invite you into self-discovery through reading.

THE POWER OF MYTH

By

JOSEPH CAMPBELL
and BILL MOYERS

CAMPBELL: People say that what we're all seeking is a meaning for life. I don't think that's what we're really seeking. I think that what we're seeking is an experience of being alive, so that our life experiences on the purely physical plane will have resonances within our own innermost being and reality, so that we actually feel the rapture of being alive. That's what it's all finally about, and that's what these clues help us to find within ourselves.

MOYERS: Myths are clues?

CAMPBELL: Myths are clues to the spiritual potentialities of the human life.

MOYERS: What we're capable of knowing and experiencing within?

CAMPBELL: Yes.

MOYERS: You changed the definition of a myth from the *search* for meaning to the *experience* of meaning.

CAMPBELL: Experience of *life*. The mind has to do with meaning. What's the meaning of a flower? There's a Zen story about a sermon of the Buddha in which he simply lifted a flower. There was only one man who gave a sign with his eyes that he understood what was said. Now, the Buddha himself is called "the one thus come." There's no meaning. What's the meaning of the Universe? What's the meaning of a flea? It's just there. That's it. And your own meaning is that you're there. We're so engaged in doing things to achieve purposes of outer value that we forget that the inner value, the rapture that is associated with being alive, is what it's all about.

MOYERS: How do you get that experience?

CAMPBELL: Read myths. They teach you that you can turn inward, and you begin to get the message of the symbols. Read other people's myths, not those of your own religion, because you tend to interpret your own religion in terms of facts—but if you read the other ones, you begin to get the message. Myth helps you to put your mind in touch with this experience of being alive. It tells you what the experience is. It's the reunion of the separated duad. Originally you were one. You are now two in the world, but the recognition of the spiritual identity is what marriage is. It's different from a love affair. It has nothing to do with that. It's another mythological plane of experience. When people get married because they think it's a long-time love affair, they'll be divorced very soon, because all love affairs end in disappointment. But marriage is recognition of a spiritual identity. If we live a proper life, if our minds are on the right qualities in regarding the person of the opposite sex, we will find our proper male or female counterpart. But if we are distracted by certain sensuous interests, we'll marry the wrong person. By marrying the right person, we reconstruct the image of the incarnate God, and that's what marriage is.

MOYERS: The right person? How does one choose the right person?

CAMPBELL: Your heart tells you. It ought to.

MOYERS: Your inner being.

CAMPBELL: That's the mystery.

MOYERS: You recognize your other self.

CAMPBELL: Well, I don't know, but there's a flash that comes, and something in you knows that this is the one.

MOYERS: If marriage is the reunion of the self with the self, with the male or female grounding of ourselves, why is it that marriage is so precarious in our modern society?

CAMPBELL: Because it's not regarded as a marriage. I would say that if the marriage isn't a first priority in your life, you're not married. The marriage means the two that are one, the two become one flesh. If the marriage lasts long enough, and if you are acquiescing constantly to it instead of to individual personal whim, you come to realize that this is true—the two really are one.

MOYERS: One not only biologically but spiritually.

CAMPBELL: *Primarily* spiritually. The biological is the distraction which may lead you to the wrong identification.

MOYERS: Then the necessary function of marriage, perpetuating ourselves in children, is not the primary one.

CAMPBELL: No, that's really just the elementary aspect of marriage. There are two completely different stages of marriage. First is the youthful marriage following the wonderful impulse that nature has given us in the interplay of the sexes biologically in order to produce children. But there comes a time when the child graduates from the family and the couple is left. I've been amazed at the number of my friends who in their forties or fifties go apart. They have had a perfectly decent life together with the child, but they interpreted their union in terms of their relationship through the child. They did not interpret it in terms of their own personal relationship to each other.

Marriage is a relationship. When you make the sacrifice in marriage, you're sacrificing not to each but to unity in a relationship. The Chinese image of the Tao, with the dark and light interacting—that's the relationship of yang and yin, male and female, which is what a marriage is. And that's what you have become when you have married. You're no longer this one alone; your identity is in a relationship. Marriage is not a simple love affair, it's an ordeal, and the ordeal is the sacrifice of ego to a relationship in which two have become one.

MAN AND HIS SYMBOLS

By
CARL G. JUNG

Because there are innumerable things beyond the range of human understanding, we constantly use symbolic terms to represent concepts that we cannot define or fully comprehend. This is one reason why all religions employ symbolic language or images. But this conscious use of symbols is only one aspect of a psychological fact of great importance: Man also produces symbols unconsciously and spontaneously, in the form of dreams.

It is not easy to grasp this point. But the point must be grasped if we are to know more about the ways in which the human mind works. Man, as we realize if we reflect for a moment, never perceives anything fully or comprehends anything completely. He can see, hear, touch, and taste; but how far he sees, how well he hears, what his touch tells him, and what he tastes depend upon the number and quality of his senses. These limit his perception of the world around him. By using scientific instruments he can partly compensate for the deficiencies of his senses. For example, he can extend the range of his vision by binoculars or of his hearing by electrical amplification. But the most elaborate apparatus cannot do more than bring distant or small objects within range of his eyes, or make faint sounds more audible. No matter what instruments he uses, at some point he reaches the edge of certainty beyond which conscious knowledge cannot pass.

There are, moreover, unconscious aspects of our perception of reality. The first is the fact that even when our senses react to real phenomena, sights, and sounds, they are somehow translated from the realm of reality into that of the mind. Within the mind they become psychic events, whose ultimate nature is unknowable (for the psyche cannot know its own psychical substance). Thus every experience contains an indefinite number of unknown factors, not to speak of the fact that every concrete object is always unknown in certain respects, because we cannot know the ultimate nature of matter itself.

Then there are certain events of which we have not consciously taken note; they have remained, so to speak, below the threshold of consciousness. They have happened, but they have been absorbed subliminally, without our conscious knowledge. We can become aware of such happenings only in a moment of intuition or by a process of profound thought that leads to a later realization that they must have happened; and though we may have originally ignored their emotional and vital importance, it later wells up from the unconscious as a sort of afterthought.

It may appear, for instance, in the form of a dream. As a general rule, the unconscious aspect of any event is revealed to us in dreams, where it appears not as a rational thought but as a symbolic image. As a matter of history, it was the study of dreams that first enabled psychologists to investigate the unconscious aspect of conscious psychic events.

It is on such evidence that psychologists assume the existence of an unconscious psyche—though many scientists and philosophers deny its existence. They argue naively that such an assumption implies the existence of two "subjects," or (to put it in a common phrase) two personalities within the same individual. But this is exactly what it does imply—quite correctly. And it is one of the curses of modern man that many people suffer from this divided personality. It is by no means a pathological symptom; it is a normal fact that can be observed at any time and everywhere. It is not merely the neurotic whose right hand does not know what the left hand is doing. This predicament is a symptom of a general unconsciousness that is the undeniable common inheritance of all mankind.

Man has developed consciousness slowly and laboriously, in a process that took untold ages to reach the civilized state (which is

arbitrarily dated from the invention of script in about 4000 B.C.).
And this evolution is far from complete, for large areas of the human
mind are still shrouded in darkness. What we call the "psyche" is by
no means identical with our consciousness and its contents.

Whoever denies the existence of the unconscious is in fact as-
suming that our present knowledge of the psyche is total. And this
belief is clearly just as false as the assumption that we know all there
is to be known about the natural universe. Our psyche is part of
nature, and its enigma is as limitless. Thus we cannot define either
the psyche or nature. We can merely state what we believe them to
be and describe, as best we can, how they function. Quite apart,
therefore, from the evidence that medical research has accumulated,
there are strong grounds of logic for rejecting statements like "There
is no unconscious." Those who say such things merely express an
age-old "misoneism"—a fear of the new and unknown.

THE ROAD LESS TRAVELED

By
M. SCOTT PECK

Life is difficult.

This is a great truth, one of the greatest truths.* It is a great truth because once we truly see this truth, we transcend it. Once we truly know that life is difficult—once we truly understand and accept it—then life is no longer difficult. Because once it is accepted, the fact that life is difficult no longer matters.

Most do not fully see this truth that life is difficult. Instead they moan more or less incessantly, noisily or subtly, about the enormity of their problems, their burdens, and their difficulties as if life were generally easy, as if life should be easy. They voice their belief, noisily or subtly, that their difficulties represent a unique kind of affliction that should not be and that has somehow been especially visited upon them, or else upon their families, their tribe, their class, their nation, their race or even their species, and not upon others. I know about this moaning because I have done my share.

Life is a series of problems. Do we want to moan about them or solve them? Do we want to teach our children to solve them?

Discipline is the basic set of tools we require to solve life's problems. Without discipline we can solve nothing. With only some discipline we can solve only some problems. With total discipline we can solve all problems.

What makes life difficult is that the process of confronting and

* The first of the "Four Noble Truths" which Buddha taught was "Life is suffering."

solving problems is a painful one. Problems, depending on their nature, evoke in us frustration or grief or sadness or loneliness or guilt or regret or anger or fear or anxiety or anguish or despair. These are uncomfortable feelings, often very uncomfortable, often as painful as any kind of physical pain, sometimes equaling the very worst kind of physical pain. Indeed, it is because of the pain that events or conflicts engender in us that we call them problems. And since life poses an endless series of problems, life is always difficult and is full of pain as well as joy.

Yet it is in this whole process of meeting and solving problems that life has its meaning. Problems are the cutting edge that distinguishes between success and failure. Problems call forth our courage and our wisdom; indeed, they create our courage and our wisdom. It is only because of problems that we grow mentally and spiritually. When we desire to encourage the growth of the human spirit, we challenge and encourage the human capacity to solve problems, just as in school we deliberately set problems for our children to solve. It is through the pain of confronting and resolving problems that we learn. As Benjamin Franklin said, "Those things that hurt, instruct." It is for this reason that wise people learn not to dread but actually to welcome problems and actually to welcome the pain of problems.

Most of us are not so wise. Fearing the pain involved, almost all of us, to a greater or lesser degree, attempt to avoid problems. We procrastinate, hoping that they will go away. We ignore them, forget them, pretend they do not exist. We even take drugs to assist us in ignoring them, so that by deadening ourselves to the pain we can forget the problems that cause the pain. We attempt to skirt around problems rather than meet them head on. We attempt to get out of them rather than suffer through them.

This tendency to avoid problems and emotional suffering inherent in them is the primary basis of all human mental illness. Since most of us have this tendency to a greater or lesser degree, most of us are mentally ill to a greater or lesser degree, lacking complete mental health. Some of us will go to quite extraordinary lengths to avoid our problems and the suffering they cause, preceding far afield from all that is clearly good and sensible in order to try to find an easy way out, building the most elaborate fantasies in which to live, sometimes to the total exclusion of reality.

✓ THE TAO OF LEADERSHIP

By
JOHN HEIDER

POTENT LEADERSHIP

Potent leadership is a matter of being aware of what is happening in the group and acting accordingly. Specific actions are less important than the leader's clarity or consciousness. That is why there are no exercises or formulas to ensure successful leadership.

Potency cannot be calculated or manipulated, nor is it a matter of trying to look good.

Three examples illustrate differing degrees of potency in leadership:

1. Potent: a conscious yet spontaneous response to what is happening in the here-and-now; no calculation or manipulation.
2. Less Potent: trying to do what is right. This is calculated behavior based on a concept of right, and manipulative behavior based on an idea of what should happen.
3. Least Potent: imposed morality. Imposed morality rests entirely on should and shouldn't. It is both calculated and manipulative, and meets resistance with punishment. It sheds no light on what is actually happening. It often backfires.

Leaders who lose touch with what is happening cannot act spontaneously, so they try to do what they think is right. If that fails, they often try coercion.

But the wise leader who loses the sense of immediacy becomes quiet and lets all efforts go until a sense of clarity and consciousness returns.

THE SOURCE OF POWER

Natural events are potent because they act in accordance with how things work. They simply are. Study natural processes: the light in the sky, the gravity of earth, the unfolding of your own ideas and insights, the emptiness of space, the fullness of life, and the behavior of saints.

Imagine what would happen if these processes were neurotic and self-centered: a lazy sky flickers; gravity varies from moment to moment; your mind is irrational; space is agitated; life is abortive; the saints are worthless models. Nothing works.

The wise leader knows better than to be neurotic and self-centered. Potency comes from knowing what is happening and acting accordingly. Paradoxically, freedom comes from obedience to the natural order.

Since all creation is a whole, separateness is an illusion. Like it or not, we are team players. Power comes through cooperation, independence through service, and a greater self through selflessness.

NOTHING TO WIN

The well-run group is not a battlefield of egos. Of course there will be conflict, but these energies become creative forces.

If the leader loses sight of how things happen, quarrels and fear devastate the group field.

This is a matter of attitude. There is nothing to win or lose in group work. Making a point does not shed light on what is happening. Wanting to be right blinds people.

The wise leader knows that it is far more important to be content with what is actually happening than to get upset over what might be happening but isn't.

THE DISOWNED SELF

By

NATHANIEL BRANDEN

When a person denies his real needs, the inevitable outcome is the creation of an unreal self—the personality he presents to the world. In this case, that personality consisted, in effect, of a work-machine and a sex-machine, not a human being. For many persons who have a strong desire for efficacy, but neurotic fear of emotional intimacy, sex can become their one bridge to other human beings, their one acceptable form of reaching out; and the more intolerable their inner state, the more anxiously unbearable their unacknowledged loneliness, the more erratically compulsive their sexual behavior is likely to be. Sex without personal involvement is often called upon to perform that same psychological function which is performed, for persons of a different psychologist, by prayer or alcohol or tranquilizers.

His mother's extreme dependency and emotionalism and his father's remote sternness both contributed to this client's animosity towards emotions—the mother's example encouraging him to associate emotions with weakness, the father's behavior and the hurt it produced in the son encouraging him to associate emotions with vulnerability, pain and rejection.

But if a person spends years repressing his emotions and denying his loneliness, if he blocks the knowledge of his need to love and be loved, if he numbs himself to the pain of his frustration, but then partially overcomes his fear of being hurt, enough to fall in love, he finds himself trapped in an anxiety-provoking dilemma: that love, which should signal the end of his loneliness and the fulfillment of his happiness, becomes instead a formidable threat. In order to fully experience the love and the potential happiness it offers him, he has to be willing to confront his past pain, the pain he never had permitted himself to acknowledge. In order to fully experience the meaning of the present, he must be able to experience the meaning of his past—including his loneliness, frustration, and feelings of rejection—which constitutes his *particular psychological context.*

Fear of such a confrontation was a major factor incapacitating this man. As soon as he began to experience and to make real his feelings for the woman, the past rose up like a terrifying specter, announcing itself by the onset of incomprehensible tears. In reverting to a state of emotional dissociation and turning to senseless infidelities, he was clearly seeking to deny the importance of the first serious relationship he had ever had with a woman. Paradoxically and tragically, his infidelity—seen in this light—was a twisted form of tribute to her.

Still another element involved in his infidelity, which became much more apparent in a subsequent session, was his fear of being hurt in the present, a fear whose origins obviously extended back to his childhood. This fear was as powerful a factor in his motivation as his dread of confronting his past suffering.

Every person who dreads emotional intimacy does so because he lives with the expectation that, in any relationship, sooner or later he will be rejected. So sometimes he "protects" himself by rejecting before he can be rejected, or by acting in such a way to imply that the relationship is less important than it actually is. Such behavior often results in bringing about the very rejection and loss he had feared, which, of course, merely intensifies his fear of future rejection and loss. This is one of the commonest forms of self-destruction men and women practice.

Few of the irrationalities people commit—the destructive behavior they unleash against themselves and against others—would be possible to them if they did not first cut themselves off from their own deepest feelings. Paradoxically, the person we sometimes describe as "ruled by his feelings"—the irresponsible, impulsive "whim-worshipper"—is as dissociated from his inner emotional life as the most inhibited "intellectualizer." The difference in personality is more of form than of essence.

To take an extreme example: a pathological murderer is not a man guided by his intellect, but neither is he a man in good, integrated contact with his emotions. Indeed, it is the brutal repression of feeling, specifically feelings of hurt, anger and rage, that sometimes leads to sudden, unexpected and seemingly uncontainable explosions of violence. A tension generated by denied feelings becomes so unbearable that it finally erupts in physically destructive behavior.

THE CRACK IN THE COSMIC EGG

By

JOSEPH CHILTON PEARCE

To be "realistic" is the high mark of intellect, and assures the strengthening of those acceptances that make up the reality and so determine what thoughts are "realistic." Our representation-response interplay is self-verifying, and circular. We are always in the process of laying our cosmic egg.

The way by which our reality picture is changed provides a clue to the whole process. A change of concept changes one's reality to some degree, since concepts direct percepts as much as percepts impinge on concepts. There are peculiarities and exceptions, such as my no-fireburn venture, by which our inherited fabric is by-passed temporarily in small private ways. These are linear thrusts that break through the circles of acceptancy for making up our reality.

Metanoia is the Greek word for conversion: a "fundamental transformation of mind." It is the process by which concepts are reorganized. *Metanoia* is a specialized, intensified adult form of the same world-view development found shaping the mind of the infant. Formerly associated with religion, *metanoia* proves to be the way by which all genuine education takes place. Michael Polanyi points out that a "conversion" shapes the mind of the student into the physicist. *Metanoia* is a seizure by the discipline given total attention, and a restructuring of the attending mind. This reshaping of the mind is the principal key to the reality function.

The same procedure found in world-view development of the

child, the *metanoia* of the advanced student, or the conversion to a religion, can be traced as well in the question-answer process, or the proposing and eventual filling of an "empty category" in science. The asking of an ultimately serious question, which means to be seized in turn by an ultimately serious quest, reshapes our concepts *in favor of* the kinds of perceptions needed to "see" the desired answer. To be given ears to hear and eyes to see is to have one's concepts changed in favor of the discipline. A question determines and brings about its answer just as the desired end shapes the nature of the kind of question asked. This is the way by which science synthetically creates that which it then "discovers" out there in nature.

Exploring this reality function shows how and why we reap as we sow, individually and collectively—but no simple one-to-one correspondence is implied. The success or failure of any idea is subject to an enormous web of contingencies. Any idea seriously entertained, however, tends to bring about the realization of itself, and will, regardless of the nature of the idea, to the extent it can be free of ambiguities. The "empty category" of science as an example will be explored later and the same function is triggered by any set of expectancies, as, for instance, a disease.

For instance, in my wife's case, a grandmother who had died of cancer was the family legend, and all the females scrupulously avoided all the maneuvers rumored to have possibly caused the horror. Then, in neat, diabolical two-year intervals, my wife's favorite aunt died of cancer; her mother developed cancer but survived the radical-surgery mutilations; her father then followed and died in spite of extensive medical machinations. Naturally, two years after burying her father, my wife's own debacle occurred, in spite of her constant submissions to the high priests for inspections, tests, and, no doubt, full confessionals. The fact that all these carcinomas were of different sorts, and on opposite sides of the family, was incidental. Few people understood my fury when the medical center that had attended my wife requested that I bring my just-then-budding teenage daughter for regular six-monthly check-ups forever thereafter, since they had found—and thoroughly advertised—that mammary malignancies in a mother tended to be duplicated in the daughter many hundred percent above average. And surely such tragic duplications *do* occur, in a clear example of the circularity of expectancy verification, the mirroring by reality of a passionate or basic fear.

The "empty category" is no passive pipe dream—it is an active, shaping force in the making of events. There are not as many hard line, brass tack qualifications to the mirroring procedure to be outlined in this book as one might think. For instance, the Ceylonese Hindu undergoes a transformation of mind that temporarily bypasses the ordinary cause-effect relationships—even those we must have for the kind of world we know. Seized by his god and changed, the Hindu can walk with impunity through pits of white-hot charcoal that will melt aluminum on contact. Recently, in our own country, hypnotically induced trance states have replaced chemical anesthesias, allowing bloodless, painless, quickly healing operations to be performed.

FROGS INTO PRINCES

By

RICHARD BANDLER *and* JOHN GRINDER

It's really interesting to me that the percentage of left-handed and ambidextrous people in the "genius" category in our culture is much higher than the percentage in the general population. A person with a different cerebral organization than most of the population is automatically going to have outputs which are novel and different for the rest of the population. Since they have different cerebral organization, they have natural capabilities that "normally organized" right-handers don't automatically have.

Woman: You talked earlier about children who spelled badly because they did it auditorily, and that you could teach them how to do it visually. And now you just talked about the auditory or ambidextrous person having something different that makes him unique. I'm wondering if it's worth the energy it takes to make those kids be able to do what other people do more easily if it's taking away from other things that they can do?

If I teach a child how to spell correctly, I'm not taking anything away. Choices are not mutually exclusive. Many people close their eyes in order to be in touch with their feelings, but that's just a statement about how they organize themselves. There's no necessity to that. I can have all the feelings that I want with my eyes open. Similarly, if I have an ambidextrous or left-handed person with a different cerebral organization, I don't have to destroy any choices they presently have to *add* to that. And that's our whole function as modelers. We assume since you all managed to scrape up whatever amount of money it cost you to come here, that you are competent, that you already are succeeding to some degree. We respect all those choices and abilities. We're saying "Good," let's *add* other choices to those choices you already have, so that you have a wider repertoire" just as a good mechanic has a full tool box.

Our claim is that you are using *all systems all the time*. In a particular context you will be *aware* of one system more than another. I assume that when you play athletics or make love, you have a lot of kinesthetic sensitivity. When you are reading or watching a movie, you have a lot of visual consciousness. You can shift from one to the other. There are contextual markers that allow you to shift from one strategy to another and use different sequences. There's nothing forced about that.

There are even strategies to be creative, given different forms of creativity. We work as consultants for an ad agency where we psychologically "clone" their best creative people. We determined the strategy that one creative person used to create a commercial, and we taught other people in that agency to use the same structure at the unconscious level. The commercials they came up with were then creative in the same way, but the content was totally unique. As we were doing the process, one of the people there even made a change in the strategy that made it better.

Most people don't have a large number of strategies to do anything. They use the same kind of strategy to do everything and what happens is that they are good at some things and not good at others. We have found that most people have only three or four basic strategies. A really flexible person may have a dozen. You can calculate that even if you restrict a strategy to four steps there are well over a thousand possibilities!

We make a very strong claim. We claim that if any human can do anything, so can you. All you need is the intervention of a modeler who has the requisite sensory experience to observe what the talented person actually *does*—not their report—and then package it so that you can learn it.

UNLIMITED POWER

By

ANTHONY ROBBINS

Have you ever wondered what a Spielberg and a Springsteen might have in common? What do a John F. Kennedy and a Martin Luther King, Jr., share that caused them to affect so many people in such a deep and emotional way? What sets a Ted Turner and a Tina Turner apart from the masses? What about a Pete Rose and a Ronald Reagan? All of them have been able to get themselves to consistently take effective actions toward the accomplishment of their dreams. But what is it that gets them to continue day after day to put everything they've got into everything they do? There are, of course, many factors. However, I believe that there are seven fundamental character traits that they have all cultivated within themselves, seven characteristics that give them the fire to do whatever it takes to succeed. These are the seven basic triggering mechanisms that can ensure your success as well:

Trait number one: Passion! All of these people have discovered a reason, a consuming, energizing, almost obsessive purpose that drives them to do, to grow, and to be more! It gives them the fuel that powers their success train and causes them to tap their true potential. It's passion that causes a Pete Rose to continuously dive headfirst into second base as if he were a rookie playing his first major-league game. It's passion that sets the actions of a Lee Iacocca apart from so many others. It's passion that drives the computer scientists through years of dedication to create the kind of breakthroughs that have put men and women in outer space and brought them back. It's passion that causes people to stay up late and get up early. It's passion that people want in their relationships. Passion gives life power and juice and meaning. There is no greatness without a passion to be great, whether it's the aspiration of an athlete or an artist, a scientist, a parent, or a businessman. . . .

Trait number two: Belief! Every religious book on the planet talks about the power and effect of faith and belief on mankind. People who succeed on a major scale differ greatly in their beliefs from those who fail. Our beliefs about what we are and what we can be precisely determine what we will be. If we believe in magic, we'll live a magical life. If we believe our life is defined by narrow limits, we've suddenly made those limits real. What we believe to be true, what we believe is possible becomes what's true, becomes what's possible. This book will provide you with a specific, scientific way to quickly change your beliefs so that they support you in the attainment of your most desired goals. Many people are passionate, but because of their limiting beliefs about who they are and what they can do, they never take the actions that could make their dream a reality. People who succeed know what they want and believe that they can get it. . . .

Passion and belief help to provide the fuel, the propulsion toward excellence. But propulsion is not enough. If it were, it would be enough to fuel a rocket and send it flying blindly toward the heavens. Besides that power, we need a path, an intelligent sense of logical progression. To succeed in hitting our target, we need:

Trait number three: Strategy! A strategy is a way of organizing resources. When Steven Spielberg decided to become a filmmaker, he mapped out a course that would lead to the world he wanted to conquer. He figured out what he wanted to learn, whom he needed to know, and what he needed to do. He had passion, and he had belief, but he also had the strategy that made those things work to their greatest potential. Ronald Reagan has developed certain communication strategies that he uses on a consistent basis to produce the results he desires. Every great entertainer, politician, parent, or employer knows it's not enough to have the resources to succeed. One must use those resources in the most effective way. A strategy is a recognition that the best talents and ambitions also need to find the right avenue. You can open a door by breaking it down, or you can find the key that opens it intact. . . .

Trait number four: Clarity of values! When we think of the things that made America great, we think of things like patriotism and pride, a sense of tolerance, and a love of freedom. These things are values, the fundamental, ethical, moral, and practical judgments we make about what's important, what really matters. Values are specific belief systems we have about what is right and wrong for our lives. They're judgments we make about what makes life worth living. Many people do not have a clear idea of what is important to them. Often individuals do things that afterward they are unhappy with themselves about simply because they are not clear about what they unconsciously believe is right for them and others. When we look at great successes, they are almost always people with a clear fundamental sense about what really matters. Think of Ronald Reagan, John F. Kennedy, Martin Luther King, Jr., John Wayne, Jane Fonda. They all have different visions, but what they have in common is a fundamental moral grounding, a sense of who they are and why they do what they do. An understanding of values is one of the most rewarding and challenging keys to achieving excellence. . . .

As you've probably noticed, all these traits feed on and interact with one another. Is passion affected by beliefs? Of course it is. The more we believe we can accomplish something, the more we're usually willing to invest in its achievement. Is belief by itself enough to achieve excellence? It's a good start, but if you believe you're going to see a sunrise and your strategy for achieving that goal is to begin running west, you may have some difficulty. Are our strategies for success affected by our values? You bet. If your strategy for success requires you to do things that do not fit your unconscious beliefs about what is right or wrong for your life, then even the best strategy will not work. This is often seen in individuals who begin to succeed only to end up sabotaging their own success. The problem is there's an internal conflict between an individual's values and his strategy for achievement.

In the same way, all four of the things we've already considered are inseparable from:

Trait number five: Energy! Energy can be the thundering, joyous commitment of a Bruce Springsteen or a Tina Turner. It can be the entrepreneurial dynamism of a Donald Trump or a Steve Jobs. It can be the vitality of a Ronald Reagan or Katharine Hepburn. It is almost impossible to amble languorously toward excellence. People of excellence take opportunities and shape them. They live as if obsessed with the wondrous opportunities of each day and the recognition that the one thing no one has enough of is time. There are many people in this world who have a passion they believe in. They know the strategy that would ensure it, and their values are aligned, but they just don't have the physical vitality to take action on what they know. Great success is inseparable from the physical, intellectual, and spiritual energy that allows us to make the most of what we have. . . .

Trait number six: Bonding power! Nearly all successful people have in common an extraordinary ability to bond with others, the ability to connect with and develop rapport with people from a variety of backgrounds and beliefs. Sure, there's the occasional mad genius who invents in a lonely warren; he will succeed on one level but fail on many others. The great successes—the Kennedys, the Kings, the Reagans, the Gandhis—all have the ability to form bonds that unite them to millions of others. The greatest success is not on the stage of the world. It is in the deepest recesses of your own heart. Deep down, everyone needs to form lasting, loving bonds with others. Without that, any success, any excellence, is hollow indeed. . . .

The final key trait is something we talked about earlier.

Trait number seven: Mastery of communication! This is the essence of what this book is about. The way we communicate with others and the way we communicate with ourselves ultimately determine the quality of our lives. People who succeed in life are those who have learned how to take any challenge that life gives them and communicate that experience to themselves in a way that causes them to successfully change things. People who shape our lives and our cultures are also masters of communication to others. What they have in common is an ability to communicate a vision or a quest or a joy or a mission. Mastery of communication is what makes a great parent or a great artist or a great politician or a great teacher.

SECTION THREE:

HEALING AND ALTERNATIVE MEDICINE

A revolution has occurred in the ways that people think about healing, nutrition and diet, and preventive medicine. One of the most important contributions that New Age thinkers have made is in the area of alternative medicine, holistic health, and healing. The risks of cancer, AIDS, and other life-threatening forms of illness have directly influenced all of us, affecting our family and friends. Traditional medicine has failed to cure or effectively treat these illnesses, forcing patients and their families to open up to new alternatives. Health problems such as cancer, heart disease, stress-related hypertension, allergies, and immune deficiency illnesses have inspired new approaches and experimental attitudes toward "wellness."

Many of the new therapies are nonscientific. They concentrate on the intangible aspects of healing such as cultivating self-love, maximizing the powerful "will to live," and discovering the spiritual and educational messages or lessons of illness and disease. These therapies are based on the idea that the true healer lies within us, and the pathway to awareness is the same as the pathway to healing. New forms of healing have their origins in ancient non-Western traditions such as meditation and relaxation, massage and visualization, acupuncture and accupressure, and the shamanic healing techniques of native cultures.

Some techniques allow for possible supernatural intervention. Faith healing, the "laying on of hands," the power of prayer, and miracle cures have been documented in such diseases as cancer, multiple sclerosis, and Parkinson's disease. Spiritual healers are active within the Christian faith, shamanic healers are very popular in South America, and many Western doctors are using holistic methods in the treatment of their patients.

This section includes alternative medicine and healing techniques from many prominent authors, psychologists, and medical doctors. Dr. O. Carl Simonton, famous for his work with cancer patients, is the pioneer in the new field of psycho-neuro-immunology. Using visualizations and imagery, his patients are encouraged to see the cancer cells in their bodies being surrounded by white blood cells that attack or eat the cancer cells. Like tiny Pac-Mans, the white blood cells clean out and eat the weaker malignant cells until the patient is in remission or totally cured. Dr. Simonton is convinced that psychology plays a vital role in the formation of cancer in the body. By using the creative power of the imagination and positive thinking, he has achieved dramatic results in his practice.

Louise Hay is a very successful seminar leader and author in California who has brought tremendous love and compassion to thousands of people who have AIDS. In her best-selling book *You Can Heal Your Life* she advocates self-love, forgiveness, and coming to terms with the pain and trauma of one's past. She leads Wednesday night sessions called "Hay Rides" where she provides an opportunity for all of those in attendance to heal themselves. She does not call herself a healer, feeling as she does that healing comes from within, assisted by self-love and self-acceptance.

In his book *Love, Medicine and Miracles,* Bernie S. Siegel, M.D., shares insights gained during many years in his surgical practice. The subtitle of the book is "Lessons Learned About Self-Healing from a Surgeon's Experience with Exceptional Patients." It is based on the stories of cancer patients who survive—the exceptional patients.

Ex–medical doctor turned author and seminar leader W. Brugh Joy is a very influential healer. In his inspirational book *Joy's Way,* he shares his personal experiences with nontraditional healing techniques such as music, light, sound, body energy, meditation, the chakra system, and transformational psychology. He has conducted healing seminars at Ski High Ranch in California that have profoundly affected many of the leaders in the New Age movement, along with thousands of other participants.

Attitudes toward death and dying have undergone a radical shift in the past decade. There is a new set of beliefs that proclaim death as a natural transition into another dimension. Funerals have become loving memorials or celebrations of life. Death is viewed as a passing, a transition, and ultimately a celebration.

In her book *Death, the Final Stage of Growth,* Elisabeth Kübler-Ross shares new attitudes about death gathered from rabbis, doctors, nurses, ministers, and sociologists. She explores the importance of living life to the fullest and accepting death as an inevitable friend who motivates us to make the most of our lives.

Who Dies? by Stephen Levine is a respected work dealing with conscious dying, forgiveness, and attitudinal healing.

Using the principles of the New Age, we accept the premise that we are all one, that God is within each of us, that we are connected and united in our highest selves. If everything is connected, then nothing ever dies—it changes form and mass. If God is the life force that shines through all things, it continues to shine forever. New Age principles such as these are valuable for living life fully in all of its stages: birth, growth, union, passage, and death.

HEALING FROM WITHIN

By

DENNIS T. JAFFE, PH.D.

Most of us take our good health for granted. We tend to pay little attention to our physical condition until pain or discomfort signals us that something has gone wrong. Our reaction usually consists of surprise and frustration at such an unwarranted intrusion, accompanied by anxiety and helplessness. We are uncertain what has gone wrong, why it happened, and how to heal it. We consider the inner workings of the body as a mystery that can be probed and repaired only by a physician.

I believe that many of our common assumptions about illness are inaccurate and sometimes dangerous. Most of us regard illness as an external invader, attacking a body that was previously healthy. Illnesses are typically blamed on defective genes, bad fortune, last night's meal, or something in the air. Using this logic, we assume that physical disorders cannot usually be prevented. There is a dim awareness that our bodies have needs and require care, but such care is nevertheless rather low on our priorities. If you're like most of us, you probably expend more energy on your house or car than on your own self-preservation.

Such attitudes ignore our own power to influence health or illness. In reality, most diseases stem from not one but a long chain of contributing factors, which intensify and multiply over a period of months or years. Our behavior, feelings, stress levels, relationships, conflicts, and beliefs contribute to our overall susceptibility to disease. In essence, everything about our lives affects our health. By improving these dimensions of ourselves over which we have control, we can maximize our well-being and our ability to resist illness. Our power to prevent and heal illness is far greater than most of us realize.

Consequently, no one should remain insensitive to his state of health or illness. If you are ill, it is essential for you to become an active participant in the therapeutic process. If you are healthy, you must be willing to work actively, every day, to maintain your well-being. While it may be reassuring to imagine that medical technology will eventually deliver you from illness, modern medicine has reached a point where it cannot guarantee good health unless you work in conjunction with your physician. Today, the key to enduring health and healing often lies in your own behavior.

This idea is not as radical as it may seem. A growing number of physicians and health professionals have arrived at the same conclusion. They agree that if an individual is to remain healthy, and avoid premature death or unnecessary disease and suffering, he must change his attitudes both toward himself and toward the health-care system. They regard disease not just as a crisis within the body, but as a process involving every aspect of life. Each person can help determine his own health status, using his physician or other health professional as an educator and guide.

YOU CAN HEAL YOUR LIFE

By

LOUISE L. HAY

In the infinity of life where I am, all is perfect, whole and complete, and yet life is ever changing. There is no beginning and no end, only a constant cycling and recycling of substance and experiences. Life is never stuck or static or stale, for each moment is ever new and fresh. I am one with the very Power that created me and this power has given me the power to create my own circumstances. I rejoice in the knowledge that I have the power of my own mind to use in any way I choose. Every moment of life is a new beginning point as we move from the old. This moment is a new point of beginning for me right here and right now. All is well in my world.

WHAT I BELIEVE

Life Is Really Very Simple. What We Give Out, We Get Back.

What we think about ourselves becomes the truth for us. I believe that everyone, myself included, is 100 percent responsible for everything in our lives, the best and the worst. Every thought we think is creating our nature. Each one of us creates our experiences by our thoughts and our feelings. The thoughts we think and the words we speak create our experiences.

We create the situations, and then we give our power away by blaming the other person for our frustration. No person, no place, and no thing has any power over us, for "we" are the only thinkers in our mind. We create our experiences, our reality and everyone in it. When we create peace and harmony and balance in our minds, we will find it in our lives.

Which of these statements sounds like you:

"People are out to get me."

"Everyone is always helpful."

Each of these beliefs will create quite different experiences. What we believe about ourselves and about life becomes true for us.

The Universe Totally Supports Us in Every Thought We Choose to Think and Believe.

Put another way, our subconscious mind accepts whatever we choose to believe. They both mean that what I believe about myself and about life becomes true for me. What you choose to think about yourself and about life becomes true for you. And we have unlimited choices about what we can think.

When we know this, then it makes sense to choose "Everyone is always helpful," rather than "People are out to get me."

The Universal Power Never Judges or Criticizes Us.

It only accepts us at our own value. Then it reflects our beliefs in our lives. If I want to believe that life is lonely and that nobody loves me, then that is what I will find in my world.

However, if I am willing to release that belief and to affirm for myself that "Love is everywhere, and I am loving and lovable" and to hold on to the new affirmation and to repeat it often, then it will become true for me. Now loving people will come into my life, the people already in my life will become more loving to me, and I will find myself easily expressing love to others.

Most of Us Have Foolish Ideas About Who We Are and Many, Many Rigid Rules About How Life Should Be Lived.

This is not to condemn us, for each of us is doing the very best we can at this very moment. If we knew better, if we had more understanding and awareness, then we would do it differently. Please don't put yourself down for being where you are. The very fact that you have found this book and have discovered me means that you are ready to make a new positive change in your life. Acknowledge yourself for this. "Men don't cry!" "Women can't handle money!" What limiting ideas to live with.

When We Are Very Little, We Learn How to Feel About Ourselves and About Life by the Reactions of the Adults Around Us.

It is the way we learn what to think about ourselves and about our world. Now, if you lived with people who were very unhappy, or frightened, guilty or angry, then you learned a lot of negative feelings about yourself and about your world.

"I never do anything right." "It's my fault." "If I get angry, I'm a bad person."

Beliefs like this create a frustrating life.

When We Grow Up, We Have a Tendency to Recreate the Emotional Environment of Our Early Home Life.

This is not good or bad, right or wrong; it is just what we know inside as "home." We also tend to recreate in our personal relationships the relationships we had with our mothers or with our fathers, or what they had between them. Think how often you have had a lover or a boss who was "just like" your mother or father.

We also treat ourselves the way our parents treated us. We scold and punish ourselves in the same way. You can almost hear the words when you listen. We also love and encourage ourselves in the same way, if we were loved and encouraged as children.

"You never do anything right." "It's all your fault." How often have you said that to yourself?

"You are wonderful." "I love you." How often do you tell yourself this?

TEACH ONLY LOVE

By

GERALD JAMPOLSKY

BEHAVIOR FOLLOWS PEACE

Consistent peace is not the same as regimented behavior. Our behavior should follow our peace of mind like a wake trailing the movements of a ship. If peace is our single aim in all we do, we will always know what to do because we will do whatever will protect and deepen our peace. This approach is in marked contrast to the exhausting attempt to decide every movement beforehand on the basis of whether it will turn out all right.

Our ego always wants to see its way clear before it acts. It prefers mental conflict now to simple action. It would rather pause and stew than move easily forward, and so it uses its favorite delaying tactic: the question of right and wrong.

Everyone wants to be moral and good, at least in his own terms, and so the ego uses this desire to engage our attention in an interminable calculation of consequences. Yet it is only now that we can be good, kind and gentle. No way exists in the present to accurately determine the future effect of the least of our actions. And it goes without saying that there is no way for us to go back in time and correct what we consider to be our past mistakes. No matter how long we try, we will not know all the people our actions will affect or whether the effect will be beneficial in the long run. Why then engage in an impossible task, no matter how well meaning it may seem, when genuine opportunities to be kind and truly helpful are all around us?

Understanding this releases us from guilty preoccupation with the future and gives us permission to consult the present urgings of peace and love within our heart. Yet it must be stressed that as we start out, this procedure will require trust. We simply begin to do what our sense of peace indicates, even though we do not know the outcome. Of course, we never knew the outcome before, but we did have a certain sense of safety in thinking we had second-guessed the results. Now we admit that a loving preference is a more reliable basis for a decision than guesses about future consequences.

Several months ago I met with Carol Chapman and her daughter, Hillary, who was hospitalized with a brain tumor at Children's Hospital in Los Angeles. Two weeks later, I received a phone call from Carol. She said Hillary was now going in and out of a coma and that when her daughter was lucid she would beg her to take her off chemotherapy and x-ray treatment. Carol was very distressed and asked me what she should do. I told her that if she had asked me this question a few years ago I would have known exactly what to advise her. Now, I said, the only thing I knew to say to her was what I would tell myself: to be still and listen to her inner voice. For I had learned from experience that the one thing that could bring a restful assurance in an extreme and painful dilemma such as this was the Voice of Peace itself.

My response did not satisfy her. She said she knew I was an expert in these matters and should therefore be able to give her a definite course of action. We talked awhile longer, but she was still unhappy with me when we hung up.

The next day Carol called me again, and this time her voice was quite serene. She told me that after we talked, she was able to quiet her mind and pray. And this, she said, was the answer she received: "There is no right or wrong. There is only love." The answer freed her mind from fear and allowed her to consult deeply her love for her daughter. What she then saw that she wanted to do was stop all treatments as her daughter had requested.

Three weeks later, Hillary died a very peaceful death. Carol received the news at a conference where several other parents who had lost children to cancer were present, and they were able to comfort her in a way that only parents who have been through it could.

Once we realize there is no right or wrong procedure, we can turn to love in complete confidence. But the peaceful preference that lies within our heart cannot be heard until we have relinquished our fearful emphasis on specific answers. First, we must see that any number of alternatives could be accompanied by the peace and love we desire. We see that we do not care personally which course of action we take, but that we do care that our way be kind, harmless and harmonious. Now our emphasis is on how we go, not where we go. And from this type of inner calm will always come a simple suggestion as to what to do. Our part is to gently do it so that we can enter once more into peace. And if a change or another course of action is needed later, we are not afraid to take it.

Instead of judging everything and trying to twist people and circumstances into appearances we like, the way of peace proceeds quietly and simply. Whenever life surprises us, our first reaction is now to consult that calm place within our heart. We stop and rest a moment in God's love. Then, if action is needed to restore our peace of mind, we take the course that comes to us from out of our calmness. We act with assurance, for indeed we have been assured. And if later we need to ask again, we do so quickly and easily. Our purpose is not to seek peace in order to make rigid decisions or set for ourselves long term rules, but rather to make those decisions that will return us to peace this instant. For it is only when we are peaceful that we can be truly kind.

JOY'S WAY

By

W. BRUGH JOY, M.D.

In modern physics, one current theory holds that all matter—and, thus, all energy—is actually trapped light. I find this suggestion intriguing, because many mystical and cosmic experiences report light of various colors emanating from all objects. This light appears to be intrinsic to an object, rather than being reflected from the object; that is, the object itself emits the light and can be seen in total darkness. Without even considering the nature of intrinsic light, with all our sophistication, we do not know what ordinary light is. Our understanding of it is still theoretical.

Light and sound are accepted in conventional medicine as energy forces capable of healing. Light, in the many frequencies that we know as colors, has been shown to be effective in influencing certain abnormalities of the body. For example, blue light is used to treat jaundiced infants, and the mechanism is clearly known: the frequency of blue light is capable of breaking up the chemical bonding of the bilirubin molecule and thus converting it into a substance less toxic to the central nervous system. For another example, ultraviolet light is used to treat certain skin disorders and, in sterilization techniques, to kill bacteria and influence virus replication. Sun tanning and sunburn are both produced by light beyond visible frequencies, and when light is produced in a single frequency—as a laser beam— it can make incisions into the body and, outside medicine, can cut metal, fabrics and other materials.

Sound is used in orthodox medicine in the form of ultrasonics—sound frequencies far above the range audible to humans. These frequencies are used to vaporize liquids in inhalation therapy for respiratory patients, in diagnostic equipment which bounces sound waves through the body to produce so-called echograms, and in direct application to the body to promote the healing of injured tissue. Down in the ordinary listening ranges, sound in the form of music is used to soothe or calm supermarket shoppers, operating-room personnel, and office and factory workers. Sonar uses sound waves in the sea in a way analogous to the diagnostic equipment that makes echograms. And I will share some further insights about sound later in the section about high-intensity sound—in the form of music played at high volume—as a tool in precipitating expanded experiences in awareness.

Although we may recognize that sound and light can influence us psychologically, most of us have not conceived that our psychological aspect, like our physical structure, may be nothing more nor less than a configuration of energies. I believe that it is. As I see it, the "density" of this psychological energy is far less than the density of what we know as matter, and therefore it is capable of interpenetrating the energy fields that make up matter.

The comparison process literally locks us into a prison filled with psychological pain. Until I could reach a state of awareness that each individual is a distinct and unique representation of form and psyche, I was trapped. Then awareness let me out of prison and led me to the astonishing truth: we are far more than we possibly could wish, but we are herded into a narrow spectrum of beliefs about who and what we are. To begin to awaken into this potential experience of our own individual wholeness demands that no comparisons be made. There is only one entity in the entire plane who can make the comparison that generates the vicious cycle, and that entity is you.

My greatest test of self-value came during the night of the full moon in February 1975 when I spent thirteen hours alone in the Great Pyramid of Cheops. One of many profound experiences that night was the presentation of every flaw of my Beingness, each one rapidly flashed before my awareness like a series of photographic slides in super vivid color and detail. Seeing them, I knew that I could choose between reacting and observing, and I chose the latter.

The totality of my Beingness then flashed before me, and, with insight into each flaw, I no longer saw them as flaws, but rather, as challenges, necessary experiences for my unfolding and awakening.

There is a quotation from Goethe: "If you treat man as he appears to be, you make him worse than he is. But if you treat man as if he already were what he potentially could be, you make him what he should be." The key word is *appears*. Rarely, if ever, do we see the totality—including the potential not yet manifest—of ourselves or of another human being; the filtering system of the outer mind is too strong. In Conferences at the ranch, after I deliver the Goethe quotation to participants, I ask that each spend an entire afternoon paraphrasing this quotation into a contemplation of: "If I treat myself as I think I appear to be, I make myself less than I am. But if I treat myself as if I already were what I potentially could be, I make myself what I should be." Only linear, time-trapped thoughts prevent us from seeing the staggering beauty of our entirety.

"Make no judgments." All judgments of the kind meant in this second injunction issue out of conditioned value systems, which in turn have roots in the emotional-reflex arc. A judgment of this kind can be only a reaction to what is experienced. Note the word *reaction* because it is the criterion to determine whether the response is a conditioned one and not an intrinsic value. Our reactions to good or bad, beautiful or ugly, talented or untalented are trained responses related to the culture and subculture of our upbringing and education. Before one commits oneself to a judgment, one must at least attempt to see whence the reaction came. If it is an idea also held by mother or father, a teacher, an authority figure in a religious institution, you must ask yourself whether it is a valid, natural response in its own right or whether it has been conditioned in you by those authorities. Do you have an alternative to the perspective from which you are viewing and experiencing the situation? The task is to discern an event, to see it clearly, at first without response. Then one's later response is a clue to one's level of development or awakening. Human consciousness becomes rigid through training. Once it has been conditioned, it cannot appreciate natural states of experience without being retrained.

LOVE, MEDICINE AND MIRACLES

By

BERNIE S. SIEGEL, M.D.

RELAXATION

By relaxation I don't mean falling asleep in front of the TV set or
unwinding with friends. The kind I'm talking about is a quieting of
mental activity and withdrawal of body and mind from external
stimulation, a way of "erasing the blackboard" of all mundane concerns in preparation for contacting deeper layers of the mind. The
goal is to reach a light trance state, sometimes called the alpha state
because in it brain waves consist mainly of alpha waves, those whose
frequency is between 8 and 12 cycles per second and which appear
during deep relaxation. Inducing this state is the first step of hypnosis, biofeedback, yogic meditation, and most related forms of mind
exploration.

There are many methods of relaxation, nearly all of them quite
similar. They are thoroughly discussed, along with their physiological effects, in Dr. Herbert Benson's bestseller *The Relaxation Response*, one of the first books to approach the subject from a medical
point of view.

One method differs somewhat from most of the others. Dr. Ainslie
Meares of Melbourne, Australia, believes that all verbal instructions,
even in the beginning, tend to stimulate too much logical thought. He
has reported several remarkable regressions of cancer using a non-
verbal quieting method based on gentle touching and reassuring

sounds by the therapist. He also believes that best results depend on a slight degree of discomfort to be overcome by the patient, such as that produced by sitting on a low stool or straight-backed chair. Healing touch can certainly be significant when the patient has someone to administer it regularly, but other ways of inducing the relaxation response also achieve excellent results. . . .

Don't be discouraged if you find relaxation procedures hard at first. Relaxation and meditation are perhaps especially difficult for Americans. Our constant mental diet of advertising, noise, violence, and media stimulation makes it very difficult to endure even a few minutes of inactivity and quiet. We have created a wall around ourselves to block out this deluge. In the process we also stop feeling and the quiet can be threatened. It gives us time to think and feel again.

MEDITATION

Someone once said, "Prayer is talking, meditation is listening." Actually, it's a method by which we can temporarily stop listening to the pressures and distractions of everyday life and thereby are able to acknowledge other things—our deeper thoughts and feelings, the products of our unconscious mind, the peace of pure consciousness, and spiritual awareness.

To call it listening makes it sound entirely passive but meditation is also an active process, although not in the usual sense. It is a way of focusing the mind in a state of relaxed awareness that, although less responsive to distraction, is more focused than usual toward things we want to pay attention to—images of healing, for example.

There are many ways of doing this. Some teachers recommend focusing your attention on a symbolic sound or word (a mantra), or on a single image such as a candle flame or mandala. Others focus on the relaxed ebb and flow of the breath, or gently restrain the mind from following the thoughts that flicker across its surface. The end of all the methods is ultimately the same: a deeply restful emptiness or trance, that strengthens the mind by freeing it from its accustomed turmoil.

With guidance and practice, meditation can lead to breathtaking experiences of cosmic at-oneness and enlightenment, but the changes in the beginning are typically gentle and subtle. As you begin meditating, you'll find that it improves your concentration. Gradually you become centered within yourself, so that you no longer react so strongly to outside stresses. When someone cuts you off on the highway you can avoid or shorten that hair-trigger surge of frustrated anger and its corresponding rise in blood pressure. The calmness also leaves you better prepared to avoid danger from other people's foolish actions.

I know of no other single activity that by itself offers such a great improvement in the quality of life. I once received a letter from a group of women who began meditating to increase their breast size. Indeed, they were able to accomplish that, but the meditation experience itself so improved their lives that breast size became secondary and they became more interested in the complete revitalization that was taking place.

The physical benefits of meditation have recently been well documented by Western medical researchers, notably Dr. Herbert Benson. It tends to lower or normalize blood pressure, pulse rate, and the levels of stress hormones in the blood. It produces changes in brain wave patterns, showing less excitability. These physical changes reflect changes in attitude, which show up in psychological tests as a reduction in the overcompetitive Type A behavior that increases the risk of heart attack. Meditation also raises the pain threshold and reduces one's biological age. Its benefits are multiplied when combined with regular exercise. In short, it reduces wear and tear on both body and mind, helping people live better and longer.

QUANTUM HEALING

By

DEEPAK CHOPRA, M.D.

The good news about neuro-transmitters is that they are material. A thought, whether sane or mad, is hard to grasp because it is so intangible; it is not something you can touch or feel. The neuro-transmitters, however, are certainly tangible, although they are extremely tiny and often short-lived. It is the neuro-transmitter's role to match up with a thought. To do that, its molecules must be just as flexible as thoughts, just as fleeting, elusive, changeable, and faint.

Such flexibility is a kind of miracle but also a curse, in that it throws up a barrier that is almost impossible to pass. No man-made drug can duplicate this flexibility, either now or in the foreseeable future. No drug actually pairs up with a thought. This is apparent just by looking at the structure of the receptor. Receptors are not fixed; they have been accurately described as looking like lily pads that have floated up from the depths of the cell.

Like lily pads their roots sink downward, reaching the cell's nucleus, where the DNA sits. The DNA deals in many many kinds of messages, potentially an infinite number. Therefore, it makes new receptors and floats them up to the cell wall constantly. There is no fixed number of receptors, no fixed arrangement on the cell wall and probably no limit to what they are tuned in to. A cell wall can be as barren as a pond in winter, or as crammed as the pond in full flower in June.

The only constraint about a receptor is its unpredictability. Research has recently discovered, for example, that a neuro-transmitter called imipramine is produced abnormally in the brains of depressed people. While looking for the distribution of the imipramine receptors they were startled to find them not only on the brain cells but on the skin cells. Why should the skin create receptors for a "mental molecule"? What did these receptors have to do with depression?

One plausible answer is that a depressed person has a sad brain, sad skin, a sad liver and so on. (Likewise, researchers have examined patients who complain of feeling jittery and discovered abnormally high levels of two chemicals, epinephrine and norepinephrine, in their brains and adrenal glands. However, high concentrations were then found in their blood platelets, meaning that they had "jittery blood cells" too.)

It has been frustrating for doctors to realize how complex this whole business is becoming. Hopes for a quick cure for schizophrenia, depression, alcoholism, drug addiction and other disorders, were dashed in the mid-1970's, just a few years after the original endorphins had been isolated in 1973. Now the chemical barrier is stronger than ever, as the true flexibility of messenger molecules is being divined.

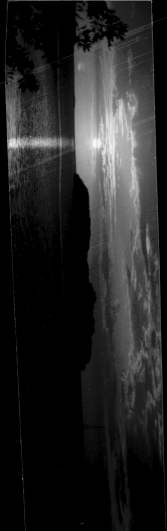

VIBRATIONAL MEDICINE

By

RICHARD GERBER, M.D.

VIBRATIONAL MEDICINE AS THE SPIRITUAL SCIENCE OF THE FUTURE: THE NEXT EVOLUTIONARY STEP IN PERSONAL AND PLANETARY TRANSFORMATION

Vibrational or energy medicine has finally found modern day scientific validation in our Einsteinian understanding of matter as energy, especially as it is applied to the examination of biological systems from the perspective of interactive energy fields. More simply stated, the Einsteinian viewpoint sees human beings from the higher dimensional perspective of fields within fields within fields. Matter itself, from the infinitesimal sub-atomic particle to the level of the physical and higher vibrational bodies, is now seen as dynamic energy contained within the constraints of fluctuating energy fields. We have observed that experimentation in the fields of high-energy particle physics, Kirlian photography, holography, and the study of the effects of psychic healing on the biological systems, have converged to teach us new ways of understanding the energetic field nature of all life processes. As we begin to think about human beings as multidimensional spiritual beings of light, we can start to comprehend the powerful effects of vibrational healing modalities which deliver specified quanta of subtle energy to promote healing through reintegration and realignment of our mind/body/spirit complexes. Vibrational healing methods work by rebalancing disturbances of structure and energy flow within the context of our multi-level interactive energetic fields.

Many of the energies that make up the etheric and higher dimensional worlds of human subtle anatomy vibrate at speeds faster than ordinary light. The physics of so-called magnetoelectric energy, predicted by Einstein's equations, holds the keys to deciphering the scientific principles which underlie the behavior of higher vibrational phenomena. Our thoughts and our emotions are indeed manifestations of this special energy. For medicine and psychology to truly advance over the next several decades, we must begin to think of our emotional problems as energetic imbalances that affect the functioning of our subtle and physical anatomy. If we can accept that these emotional disturbances are partly due to problems within the subtle fields of human physiology, then we can begin to utilize other natural forms of subtle energy that can remove or correct the problematic imbalances. Because homeopathic remedies, flower essences, gem elixirs, crystals, and color energies affect the subtle energy fields of the human body, such vibrational therapies can have powerful impacts on the stress and illness. Over the next twenty years, we will see the creation of a whole new science of energy as it applies to human consciousness and subtle physiology. Spiritual scientists will begin to extend the limits of known science to incorporate higher energy phenomena.

Humankind is at a unique turning point in history. The development of new technologies in pharmacology, surgery, and electronic imaging systems for diagnosis has allowed traditional medicine to evolve in this century toward tremendous breakthroughs in the treatment of serious illness. We have come far in treating many common infectious diseases, in providing relief from various types of cancer and heart disease, as well as in knowing better ways of controlling hypertension and kidney ailments. Orthodox medicine is a truly marvelous field of continual discovery. We cannot deny that modern medicine has uplifted the human condition significantly, for many people would have died prematurely had it not been for some of the miracles of its scientific discoveries and applications. The problem lies in the fact that the orthodox medical approaches still fall short of treating the true cause of illness. Traditional physicians can treat the effects of the disease; but can they really approach the emotional, mental, bioenergetic, and spiritual precursors of disease?

KEY POINTS TO REMEMBER

1. Human beings are dynamic energy systems which reflect evolutionary patterns of soul growth. Human consciousness is constantly learning, growing, and evolving. As spiritual awareness of this dynamic process of change becomes more prevalent, there will be a ripple effect that will shift the energetic dynamics of the human race as a whole.

2. In general, most people go to physicians to be treated for their ills without thinking about the need for themselves to somehow change their lifestyles or mindstyles. The physician-patient interaction is only healing to the extent that there is mutual cooperation and increased awareness on the parts of both parties. People must take responsibility for their own lives, in part by following the advice of their physicians.

3. Our illnesses may often be a symbolic reflection of our own internal states of emotional unrest, spiritual blockage, and dis-ease. Although there may be external factors operating which have negative effects, these effects are only able to create disease where there is an underlying susceptibility. Our subtle energetic components, i.e., the chakras and the meridian system, translate our emotional and spiritual difficulties into physiological weaknesses which may eventually result in a localized system breakdown in the physical body, i.e., disease.

4. When disease occurs, it is a sign that we are constricting the natural flow of creative consciousness and subtle life-energies through our multidimensional body/mind/spirit complexes. It is a symbolic warning message that something has gone wrong in the system. The area of constriction needs to be rebalanced if lasting health is to be achieved.

5. Many of the basic emotional/spiritual issues that human beings are trying to work through are reflections of the key lessons of the

chakras. These chakric issues relate to grounding, sexuality, personal power, love, will, creative expression, inner vision, and spiritual seeking.

6. When the individual has a blockage in working through one of these key life issues, it may result in a blocked flow of energy in the corresponding major chakra, thus constricting the flow of life-energy to the associated bodily organ system(s). Such blockages may eventually express themselves as illnesses if the problem becomes chronic and is an important learning experience for the incarnating personality.

7. Of the chakric issues, none is more important than the lesson of the heart chakra, for it involves being able to freely express love toward oneself, as well as to others, both strangers as well as meaningful others. Personal and spiritual transformation are ultimately dependent upon the opening and blossoming of the flower-like heart chakra.

8. Fear and misunderstanding are the root causes of much illness, distress, and suffering in the world. Often, when we are functioning in the lower aspects of our awareness, we are blind to our own fears and we project them onto the world, when in fact the problem lies within. The key toward dissolving and healing these fears is to release the blockages of the heart chakra and to operate from a position of love and forgiveness. As we open our heart center and the higher spiritual energies can more easily flow through us, it is a catalyst to healing not only ourselves, but also those around us.

9. Reincarnation is a system by which souls, the particularizations of God's own energy, can evolve, learn, and spiritually mature, thus adding to the total knowledge and experience banks of both God and the individuated consciousness that are the souls. Because of the holographic connectivity between God and all aspects of creation, the vast consciousness which is God is always aware of everything that happens in the universe.

10. The system of reincarnation allows souls to learn by trial and experience through many lifetimes in physical bodies. Both positive and negative life experiences are stored in the causal body, and through karma, may affect the outcome of future lives.

11. The misdeeds and tormenting behavior of one lifetime may be translated into an appropriate handicap in future lifetimes, thus

teaching the lesson of seeing both sides of the issue. Similarly, the incarnating personality may achieve wealth, position, and social advancement partly as a consequence of the grace of their positive deeds in previous lives. The philosophy of reincarnation allows one to see the various physical and socioeconomic handicaps as learning experiences chosen by the soul for the growth and spiritual maturation of the physical personality. How each person chooses to act in a particular setting, as to whether or not they will use that circumstance as an opportunity for soul growth, will vary according to the free will of the individual.

12. There have been many past civilizations which knew the truth about reincarnation and human multidimensional anatomy. These included Atlantis, Lemuria, and the various mystery schools of Egypt and Greece. In spite of human perversion, wars, and corruption, there have always been secret outposts teaching the divine nature of humanity and the full range of extended human potential.

13. Over the centuries, there have been incarnated great teachers who came to rekindle the ancient spiritual wisdom. These included Lao-Tze, Confucius, Buddha, Zoroaster, Mohammed, and Jesus of Nazareth. In their wake have sprung up many world religions, each teaching the same basic principles in a slightly different tongue and version, but all speaking the same truth. What has been lost over the years is the symbolic nature of the lessons they came to teach. Their metaphorical words have been literalized, often to the extent that the basic spiritual meanings have been altered or lost.

14. Vibrational medicine is a healing approach which is based upon the Einsteinian concept of matter as energy, and of human beings as a series of complex energy fields in dynamic equilibrium. The physical matter field is in equilibrium with these negative space/time, higher dimensional fields. These fields of etheric, astral, mental, causal and even higher frequency matter operate to provide energetic information, structure, and higher knowledge to the incarnating personality from its spiritual source. The purpose of the entire structural arrangement is to provide a vehicle of expression for the soul to grow through experiences in the worlds of matter.

15. Vibrational medicine seeks to reunite the personality with the Higher Self in a more meaningful, connected way. Vibrational modalities help to strengthen the energetic connections between the

personality and the soul itself, by rebalancing the body/mind/spirit complex as a whole. Not all vibrational healing tools work at the higher energetic levels, but it is the intent and goal of the vibrational healer/physician to seek and assist this alignment within his or her patients.

16. As the New Age technologies evolve, and imaging systems are developed which can substantiate this author's picture of extended multidimensional human anatomy, vibrational medicine will become more widely accepted by those within the more orthodox medical establishment.

HANDS OF LIGHT

By

BARBARA ANN BRENNAN

HEALING WITH COLOR AND SOUND

HEALING WITH COLORED LIGHT, COLOR MEDITATION

There are many times when a healer will need to hold a certain color that is being channelled through her. Holding a color also means holding your field in a certain frequency range, which you really must do throughout the entire healing. You need to be sensitive enough to keep your energy level at the range that is needed at any given time by the patient. Some examples of holding a certain color have already been given in previous chapters on etheric template healing, Ketheric template healing (holding gold), sixth level healing in which you go up into the celestial frequencies, spine cleaning and chakra charging, in which you hold the specific color of a chakra until it is charged. At other times, you may be requested by the guides to pour certain colored light into your patient whenever and wherever it is needed. At these times, you must learn to be in a specific color and hold it.

In the last chapter I stated that it takes practice to learn to produce a color of your choosing and use in healing. For beginning students it is very important to practice color modulation before trying to control the color coming through you. Most chelation is done without color control. However, later in a healing the guides may want you to "sit in" or hold steady a certain color they wish to use. This means that if you do not learn to control color, you may very well interfere with the color being sent through you by changing your field unconsciously. Thus you need to be able to hold your field steady in one particular color.

Dolores Krieger in her book *Therapeutic Touch* gives some very good color modulation exercises. Essentially you must learn what it is like to "be in" a certain color. It is not a matter of thinking the color as in visualization. If you think red, you will make yellow. If you think blue, you will make yellow. Healers call this "doing it in yellow" because when you think you make yellow. Many beginners do it in yellow. Thus to make blue, you must "be" blue, whatever that means to you so you need to experiment for yourself what it is like to be in a state of blue.

EXERCISES TO CONTROL THE COLOR YOU SEND

How do you feel when you wear blue clothes or sit in blue light that comes from a cathedral window? What does blue mean to you? Again, you must use the sense that you are accustomed to using. Do you best access information through seeing, hearing, or feeling? What does blue look like, sound like, or feel like? Get one of those leaded glass crystals that you can hang in your window. Put your fingers in each of the colors of the rainbow it produces. How does each color feel? Get plates of colored glass, or sheets of colored, clear plastic. Hold them in the sunlight. Explore your relationship to each other. Take colored pieces of paper or material all the same size. Mix them up in a pile. Close your eyes and pick out two of them. Keep your eyes closed. Explore your relationship to that color. What does it feel like? Do you like it? Dislike it? Does it provoke any feelings in you? Does it energize or deenergize you? Does it make you feel calm or uncomfortable? Place it on different parts of your body. Would you like to wear this color? Then after this, with eyes closed, decide which color you like the best. If you like, you can guess what color it is. Then open your eyes. You will be surprised at how much information you now have about your relationship to each color. You will find that you carry prejudice about what each color is "supposed" to do but didn't.

Get a partner, hold hands, and each take a turn at running energy to the other in a certain color. See if your partner can tell what color it is. Practice, practice, practice. Remember that in order to run red, you must have your first chakra clear. To run orange, you must have your second chakra clear, etc. You should clear your chakras before doing these exercises. The exercises to clear your chakras are given in Chapter 21.

THE MEANING OF COLOR IN THE AURA

Many people come up to me and say, "What color is my aura?" And then they ask, "What does that color mean?" Many people get "Aura Readings" in which the reader will say, "Your aura is such and such a color and that means such and such." As you can see from this book, I don't normally do that. If someone says, "What color is my aura?" I usually say, "On which layer?" Or I will simply read the predominant colors on the unstructured levels and say something like, "Primarily blue, with some yellow and purple."

My colleague Pat (Rodegast) de Vitalis, who channels a guide named Emmanuel, reads colors on the "soul" level. Emmanuel simply shows her the "aura" of the person on the soul level as it connects to the task in this lifetime. These colors have a specific meaning to Pat, and that is how she interprets what she sees. Her color meaning list is given in Figure 32-1. Remember that to use this list to interpret what you are seeing, you must be looking at the same level Pat is.

To read the colors of the soul level, clear your mind through deep meditation, and then ask to be given the colors of the soul level. After some practice, these colors will appear on your mind-screen. You may also see forms or figures with these colors that you can describe to your patients in order to help them understand the meaning of the colors. If you see red, it means passion or strong feelings. When mixed with rose, it means love. Clear red means free or expressed anger; dark red, held anger; red-orange implies sexual passion. When the color is orange, the person has ambition. When it is yellow, it refers to intellect. A person with a lot of green has a lot of healing and nurturing energy. Blue is the color of the teacher and of sensitivity. When purple is seen on the soul level, the person has a deeper connection to spirit, while indigo means moving toward a deeper connection to spirit. Lavender refers to spirit, and white to truth. Gold is connection to God and the service of humankind with godlike love. When a person has silver in her soul level, it means she is connected to or has gifts in communication and is able to communicate well. Velvet black is like holes in space, which are doorways to other realities. Maroon means moving into one's task. Black is the absence of light, or profound forgetting, which leads to cancer, and which is seen on the soul level as thwarted ambition.

THE HEALING ARTS

By

TED KAPTCHUK AND MICHAEL
CROUCHER

The ceremony begins as the sun disappears over the horizon, the symbol of time entering the realm of dreams. From now on there is to be no quarreling, eating of corn dumplings, or, for specifics, urinating facing north. The first two days are consumed in the purification ritual of the sweat baths. Four pokers point out of the fire to the four corners of the earth. Dancing over these, the assembled purify themselves of worldly faults accumulated over a lifetime.

Now it is the patient's turn. He is made to vomit and to clean his bowels by taking herbs. The suds from the soapy yucca cactus clean him, and fragrant herbs anoint him. A cacophony of drums, rattles, whistles made of the largest bone of the eagle wing (to make his spirit soar), and "bullroarers" made of wooden slats (to cleanse and strengthen him with their screeching) fill the room. The patient is moved to a public confession of his sins and his violations of taboos. The climax of the ceremony is now about to be reached, and the arena is purified and readied.

The third day begins with a new forcefulness in the drums and rattles. Now the songs begin, acted out with gestures and stances. Reeds are lit—filled with fragrant plants, bluebird feathers, and native tobacco—as a sign to the gods. And the patient is identified to the gods by the eagle and owl feathers, as well as snakelike painted sticks, placed on him. The gods are also offered refreshments in the form of cornmeal figurines in the shape of porcupines and snakes. If everything is done precisely the gods will perform the healing act.

The chanter is the key. His songs tell the story of Rainboy, a Navaho hero. Sometimes it sounds like a morality play, at other times like Star Wars. It starts with the simple Rainboy, an innocent gambler, getting into all sorts of small scrapes. Rescued by the humblest of the Navaho Holy People, the bat, Rainboy eventually wanders to a strange land ruled by the White Thunder God, master of the rare winter thunder. Out of nowhere, the wife of White Thunder lassoes Rainboy with a preternatural rainbow and seduces him. Contorted by jealousy, White Thunder takes revenge. He smashes Rainboy into small pieces, scattering them in all directions. But the other gods take pity on the innocent Rainboy and a war ensues between them, and kindly Holy People, and the angry White Thunder and his allies. This cosmic clash creates the Navaho map and their customs once and for all. The battlefield is the sacred space of the Navaho; the only real time in this "main event." A truce is finally established so that healing rites can be performed. . . . The Navaho firmly believes that the chanter knows what he's doing, just as the angina patient has complete confidence in the art and science of surgical procedures. The distinction is that the surgeon has a different viewpoint on how he heals. I don't mean to suggest that face surgery is an effective or ethical way to deal with disease; my point is that there is a strong ritual element in much of modern medicine. Ritualistic healing is not being squarely faced and examined.

BODYWORK: CHOOSING AN APPROACH TO SUIT YOUR NEEDS

By

JOSEPH HELLER

and WILLIAM A. HENKIN

America's perennial concern with physical fitness has once again been making headlines. Yet a true appreciation of the value of bodywork has still not become a part of our national way of thinking.

Our well-intentioned efforts at exercise are designed for the most part to improve certain body systems—and some of them certainly benefit some of the people some of the time. Frequently, however, physical fitness programs are more concerned with building up our armor, our images and our self-protective attitudes than with providing any lasting physical benefit. Many programs, for example, concentrate on developing the outer musculature, which is useful for rapid defense. But its speed and strength are not as useful for more refined sensitivity, for subtler forms of movement or for making love.

Nor can the outer musculature alone—even in conjunction with the cardiovascular system—maintain the kinds of balance that makes for easy living. Indeed, the efforts of many fitness programs to encourage speed and aggressiveness are diametrically opposed to the major thrust of bodywork, which is to reduce the muscular tensions that both hold and produce physical and psychological armor. Body-

From "Bodywork: Choosing an Approach to Suit Your Needs," by Joseph Heller and William A. Henkin, in *Choices and Connections*. Excerpt used by permission of the publishers, Human Potential Resources, P. O. Box 1057, Boulder, CO 80306.

work seeks to make immaterial the images we have learned to carry around with us and to free us physically and somatically from the restrictions imposed on us by our attitudes. In other words, the purpose of bodywork is to free us by *balancing* rather than tightening the body.

The diverse forms of bodywork all derive from four principal traditions: the *energetic,* the *mechanical,* the *psychological,* and the *integrative.* These traditions, like the individual disciplines themselves, are far more thorough and complex than a brief overview can hope to convey. But at least such an overview, with a cursory description of a few representative forms, will identify some features that make these different schools of thought valuable in their own ways.

THE ENERGETIC TRADITION

Probably the oldest of the four bodywork traditions, the energetic is closest to the primitive rites of religion, magic and myth in its notion that human energy is related to and can be affected by divine, cosmic, or universal energy. At its least systematic, this tradition comprises the simple belief that higher energy will flow through the hands of a person especially attuned to it—a healer to make another person's ailing body well. With techniques that appear to vary little from one culture to another, the tradition encompasses faith healing, psychic healing, laying on of hands, calling up of spirits, and various forms of shamanism.

To contemporary Westerners, the energetic traditions that seem most systematic are those based on the Indian notion of chakras and those based on the Chinese idea of acupuncture meridians. The Hindu chakra system best known in the West today through Kundalini Yoga identifies seven primary energy points situated within the hollow central channel of the spine.

All chakras can be activated to varying degrees, and ailments of the body are understood to express energetic imbalances. As a result, some healers claim to be capable of curing physical maladies by cleaning, balancing and adjusting the chakras.

Acupuncture, an ancient Chinese healing system, also assumes the existence of energy channels within the body, called *meridians*. According to acupuncture theory, health results when the flow in the meridians is properly balanced between masculine (yang) and feminine (yin) energies. Pain, disease and disability can result when the energy is blocked or imbalanced. To right the balance, the acupuncturist stimulates the appropriate meridians by inserting and withdrawing extremely fine needles. . . .

Like acupuncture and the chakras, iridology, reflexology and a host of other holistic healing systems also rely for their coherence on the concept of balance—the balance of seasons, of the elements, of food groups, of patterns of human activity. What these approaches all have in common is their appreciation and use of energy configurations.

THE MECHANICAL TRADITION

The mechanical tradition in body work is based on an appreciation of the body's tangible parts and their interrelatedness. Unlike practitioners who focus on the energetic tradition, those who work with body mechanisms usually neither acknowledge nor use systems broader than the strictly physical. For the most part, they are concerned with the body as an interrelated system of pulleys, levers, hinges and plates which, because of stress and tension, may become worn or misaligned and therefore require adjustment.

Different schools within the mechanical tradition have focused on different facets of the body's mechanical components in their endeavors to correct imbalances. For example, Frederick Matthias Alexander sought to shift a person's attention from the end he or she sought to the means by which he or she sought that end, with the intention of enhancing sensory awareness. . . .

Since Alexander's time, others have devised means to balance the mechanisms of the body. Milton Trager, for instance, discovered that one can release tension from the joints by shaking each part of the body in a gentle, rhythmic way that permits the movement to transfer itself throughout the entire body. Rigidity in any portion of the anatomy blocks the natural path this movement tries to follow. This block is apparent to a Trager practitioner, who then works with his or her client to encourage release of the tension that creates the block. When all the blocks have been released in this fashion, the body can assume its proper, free-flowing structure and functioning.

The mechanical system developed by Moshe Feldenkrais aims to reprogram the nervous system through movement augmented by physical pressure and manipulation. Feldenkrais points out that people get into habit patterns that result in a reduced potential for movement. Feldenkrais developed a system of re-educating the body. His exercises, which start to unhook established mechanical connections from their nervous system programs, result in freer movement of the entire body. . . .

Generally better known than Alexander, Trager or Feldenkrais, and more mechanical as well, are the practices of chiropractic and osteopathy. Chiropractic is a mechanical realignment of the bones, particularly of the spine, and most particularly—according to Daniel Palmer, one of the originators of chiropractic—of the atlas, or first vertebra.

Osteopathy is also based on the manipulation of bones, but in a broader fashion than chiropractic. Whereas chiropractic focuses primarily on the spine, osteopathy concerns itself with all the bones and joints. For example, a chiropractor would be unlikely to treat a club foot, but an osteopath might well attempt to manipulate the foot's bones and joints into a more useful arrangement of parts, alleviating the condition to some degree.

The founder of Rolfing, Ida Rolf, was familiar with osteopathy and borrowed some of its techniques in the course of developing her own bodywork. One of the features that distinguished Rolf's system of structural integration from virtually every other practice in the mechanical tradition, however, is that she sought a unifying element for her work in the body itself. Where the chiropractor would not deal with a club foot, and the osteopath would deal with it as an isolated problem, Rolf looked for the connection between the misshapen part and the rest of the body. . . .

THE PSYCHOLOGICAL TRADITION

Although Ida Rolf clearly had something to say about it, the psychological tradition in bodywork is not concerned with the health and functioning of the body *per se*. Rather, its primary concern is the healthy functioning of the mind, which it reaches *through* the body by removing psychological blocks that manifest themselves in the living flesh. The psychological tradition was largely founded and promulgated by the work of two psychoanalytically trained physicians, Wilhelm Reich and Alexander Lowen.

Reich, at one time a prominent member of Freud's inner circle in Vienna, was the first Westerner to concentrate attention on the relationship between body tension, or rigidity, and psychological limitations to a person's well being. In the therapy he developed, a person lies on a table and breathes in specific ways dictated by the therapist, who monitors observable reactions in the body indicating blocks in the energy flow. Reich discovered that such blocks could be detected, for example, by the ways in which skin temperature or color may change on only one side of an apparently arbitrary line on the body, beyond which it would remain unaffected by the person's breathing. Reich saw that these blocks could be released directly by physical manipulations, which, when accompanied by psychoanalysis, enhanced therapy. . . .

Alexander Lowen—Reich's client, student and colleague, and, like Reich, a physician and psychiatrist—defined the psychological tradition in bodywork with great clarity.

Psychoanalysis, he said, throughout its development, has never been able to dissociate itself from the physical manifestations of emotional conflicts. Yet with respect to the physical function of the organism, the psychoanalytic attitude has been to approach it from its psychic reflection. One can proceed in the reverse direction with greater effectiveness, that is, from the physical problem to its psychic representation. . . .

THE INTEGRATIVE TRADITION

Integrative practices usually entail some attention to balancing the body mechanics, some to exploring the psychological connections between physical misalignment and the emotional or mental distress, and some to balancing the body's energy fields. In addition many include meditative, clearing or centering exercises that lead to peace of mind. Most of the meditative forms of bodywork start from the premise that life is flowing, fluid and constantly changing; and most are, or are based on, Eastern disciplines such as yoga and the martial arts.

Defined by Patanjali as union with God, yoga is often understood to be the path of union between an individual and the cosmos. No matter what form of yoga one practices, the ultimate purpose is to experience oneness with the whole universe: to have an integral experience of the hologram of one's being. Often in the practice of yoga, a kind of psychic meditation is combined with physical exercises that realign the body, so that the integration of body, mind and spirit takes place all in a single, balanced self.

The martial arts, too, are based on the balance of physical, psychological and energetic elements: as one's body is balanced, both at rest and in motion, one learns to recognize that outer and inner environments reflect one another, and that the person is the embodiment of both, as well as the fulcrum around which they hover. By maintaining balance and poise, one learns to direct one's energy so that it can influence one's surroundings, and in so doing, one learns how the surrounding energy affects one's own state of balance. The very fact of being balanced obviates many psychological issues and allows other issues to appear in such a new light that they cease to be experienced as problems. To be integrated is to be complete and whole, and it is exactly the end of completeness and wholeness that the integrative bodywork traditions serve.

Like the practice of yoga, the structural bodywork developed by Joseph Heller is based on the experience of the body as a hologram of the being; like the martial arts, it is designed to integrate the principles of the mechanical, psychological and energetic traditions, not just in exercises or in a teaching or bodywork session, but in the practical tasks and functions of daily life. . . .

Hellerwork combines the sort of deep-tissue bodywork pioneered by Rolf with movement awareness based on the principles of Aston patterning. To counteract the human tendency to drift back to the way things used to be, Hellerwork teaches people to sit, stand, bend, walk and balance themselves in keeping with their new structures. . . .

Hellerwork encourages a person to explore his or her past to discover where and when he or she began to adopt the mental attitudes and beliefs that led to such a presentation of self. Without such exploration, old habits can dominate even some of the restructuring that bodywork can accomplish.

DEATH, THE FINAL STAGE OF GROWTH

By

ELISABETH KÜBLER-ROSS

Death always has been and always will be with us. It is an integral part of human existence. And because it is, it has always been a subject of deep concern to all of us. Since the dawn of humankind, the human mind has pondered death, searching for the answer to its mysteries. For the key to the question of death unlocks the door of life.

In times past, human beings died in numbers too large for most of us to comprehend, the luckless victims of war and pestilence. Just living was an accomplishment of fate, and death was a feared and dreaded enemy who struck indiscriminately at rich and poor, good and bad alike. The thinkers of the past, pious people and representatives of Enlightenment wrote books about death. They tried to rob it of its strangeness and terror by studying it seriously. They tried to find its meaning in the lives of human beings. And at the same time that they clarified the meaning of death, they also contributed to understanding the significance of life.

Now, when humankind is surrounded by death and destruction as never before, it becomes essential that we study the problems of death and try to understand its true meaning.

For those who seek to understand it, death is a highly creative force. The highest spiritual values of life can originate from the thought and study of death.

We can see from studies of different religions that the thought of

death forms the kernel of all creeds, myths, and mysteries. . . . [D]if-
ferent views of death mold the lives of those who hold those views.
The most persistent questions that human beings explore through
their myths and religions are those pertaining to rebirth, resurrection, and a life hereafter: Is there another life after this one? And if
there is, what is the relationship between that one and the way you
live this one? It's not just a question of good and evil, heaven or
hell. . . . It's also a question of growth and the level of enlightenment
reached in this lifetime.

From the Indian Vedas (sacred texts of the earliest phase of
Indian religion, 3000 years ago) to the words of our contemporary
thinkers, the aim of all philosophers has been to elucidate the meaning of death, thus helping human beings to overcome their fear.
Socrates, Plato, and Montaigne have taught: to philosophize means
nothing more than to study the problem of death. And Schopenhauer
called death "the truly inspiring genius of philosophy."

Thomas Mann once said: "Without death there would scarcely
have been poets on earth." Any person who studies poetry through
the centuries can verify this. The first epic, the Babylonian
Gilgamesh, and the first-known lyric poem of world literature, a
poem by Sappho, dealt mainly with death. From then until now, no
great poet has existed who failed to dedicate some of his most beautiful verses to death. And all of them touched the deepest secret of
life while talking about death.

"No thought exists in me which death has not carved with his
chisel," said Michelangelo. From the Egyptian, Etruscan, and Attic
beginnings of art to modern surrealism, death has played an important part.

And as in philosophy, literature, and art, death was also the great
inspirer of music. The first songs were funeral dirges, and the great
music of Bach, Gluck, Mozart, Beethoven, Schubert, Liszt, Verdi,
Mahler, Moussorgsky, and the modern composers frequently has
death as its leading motif.

Death is, however, not only the inspirer of artistic imagination. It
has strongly influenced the ethical attitude of human beings as well.
Death was the great instructor of those noble characters in history
who we venerate as heroes, saints, or martyrs of science.

I hope to convey one important message to my readers: namely, that death does not have to be a catastrophic, destructive thing; indeed, it can be viewed as one of the most constructive, positive, and creative elements of culture and life.

This book attempts to familiarize the reader with some other aspects of death and dying, with the viewpoints of other people, other cultures, other religions, and philosophies. I hope that one thing comes through all these pages—namely, that all people are basically alike; they all share the same fears and the same grief when death occurs. We are finite little beings who could help each other if we would dare to show that we care, if we maintain some compassion and, last but not least, if we stop being judgmental and try to learn *why* people behave as they do in crisis. For this we need a sound understanding not only of human (general) behavior, but also of the individual's cultural and religious background.

In the decades to come we may see one universe, one humankind, one religion that unites us all in a peaceful world. It is up to each of you to lay the groundwork for this future generation, by making an attempt *now* to comprehend and care for your fellow humans, no matter what their creed, color, or philosophy. Through understanding that in the end we all share the same destiny—we may come also to understand that in life also we must be as one, aware and appreciative of our differences and yet accepting that in our humanness, we are all alike.

WHY IS IT SO HARD TO DIE?

Dying is an integral part of life, as natural and predictable as being born. But whereas birth is cause for celebration, death has become a dreaded and unspeakable issue to be avoided by every means possible in our modern society. Perhaps it is that death reminds us of our human vulnerability in spite of all our technological advances. We may be able to delay it, but we cannot escape it. We, no less than other, nonrational animals, are destined to die at the end of our lives. And death strikes indiscriminately—it cares not at all for the status or position of the ones it chooses; everyone must die, whether rich or poor, famous or unknown. Even good deeds will not excuse their doers from the sentence of death; the good die as often as the bad. It is perhaps this inevitable and unpredictable quality that makes death so frightening to many people. Especially those who put a high value on being in control of their own existence are offended by the thought that they, too, are subject to the forces of death.

But other societies have learned to cope better with the reality of death than we seem to have done. It is unlikely that any group has ever welcomed death's intrusion on life, but there are others who have successfully integrated the expectation of death into their understanding of life. Why is it so hard for us to do this? The answer may lie in the question. It is difficult to accept death in this society *because* it is unfamiliar. In spite of the fact that it happens all the time, we never see it. When a person dies in a hospital, he is quickly whisked away; a magical disappearing act does away with the evidence before it could upset anyone. But . . . being part of the dying process, the death, and the burial, including seeing and perhaps interacting with the body, is an important part of coming to grips with death—that of the person who has died and your own.

We routinely shelter children from death and dying, thinking we are protecting them from harm. But it is clear that we do them a disservice by depriving them of the experience. By making death and dying a taboo subject and keeping children away from people who are dying or who have died, we create fear that need not be there. When a person dies, we "help" their loved ones by doing things for them, being cheerful, and fixing up the body so it looks "natural." Again our "help" is not helpful; it is destructive. When someone dies, it is important that those close to him participate in the process; it will help them in their grief, and it will help them face their own death more easily.

It *is* hard to die, and it will always be so, even when we have learned to accept death as an integral part of life, because dying means giving up life on this earth. But if we can learn to view death from a different perspective, to reintroduce it into our lives so that it comes not as a dreaded stranger but as an expected companion to our life, then we can also learn to live our lives with meaning—with full appreciation of our finiteness, of the limits on our time here. I hope that this book will help you understand death and dying better and will make it a little less hard for you to die and a little easier for you to live.

WHO DIES?

By

STEPHEN LEVINE

What most people call freedom is just the ability to satisfy desire. Many say, "I want more freedom," and what they mean is they want to be able to have more of what they want. But that is not freedom, that is a kind of bondage. Freedom is the ability to have or *not have* what you want without it closing your heart. Freedom is not to act compulsively on all the contents of the mind, to let the contents flow away and tune to the unfolding. The content of your mind and the content of my mind may be different but the process by which it unfolds is precisely the same. Tuning to that process we enter the Tao.

This, again, is Suzuki Roshi:

"I went to Yosemite National Park, and I saw some huge waterfalls. The highest one there is 1,340 feet high, and from it the water comes down like a curtain thrown from the top of the mountain. It does not seem to come down swiftly, as you might expect; it seems to come down very slowly because of the distance. And the water does not come down as one stream, but is separated into many tiny streams. From a distance it looks like a curtain. And I thought it must be a very difficult experience for each drop of water to come down from the top of such a high mountain. It takes time, you know, a long time, for the water finally to reach the bottom of the waterfall. And it seems to me that our human life may be like this. We have many difficult experiences in our life. But at the same time, I thought, the water was not originally separated, but was one whole river. Only when it is separated does it have some difficulty in falling. It is as if the water does not have any feeling (of being separate) when it is one whole river. Only when divided into many drops can it begin to have or express some (separate) feeling.

"Before we were born we had no such feeling; we were one with the universe. This is called 'mind-only,' or 'essence of mind,' or 'big mind.' After we are separated by birth from this oneness, as the water falling from the waterfall is separated by the wind and rocks, then we have such feelings. And you have difficulty because of such feelings. You attach to the feeling you have without knowing just how this kind of feeling is created. When you do not realize that you are one with the river, or one with the universe, you have fear. Whether it is separated into drops or not, water is water. Our life and death are the same thing. When we realize this fact, we have no fear of death anymore and we have no actual difficulty in our life."

Letting go of the little mind, of your suffering, is simpler than you think, though it's the hardest work you will ever do. Cultivating that "don't know," we enter the process and become the Tao.

The contemplation of death encourages us to let go of our specialness. The fact of death, of having to leave this world behind, makes us see that we have the opportunity now to let go of all that stays the flow. Or will you try to take your specialness with you? Will death be a struggle and a tragedy? The contemplation of death can be used as an opportunity, even as a technique, to leave specialness behind and dissolve into that which is universal. As you die there seems to be an experience of melting, sometimes gradual, sometimes rapid, that frightens people who want to hold on to who they think they are. But it brings joy to those who wish to go beyond the clinging mind. For some death is the great initiation, an opportunity to let go yet deeper. At death your priorities become very clear. If it is to control the universe, to get all the juice you can, then you will go for the objects of your desires and lose touch with the deathless. Perhaps this is what Jesus meant when he said, "For what is a man profited, if he shall gain the whole world, and lose his own soul." Fear will block the wisdom and unity available in the experience. But if you want the truth more than anything else, your death will be another opportunity to let go of control, to merge with the mystery.

Indeed, those who seem most alive are those who want the truth more than life itself. It you want life more than truth, you will seldom touch the truth of your life. But if the truth is the priority, death will dissolve and only the truth will continue.

Our original nature is like a clear water. By imagining that we are something separate from the whole, that imagining seeks yet another body. Yearning for experience we exit the womb. We seek to "fulfill our destiny" rather than empty it.

Born again into a world of wildly changing forms, though having no essential form of our own, we take on the shapes of the containers we are poured into. We become "sons" or "daughters" and are told to think of ourselves in that manner. We are thought to be "responsible." Acculturated, we bend to the curves of that arbitrary modality. Slowly we solidify to fit the "acceptable" shape we are told we should think of ourselves as being. We take on the bends and curves, the hard edge of the container. Slowly we freeze into that shape. The straighter and harder the edge the more we are praised as being "someone" of merit. Eventually the mold can be removed and we stay frozen in that shape—this learned self-image is from that time on applied as the measure of all other forms. We become freeze-dried. Our mind like a wild river, our heart like a desert.

But water is water, no matter what its shape or form. The solidity of ice imagines itself to be its edges and density. Melting, it remembers; evaporating, it ascends.

When you let go of control of the universe, when you let go of everything, only the truth remains. And like a roshi you start responding from the moment. Your actions come out of the present. There is no force. Your boat is empty. The currents move you to the left, "Ahhh, the left." They move you to the right, "Ahhh, the right." But you never feel as though you are to the left or to the right, you only feel that you are here now, in the present. Open to all possibilities and opportunities of the moment. Fully present. Able to respond, not out of personal desire, but out of a sense of the appropriateness of things. You respond from the flow itself, or perhaps better stated, the flow responds to itself. No separation anywhere. Nowhere to go. Nothing to do. No one to be.

RETURN TO CENTER

By

BOBBIE PROBSTEIN

The first notes I wrote down were, "Hypnosis is a natural state of mind. The mind and body are inseparable; if your mind does not work for you, it will work against you. The three signals when you're out of step with your nature are: pain, unhappiness and frustration. *Everything you think vibrates through your body.* What you think of as your 'mind' is composed primarily of two parts, the conscious and the subconscious. By far the smaller of the two, the conscious mind is the thinking, rational part which deals with logical thought and responses to the outer world. The larger subconscious is the feeling, uncritical, obeying part, which operates whether you are awake or asleep. Its food is images, and that's what you're going to feed it."

I was inundated with more information and excited by the possibility that I might be able to change my body responses. If I could lessen my allergies, I would become a believer. It was the perfect test: I had nothing to lose, everything to gain. I'd had severe allergies at intervals in my life; I had often been incapacitated by the sneezing and wheezing, or listless and drugged from antihistamines taken to relieve symptoms. A year ago, a doctor had told me I was on the verge of bronchial asthma and since then I had been getting allergy shots; they helped, but I didn't like being dependent on them.

During the break, I asked Jim how I could use my mind to eliminate allergies. He surprised me by saying, "Well you can't tell yourself you don't have them if you do. Go after it another way."

I told him about the shots, and he said, "Each time you hypnotize yourself, visualize—in every minute detail—going to the allergist. *See* yourself getting the shots, but don't actually take them. Practice this twice a day, and you'll see how well it works."

At the end of the session, he gave us our first instructions in self-hypnosis: "Loosen your belts, put your feet flat on the floor, shut your eyes and visualize each part of your body, telling it to relax. I'll lead you through it in class; you practice at home. Now, give yourself the suggestion that you'll be wide awake in twenty minutes, feeling wonderful."

It worked fairly well; I did relax even though the hard chair was quite uncomfortable. It worked better at home where I was able to lie down, make myself comfortable and feel less self-conscious. Each time I visualized myself driving to the allergist, I wore different clothes and had a current conversation with the nurse. It was so real, I actually winced as I pictured the long, thin needle going in each arm and the redness and swelling that always followed the shots. It was too soon to know whether or not it would work.

I could hardly wait for the second class. Jim said, "The most important thing to remember is that any idea you hold to be true in your subconscious mind becomes binding upon you and determines the outcome of your behavior. Know that it may *not* be true—our subconscious can't judge that for itself. When you believe an incident or reinforce a condition, you're living in the past. When you change your imagery you can live in the present. So use it to your advantage!"

THE HARMONY OF HEALTH

By

O. CARL SIMONTON, M.D.

The healing process is a creative process; you must be sensitive and able to improvise and draw on your knowledge as the situation unfolds. If you are tuned in, you can do whatever presents itself at the time. You can learn to follow the inner self, the inner physician that tells you where to go. Healing is simply attempting to do more of those things that bring joy and fewer of those things that bring pain. Someone once said: "Let joy be your compass heading." This means that you should follow those things that bring joy into your life. Not just superficial joy, but deep fulfillment.

Implementing this at a pace that is comfortable is very important. People often want to do things in a hurry. I'm one of those people. I recognize it quickly in my patients, because we most readily see in others those problems that exist in ourselves. I am very sensitive to the side of my patients that wants to do things too fast and to excess, because that tendency is part of my own personality.

That brings us to the question of wisdom, and in particular the wisdom of how to integrate joy and not overdo it. One of my problems is that I tend to do things I like to excess. I sail to excess; I exercise to excess; I work to excess. So I have to learn to balance. Fortunately, I have people around me to remind me when I stray and to support my efforts to regain balance. My greatest help, however, is my own awareness.

Support systems are critical. In my case, my family is a significant part of my support system. When they are not supportive, it takes a huge toll on me. When they are supportive, it enhances my life. I've been involved in a fair amount of controversy in my work. In the first three or four years of this work, my family was suspect of what I was doing and of my motivations. That was a troubling time for me. But, as my parents and siblings began to understand what I was doing and became excited and supportive of my work, they were a great resource for me. Later on, when I went through other times of controversy and difficulty I had the family support to draw upon.

I believe that the attitudes and beliefs of the people we live with have a huge impact on what we do. For instance, in the case of illness, if my family believes that I'm going to die and there is nothing that I can do about it, this makes the process of getting well incredibly difficult. On the other hand, if they believe that I can become healthy again, their beliefs strengthen my ability to achieve it. This is true in any significant relationship, including the one between patient and healer.

The attitude of the healer is almost as important as the attitude of the person being healed. I think that's why it is important to separate the healer from the physician. You do not need any credentials to be a healer, whereas you do need credentials to be a physician. But physicians are not necessarily healers.

It is important to understand the position of the physician. This is particularly true if the physician is not a healer and does not understand the importance of attitude in healing. The physician is trained in the prevailing beliefs of the medical profession. If the patient can learn to view those beliefs as simply one person's beliefs rather than being overwhelmed by the doctor's authority and taking those beliefs as truth, he can be more aware of the type of care he is receiving. This becomes very important in helping a person deal with a physician who believes that there is no chance for a cure or even any significant chance for improvement.

If you, as a healer, can help the patient understand this, you will be doing a real service. Because you are not limited by the physician's or the health-care team's beliefs, you can help the patient get much more out of whatever treatment is being offered than the physician would even guess is possible.

THE EMPATHETIC RELATIONSHIP: A FOUNDATION OF HEALING

By

ROLLO MAY

In my view, the fundamental element of all healing is empathy. The word *empathy* sounds like *sympathy*, but its meaning is actually quite different. In the present context, it means that the healer does not promote healing in the patient by commiseration or sentimental feeling, but by a kind of subtle communication. In empathy there is nonverbal interchange of mood, belief, and attitude between doctor and patient, therapist and client, or any two people who have a significant relationship.

Empathy is the experience of understanding that takes place between two human beings. If you go into a music shop and pluck one string of a violin, each of the other instruments in the store will resonate with sound. Similarly, human beings can resonate with each other to such an extent that they can exchange understanding at a subtle level. In extreme terms, this exchange may take the form of telepathy.

Empathy is the basis of both human love and human hatred. It is the way in which one person can intuitively and directly understand or "reach into" another person without using words.

Native peoples in Central Africa serve as a vivid example of the way in which empathy works. In Pygmy societies, when the tribe as a whole believes a person is going to die soon, that person usually does. One explanation is that the force of the tribe's collective mood and attitude exerts a tremendous pressure on the person to die, and he or she usually obliges. Empathy, in this sense, sets the mood for what is going to happen.

Although I have discussed these sorts of destructive effects of empathy in greater detail in *The Meaning of Anxiety* and in *Love and Will*, it is important to mention here that empathy also can provide a positive healing effect. For instance, if a doctor, therapist, or group of individuals believes that such a person can be healed, there is a good chance that such healing will occur. As more and more individuals feel that healing is a possibility, the feeling is transferred, through empathy, to the person in need of healing.

The strange thing about healing, however, is that it often occurs with negative emotions as well. Negative emotions can be the trigger for someone to express honest thoughts in psychotherapy and in other healing modalities. In certain cases, negative emotions are essential to the healing process and are the only vehicle capable of taking the patient in a healing direction.

For example, my friend Dr. Irving Yalom, who used to work with people with severe cases of cancer, found that all his patients died except one: a woman who got very angry at her disease. Her anger kept her alive.

SECTION FOUR:

LOVING RELATIONSHIPS

Human love is not a substitute for spiritual love. It is an extension of it.

EMMANUEL

In India, the spiritual path is said to have two branches. One is the path of the Saddhu, the renunciate or monk. The other is the path of the householder, the husband and wife who choose to live in the world while keeping a spiritual focus in their lives.

Couples with New Age inclinations have often come together by pursuing their individual spiritual paths. Or they might have met through a shared therapeutic experience—perhaps a workshop or seminar. New Age networking groups and singles organizations have formed to help like-minded individuals find each other. An interest in growth and personal transformation, curiosity about shamanism or crystal healing, traveling on one of the many sacred sites tours, or some other "accident of fate" may have brought two New Age people together. Now they face the challenges of creating an ever-deepening, committed spiritual partnership.

New Age couples are not different from other couples, except that they attempt to apply the self-realization techniques that they have learned to their relationship. The connections between the partners are based on objectives such as honesty, intimacy, commitment, fidelity, shared spiritual values, and co-creation of a shared life purpose. They have an increased commitment to emotional awareness and spiritual growth, both together as a couple and individually.

These couples seek to break old destructive patterns in relationships and to create new healthy models of loving relationships.

There are many books and workshops that deal with healing dysfunctional families and relationships. The various twelve-step programs that address all forms of addiction have been useful to many couples in breaking old patterns. New Age couples strive to view all their difficulties, problems, and challenges as life training and growth opportunities. They hold the relationship as central to their spiritual path and practice love for each other as a mirror of their love for God.

The selections included in this section cover a range of concepts and approaches to creating healthy, happy partnerships. Richard Sutphen, in *You Were Born Again to Be Together,* shares stories of couples he has worked with in past life regressions who discovered their past lives together. This discovery of "karmic destiny" helped the partners to understand each other better and to clarify the purpose of their partnership.

In Robert A. Johnson's *We,* the myth of Tristan and Iseult is shared as a metaphor for the understanding of romantic love.

The End of Sex by George Leonard is a moving account of the power of commitment and "high monogamy" in marriage and partnership.

The Game of Life is a beautifully simple book that is a metaphysical primer. The major tenets of Science of Mind are presented in a simple yet poetic way. This book has been a favorite since it was published many years ago.

In his book *The Conscious Person's Guide to Relationships,* Ken Keyes speaks about creating "delightful relationships" by giving up all forms of addictions.

Dr. Barbara De Angelis shares wonderful tools and techniques from her popular workshop, "Making Love Work," in her resource book, *How to Make Love All the Time.*

Sondra Ray, founder of "The Loving Relationships Trainings," has written many excellent books that are New Age staples. In *Loving Relationships,* she shares ideas on how to find, achieve, and maintain fulfilling relationships. *I Deserve Love* is a primer for the end of guilt and the beginning of sexual satisfaction in relationships.

The New Age movement is filled with workshops and trainings, but the most successful of these deal with issues of family, forgiveness, self-esteem, and loving relationships. There is an enormous void in contemporary American culture in the creation of successful role models for family and relationships. Those trainings and authors who are addressing this void are offering valuable information to people who want to find loving relationships or improve the quality of the relationships they are in.

Kahlil Gibran's *The Prophet* has been quoted often and used in countless wedding ceremonies because his poetic descriptions of love strike such a harmonious chord in our hearts. "For the pillars of the temple stand apart and the cypress and the oak grow not in each others shadow..." *The*

Prophet is a true classic, the kind of book you read again and again, and then read aloud to your lover.

These books can assist couples by offering tools and techniques for creating and maintaining conscious relationships. The truly successful loving relationship is one of the most challenging and rewarding endeavors two human beings can share.

THE PROPHET

By

KAHLIL GIBRAN

Love gives naught but itself and takes naught but from itself.

Love possesses not nor would it be possessed; for love is sufficient unto love.

When you love you should not say, "God is in my heart," but rather, "I am in the heart of God."

And think not you can direct the course of love, for love, if it finds you worthy, directs your course.

Love has no other desire but to fulfil itself.

But if you love and must needs have desires, let these be your desires:

To melt and be like the running brook that sings its melody to the night.

To know the pain of too much tenderness.

To be wounded by your own understanding of love;

And to bleed willingly and joyfully.

To wake at dawn with a winged heart and give thanks for another day of loving;

To rest at the noon hour and meditate love's ecstasy;

To return home at eventide with gratitude;

And then to sleep with a prayer for the beloved in your heart and a song of praise upon your lips.

Then Almitra spoke again and said, And what of Marriage, master?
And he answered saying:
You were born together, and together you shall be forevermore.
You shall be together when the white wings of death scatter your days.
Ay, you shall be together even in the silent memory of God.
But let there be spaces in your togetherness,
And let the winds of the heavens dance between you.

Love one another, but make not a bond of love:
Let it rather be a moving sea between the shores of your souls.
Fill each other's cup but drink not from one cup.
Give one another of your bread but eat not from the same loaf.
Sing and dance together and be joyous, but let each one of you be alone.

WE
By
ROBERT A. JOHNSON

For romantic love doesn't just mean loving someone; it means being "in love." This is a psychological phenomenon that is very specific. When we are "in love" we believe we have found the ultimate meaning of life, revealed in another human being. We feel we are finally completed, that we have found the missing parts of ourselves. Life suddenly seems to have a wholeness, a super-human intensity that lifts us high above the ordinary plane of existence. For us, these are the sure signs of "true love." The psychological package includes an unconscious demand that our lover or spouse always provide us with this feeling of ecstasy and intensity.

With typical Western self-righteousness we assume that our notion of "love," romantic love, must be the best. We assume that any other kind of love between couples would be cold and insignificant by comparison. But if we Westerners are honest with ourselves, we have to admit that our approach to romantic love is not working well.

Despite our ecstasy when we are "in love," we spend much of our time with a deep sense of loneliness, alienation, and frustration over our inability to make genuinely loving and committed relationships. Usually we blame other people for failing us; it doesn't occur to us that perhaps it is we who need to change our own conscious attitudes—the expectations and demands we impose on our relationships and on other people.

This is the great wound in the Western psyche. It is the primary psychological problem of our Western culture. Carl Jung said that if you find the psychic wound in an individual or a people, there you also find their path to consciousness. For it is in the healing of our psychic wounds that we come to know ourselves. Romantic love, if we truly undertake the task of understanding it, becomes such a path to consciousness. If Westerners will free themselves from their automatic servitude to their unconscious assumptions and expectations they will not only find a new awareness in their relationships but a new awareness of their own selves.

Romantic love has existed throughout history in many cultures. We find it in the literature of ancient Greece, the Roman Empire, ancient Persia, and feudal Japan. But our modern Western society is the only culture in history that has experienced romantic love as a mass phenomenon. We are the only society that makes romance the basis of our marriages and love relationships and the cultural ideal of "true love."

The ideal of romantic love burst into Western society during the Middle Ages. It first appeared in our literature in the myth of Tristan and Iseult, then in the love poems and songs of the troubadours. It was called "courtly love"; its model was the brave knight who worshiped a fair lady as his inspiration, the symbol of all beauty and perfection, the ideal that moved him to be noble, spiritual, refined, and high-minded. In our time we have mixed courtly love into our sexual relationships and marriages, but we still hold the medieval belief that true love has to be the ecstatic adoration of a man or woman who carries, for us, the image of perfection.

Carl Jung has shown us that when a great psychological phenomenon suddenly appears in the life of an individual, it represents a tremendous unconscious potential that is rising to the level of consciousness. The same is true for a culture. At a certain point in the history of a people, a new possibility bursts out of the collective unconscious; it is a new idea, a new belief, a new value, or a new way of looking at the universe. It represents a potential good if it can be integrated into consciousness, but at first it is overwhelming, even destructive.

Romantic love is one of these truly overwhelming psychological phenomena that have appeared in Western history. It has overwhelmed our collective psyche and permanently altered our view of the world. As a society, we have not yet learned to handle the tremendous power of romantic love. We turn it into tragedy and alienation more often than into enduring human relationships. But, I believe, if men and women will understand the psychological dynamics behind romantic love and learn to handle them consciously, they will find a new possibility of relationship, both to themselves and to others.

THE END OF SEX

By

GEORGE LEONARD

AN UNCOMMON OPTION

High Monogamy is not for everyone, nor is it the only path to creative, transformative love. Sometimes the most fleeting erotic encounter can strike the chord of poignancy and delight that has the power to transform lives, and in youth a certain amount of erotic exploration is a natural urge. High Monogamy deserves a brief discussion here simply because, in an age that is fascinated with erotic options, it is one option that is rarely mentioned. I define it as a long-term relationship in which both members are *voluntarily* committed to erotic exclusivity, not because of legal, moral or religious scruples, not because of timidity or inertia, *but because they seek challenge and an adventure.*

High Monogamy requires, first of all, a goodly supply of self-esteem in both partners. Psychologist Nathaniel Branden, one of the rare modern writers who advocates romantic love, argues that no other factor is more important.

It has become something of a cliché to observe that, if we do not love ourselves, we cannot love anyone else. This is true enough, but it is only part of the picture. If we do not love ourselves, it is almost impossible to believe fully that we *are loved* by someone else. It is almost impossible to *accept* love. It is almost impossible to *receive* love. No matter what our partner does to show that he or she cares, we do not experience the devotion as convincing because we do not feel lovable to ourselves.

*   *   *

Self-esteem, no matter how important, is not all that is required of those who would take the path of High Monogamy. It is essential that both partners have mutual interests and share a common vision of life's purpose and how to achieve it. Each partner needs the ability to celebrate and support the other, not only in low moments but also in high. "Never marry a person," Nathaniel Branden tells his clients, "who is not a friend of your excitement." The High Monogamist is not blindly approving but rather is dedicated to an uncommon openness and honesty. At the same time, he or she knows *how* to be open and honest without being abrasive or dogmatic.

Some of the virtues needed for High Monogamy—such things as enthusiasm, loyalty, courtesy, and patience—have become so platitudinous as to fade into the background noise of the modern world. And yet, unacknowledged, their presence or absence shapes the outcome of every relationship. In a book on marriage, the great psychologist Carl Rogers tells us that when he turned forty he mysteriously became impotent. This condition lasted a year, during which his wife remained cheerful, loving, and supportive. At the end of the year, his impotence disappeared, never to return. His wife's uncanny patience so touched Rogers that he knew he would love her until the end of her days.

Still, it is not merely the exercise of the common virtues that marks the High Monogamist, but rather a sort of towering, vertiginous daring. For this state requires that we look directly and unflinchingly at our every weakness and flaw, straight down through layer after layer of cowardice and self-deception to the very heart of our intentionality. And in High Monogamy we are forced, as well, to confront something even more terrifying: our beauty and magnificence, our potential to love and create and feel deeply, and the daily, hourly, moment-by-moment waste of that potential. And when we achieve the unnerving clarity that High Monogamy demands, we must either beat a fast retreat or undertake to transform ourselves.

Simone de Beauvoir has argued that eroticism "is a movement toward the *other*, this is its essential character, but in the deep intimacy of the couple, husband and wife become for one another the *same*; no exchange is any longer possible, no giving and no conquering." De Beauvoir in this case failed to look deeply enough into the possibilities of the monogamous situation. High Monogamy is not a mere fusion, not a mutual loss of self. It is the reassertion of a more fundamental self, explainable only through the paradox: *The more I am truly myself, the more I can be truly one with you. The more I am truly one with you, the more I can be truly myself.* The paradox is inescapable. In High Monogamy, the couple constitutes a single entity made of two autonomous entities. For each person, the partner is both the Same and the Other. In this regard, the couple models the ancient mystery of multiplicity within unity, identity within holonomy.

It is easy to associate multiple sexual partners with personal change and monogamy with personal stasis. This can at times be called Low Monogamy; having an affair can reawaken dulled perceptions and trigger a transformation of sorts. But extramarital affairs or the pursuit of recreational sex are far more likely to be associated with the avoidance of change. After superficial erotic novelty has faded, after ego has had its full run (all the life stories told, all the sexual tricks displayed), *then* the adventure of transformation and a deeper eroticism can begin. But it is precisely at this point that most of us are likely to lose our nerve and leap into another bed, where we can once again tell our stories, display our tricks, do *anything* rather than see ourselves clearly and start doing something about it.

Indeed, one glimpse into the powerful mirror of High Monogamy might be all it takes to send us back into the desolate comfort of Low Monogamy or out in hot pursuit of the-same-thing-another-time-around. In either case, the underlying, unacknowledged aim is to avoid change, to be allowed to lead an essentially predictable life. High Monogamy, merciless in its presentation of self-knowledge, demands that we change, that we have the courage to lead an essentially unpredictable life.

Advocates of multiple sex have a saying: "Why should I be satisfied with a sandwich when there's a feast out there?" Obviously, they have never experienced High Monogamy. Those of us who have tried both tend to see it differently. Casual recreational sex is hardly a feast—not even a good hearty sandwich. It is a diet of fast food served in plastic containers. Life's feast is available only to those who are willing and able to engage life on a deeply personal level, giving all, holding back nothing.

It would be a mistake to over praise High Monogamy. Nothing is quite as glorious as it can be made to sound, and human beings are ingenious in discovering ways to sabotage their own joy. Still, for those adventurers who can make the leap into commitment, the rewards are great: a rare tenderness, an exaltation, a highly charged erotic ambience, surprise on a daily basis, transformation. But there is no insurance policy.

No wonder High Monogamy is so rare and so rarely even mentioned. The survey takers, in fact, suggest that it is virtually impossible. Romance fades, they proclaim, after an average of fifteen months. Or is it eighteen months, or three years? In any case, romance fades. And they are often right.

THE CONSCIOUS PERSON'S GUIDE TO RELATIONSHIPS

By

KEN KEYES

"I love you" really means "When I'm with you, I'm
in touch with the beautiful, capable and lovable parts
of me."

When going into a relationship, it is helpful to have a clear understanding of what the words "I love you" really mean. Of course, if
you are a saint who has completed the inner work of upleveling
addictions to preferences, the words "I love you" are more likely to
be an expression of the oneness that is being experienced with everything everywhere. Since this book was not written for saints, let's
look at what the rest of us mean by "I love you."

What is really happening inside my nervous system when I say "I
love you"? What's happening is that when I am with you, things you
say and do help me experience parts of me that I regard as beautiful,
capable and lovable. In other words, what I am loving is my own
experience of me. You're mirroring me and letting me see the beautiful, capable and lovable parts of me.

Now let's turn it around. If I create the experience of hating you instead of loving you, it means that the things you are doing and saying are more or less continuously putting me in touch with thoughts and actions that I would addictively reject in me if I were to say or do them. For example, if after much effort I finally manage to quit smoking, the sight of your smoking may touch off addictive programming that makes me dislike you for smoking because I now reject this type of behavior in myself—or perhaps because being with smokers makes it difficult for me to resist my addiction. Perhaps a while back when I was smoking, I may have loved you for your smoking because it then reminded me of behavior I was still accepting in myself.

Thus we see that other people simply act as a mirror for what we are accepting or rejecting in ourselves. Unfortunately the illusion that we create through the operation of our minds is that we credit the mirror (the other person) for what we see reflected there. The big game of the ego-mind is to keep us trapped in the illusion that its feelings and judgments refer to external realities. We thus see that we create the experience of love or hate based on what we accept or reject in ourselves (or would accept or reject in ourselves if we were doing these things).

Since this is a rather sloppy and self-centered procedure for determining the quality and quantity of our love, we increasingly see how important it is to learn to accept and love ourselves—and I mean unconditionally. When we burden our perception of ourselves with all these shoulds and shouldn'ts, rights and wrongs, and goods and bads, we really destroy our ability to perceive other people clearly— and to create the experience of love when we are with them.

We thus see that when we reject someone, we are really rejecting something in ourselves—and we are thus blaming an innocent person. As we become more skillful in creating our experience, we increasingly learn to create the continuous experience of ourselves and others as beautiful, capable, and lovable. As we become more aware of the inner workings of our minds, we increasingly understand how "I love you" basically means, "When I'm with you, I get in touch with the parts of me that I experience as beautiful, capable and lovable."

There are over four billion people on this earth. So how do we choose whom to be involved with? Obviously selection is needed. It makes sense to get to know your own addictive demand patterns and those of the person you're thinking of being with. In a relationship, you'll have to live with each other's addictive demands. You have to ask yourself if you can be with her/his demands for the rest of your life.

I strongly recommend that you don't go into a relationship with a secret program in your head that you're going to change the other person so that you can live happily with him/her. I've tried it and it doesn't work! There's nothing wrong with asking a person to change. But if you must have someone change in order for you to be happy, you're just setting up trouble in your life.

It's okay to be selective when deciding on a partner. Some people's addictive demands will be easier for you to live with than others. But above all, develop your body, mind and living spirit so you don't blow apart when strong emotions are triggered.

Don't fall into the trap that there is only one special person that you are able to love. Instead, try to develop the expectation that the world is full of people that you can love and that can love you—even in the deeper levels of relationships. Since "I love you" really means "When I'm with you, I'm in touch with the beautiful, capable and lovable parts of me," you will greatly increase the number of people with whom you can establish a deep love relationship by more deeply accepting and loving yourself!

Since your partner is a projection of your mind of what you want and don't want in your life, the simplest way to change your experience of your partner is to work on what you're judgmentally rejecting about yourself. This neat strategy involving your own inner development can make you the master of your experience—instead of being an effect of the person you choose to be in a relationship with. This helps you to stay out of the dead-end you get yourself into when you create the illusion that you've got to find the one person that is your soul-mate—and on whom your happiness depends.

THINK ON THESE THINGS

By
J. KRISHNAMURTI

FREEDOM AND LOVE

I don't know if any of you have noticed, early in the morning, the sunlight on the waters. How extraordinarily soft is the light; and how the dark waters dance, with the morning star over the trees the only star in the sky. Do you ever notice any of that? Or are you so busy, so occupied with the daily routine, that you forget or have never known the rich beauty of this earth—this earth on which all of us have to live? Whether we call ourselves communists or capitalists, Hindus or Buddhists, Moslems or Christians, whether we are blind, lame, or well and happy, this earth is ours. Do you understand? It is our earth, not somebody else's, not some rich man's earth, it does not belong exclusively to the powerful rulers, to the nobles of the land, but it is our earth, yours and mine. We are nobodies, and yet we also live on this earth, and we all have to live together. It is the world of the poor, as well as of the rich, of the unlettered as well as of the learned; it is our world, and I think it is very important to feel this and to love the earth, not just occasionally on a peaceful morning, but all the time. We can feel that it is our world and love it only when we understand what freedom is.

There is no such thing as freedom at the present time, we don't know what it means. We would like to be free, but if you notice everybody—the teacher, the parent, the lawyer, the policeman, the soldier, the politician, the business man—is doing something in his own little corner to prevent that freedom. To be free is not merely to do what you like, or to break away from outward circumstances which bind you, but to understand the whole problem of dependence. Do you know what dependence is? You depend on your parents don't you? You depend on your teachers, you depend on the cook, the postman, on the man who brings you milk, on so on. That kind of dependence one can understand fairly easily. But there is a far deeper kind of dependence which one must understand before one can be free; the dependence on another for happiness. Do you know what it means to depend on somebody for your happiness? It is not the mere physical dependence on another that is so binding, but the inward psychological dependence from which you derive so-called happiness, for when you depend on somebody in that way, you become a slave. If, as you grow older, you depend on your parents emotionally, on your wife or husband, on a guru, or on some idea, there is already the beginning of bondage. We don't understand this—although most of us, especially when we are young, want to be free.

To be free we have to revolt against all inward forms of dependence, and we cannot revolt if we don't understand why we are dependent. Until we understand and really break away from all inward dependence we can never be free, for only in that understanding can there be freedom. But freedom is not a mere reaction. Do you know what a reaction is? If I say something that hurts you, if I call you an ugly name and you get angry with me, that is a reaction—a reaction born of dependence; and independence is a further reaction. But freedom is not a reaction, and until we understand reaction and go beyond it, we are never free.

Do you know what it means to love somebody? Do you know what it means to love a tree, or a bird, or a pet animal, so that you take care of it, feed it, cherish it, though it may give you nothing in return, though it may not offer you shade, or follow you, or depend on you? Most of us don't love in that way, we don't know what that means at all because our love is always hedged about with jealousy, anxiety, fear—which implies that we depend inwardly on each other, we want to be loved. We don't just love and leave it there, we ask something in return; and in that very asking we become dependent.

So freedom and love go together. Love is not a reaction. If I love you because you love me, that is a mere trade, a thing to be bought in the market; it is not love. To love is not to ask anything in return, not even to feel that you are giving something—and it is only such love that can know freedom.

I DESERVE LOVE

By

SONDRA RAY

At the very beginning of our relationship I wrote "I am now developing a loving, harmonious lasting relationship," and I also did most of the affirmations in this chapter. Our relationship has continued for two years and has been completely nourishing and effortless for both of us.

If you have a good relationship with *yourself*, you will automatically have a good relationship with others. "The soul attracts that which it secretly harbors." In other words, you will attract the person who has harmony with your thought structures. If you feel really good about yourself, you'll attract someone who also feels good about him/her self. By the universal law of attraction someone will respond to the mental vibrations you exude.

You can create the perfect relationship for yourself by sitting down and listing the things you want in such a relationship. Meditate on them. Imagine already having such a relationship. Imagine the person you want for a partner. If you really are willing for it to happen, someone will come into your life just as you imagine, by this universal law of attraction. Thought creates vibrations which inevitably attract that which is in its image.

If you are already in a relationship, the same procedure will work. Pictures these positive, divine qualities coming out in him or her. Your partner will soon develop and become as you imagine. Jesus often spoke of the law of attraction. "As ye believe, so shall it be done unto you." "Unto him who hath, shall be given." When you come to understand that there is only one universal mind which is every place at the same time and in all things, you will see that the differences between you and others are illusionary. We are all just vibrating at different levels. Raise your vibration level and you will attract people on higher and higher levels.

Do not dwell on thoughts of the lack of things. There are no limitations. There is no lack in the universal mind (God) of which we are all part. Whatever you dare ask for you will be given. Watch yourself. Watch your thoughts. If you are thinking "I'll never meet somebody who————" etc., you never will. Immediately invert the thought to someone like this: "I am now attracting someone who ————" etc.

What you are willing to accept comes your way. Ken Keyes said "Happiness is experienced when your life gives you what you are willing to accept." So take responsibility for the thoughts you choose to think regarding relationships. Remember, we really are all related so you don't have to search and make effort. You can bring people you like into your life with your thoughts. The logical person to put into your circle is someone with whom you are in harmony—whomever you think you deserve.

Let's say you are now in a relationship. You may wonder how to make or keep it successful. It's easy. A successful relationship is based upon one being nourished by the other person's presence. That is enough. You don't have to do anything else except set up certain agreements; make it a game. Don't get stuck in the rules, however. You might want to change them as frequently as every week. All you have to do is negotiate.

It is important to remember that you must experience your own self-love before you can experience another's. A loving relationship is when two people experience each other's *being*. In a loving relationship, the loving is absolute already. It is in the "relationship" that the action comes in.

Loving relationships can benefit you immensely. (So don't deprive yourself.) Another person can enrich you. Another can assist

you to grow faster. Another person can enlighten you, fast. Your
negative patterns are likely to come up quickly for you to see. Since
you attract what you are, you have a mirror at all times to see
yourself. Your partner can be your personal Guru. You always get
value.

HOW TO MAKE LOVE ALL THE TIME

By

BARBARA DE ANGELIS, PH.D.

SEX: THE BIG COVER-UP

If you think that the biggest problem in your relationships has a lot to do with sex, you are probably wrong. Don't feel too bad, though, because you are not alone. One of the most serious mistakes most people make in their relationships is attempting to isolate a part of the relationship, like sex, from the whole, thinking that when one part is fixed, the whole relationship will be better. I call this the "cover-up" approach to dealing with problems.

Secret: Most sexual problems are just symptoms of problems in other areas. If you try to suppress or hide the weaknesses or problems in your relationship, they will emerge in bed!

Here is how one of my clients described his relationship:

"Everything is very good in my relationship with my wife. We are very close; she is a great companion, a wonderful mother to our children, and extremely intelligent. Things are very smooth in our life, and I think we are pretty happy. But there is one thing I wanted to discuss with you. You see, I'm no longer really turned on to my wife sexually. We still have sex, but it feels like we are just doing it to live up to our expectations of how many times a happily married couple should make love. And it feels pretty mechanical.

"It wasn't always like this. When we first met, we were quite passionate and I felt very attracted to her. Things are certainly different now, but other than that, we have a wonderful marriage. I came to you because I hoped you could teach me some techniques to enjoy sex again."

My answer to this man was simple and very surprising to him: "Your real problem lies in your relationship, and not in bed!" Yes, I could suggest many things to create more excitement in this man's sex life, but they wouldn't work. *Sex is just a mirror of the rest of your relationship.* There is no such thing as a great relationship which just happens to have a big sexual problem.

THE REAL SOURCE OF LASTING SEXUAL EXCITEMENT

As human beings, we are very skilled at fooling ourselves and others when it comes to knowing what we are feeling. But there is one area which you cannot control so easily, and that is your body. If you insist to me that you are not upset about something, and I hook you up to an instrument that measures physiological responses, your body would not lie. It would tell me that you were upset, even if you denied it.

The same thing happens during sex. *Sexual excitement is a natural reaction to certain conditions.* When those conditions are absent or inhibited, so is your natural sexual response. In this way, you're most fortunate: Sex is a great barometer for telling you how well your relationship is working, and when it needs more attention.

I'm not saying that nothing can be done to bring about sexual rejuvenation in a relationship. Some books will tell you that if you aren't turned on by your partner, you should fantasize about someone else while having sex, or try having an affair. These things may work to improve your sex life on a superficial and temporary level. But beware of the great danger in superficial sexual remedies! *As you become more and more dependent on outside stimulation (fantasy, other people, vibrators, etc.) you decrease your natural ability to feel turned on by* *your partner. You may feel turned on **with** another partner, but not **by** him or her.* Two people who are turned on within themselves, but not by the other person, are two people who are having sex, but not making love.

If you feel you have sexual problems in your relationship, and your sexual functions were normal, healthy, and exciting in the beginning of your relationship with your partner, then your problems most likely have little or nothing to do with sex. They are symptoms of something deeper in the relationship, such as unexpressed anger or disappointment, lack of trust, unresolved conflicts, or fear of failure. By discovering the real problems and working together with your partner to heal them, you will see your sexual "problems" diminish and eventually disappear.

Lisa and Tom were instantly attracted to one another when they met. They were thrilled that they had at last found a relationship with the right sexual chemistry. Lisa and Tom fell madly in love and soon moved in together.

One year later, Lisa and Tom had practically stopped having sex, and neither of them could figure out why. Tom felt frustrated because he had been rejected so many times by Lisa. Lisa felt afraid of Tom, and the more he complained about their nonexistent sex life, the more defensive she became. Lisa and Tom came to me for help because they loved each other very much and were desperate to change their passionless relationship.

The first thing I taught Lisa and Tom was that sex was not their problem, but a symptom of other problems they hadn't dealt with. Then I taught them everything I'll be teaching you in this book, especially how to make love all the time in their relationship, and not wait until they got into bed to do so. Three months later, Lisa and Tom were having sex again and loving it. The passion was back.

Passionate sex is a symptom of a passionate relationship. And a passionate relationship means knowing how to make love with your partner all the time, and not waiting until you get into bed to start.

In this book, I call the conditions that support making love all the time "secrets," because I feel that the knowledge of how to create the right conditions for lasting love *is* hidden from most people. When you read these "secrets," you will find they make so much sense that you may ask yourself, "Why didn't I think of that?" or "It's so simple — I wonder why I never saw it this way before?" The truth is usually simple. But these simple truths about how to make love all the time are things we just aren't taught.

THE GAME OF LIFE

By
FLORENCE SCOVEL SHINN

Every man on this planet is taking his initiation in love. "A new commandment I give unto you, that ye love one another." Ouspensky states, in "Tertium Organum," that "love is a cosmic phenomenon," and opens to man the fourth dimensional world, "The World of the Wondrous."

Real love is selfless and free from fear. It pours itself out upon the object of its affection, without demanding any return. Its joy is in the joy of giving. Love is God in manifestation, and the strongest magnetic force in the universe. Pure, unselfish love draws to itself its own; it does not need to seek or demand. Scarcely anyone has the faintest conception of real love. Man is selfish, tyrannical or fearful in his affections, thereby losing the thing he loves. Jealousy is the worst enemy of love, for the imagination runs riot, seeing the loved one attracted to another, and invariably these fears objectify if they are not neutralized.

For example: A woman came to me in deep distress. The man she loved had left her for another woman, and said he never intended to marry her. She was torn with jealousy and resentment and said she hoped he would suffer as he had made her suffer; and added, "How could he leave me when I loved him so much?"

I replied, "You are not loving that man, you are hating him," and added, "You can never receive what you have never given. Give a perfect love and you will receive a perfect love. Perfect yourself on this man. Give him a perfect, unselfish love, demanding nothing in

From *The Game of Life* by Florence Scovel Shinn.

return, do not criticize or condemn, and bless him wherever he is."

She replied, "No, I won't bless him unless I know where he is!"

"Well," I said, "that is not real love. When you send out real love, real love will return to you, either from this man or his equivalent, for if this man is not the divine selection, you will not want him. As you are one with God, you are one with the love which belongs to you by divine right."

Several months passed, and matters remained about the same, but she was working conscientiously with herself. I said, "When you are no longer disturbed by his cruelty, he will cease to be cruel, as you are attracting it through your own emotions."

Then I told her of a brotherhood in India, who never said, "Good morning" to each other. They used these words: "I salute the Divinity in you." They saluted the divinity in everyman, and in the wild animals in the jungle, and they were never harmed, for they saw only God in every living thing. I said, "Salute the divinity in this man, and say 'I see your divine self only. I see you as God sees you, perfect, made in His image and likeness.' "

She found she was becoming more poised, and gradually losing her resentment. He was a Captain, and she always called him "The Cap."

One day, she said, suddenly, "God bless the Cap wherever he is."

I replied: "Now, that is real love, and when you have become a 'complete circle,' and are no longer disturbed by the situation, you will have his love, or attract its equivalent."

I was moving at this time, and did not have a telephone, so was out of touch with her for a few weeks, when one morning I received a letter saying, "We are married."

At the earliest opportunity, I paid her a call. My first words were, "What happened?"

"Oh," she exclaimed, "a miracle! One day I woke up and all suffering had ceased. I saw him that evening and he asked me to marry him. We were married in about a week, and I have never seen a more devoted man."

There is an old saying: "No man is your enemy, no man is your friend, every man is your teacher."

So one should become impersonal and learn what each man has to teach him, and soon he would learn his lessons and be free.

The woman's lover was teaching her selfless love, which every-man, sooner or later, must learn.

Suffering is not necessary for man's development; it is the result of violation of spiritual law, but few people seem able to rouse themselves from their "soul sleep" without it. When people are happy, they usually become selfish, and automatically the law of Karma is set in action. Man often suffers loss through lack of appreciation.

YOU WERE BORN
AGAIN TO BE
TOGETHER

By

DICK SUTPHEN

Karma is totally just. No one can argue that. It explains the supposed inequality we see around us daily. It explains sickness, health, affliction, fame, fortune, poverty, and life and death. As Kahlil Gibran said in *The Prophet*, ". . . the murdered is not unaccountable for his own murder." He meant that karma was being balanced.

Let's look at karma from the "reward" side. Take a man who has made a great deal of money . . . is this a reward, or is it a test? Did he make the money fairly, without hurting others or taking advantage of situations that in some way harmed others? Did he make it at the sacrifice of devoting some time to things that are more important than money? Is he using his resources beneficially or is he piling up negative karma on a personal power trip? He has been given his opportunity to grow in a special way. How he handles it will be balanced in the future.

If you've made mistakes in a personal relationship or marriage, you can use the time you have to learn from them. You do have the choice to rise above such negative karma—now.

I believe some marital relationships are destined to end, that the two individuals have learned all they can from each other in this life and that new opportunities are waiting for both.

If two people know it is over and feel divorce is the only answer, it is most important to achieve the parting without developing negative karma. Negative actions and emotions will produce negative karma. If this is the result, the two will have to go through it all over again and probably with the same individual . . . in another life and in other bodies, until they've learned the lessons they set out to learn.

It seems that divorce, in some cases, is the primary reason for two people having come together in the first place. They have predetermined the situation as a test of their own soul's growth — to see if they have evolved to the point of parting under positive circumstances.

SECTION FIVE:

SCIENCE

Science, from a New Age perspective, could be loosely defined as a scientific quest to save the planet, and a scientific search for God. This search is conducted through the study of new physics, astronomy, cybernetics, computers, the environmental Gaia movement, and brain research.

New Physics is a tremendously interesting area of science. Studying atoms, molecules, and electrons has given way to discovery of even tinier particles of energy called quarks. At the edge of scientific discovery are the questions about the "reality" of time, the "big bang theory," and the existence of "life force energy." Unexplainable in scientific terms, yet increasingly obvious in scientific experiments and discoveries is an "intention toward life," an inclination of movement, of growth or evolution. Books such as *Parallel Universes* by Fred Allen Wolf and *The Universe Is a Green Dragon* by Brian Swimme inspire readers to think about life, energy, and time in new ways.

French Jesuit Pierre Teilhard de Chardin (1881–1955) has had a profound influence on New Age thinkers. His theory of evolution (vastly generalized and simplified here) states that matter and energy are two aspects of one principle, that spirit is a function of matter, and that evolution moves toward increasing complexity. In *The Aquarian Conspiracy*, Marilyn Ferguson says "Teilhard prophesied the phenomenon central to this book: a conspiracy of men and women whose new perspective would trigger a critical contagion of change." Teilhard's books were forbidden, banned by the Catholic church, in his own lifetime. Now they are hot sellers in the bookstores all over the country.

The scientific discoveries made about the human brain in the past decade have been extremely exciting. Evidence supports the existence of a split between brain functions; the right brain housing the neurological functions determining creativity, intuition, and access to deeper subconscious influences, while the left brain determines the logical, systematic, rational, more scientific types of reasoning and analysis. "Right- and left-brain thinking" have become part of everyday language.

Brain research has led to new forms of psychology such as Neuro-Linguistic Programming, a leading edge behavioral technology for creating instant change, reframing past traumas, and assuring success in personal and professional situations.

There is even newer evidence to suggest that the brain is made up of four quadrants rather than two. We can look forward to more discoveries as brain research continues.

It is very exciting to read the work of these authors and scientists and realize that the field of physics and the field of metaphysics are starting to merge.

THE TAO OF PHYSICS

By

FRITJOF CAPRA

In the Chinese view, it is better to have too little than too much, and better to leave things undone than to overdo them, because although one may not get very far this way, one is certain to go in the right direction. Just as the man who wants to go farther and farther East will end up in the West, those who accumulate more and more money in order to increase their wealth will end up being poor. Modern industrial society, which is continuously trying to increase the "standard of living" and thereby decreases the quality of life for all its members is an eloquent illustration of this ancient Chinese wisdom. . . .

The idea of cyclic patterns in the motion of the Tao was given a definite structure by the introduction of the polar opposites Yin and Yang. They are the two poles which set the limits for the cycles of change. . . .

The more one studies the religious and philosophical texts of the Hindus, Buddhists, and Taoists, the more it becomes apparent that in all of them the world is conceived in terms of movement, flow, and change. This dynamic quality of Eastern philosophy seems to be one of its most important features. The Eastern mystics see the universe as an inseparable web, whose interconnections are dynamic and not static. The cosmic web is alive; it moves, grows and changes continually. Modern physics, too, has come to conceive of the universe as such a web of relations and, like Eastern mysticism, has recognized the web is intrinsically dynamic. The dynamic aspect of matter arises in quantum theory as a consequence of wave-nature of sub-atomic particles, and is even more essential in relativity theory, as we shall see, where the unification of space and time implies that the being of matter cannot be separated from its activity. The properties of sub-atomic particles can therefore only be understood in a dynamic context; in terms of movement, interaction, and transformation.

THE UNIVERSE IS A GREEN DRAGON

By

BRIAN SWIMME

THOMAS: When we reflect on the creativity and forgiveness, the wisdom, insight, and perdurance required of humans in our moment of crisis, we understand the need for the tremendous power of the universe for our work, our survival, and our celebration of life. To become fully mature as human persons, we must bring to life within ourselves the dynamics that fashioned the cosmos. We must become these cosmic dynamics and primordial powers in new human form. That is our task: to create the human form of the central powers of the cosmos.

YOUTH: Wait! The *human* form of the powers of the cosmos?

THOMAS: The same dynamics that created the galaxies created the stars and the oceans. The powers that build the universe are ultimately mysterious, issuing forth from and operating out of mystery. They are the most awesome and numinous reality in the universe. Humans *are* these dynamics, brought into self-awareness, becoming now fully aware of our creative work. We already have these powers in the forms of stars, mountains, atoms, and elephants, but we do not yet have them in human form. We are probing still, exploring, experimenting. Having only just arrived on this planet, we are still learning what it means to become fully human.

We have already discussed the most primordial of these powers, that of alluring activity. There are five other powers central to the creativity of the universe that are now needed in our task of world-building. These—the powers of Sea, Land, Life Forms, Fire and Wind—are the cosmic dynamics that, when woven together in a new form, will show the universe the human person.

We can begin by considering the sea. When I say the sea, I mean one activity of the sea above all: its powers to absorb. Water absorbs minerals and draws them into the life of plants, absorbs the soils of the plains, and deposits silt in river mouths. Put a lump of salt in water and it slowly disappears. New York City at the bottom of the sea would also slowly vanish. The sea demonstrates the power of the universe, extant at all levels, to *dissolve the universe*.

YOUTH: What would be another example?

THOMAS: We could consider the elementary particles. When electrons and protons interact with each other, protons are fundamentally and intrinsically changed. We say that the state vector is new, which means that we have a different reality than before. Why? The proton picks up something from its interaction with the electron. This is called quantum stickiness, and is central to the entire theory of quantum mechanics. If the proton is "sticky," it can't just slide by the electron. It absorbs something, assimilating it into its own state of being. It becomes new because, through its interaction with the electron, it has dissolved something into itself.

YOUTH: But it's still the same proton, isn't it?

THOMAS: The situation is similar to water rushing down a mountainside. The water picks up minerals and salts in its journey, becoming something new. When I say it is new, I mean that it enters into new relationships with the Earth. That is how we study the reality of a thing, through its interactions and relationships. If these relationships are new, we have a new entity. An electron passing through hot plasma enters into different relationships; an atom in a highly charged electric field enters into new relationships; so does water passing down a mountain.

YOUTH: But if you wanted to, you could separate the water from the minerals again, right? Then you'd have minerals in one jar, and water in another.

THOMAS: That's true. We tend to define something in terms of the parts it can be broken down into. But that's only half the story. Mineral water can be broken down into its parts, and we can learn something from that. But mineral water as an entity shows itself in ways that its parts can not. Breaking down water itself into its parts of hydrogen and oxygen gives us some knowledge of water, but water as an integral entity reveals things about itself that its parts do not. Learning by analysis has been emphasized over the last two centuries, but we also learn by examining things as wholes.

Notice how this conversation has proceeded: By looking at the sea, we begin to appreciate the manner in which the universe dissolves itself. But when we learn that this activity exists in a different form in the realm of elementary particles, we are assured that we are speaking of reality. This reveals our cultural basis for analysis—the dynamic is as real in the life of the seas as it is in the realm of elementary particles. Each realm has its own integrity; the ocean can not be reduced to elementary particles. If you decompose the ocean into elementary particles, the ocean disappears.

In any event, as we glance at the sea, as we explore the world of elementary particles, we see how the universe assimilates qualities spontaneously. What name should we give this cosmic dynamic? We could call it quantum stickiness, if we wished to keep our attention tuned to the quantum realm. Or we could call it solvency properties of water, if we wished to take the sea, and liquids in general as our reference point. But in order to indicate the universal aspect of this dynamic, we will use the word *sensitivity*.

YOUTH: So protons are sensitive.

THOMAS: They show a minimal sensitivity for each other, yes. The universe is sensitive—it's a realm of sensitivity. Matter is sensitive. To say that an electron is sensitive means that an electron notices things. The electron responds to situations and is intrinsically altered by them. I don't mean that the electron is self-reflexively aware as a human is, however. Perhaps we could use the phrase *quantum sensitivity* to make the same point. All I'm saying is that the electron absorbs something from the world, assimilating it into itself.

YOUTH: I'm confused. This sensitivity, this power of absorbing . . . What are we getting at?

THOMAS: We're investigating the way humans will mature into their destiny as the human form of cosmic dynamics.

YOUTH: And we've already discussed allurement, and how our destiny is to become allurement. OK. Now it's cosmic sensitivity. But if the *universe* is sensitive, then *we're* already sensitive, right?

THOMAS: Yes. But remember, cosmic unfolding has not ended. If you think of the Earth as forty-six-years old, it has only developed flowers in the last year and a half. There is much more to come, but right now the Earth is having difficulty with its most recent creation, *Homo sapiens*. Evolutionary dynamics are blocked until they can bloom in the human form. We are to become allurement, we are to live a cosmic sensitivity, but we're not there yet.

OTHER WORLDS

By

PAUL DAVIES

Scientific revolutions tend to be associated with a major restructuring of human perspectives. Copernicus' claim that the Earth did not occupy the center of the universe began a disintegration of religious dogma that tore Europe apart; Darwin's theory of evolution upset centuries of belief in the special biological status of humans; Hubble's discovery that the Milky Way is but one among billions of galaxies scattered throughout an expanding universe opened up new vistas of celestial immensity. It is therefore remarkable that the greatest scientific revolution of all time has gone largely unnoticed by the general public, not because its implications are uninteresting, but because they are so shattering as to be almost beyond belief—even to the scientific revolutionaries themselves.

The revolution concerned took place between 1900 and 1930, but over forty years later controversy still rages over precisely what it is that has been discovered. Known broadly as the quantum theory it began with an attempt to explain certain technical aspects of subatomic physics. Since then it has grown to incorporate most of modern microphysics, from elementary particles to lasers, and nobody seriously doubts that the theory is correct. What is at issue are the extraordinary consequences that follow if the theory is taken at face value. If accepted completely literally, it leads to the conclusion that the world of our experience—the universe that we actually perceive—is not the only universe. Co-existing alongside it are countless billions of others, some almost identical to ours, others wildly different, inhabited by myriads of near carbon-copies of ourselves in a gigantic, multifoliate reality of parallel worlds.

To avoid this startling spectre of cosmic schizophrenia, the theory can be interpreted more subtly, though its consequences are no less mind-boggling. It has been argued that the other universes are not real, but only contenders for reality—failed alternative worlds. However, they cannot be ignored for it is central to the quantum theory, and can be checked experimentally, that the alternative worlds are not always completely disconnected from our own: they overlap our perceived universe and jostle its atoms. Whether they are only ghost worlds, or as real and concrete as our own, our universe is actually only an infinitesimal slice from a gigantic stack of cosmic images—a "superspace." . . .

Science, it is usually believed, helps us to build a picture of objective reality—the world "out there." With the advent of quantum theory, that very reality appears to have crumbled, to be replaced by something so revolutionary and bizarre that its consequences have not yet been properly faced. As we shall see, one can either accept the multiple reality of the parallel worlds, or deny that a real world exists at all, independently of our perception of it. Laboratory experiments performed in the last few years have demonstrated that atoms and subatomic particles, which people usually envisage as microscopic *things*, are not really things at all, in the sense of having a well-defined, independent existence and a separate, personal identity. Yet we are all made of atoms: the world about us seems to be directed inevitably to an identity crisis.

In the mid-1960s a remarkable mathematical formula was discovered by the physicist John Bell. Any logical theory based on the independent reality of subatomic particles which adheres to the well-established principle that faster-than-light signaling is impossible obeys this formula. Quantum theory on the other hand does not. Recent experiments in which pairs of photons (particles of light) are sent simultaneously through two pieces of polarized material set obliquely to one another confirm that Bell's formula is indeed violated.

These studies show that reality, inasmuch as it has any meaning at all, is not a property of the external world on its own but is intimately bound up with our perception of the world—our presence as conscious observers. Perhaps more than anything else this conclusion carries the greatest significance of the quantum revolution, for unlike all the previous scientific revolutions, which have successively demoted mankind from the center of creation to the role of mere spectator of the cosmic drama, quantum theory reinstates the observer at the center of the stage. Indeed some prominent scientists have even gone so far as to claim that quantum theory has solved the riddle of the mind and its relation to the material world, asserting that the entry of information into the consciousness of the observer is the fundamental step in the establishment of reality. Taken to its extreme, this idea implies that the universe only achieves a concrete existence as a result of this perception—it is created by its own inhabitants!

PARALLEL UNIVERSES

By
FRED ALLEN WOLF

CLASSICAL PHYSICS HAS NO TIME ORDER

If the world we observe were to actually follow the equations of classical physics, there would be processes which we could observe that would contradict our usual "sense" of time order. We would see objects that normally rise, fall. Objects that normally go toward the right, proceed to the left. For example, a ball lying on the floor could suddenly begin hopping, with each hop getting higher and higher until it just leaped into my hand. While this would certainly look strange, there is nothing in the classical laws of physics to prevent this from happening. However, looking at the most microscopic phenomena observable that we are usually not accustomed to watching, we probably would not be struck by anything strange going on. I mean, who cares if that amoeba spits out that piece of food or not.

But watching a hungry man eating chicken, proceeding backward-through-time, would indeed be a strange experience. We would see him pick up an empty bone from his plate, shove it into his mouth and then watch him chew. As we glimpsed inside his mouth from time to time, as we usually are prone to do when we watch a hungry man eat, we would find that pieces of meat would be adhering to the bone, layer upon layer, rather than being pulled from the bone by a voracious appetite.

As soon as the man was "full" he would stop eating, pull the bone completely covered by hot chicken meat from his colder mouth, and put the hotter assembled chicken leg down on the plate. Of course, the man would appear a little strange after his meal. He would actually look hungrier after "eating" than before he started. And most likely he would be hungrier, although I don't really know that, for the man eating backward-in-time would be simply time-ordering his meal in the opposite sense from our time order.

Imagine a person living backward in time day before day. If he walked through the streets of San Francisco, he would appear quite strange because he would be walking backward. Only if he decided to climb Nob Hill, step by step, looking in the direction from which he came, would he appear to the outside world of sophisticated San Franciscans as normal. They would see him walking down the hill, even though he would actually be climbing it with his back toward the incline.

I am sure the reader can imagine even more bizarre scenarios for our time-reversed hero. Such scenarios could actually occur if the world were completely described by the classical equations of motion. Of course, most sequences involving large numbers of events, such as a ball spontaneously hopping off the floor, would appear highly unlikely even in classical physics. Broken eggs do not reassemble and jump off the floor into a tipping bowl on the table. Such sequences usually involve a degree of randomness associated with the lack of specification of the initial or boundary conditions associated with them. If we could specify the egg's broken shells, bits of white and yellow matter, and bounce the floor with the right amount of energy and momentum, nothing in classical physics would prevent the egg from reassembling and doing its time-reversed thing.

The air molecules in a room, for another example, could all speed to the nearest corner, leaving the rest of the room devoid of air, if those initial conditions were designed in the right way. However, given a random distribution of the speeds of the molecules, we are assured that none of us will suffocate. My point is that classical physics appears to contain the experience of time order we have all come to know as the "march of time," not because it does contain a time order, but because the boundary or initial conditions governing the behavior are largely random and uncontrollable. Even though the classical equations would allow time reversal to occur, it is statistically not the case that those conditions that would send all the molecules in the room to the corner would ever occur.

QUANTUM PHYSICS HAS NO TIME ORDER

When quantum physics is used, a similar situation arises. Again time order is arbitrary, and sequences of "events" can arise in which a reversal of time order occurs. The events in quantum physics equations are, however, not existential as they are in classical physics. In classical physics an event is described by one possibility and one possibility only. The event actually occurred, will occur, or is occurring. In quantum physics the "things" calculated have not occurred, they will not occur, nor are they occurring. They have not taken place in the past, the future, or in the present. They are ghosts — probabilities of what was, what is, or what will be.

These "things" are quantum wave functions. They describe distributions in space of possible occurrences of real events. To do so these quantum waves not only must be nonexistential, but must also be capable of traveling both forward and backward through time and be able to link one parallel universe with another.

SECTION SIX:

SHAMANISM AND NATIVE TRADITIONS

Some of the most famous New Age writers and thinkers are conducting their own personal journeys through shamanic terrain. Carlos Castaneda has enthralled readers for the past two decades with stories of his work with the Yaqui sorcerer and medicine man Don Juan. Lynn Andrews has drawn an enormous following for her work with various shaman women who are members of the Sisterhood of the Shield, including stories of her own teacher, Agnes, the Manitoba medicine woman. These books share the deep personal quest of each of their authors for spiritual connection with nature and the elements, for new uses of power and energy, and for healing insights that can address the issues that concern all human beings. New Age seekers are drawn to the ancient wisdom that these shaman teachers are sharing. Practices that have been held secret to tribal members and initiates for centuries are becoming available to the masses for the first time through the work of the authors included in this section.

When Lynn Andrews, a successful art dealer from Beverly Hills, follows her quest for the mysterious marriage basket, she includes all her readers in her personal spiritual journey. As she undergoes trials and tests, the reader shares her confusion, awakening, and eventual understanding of her higher self. This type of shared shamanic experience brings powerful vicarious fulfillment to the reader, offering insights and metaphors to apply to his or her own life.

The shamans of each culture represented in this collection are unified in their explanation that these ancient, previously guarded secrets for healing and growth are now being made available because there is such a profound need for this information. If we are to save planet Earth and her inhabitants, the Native American, South American, and Hawaiian shamans agree, the powerful medicine and healing energy contained in these teachings must be shared with all who are interested.

Shamans are healers, and that has been and continues to be their primary function. In primitive tribes and villages, the shaman (or medicine man or woman) was often the doctor, therapist, counselor, or priest. Performing many or all of these duties, the shaman also held the ear of the king or chief. He or she held tremendous political power for as long as the healing techniques were successful.

Michael Harner offers an excellent description of shamanism in his book *The Way of the Shaman.*

"Shamanism represents the most widespread and ancient methodological system of mind-body healing known to humanity. Shamans are especially healers, but they also engage in divination; seeing into the past, present, and future for other members of the community. A Shaman is a *seer*. . . . The shaman moves between realities, a magical athlete of states of consciousness engaged in mythic feats. The shaman is a middle man between ordinary reality and nonordinary reality, as Castaneda has dramatically described. The shaman is also a power-broker in the sense of manipulating spiritual power to help people and put them into a healthy equilibrium."

A shaman, after learning basic principles and healing methods, builds power and ability by learning his or her art through direct experience. One becomes a shaman by heeding an inner calling, exploring states of nonordinary reality by firsthand experience, and learning to move back and forth between states of consciousness with serious intention to heal people, places, or situations. Shamans go through a period of initiation, which can include long periods of fasting, water and sleep deprivation, use of powerful psychotropic drugs to obtain visions, and physical trials. Physical trials have included such horrors as being buried in red ants, sealed alive in caves, abandoned in the wilderness with no survival tools, hanged, beaten, tattooed and tortured, and sexually mutilated. These trials were then followed by a dramatic form of awakening, rebirth, and spiritual transformation.

The newer approaches to shamanism waive the need to go through rigorous initiation. Very few trials are experienced, and those are usually undergone only at the request of the zealous initiate. These trials are not seen as necessary components to the learning process, perhaps because day-to-day life is so confrontational in modern times that it is not necessary to intensify the stages of initiation and passage.

People who are drawn to New Age concepts are also experiencing stages of initiation, growth, and realization. As the old ways of believing are changing, these people feel a personal, often spiritual, transformation taking place. Perhaps this is why the primitive tribal practices of ancient shamans are so fascinating. New Agers feel a kinship with all humans who have experienced similar stages of growth, psychological and physical healing, and spiritual evolution. Primitive myths and stories of power animals and shamanic journeys are useful metaphors that are helping modern men and women to understand and integrate new states of consciousness.

The shaman's altered state of consciousness is achieved by entering varying degrees of trance, ecstasy, and states of visionary inspiration. These altered states of consciousness are achieved by drumming, dancing, shaking rattles, chanting, meditation, and sometimes use of psychotropic plants. To a shaman, everything in the universe is alive.

Early shamans gave the tribe a way of understanding the world around them. Shamans were storytellers and mythmakers, keepers of the traditional cultural heritage, and creators of rituals and ceremonies to explain nature and the mystery of life. Shamans were also the healers and psychotherapists of their villages, tending the diseases of body and spirit. They were preoccupied with birth, marriage, death, and other rites of passage. They presided over religious events and attempted to control the weather and divine the future. They communicated with spirits and power animals for the purpose of drawing power and energy to the village activities and individual members of the tribe.

Most important, shamans were the earliest holistic healers; approaching the mind, body, emotions, and spirit in the treatment program. In the same way that modern holistic healers take the entire mind/body into account when they work with a patient, the early shamans treated the whole human being and not just the disease or illness.

The use of dreams is a recurring theme throughout shamanic healing. Dream states are used for many healing purposes: to determine shamanic calling, to use dream imagery in the treating and healing of illnesses, to create myths, chants, and new dances.

"Their frequent use of dreams underscores the shaman's status as a unique person in his or her tribe. As a result of physical, psychological, or social factors, the shaman was highly imaginative, recalling dreams more frequently than other tribe members and dealing with them creatively. This imaginative ability included identification of synchronous events, the talent for telling stories incorporating cultural myths, the power of visual imagery, and the susceptibility for entering culturally sanctioned altered states of consciousness quickly, deeply, yet with some degree of lucidity and control" (from *Healing States* by Alberto Villoldo, Ph.D., and Stanley Krippner, Ph.D.).

The work of many fascinating "urban shamans" is included in this section. These authors have researched or directly experienced the shamanic practices that are still in existence. The books range from thrilling personal adventure stories to useful resource materials.

Sun Bear and Wabun's *The Medicine Wheel* explains how the directions (north, south, east, west) and forces (wind, fire, earth, and water) are harnessed for personal guidance and counseling by creating a medicine wheel in nature.

Serge Kahili King is an urban shaman trained in the ancient ways of Hawaiian Huna, which means "the secret." The Kahunas of Polynesia are "the keepers of the secret." In his book *Mastering Your Hidden Self,* Serge King shares the Hawaiian approach to the shamanic use of dreams.

Are these stories and adventures true? This is a question that has caused much speculation in the New Age movement. To answer that question I would have to say, "I don't know, only the authors know for sure." Perhaps a better question would be, "Are these questions useful as metaphors that we can learn from?" The answer to that question is, "Absolutely, without a doubt." And so, with that in mind, read and enjoy these interesting excerpts, and enter the shamanic journey.

THE WAY OF THE SHAMAN

By

MICHAEL HARNER

The shamanic approach to power and healing was maintained in a basically similar form in primitive cultures that otherwise represented radically different adaptations to contrasting environments and to distinctly different problems of material survival. Through pre-historic migrations and isolation, many such groups were separated from other divisions of the human family for ten or twenty thousand years. Yet, through all those years, the basic shamanic knowledge did not seem to change significantly.

Why was this? It was obviously not due to lack of imagination on the part of primitive peoples, for there is great contrast and variation in their social systems, art, economics, and many other aspects of their cultures. Why, then, is shamanic knowledge so basically consistent in different parts of the primitive world?

I suggest that the answer is, simply, because it works. Over many thousands of years, through trial and error, people in ecological and cultural situations that were often extremely different came nonetheless to the same conclusions as to the basic principles and methods of shamanic power and healing.

Shamanism flourished in ancient cultures that lacked the technological innovations of modern medicine. In my opinion, the low technological level of those cultures compelled their members to develop to the highest degree possible the ability of the human mind to cope with serious problems of health and survival. Some of the most interesting methods that humans possess with regard to the health and healing potentialities of the mind are those of the shamans in these low-technology cultures.

To perform his work, the shaman depends on special, personal power, which is usually supplied by his guardian and helping spirits. Each shaman generally has at least one guardian spirit in his service, whether or not he also possesses helping spirits. In her classic work on the concept of the guardian spirit in native North America, Ruth F. Benedict observes, shamanism "is practically everywhere in some fashion or in some aspect built around the vision-guardian spirit complex . . ."

Outside of North America, the guardian spirit is similarly important, but is often called by other names in the anthropological literature, such as "tutelary spirit" in the works on Siberian shamanism, such as "nagual" in Mexico and Guatemala. In the Australian literature it may be referred to as an "assistant totem," and in the European literature as a "familiar." Sometimes the guardian spirit is just called the "friend" or "companion." Whatever it is called, it is the fundamental source of power for the shaman's functioning.

The best-known way to acquire a guardian spirit is in a spirit quest in a remote place in the wilderness. The location may be a cave, the top of a mountain, or a tall waterfall or an isolated trail at night, as among the Jivaro. There are also involuntary as well as special shamanic ways to secure a guardian spirit.

Without a guardian spirit it is virtually impossible to be a shaman, for the shaman must have this strong, basic power source in order to cope with and master the nonordinary or spiritual powers whose existence and actions are normally hidden from humans. The guardian spirit is often a *power animal,* a spiritual being that not only protects and serves the shaman, but becomes another identity or alter ego for him.

The fact that a person has a guardian spirit does not in itself make him a shaman. As the Jivaro point out, whether an adult knows it or not, he probably has, or has had, the aid of a guardian spirit in his childhood; otherwise he would not have had the protective power necessary to achieve adulthood. The main difference between an ordinary person and a shaman with regard to their guardian spirits is that the shaman uses his guardian spirit actively when in an altered state of consciousness. The shaman frequently sees and consults with his guardian spirit, travels with it on the shamanic journey, has it help him, and uses it to help others to recover from illness and injury.

In addition to the guardian spirit, a powerful shaman normally has a number of spirit helpers. These are individually minor powers, compared to the guardian spirit, but there may be hundreds of them at a particular shaman's disposal, providing great collective power. These helping spirits have specialized functions for particular purposes. It usually takes years for a shaman to accumulate a large crew of them.

There does not seem to be any obvious difference between the sexes in terms of shamanic aptitude and potentiality. In many societies, such as that of the Jivaro, most of the shamans are men for economic and social reasons that have little connection with the practice of shamanism itself. But even Jivaro women, after they have finished raising their children and reach middle age, sometimes become shamans, indeed very powerful ones. In medieval and Renaissance Europe, widows and elderly women similarly often became healing shamans, partly to support themselves. Of course, the Inquisition termed them "witches," as Christian missionaries commonly still call shamans in non-Western societies.

Shamans are especially healers, but they also engage in divination, seeing into the present, past, and future for other members of the community. A shaman is a *see-er*. Our word "seer" refers to this kind of activity, a survival of our almost vanished European shamanic heritage. A shaman may also engage in clairvoyance, seeing what is going on elsewhere at the present moment.

The shaman moves between realities, a magical athlete of states of consciousness engaged in mythic feats. The shaman is a middle man between ordinary reality and nonordinary reality, as Castaneda has dramatically described. The shaman is also a "power-broker" in the sense of manipulating spiritual power to help people, to put them into a healthy equilibrium.

A shaman may be called upon to help someone who is *dispirited*, that is, who has lost his personal guardian spirit or even his soul. In such cases, the shaman undertakes a healing journey in nonordinary reality to recover the lost spirit or soul and return it to the patient. Or a shaman's patient may be suffering from a localized pain or illness.

In such a case, the shaman's task is to extract the harmful power to help restore the patient to health. These are the two basic approaches to shamanic healing: restoring beneficial powers and taking out harmful ones.

Shamans have to be able to journey back and forth between realities in these healing tasks. To do this, in some cultures, shamans take mind-altering substances; but in many other cultures they do not. In fact, some psychoactive material can interfere with the concentration shamanic work demands.

One of the interesting things about shamanism is that, when a drug is used, it is taken by the curer or healer rather than the patient, although there are exceptions when both partake. This contrast with modern Western medicine is easily understood if one considers that the shaman must do his healing work in an altered state of consciousness. The idea is to provide access to the hidden reality. Such work is the responsibility of the shaman, not the patient.

In its essence, shamanic initiation is experiential and often gradual, consisting of learning successfully how to achieve the shamanic state of consciousness, and to see and journey in that state; acquiring personal certainty and knowledge of one's own guardian spirit, and enlisting its assistance while in the shamanic state of consciousness; and learning successfully to help others as a shaman. A characteristic phase of more advanced shamanism is having personal certainty and knowledge of one's own spirit helpers. There are even more advanced phases, as well as some important kinds of shamanic experiences, that are not dealt with in this book. If you succeed in experiencing the first three phases listed above, however, you can probably call yourself a shaman. But shamanic initiation is a never-ending process of struggle and joy, and the definitive decisions about your status as a shaman will be made by those you try to help.

CRYSTAL WOMAN

By

LYNN ANDREWS

I saw something near the mouth of the cave. There was a movement on top of the Woman's Stone and I heard sharp, clicking sounds. I sat up and scared away whatever it was. I next heard scraping noises and a lot of whooshing sounds. Something threw a gigantic shadow onto the left wall of the cave. My mouth fell open to scream, but nothing came out. My gooma stone dug painfully into my hand as I held onto it as if I were grasping onto my very life. The shadow jumped up and down and then large, fringed shadows flapped like two giant wings. I saw the head of a tall crow the size of an ostrich. It was hopping to the top of the rock. It was looking from side to side until it saw me. The crow's large, reddened eyes held my gaze like a stick in a vise. The bird loomed up and flapped its huge wings in an attempt to swoop down on me. It was screaming and I was screaming too as I ran through the fire toward the dark cave. From the right came an ear-splitting yell, and I saw a spear tether the bird to a desert oak. I turned just as another spear pierced my throat. The pain was excruciating and I fell.

The next thing I remembered was a tall, bearded warrior with a red band around his head. He was covered with surreal red-ochre designs and carried me into the cave over his shoulder like a sack of millet. He walked a long time as I drifted in and out of consciousness. I felt my blood running over my face and down onto his back and legs. I knew I was dying, but I was too weak to move.

That was the last I remembered until I awoke lying by a river in a grassy meadow. I listened to the sounds of the water, and to the bellbirds chirping in the bush, their voices like tiny, clear chimes. When I opened my eyes, everything seemed vague and far away. The sun was shining and the sky was blue, but I knew that this was a different world and that I was dead. I was no longer frightened or in pain. The big crow was standing nearby and the tall warrior was taking several crystals out of his own chest and putting them into the wound in my neck.

He stood up and, taking his stone ax, he sliced my body open from top to bottom as if I were a rainbow trout. The crow hopped over and the two of them pulled out my heart, stomach, and all my intestines. Everything they did seemed perfectly understandable. The warrior had smoothed the sand next to me so that now as they lay my entrails onto the ground they began to form designs. The crow leaped around, joyously picking up my intestines and laying them this way and that until several spirals were formed. The warrior added sacred stones to the design.

"My name is Oruncha of Chauritzi. I am a medicine spirit warrior. I am Crazy One, the Hermaphrodite. I have killed you that you may live. This is Crow, your nari, your medicine familiar. He is a clever bird and he will guard you always. Your gooma, your teacher's sacred stone, has much power. It called me well. I will give you your own gooma now. You have earned it. For all time walk in balance on our mother. Look at the design in the sand."

My spirit seemed to rise up out of my broken body and I looked down at the multicolored patterns made by my own insides. I was fascinated by the curves and their beauty.

"Give me your fingers," he said. As I traced my fingers over my large intestines I went into a dream that must have lasted for days. I saw the totality of my early life.

When I returned, he directed my fingers over a large rectangular design. "This represents the birth of your daughter and the life with your family and your friends." Again I slipped away into the years of experience. When I came back I traced a star design that was my heart shaped like a star.

Oruncha's kind eyes, like burning coals, looked into me. Finally we traced the design that marked the end of this life and the next life that was coming up.

"Whenever you retrace this design on your sacred stone you will recall perfectly the dream that is you. In knowing your dream, you can kill the dream. In taking your power, you can balance your power. You see, my sister, our sacred sand paintings are the ceremonies of our sky beings, or alcheringa, but if you look closely you will see the galaxies. See, here are the Seven Sisters just as they are in the Pleiades." I looked down and saw that he was right. The patterns looked like stars and protozoa all wrapped into one picture. I realized that I was made from stars and that the universe was within me and that it had always been that way.

"If you see clearly it will come true. What you design in your inner life will manifest in your outer life. See, it is all here. These markings are the designs of your tiniest cells that make up your body. These designs are also the sacred pattern of your destiny. Never forget what is here in the Dreamtime."

Then he placed a flat stone in my hand. It held the exact design of my intestines in the sand.

"This is your own gooma stone, a spirit-haunted stone from a sky warrior of the Dreamtime."

Very carefully he took all of my intestines, my heart, and my stomach and washed them clean of sand. He took a few more crystals from his own body and a few magical objects and closed me up, using his magic shell and other instruments and leaving the crystals inside of me.

After the incision was fully closed Crow hopped over by my side. He was still very much larger and more fierce-looking than any crow I'd ever seen. He looked like a crow-eagle. He had a handful of white feathers in his beak. He dropped them onto my stomach and Oruncha put the feathers along the incision and the hole in my neck. Then he took a fire stick from the fire, called a madagor, and ran it along the cut flesh to heat it and heal it. He sang many songs into me and into the cut. The crow cawed, but it didn't sound like cawing. He wailed and cried and turned his head so it lay on his shoulder and sort of groaned. I could smell my own flesh burning and my insides moving with a new life of their own.

The only real pain I had felt was the agonizing pierce of Oruncha's spear. When the blood had been pouring out of me, I had felt like a balloon deflating, and during the rest of my time with Oruncha I had felt very weak and hazy as if I were floating on a cloud faraway. But pain had not been part of this experience until now. Under the aegis of Oruncha I knew I could learn how to use these crystals inside of me. His herculean abilities were beyond anything I had ever known and I felt a strong bond with this being. I didn't want to return from this valley of knowledge.

Oruncha touched me gently with his hands and made sure that I was healing. I felt prickly heat and a pulling sensation, but that was all.

"I will bring you back to life now. Is there anything you want to ask me, my sister?"

"Yes, Oruncha, how do I use the sacred objects inside of me?" I said, coughing and testing my voice. I did not sound like myself.

"I have shown you how to heal someone. Your personal gooma lives in your mind. To use its power, extract it from your body through your alcheringa eye." He pointed to his third eye.

"If a fella come to you sick in body, I have placed crystals all through you so you can help. Feel this one now."

Oruncha pressed my stomach.

"Yes, I can feel it. There's a clear feeling." I was crying with excitement. He pressed several other parts of my body and again in each place I could feel the sensation of clarity.

"If a fella has a sick stomach, use the crystal in your stomach to heal. That's why I have put magical objects all over you. Keep your sacred gooma in your clever bag. You are a clever woman now." Before I could say anything else, he had slung me over his shoulder and was striding out of the valley, toward the entrance to the cave.

The next thing I knew it was morning. I was still wrapped in kangaroo and lying at the mouth of the cave. The sun was warming my face and I opened my eyes. At first it was hard to see and I felt a little nauseated. Ginevee and Agnes were helping me to a sitting position.

Then I remembered Oruncha and I tore open the kangaroo hide.

There was no scar on my midsection, but dozens of white feathers were stuck in me. Suddenly I felt sick and threw up. Afterward, I felt better and struggled to my feet but I could hardly walk. I heard a forlorn cry of a crow. I looked off to the left, but all I saw was the shadow of a bird in flight.

THE WAY OF THE PEACEFUL WARRIOR

By
DAN MILLMAN

Pointing to the shadows, Socrates said, "These shadows in the cave are an *essential image* of illusion and reality, of suffering and happiness. Here is an ancient story popularized by Plato:

There once was a people who lived their entire lives within a Cave of Illusions. After generations, they came to believe that their own shadows, cast upon the walls, were the substance of reality. Only the myths and religious tales spoke of a brighter possibility.

Obsessed with the shadow-play, the people became accustomed to and imprisoned by their dark reality.

I stared at the shadows and felt the heat of the fire upon my back as Socrates continued.

"Throughout history, Dan, there have been blessed exceptions to the prisoners of the Cave. There were those who became tired of the shadow play, who began to doubt it, who were no longer fulfilled by shadows no matter how high they leaped. They became seekers of light. A fortunate few found a guide who prepared them and who took them beyond all illusion into the sunlight."

Captivated by his story, I watched the shadows dance against the granite walls in the yellow light. Soc continued:

"All the peoples of the world, Dan, are trapped within the Cave of their own minds. Only those few warriors who see the light, who cut free, surrendering everything, can laugh into eternity. And so will you, my friend."

"It sounds unreachable, Soc—and somehow frightening."

"It is beyond searching and beyond fear. Once it happens, you will see that it is only obvious, simple, ordinary, awake, and happy. It is only reality, beyond the shadows."

We sat in a stillness broken only by the sound of crackling logs. I watched Socrates, who appeared to be waiting for something. I had an uneasy feeling, but the faint light of dawn, revealing the mouth of the cave, revived my spirits.

But then the cave was again shrouded in darkness. Socrates stood quickly and walked to the entrance with me right behind. The air smelled of ozone as we stepped outside. I could feel the static electricity raise the hairs on the back of my neck. Then the thunderstorm struck.

Socrates whirled around to face me. "There's not much time left. You must escape the cave; eternity is not so far away!"

Lightning flashed. A bolt struck one of the cliffs in the distance. "Hurry!" Socrates said, with an urgency I'd not heard before. In that moment, the Feeling came to me—the feeling that had never been wrong—and it brought me the words, "Beware—Death is stalking."

Then Socrates spoke again, his voice ominous and strident. "There's danger here. Get further back into the cave." I started to look in my pack for my flashlight, but he barked at me, "Move!"

I retreated into the blackness and pressed against the wall. Hardly breathing, I waited for him to come get me, but he had disappeared.

As I was about to call out to him, I was jarred almost unconscious as something vise-like suddenly gripped me behind my neck with crushing force and dragged me back, deeper into the cave. "Socrates!" I screamed. "Socrates!"

The grip on my neck released, but then a far more terrible pain began: my head was being crushed from behind. I screamed, and screamed again. Just before my skull shattered with the maddening pressure, I heard these words—unmistakably the voice of Socrates: "This is your final journey."

With a horrible crack, the pain vanished. I crumpled, and hit the floor of the cavern with a soft thud. Lightning flashed, and in its momentary glare I could see Socrates standing over me, staring down. Then came the sound of thunder from another world. That's when I knew I was dying.

One of my legs hung limp over the edge of a deep hole. Socrates pushed me over the precipice, into the abyss, and I fell, bouncing, smashing against the rocks, falling down into the bowels of the earth, and then dropping through an opening, I was released by the mountain out into the sunlight, where my shattered body spun downward, finally landing in a heap in a wet green meadow, far, far below.

The body was now a broken, twisted piece of meat. Carrion birds, rodents, insects, and worms came to feed on the decomposing flesh that I had once imagined to be "me." Time passed faster and faster. The days flashed by and the sky became a rapid blinking, an alternation of light and darkness, flickering faster and faster into a blur; then the days turned to weeks, and the weeks became months.

The seasons changed, and the remains of the body began to dissolve into the soil, enriching it. The frozen snows of winter flashed by in ever more rapid cycles, even the bones became dust. From the nourishment of my body, flowers and trees grew and died in that meadow. Finally even the meadow disappeared.

I had become part of the carrion birds that had feasted on my flesh, a part of the insects and rodents, and part of their predators in a great cycle of life and death. I became their ancestors, until ultimately, they too were returned to the earth.

The Dan Millman who had lived long ago was gone forever, a flashing moment in time — but I remained unchanged through all the ages. I was my Myself, the Consciousness which observed all, was all. All my separate parts would continue forever; forever changing, forever new.

I realized now that the Grim Reaper, the Death Dan Millman had so feared, had been his great illusion. And so his life, too, had been an illusion, a problem, nothing more than a humorous incident when Consciousness had forgotten Itself.

While Dan had lived, he had not passed through the gate; he had not realized his true nature; he had lived in mortality and fear, alone.

But I knew. If he had only known then what I know now. I lay on the floor of the cave, smiling. I sat up against the wall then gazed into darkness, puzzled, but without fear.

My eyes began to adjust, and I saw a white-haired man sitting near me, smiling. Then, from thousands of years away, it all came back, and I felt momentarily saddened by my return to mortal form.

Then I realized that it didn't matter—nothing could possibly matter!

This struck me as very funny; everything did, and so I started to laugh. I looked at Socrates; our eyes gleamed ecstatically. I knew that he knew what I knew. I leaped forward and hugged him. We danced around the cavern, laughing wildly at my death.

Afterward, we packed and headed down the mountainside. We cut through the passageway, down through ravines and across fields of boulders toward our base camp.

I didn't speak much, but I laughed often, because every time I looked around—at the earth, the sky, the sun, the trees, the lakes, the streams—I remembered that it was all Me!

All these years Dan Millman had grown up, struggling to "be a somebody." Talk about backwards! He had been a somebody, locked into a fearful mind and a mortal body.

"Well," I thought, "now I am playing Dan Millman again, and I might as well get used to it for a few more seconds in eternity, until it too passes. But now I know that I am not only the single piece of flesh—and that secret makes all the difference!"

There was no way to describe the impact of this knowledge. I was simply awake.

And so I woke to reality, free of any meaning or any search. What could there possibly be to search for? All of Soc's words had come alive with my death. This was the paradox of it all, the humor of it all, and the great change. All searches, all achievements, all goals, were equally enjoyable, and equally unnecessary.

Energy coursed through my body. I overflowed with happiness and burst with laughter; it was the laugh of an unreasonably happy man.

And so we walked down, past the highest lakes, past the edge of the timberline, and into the thick forest, heading down to the stream where we'd camped two days—or a thousand years—ago.

I had lost all my rules, all my morals, all my fear back there on the mountain. I could no longer be controlled. What punishment could possibly threaten me? Yet, though I had no code of behavior, I felt what was balanced, what was appropriate, and what was loving. I was capable of loving action, and nothing else. He had said it; what could be a greater power?

I had lost my mind and fallen into my heart. The gate had finally opened, and I had tumbled through, laughing, because it, too, was a joke. It was a gateless gate, another illusion, another image that Socrates had woven into the fabric of my reality, as he'd promised long ago. I had finally seen what there was to see. The path would continue, without end; but now, it was full of light.

HEALING STATES

By
ALBERTO VILLOLDO
and STANLEY KRIPPNER

Dreams represent a less dramatic but more universal altered state of consciousness in which healing can take place or in which diagnosis can occur. Many shamans are called to their profession through dreams. Dreams of dead relatives are held to mark one's call to shamanism among the Wintu and Shasta tribes of California. Among two other California tribes, the Diegunos and Liusanos, future shamans supposedly can be identified as early as nine years of age on the basis of their dreams. Among several other American Indian tribes, initiatory dreams contain such creatures as bears, deer, eagles, and owls that instruct the dreamer to draw upon their power and begin shamanic training.

Among Peru's Cashinatua Indians, the tribal hunters request herbalists to give them medicines to keep them from dreaming because they believe that the process interferes with their skill in hunting. Cashinatua shamans, however, believe that the more dreams they have, the greater their power will become; therefore, they develop methods to "pursue dreams." The Iroquois of North America had a sophisticated theory that dreams represented one's hidden desires. Thus they contained clues for the shamans to decipher as to what could be done to restore a person's health by fulfilling the desires in a manner consistent with the tribal social structure. A yearly ceremony was held in which everyone was required to relate important dreams. This was another socially approved manner in which unconscious wishes could be released.

Unpleasant dreams are held to be causes of disease among the Maricopa Indians, bringing on colds, diarrhea, and aches. Paviotso Indian children can become ill if their parents' dreams are unfavorable or if unpleasant dreams occur to visitors in the house. Shamanic intervention is asked for in either event to halt the effect. The Taulipang shamans in the Caribbean are called upon to interpret dreams of tribal members. When the Cuna Indians of Panama have dreams of an impending illness or disaster, the shaman administers a variety of cures to prevent the problem from occurring. The Cuna shaman may employ a unique out-of-body experience for purposes of diagnosis—leaving his own body and entering the body of the client to inspect possible physical difficulties. Thus the shaman may use his or her own dreams, and those of the tribe, for many purposes: to determine his or her shamanic calling, to diagnose and treat illness, to create songs and dances, to discover new charms and cures, to identify criminals, to locate lost objects, to plan military campaigns, and to name newborn children.

Their frequent use of dreams underscores the shaman's status as a unique person in his or her tribe. As a result of physical, psychological, and/or social factors, the shaman was highly imaginative, recalling dreams more frequently than other tribal members and dealing with them creatively. This imaginative ability included identification of synchronous events, the talent for telling stories incorporating cultural myths, the power of visual imagery, and the susceptibility for entering culturally sanctioned altered states of consciousness quickly, deeply, yet with some degree of lucidity and control.

If such an individual were to become an integral part of the society, he or she would need to serve a social function. She may not have been content with the prescribed female role. He may have lacked the physical dexterity to be a valuable hunter, or the leadership skills to become a chief. But probably neither the hunter nor the chief possessed the sensitivity and insight required to tend the sick, contact the spirits, or predict changes in the weather. These were tasks for a "technician of the sacred," and this was the role that these highly imaginative individuals assumed if they were to survive.

Later, many of their functions would be assumed by the priest, the diviner, and the sorcerer. Later still, with the institutionalization of religions, private visions were discouraged or even punished; sacred functions became the province of the priest, while techniques of magic were the province of the sorcerer. The diviner still maintained a direct contact with the spirit world, but assumed no responsibility for the contents of his or her utterings, ascribing them to whatever spirits took possession at that moment. The diviner usually claimed not to remember the messages once he or she returned to ordinary consciousness, again disowning much of the experience.

We live in a world alienated from its sacred dimensions. Perhaps the healing states developed by shamans and diviners through the centuries still have something to offer not only their individual clients, but entire societies as well.

MASTERING YOUR HIDDEN SELF

By
SERGE KAHILI KING

DREAM TALK

A Chinese philosopher once dreamed that he was a butterfly dreaming that he was a man. When he woke up he was not sure whether he was still the butterfly dreaming that he was a man or a man who had dreamed that he was a butterfly.

The point of this story is that the world of dreams into which we slip off and on every night is every bit as real as this conscious, orderly one to which we are more accustomed. Most of us have been conditioned by our culture to pay very little attention to dreams, and in the process we end up ignoring at least one third of our life. For sleep is not oblivion. It is a time of learning, of play, of praise, criticism, and balancing—of communication with our Higher Self and other forces, powers, and people. It is another dimension where we are often more active than we are in this one.

If you have never explored the world of dreams, now is the time to start. You will find adventure, a great many surprises, tremendous beauty, and probably a share of ugliness and evil. You will be exploring the vast, uncharted territory of your own mind, meeting friends and enemies and yourself in many guises.

THE DREAMING PROCESS

Every human being dreams every night. There is much evidence to indicate that animals do, too, but we are concerned now with humans. Even if you cannot recall a single dream that you have ever had, this does not mean that you do not dream. It only means you do not remember dreaming.

The fact that everyone dreams has long been known to students of the esoteric sciences, and research scientists have proven it to their satisfaction in the laboratory as well. According to these studies, we dream in cycles throughout the night, and we dream two distinct types of dreams. One is a "straight" dream that reflects activities like those in the fully waking state without distortion. The other type is longer, more vivid, and seems to break all the rules of time, space, and logic. It is precisely because of this type that dreams have so often been considered unreal and unworthy of attention.

Research shows we *have* to dream—it is vital to our physical and mental health. When people are experimentally deprived of dreaming for a certain period, they dream even more when next allowed to sleep uninterruptedly, as if to make up for what was lost. If the dreaming is interrupted for longer periods, they begin to dream on their feet, in which case the dreams are called hallucinations.

Actually we all dream all the time. I am not speaking about the idea that this outer life is but a dream, though a very good case could be made for that. What I mean is that dreams—inner experiences both "straight" and strange—are occurring all the time just beneath our usual waking consciousness. Most people have been conditioned not to pay attention to them. But if you just sit down, close your eyes, and watch what happens, you will experience a dream of some kind, even while you are wide awake. It may happen immediately or it may take a while, depending on your present state and previous conditioning. But dream you surely will. There is even good reason to believe that frequent recourse to "waking dreaming" will lessen the need for "sleep dreaming." Thomas Edison, for instance, used to take about seventeen very brief naps a day and only needed three hours of sleep at night. He didn't take the naps to sleep or rest but purposely to dream.

THE HUNA VIEWPOINT

The most common word for "dream" is "moe'uhane" which literally means "spirit sleep." A code meaning is "the spirit breaks
away and goes elsewhere." Specifically, it refers to the dreams you
have during a deep, sound sleep. According to Hawaiian tradition,
your spirit goes traveling, seeing persons and places, encountering
other spirits, experiencing adventures, and passing on messages
from your aumakua or High Self. All of these events you remember as dreams.

Among the many sorts of dream experiences are messages from
the subconscious relating to our state of health and suggesting how
to improve it. Other dreams from the same source concern our relations with other people and the state of our beliefs about ourselves
and the world we live in. Certain dreams come directly from the
High Self, though still interpreted by the subconscious. These tell us
about our spiritual progress and sometimes give us foreknowledge of
things to come.

There are telepathic dreams that come from people we know in
this dream dimension, and even from situations that involve people
we don't know. Often these deal with tragedy or danger because
high emotions produce the extra mana that can activate telepathic
awareness, but this is not always the case. In addition, there are
dreams which consist of receiving instructions or information from
more advanced entities, and dreams in which we travel in our aka
body to another place in this or other dimensions.

In Huna different words describe different kinds of dreams. Hi-
hi'o refers to hypnagogic-type dreams, those you have when half
awake or half asleep, when dozing lightly, or when in a light trance.
The code meaning is "to capture truth or reality." It is identical to the
state a psychic uses to tune in to people or events.

In the ordinary language kaha'ula is usually associated with
erotic dreams, but in the code it means "sacred place" or "soaring
spirit." The idea here is that sexual dreams have to do with self-
integration, a concept understood by the kahunas but seldom by
others.

Moemoea is what would nowadays be called a "programmed"
dream, one purposely sought or stimulated to help bring about a

cherished desire. In the code it means "to set a line or net" and "to go straight toward something."

Finally, there was the ho'ike na ka po, "revelations of the night," dreams which are messages or guidance from the High Self or aumakua.

THE MEDICINE WHEEL

By

SUN BEAR AND WABUN

We invite you to open your eyes, your ears, your minds and your hearts to see the magic that is always there. Today we tend to see the earth as a stable backdrop for all of the affairs of humankind. We see the minerals, the plants and the animals as servants of man. We have forgotten that they can be our teachers as well; that they can open us to ideas and emotions that have been blocked from the human heart for too long a time.

We have forgotten that we are connected to all of our relations on the earth, not just our human family. We have forgotten that we have responsibilities to all these relations, just as we have them to our human families. We have imprisoned ourselves in tight little worlds of man-made creations.

We have forgotten how to hear the stories and songs that the winds can bring to us. We have forgotten to listen to the wisdom of the rocks that have been here since the beginning of time. We have forgotten how the water refreshes and renews us.

We have lost the ability to listen to the plants as they tell us which ones of them we should eat to live well. We have lost the ability to listen to the animals as they give us their gifts of learning, laughter, love and food. We have cut ourselves off from all of these relations, and then we wonder how we can so often be bored and lonely.

The Medicine Wheel is a magic circle that encompasses all of that world. As you journey around it, you will find wonders both within and without. With tenacity you will even discover the wonder of knowing about yourself: who you are, what you know and what you can do in this lifetime.

The Native people knew about this magic circle. They respected it and used it often in their everyday lives so they would always remember all of the things that they had learned. When they built their homes, most often these were circles, whether they were tipis, wigwams or hogans. When they went to purify their bodies and their minds, they did so in the circle of the sweat bath, a cleansing lodge which represented the womb of the human mother from whom they came, and the womb of the Earth Mother, who sustained them throughout their lives. When they came together in council, they sat in a circle, so that everyone was included, as an equal, with an equal voice.

When they made music, they made it upon a round drum. They danced in a circle. The beat of the drum represented the beat of their hearts and the beat of the Earth Mother. They raised their arms and legs toward the heavens, and then placed them upon the earth, creating a circle that extended from the earth to the sky and back to the earth, with their bodies as the transmitters.

They saw life as a circle, from birth to death to rebirth. They knew how to acknowledge and celebrate the circles of their own lives so that they were able to flow and change with the changing energies that came with different ages. They knew that they, like the seasons, passed through several phases as the circle of life and time passed around them. They knew that to fall out of this circle was to fall out of rhythm with life and to cease to grow.

The circle was so important to them, so essential to life continuing in the ways that it should, that they immortalized this figure in their ceremonies and structures. The mounds of the mound-building culture were round. The calendars of the Aztecs were round, and the medicine wheels of stone were round. In everything they reminded themselves that the earth and everything on her were part of the magic circle of life.

To remind yourself now of this circle, remember that you are always traveling around it. You enter the circle at one point, and the entrance gives you certain powers, gifts and responsibilities. Your starting point is determined by the moon or month under which you were born. Different starting points are governed by different elemental clans which tell you the element to which you are attached. This clan has nothing to do with the clans of kinship that existed in most tribes. Those were determined by the clans of one's parents, and they, in turn, could govern the earthbound responsibilities one would have, as well as those one could marry. The elemental clans determine your relationship to the elements solely, and like all of the other points on the Medicine Wheel, these are not static. The starting points are also governed by the Spirit Keeper of their direction.

It was essential for people in the old days to live their lives in such a way that they would continuously be journeying around the wheel. This is equally essential now. To stay with only one moon, one totem, one element, is to become static. To become static is to cease to grow, to cease to know that one has a connection with all of the wheel. It is tantamount to stopping the flow of the life force through your being.

As you pass around the wheel, you have the responsibility of learning about the different moons, totems, plants and elements through which you pass. By this learning you keep your own life in constant change, you keep the life force beating within your heart.

BLACK ELK SPEAKS

By

JOHN G. NEIHARDT

This, then, is not the tale of a great hunter or of a great warrior, or of a great traveler, although I have made much meat in my time and fought for my people both as a boy and man, and have gone far and seen strange lands and men. So also have many others done, and better than I. These things I shall remember by the way, and often they may seem to be the very tale itself, as when I was living them in happiness and sorrow. But now that I can see it all as from a lonely hilltop, I know it was the story of a mighty vision given to a man too weak to use it; of a holy tree that should have flourished in a people's heart with flowers and singing birds, and now is withered; and of a people's dream that died in bloody snow.

But if the vision was true and mighty, as I know, it is true and mighty yet; for such things are of the spirit, and it is in the darkness of their eyes that men get lost.

So I know that it is a good thing I am going to do; and because no good thing can be done by any man alone, I will first make an offering and send a voice to the Spirit of the World, that it may help me to be true. See, I fill this sacred pipe with the bark of the red willow; but before we smoke it, you must see how it is made and what it means. These four ribbons hanging here on the stem are the four quarters of the universe. The black one is for the west where the thunder beings live to send us rain; the white one for the north, whence comes the great white cleansing wind; the red one for the east, whence springs the light and where the morning star lives to give men wisdom; the yellow for the south, whence comes the summer and the power to grow.

But these four spirits are only one Spirit after all, and this eagle feather here is for that One, which is like a father, and also it is for the thoughts of men that should rise high as eagles do. Is not the sky a father and the earth a mother, and are not all living things with feet or wings or roots their children? And this hide upon the mouthpiece here, which should be bison hide, is for the earth, from whence we came and at whose breast we suck as babies all our lives, along with all the animals and birds and trees and grasses. And because it means all this, and more than any man can understand, the pipe is holy.

SHAPESHIFTERS: SHAMAN WOMEN IN CONTEMPORARY SOCIETY

By

MICHELE JAMAL

PROFILE 1: JOAN HALIFAX

In the mid-1970's I met a Zen master whose dharma was very simple, very direct. I began to practice Buddhism; first, the practice of Zen, and then years later the practice of Vajrayana. Now I try to blend the earth wisdom of the shamanic world with the sky wisdom of the Buddhist world.

Things become simple when you have a taste of both the Absolute and the richness of the relative truth. There between the two truths, one finds the path of the "Awakening Warrior." One realizes that one is not simply to be a solitary realizer just to obtain simplicity and some degree of luminosity for oneself. One should also help other people to work in the world in a good way and do whatever one can to foster harmony and beauty, and try to help reduce the complexity. Having been with different teachers as student, friend, and co-teacher, I find myself appreciating everyday existence and trying to foster that appreciation in others.

There is a trap in the extraordinary. One begins to feel special and self-important, along with an absence of compassion. Maybe it is disappointing, this talk of simplicity in favor of the more dramatic aspects of being a shaman. What we all want at our core is to be free from suffering; we want to be in a situation of simplicity. We don't want to be driven by desire or hate; nor do we wish to be caught in confusion. Moving past these three poisons means that we discover simplicity, harmony, relaxation, compassion, and wisdom. From this awakening arises the impulse to help others.

Years ago, when I was in a state of acute suffering, part of the release from the conditioning of my past involved the opening a desire to help others. Later, in the 1970's and 1980's, much time was devoted to the healing of my own body. In the summer of 1984, however, a shift occurred. I went hiking on the Swiss Alps with a friend. When we reached a place where we were going to stay, at three o'clock in the morning, he was in extreme physical pain. His lower back was in a severe spasm.

Although I had not done any laying on of hands for many years, I realized that since our friendship was very subtle yet uncomplicated, I loved him unconditionally. Suddenly something happened in my belly, my heart, and my hands; I knew that I could help facilitate his healing. He was in such difficulty that he could neither walk nor stand. So I began to work on his body. It was as though I were guided by his condition to do exactly what needed to be done.

I cannot begin to tell you how deep this feeling was for me. In part it was because of the simple nature of our relationship and in part it was because of my work with people dying of cancer. I could love dying people unconditionally. How could there be conditions when I realized how important our relationship was? I realized that there was nothing that I could expect from that friendship except what was happening at that very moment. Thus, I was able to give away everything that blocked my helping him. For several hours I worked and then I realized that what I experienced in that interaction could inform my relationship with all beings.

An aspect that calls to be examined in our lives now has to do with the feminine and the earth. We need to look at our role as women in relation to helping people in our culture to discover the extraordinary beauty of the earth. Part of this has come about for me because I have made a friend of my womanhood. I've discovered my woman shield to be deep and profoundly creative. I am not afraid of my woman, I have a strong sense of great joy at being her. By the same token, I have a strong relationship with my man shield, the healer.

Now I am bringing a sense of equanimity and harmony between these pairs of opposites to others. It is not so much something to teach, as something to be. Those who walk in the wilderness will sense that balance directly. One feels no need to build statues to the goddess. One can sit under a tree. One feels no need to create a throne for her to sit on. Her throne is everywhere on this earth.

SECTION SEVEN:

CHANNELS AND PSYCHICS

As the American media reported the growth and evolution of the New Age movement, channeling was the area most often ridiculed and attacked. Shirley MacLaine was the brunt of cruel and unusual punishment after the publication of her extremely popular books *Out on a Limb* and *Dancing in the Light,* primarily because of her association with such channels and psychics as Kevin Ryerson, Ramtha and Lazaris.

But channeling was hot news.

Hollywood celebrities reported loyalty and reverence to such entities as Ramtha, Mafu, and Lazaris. All over the country, thousands of people were consulting channels and taking to heart the advice of entities, light beings, angels, extraterrestrials, and others with such names as Ophelia, Aurora, Michael, St. Germain, Orin and DaBen. While this may have seemed like a new phenomenon, channeling actually harkens back to ancient times. In Ancient Greece, the much-respected Oracle at Delphi provided counsel and guided generals and kings. The Oracle is an example of channeling.

The interest in psychics and mediums, seers and prophecy has appeared in cycles throughout the time-line of Western history. There was interest in seances and "table-tipping" in the mid-1800s, and in the early 1920s a great many "psychic" books were published.

The Edgar Cayce phenomenon continues to fascinate people all over the world. Cayce, known as "the sleeping prophet," diagnosed ailments and offered cures during a trance state. An enormous amount of channeled material came through Edgar Cayce, much of which has been proven and documented by the A.R.E. foundation, which has collected approximately thirty thousand case histories of those Cayce helped during his lifetime. The material is as enlightening today as when it was first received and published.

Several excerpts from the Seth material, as received by Jane Roberts (1929–1984), are included in this section. In *Seth Speaks,* this highly intellectual "energy-personality-essence" shares valuable information. Seth has also been described as a "spirit personality no longer focused in the physical reality."

Channeling takes many different forms. One form that all artists and musicians can verify is the calling of the "muse," the moment when creative genius strikes, when art is born. Brilliant problem-solving can also be considered a form of channeling—suddenly it seems that you are privy to information and answers you couldn't imagine having.

The most remarkable form of channeling occurs when an outside "entity" or personality channels through a "normal" human being to literally use his or her body and voice to relay information from other realities and dimensions. These channels claim to be from the distant past or from another planet. They say they are here to act as inspirational spiritual advisors. The entities have personalities, mannerisms, accents and vocal qualities that are totally different from those of the humans through whom they channel. They may be light forms, spirits, aliens, angels, or some energy form for which we have no name. These entities have been described as beings that exist on "another plane" but in the "same reality" as the one we humans inhabit. Channelers, or channels, go into a trance and establish contact with a spirit, ascended master, higher consciousness, animal, evolved entity, or interplanetary being and receive messages and impressions from another reality.

Another popular form of channeling involves learning to connect with one's personal guide, guardian angel, or higher self. There are classes teaching eager students "How to Channel," and most of the techniques are not outwardly difficult. One must be able to meditate, go into a deep trance state, and set aside the thoughts and concerns of one's own personality. One must surrender and allow a different consciousness to speak through the body and voice.

Ramtha is a highly flamboyant spirit entity channeled by former housewife J. Z. Knight. In *Ramtha: An Introduction,* a rich sampling of the beauty and wisdom of Ramtha's messages is shared.

Lazaris is a light being, "spark of love," and "friend" who speaks through Jack Purcel. Lazaris speaks about our "spiritual journey home to God/ Goddess/All That Is." In this section, Lazaris thoroughly answers the questions "Why so many channels?" and "Why now?"

Opening to Channel by Sanaya Roman and Duane Packer, who channel Orin and Daben, shares a definition of the purpose of channeling and information on the value of learning to channel. The excerpts in this section on channeling are often poetic and sometimes emotional. Clearly, the intention of these channeled entities is to instruct and inspire human beings—at least the books seem to reflect this attitude.

*　　*　　*

The most widespread current belief about channeling is that the individual having the channeled experience is actually connecting with his or her own Higher Self.

As with any form of self-exploration, the reader is advised to take this information with the proverbial "grain of salt." The possibility exists that the hosts channeling these flamboyant entities are actually excellent actors putting on well-intentioned performances. Similarly, the possibility exists that these other-world spirit entities are speaking to us directly and that they do indeed exist. And, as mentioned above, the possibility exists that the channel is receiving powerful insights and information, that is guidance from his or her own Higher Self.

Regardless, the information shared has been useful and healing to many and can be viewed as positive, on the one end of the spectrum, to simply harmless on the other. Channeling can be another key to the gateway of spiritual self-discovery.

THRESHOLD TO TOMORROW

By

RUTH MONTGOMERY

Planet Earth is currently on the cusp between the Piscean and Aquarian Ages, and just as a person born on the cusp between two astrological signs is said to reflect some characteristics of both, so we earthlings are precariously balanced between the materialism of recent centuries and the idealism of the future.

We are indeed on the threshold of a New Age, which the Guides say will be ushered in by a shift of the earth on its axis at the close of the century. Our globe is spinning its way out of the water sign denoted by a fish, the symbol by which the early Christians identified themselves to each other, and into the air sign of Aquarius, when we will be able to communicate as easily by thought as by the spoken word.

The Guides foresee one more brutalizing war in this century, unless herculean efforts are exerted by people of goodwill to avert it. Then comes the New Age, fulfilling the biblical prophecy of a thousand years of peace and the second coming of the Christ Spirit to establish God's kingdom on earth.

It is to prepare us for these awesome events that Walk-ins are said to be returning at a rate unprecedented since the dawn of recorded history. They wish to alert us to potential dangers, and teach us how to prepare ourselves not only for survival in physical body, but for our eventual crossover into the spirit plane. They are our friends, and because they bring directly from spirit, they are more farsighted than

most of us. Their mission is humanitarian, and they are so highly en-
ergized that almost any problem to them seems surmountable.

One of their goals is to forestall World War III, and if enough
like-minded people around the world will meditate and work for
peace, it can be prevented. The Guides are highly in favor of the
psychic seminars that are mushrooming throughout the world, and
say of them: "They are good for bringing to a focus the love of all
humanity with the Creative Force of the universe. If people meditate
together they are releasing energies that help to move the mountains
of fear and anger." All of us have free will, except where it conflicts
with universal law. In other words, the Guides say that we cannot
prevent the shift of the earth on its axis, which is inevitable and will
provide a cleansing process for Mother Earth.

THE NATURE OF PERSONAL REALITY: A SETH BOOK

By
JANE ROBERTS

AFFIRMATION, LOVE, ACCEPTANCE AND DENIAL

Now: Affirmation means saying "yes" to yourself and to the life you lead, and to accepting your own unique personhood.

(*Pause.*) That affirmation means that you declare your individuality. Affirmation means that you embrace the life that is yours and flows through you. Your affirmation of yourself is one of your greatest strengths. You can at times quite properly deny certain portions of experience, while still confirming your own vitality. You do not have to say "yes" to people, issues, or to events with which you are deeply disturbed. Affirmation does not mean a bland wishy-washy acceptance of anything that comes your way, regardless of your feelings about it. Biologically, affirmation means health. You go along with your life, understanding that you *form* your experience, emphasizing your ability to do so.

(*11:00.*) Affirmation does not mean sitting back and saying, "I can do nothing. It is all in Fate's hands, therefore whatever happens, happens." Affirmation is based upon the realization that no other consciousness is the same as your own, that your abilities are uniquely yours and like no other's. It is the acceptance of your individuality in flesh. Basically it is a spiritual, psychic, and biological necessity, and represents your appreciation of your singular integrity.

From *The Nature of Personal Reality A Seth Book* by Jane Roberts. Prentice-Hall Publishing, Englewood Cliffs, N. J., 1974.

(*Amused.*) An atom can take care of itself, but atoms themselves are somewhat like domesticated animals; joining in the biological family of the body, to some extent they become like friendly cats or dogs under your domain.

Animals pick up the characteristics of their owners. Cells are highly influenced by your behavior and beliefs. If you affirm the rightness of your physical being, then you *help* the cells and organs in your body, and without knowing it treat them kindly. If you do not trust your physical nature you radiate this feeling also, regardless of what health procedures you may take. The cells and organs know that you do not trust them, even as animals do. In a way you set up antibodies against yourself, simply because you do not confirm the rightness of your physical being as it exists in space and time.

SETH SPEAKS

By

JANE ROBERTS

—My work and those dimensions of reality into which it takes me

(*9:43.*) Now I have friends even as you do, though my friends may be of longer standing. You must understand that we experience our own reality in quite a different manner than you do. We are aware of what you would call our past selves, those personalities we have adopted in various other existences.

Because we use telepathy we can hide little from each other, even if we wished to. This, I am sure, seems an invasion of privacy to you, and yet I assure you that even now none of your thoughts are hidden, but are known quite clearly to your family and friends—and I may add, unfortunately, to those you consider enemies as well. You are simply not aware of this fact.

This does not mean that each of us is like an open book to the other. Quite the contrary. There is such a thing as mental etiquette, mental manners. We are much more aware of our own thoughts than you are. We realize our freedom to choose our thoughts, and we choose them with some discrimination and finesse.

(*Pause at 9:49.*) The power of our thoughts has been made clear to us, through trial and error in other existences. We have discovered that no one can escape the vast creativity of the mental image, or of emotion. This does not mean that we are not spontaneous, or that we must deliberate between one thought or another, in anxious concern that one might be negative or destructive. That, in your terms, is behind us.

Our psychological structure does mean that we can communicate in far more various forms than those with which you are familiar, however. Pretend, for example, that you meet a childhood friend whom you have long forgotten. Now you may have little in common. Yet you may have a fine afternoon's discussion centered about old teachers and classmates, and establish a certain rapport.

So, when I "meet" another, I may be able to relate to him much better on the basis of a particular past life experience, even though in my "now" we have little in common. We may have known each other, for example, as entirely different people in the fourteenth century, and we may communicate very nicely by discussing those experiences, much as you and your hypothetical childhood friend established rapport by remembering your past.

We will be quite aware that we are ourselves, however—the multidimensional personalities who shared a more or less common environment at one level of our existence. As you will see, this analogy is a rather simple one that will do only for now, because past, present, and future do not really exist in those terms.

Our experience, however, does not include the time divisions with which you are familiar. We have far more friends and associates than you do, simply because we are aware of varying connections in what we call for now "past" incarnations.

(*10:00.*) We have of course therefore more knowledge at our fingertips, so to speak. There is no period of time, in your terms, that you can mention, but some of us have been from there, and carry within our memories the indelible experience that was gained in that particular context.

We do not feel the need to hide our emotions or thoughts from others, because all of us by now well recognize the cooperative nature of all consciousness and reality, and our part in it. We are highly motivated (*humorously*): could spirits be anything else?

(*"I guess not."*)

Simply because we have at our command the full use of our energy, it is not diverted into conflicts. We do not fritter it away, but utilize it for those unique and individual purposes that are a basic part of our psychological experience.

Now, each whole self, or multidimensional personality, has its own purposes, missions, and creative endeavors that are initial and basic parts of itself and that determine those qualities that make it eternally valid and eternally seeking. We are finally free to utilize our energy in those directions. We face many challenges of quite momentous nature, and we realize that our purposes are not only important in themselves, but for the surprising offshoots that develop in our efforts to pursue them. In working for our purposes, we realize we are blazing trails that can also be used by others.

We also suspect—certainly I do—that the purposes themselves will have surprising results, astounding consequences that we have never realized, and that they will merely lead to new avenues. Realizing this helps us keep a sense of humor.

(*10:11.*) When one has been born and died many times, expecting extinction with each death, and when this experience is followed by the realization that existence still continues, then a sense of the divine comedy enters in.

We are beginning to learn the creative joy of play. I believe, for example, that all creativity and consciousness is born in the quality of play, as opposed to work, in the quickened intuitional spontaneity that I see as a constant through all my own existences, and in the experience of those I know.

I communicate with your dimension, for example, not by willing myself to your level of reality, but by imagining myself there. All my deaths would have been adventures had I realized what I know now. On the other hand you take life seriously, and on the other, you do not take playful existence seriously enough.

We enjoy a sense of play that is highly spontaneous, and yet I suppose you would call it responsible play. Certainly it is creative play. We play, for example, with the mobility of our consciousness, seeing how "far" one can send it. We are constantly surprised at the products of our own consciousness, of the dimensions of reality through which we can hopscotch. It might seem that we use our consciousness idly in such play, and yet again, the pathways we make continue to exist and can be used by others. We leave messages to any who come by, mental signposts.

I suggest your break.

FACE TO FACE
EDGAR CAYCE READINGS

The Work interpreted by Herbert Bruce Puryear, Ph.D.

When examining an Edgar Cayce reading it is very important for you to study carefully the wording of the suggestion given by the conductor prior to the beginning of the discourse. On this occasion the members in attendance desired to bring spiritual enlightenment to others, and they asked for a discourse on "how we may best present these truths to others." This question is of the utmost importance to all of us who have become interested in this information and want to apply it.

In what spirit and in what manner may we best share with others what we have gained from this remarkable source? In this reply through the channel of Edgar Cayce, we are told "this might be answered in the one sentence, 'As ye have received, so give.'" The work is very simple: If something has brought you to a closer understanding of the Divine within, then out of the abundance of that experience, give likewise to others who seek. This is an amazing and beautiful and simple statement of this great work.

We are then encouraged to work with one purpose, one aim, one desire, yet each in his own way and manner, and are warned "though someone may laugh or scoff at what ye say, *be* not dismayed; for so did they at the Lord." Remember the statement of the Master in the beatitude, "Blessed are ye, when men shall revile you, and persecute you . . . for my sake" (Matthew 5:11). How rarely do we claim that blessing, or how often do we let it slip by when we are reviled and persecuted? Do we not for lack of the right spirit fail to receive the promised blessing? How often do we fail to share that which has been helpful to us which might, to our surprise, be beneficial to another, because we are fearful of being scorned, rejected, persecuted?

Then we are told, "What ye *find* to do, with willing hands, *do* ye." Although this is familiar advice for us all, we may not have sensed the deeper lawfulness of our need, in our own proper place and with our own special abilities, to make an appropriate input in to the circumstances of the moment in which we lawfully find ourselves. These opportunities, rather than being by chance, are specific occasions for each of us to bring the manifestation of the Spirit into the earth in that particular finite manner. Then we are warned, "realizing that each and every chain is only as strong as the weakest link. Thou art abortion. Hast thou fulfilled, *wilt* thou fulfill, that as is shown thee by thine own *experience* with same?"

The individual likened to a link in a chain is a very instructive analogy. However, it may also be misleading if we think that every link in the chain is identical. Each is unique and has a unique purpose, and when the greater work of all the parts is considered, much may be lost when *anyone* fails to fulfill his portion. As we come face to face with this challenge and its implications for ourselves, we see that in a very specific way and manner we have a work to do in the place, time, and circumstance in which we find ourselves.

How are we to know exactly of what our own individual work consists? *"Act!* Act as thy conscience and thy heart dictate; as thou hast received, so give." And we are invited to remember, "man may make *all* efforts, all activity, but only the Spirit of Truth, only God may give the increase . . ." As each of us then does what is at hand, a little leaven leavens the whole lot and the great work in the world is accomplished.

Question: What should be the central purpose, the central ideal in presenting the work?

Answer: The Truth that shall make you free in body, in mind, and one *with* the living force that may express itself in *individual* lives.

Where there is illness of body, then give that which may make it free from those adapting of itself *to* that which has bound it in his material expression.

Where there are those troubled in mind, with many cares, if they are seeking for the *spiritual* way, they, too, may find *how* in their *own* experience they may give the greater expression *their* application of that they have in hand.

Where there are those who seek for the channel in which they may be the greater expression in this material plane in the present experience, they, too, may find their own selves and *their* relationships to the holy within.

These should be the central themes. As to the choice of this or that manner to be used, follow the manners which have been set through which individual groups here and there may receive enlightenment or aid in a better understanding or concept of what such information is that may be supplied through such a channel, and how it is of help. These are being opened.

Those that are seeking for channels to aid those who in body have become under the bond of this or that affliction, this or that ill or ailment, may stress this particular line of endeavor in their activity. And some who are already aiding in such directions will soon seek the concept of some that are here. Give expression in mind. As ye have received, give out.

You who feel that you are of little help here or there, or in manner of giving expression in thy words of mouth, then so live that ye have received that Spirit of Truth—*not* of any body but of Truth, or Christ—may be manifested. And those seeing—though ye struggle with the cares of earth, the cares of life—will, too, take hope and find in thine effort, in thine endeavor—through stumbling it may be—*hope*, and find the face of Him who has set a way for all who will enter in, who will sit at last upon the judgment within thine self. For, "As ye have done it unto the least of these, ye have done it unto me."

Question: Should we try to inform or teach children about spiritual enlightenment or merely show the way by example?

Answer: By precept *and* example. More and more will there be that preparation. For in the present, as we have given, the more oft is the mind of the young trained to the material rather than to the spiritual! But in thine training do not say one thing and live another!

LAZARIS INTERVIEWS BOOK II

By
LAZARIS

WHY SO MANY CHANNELS?

Q: Why are you and many other channeled entities appearing at this time?

Lazaris: The reasons are numerous. First because you have invited us. What we mean is that you as a consciousness individually and, indeed, collectively as a humanity, nationally and internationally, have basically said, "We are ready to grow. We are ready to reach and to stretch. We want to understand ourselves and our reality more completely and more fully, and we welcome, indeed we invite, the opportunity to learn, the opportunity to stretch, the opportunity to become more of who we are."

That invitation, spoken unconsciously, subconsciously, and indeed by many very consciously, is the invitation that at this time has been put forth. Many are now coming forth to impart, to give knowledge, to help you understand yourself and your world more completely.

Secondly, we would suggest that you have put yourselves, as a world community, into a corner whereby the traditional solutions simply don't work. The traditional, linear solutions to problems that have been readily available and rather nonchalantly applied no longer work. More and more you are confronted with what we call a Rubik's Cube reality. More and more you are confronted with a solutionless world where indeed every solution seems to produce five or six more problems.

Even though you're off there rather nicely protected on your own island (Australia), you nonetheless are still part of a world community, and you realize that what happens in Africa and what happens in South America affects you, directly and indirectly. What happens among what are called the Superpowers affects you on a regular and daily basis.

The problems have gotten to a point that there seem to be no more solutions. Therefore, in that sense, we are here not to give you the solutions on a silver platter, clearly not, but to teach you, to teach you how to find those solutions, to teach you the changes that you need to make in your own consciousness in order to allow new solutions to become evident.

We're here in our own specific energy very much to teach people how to transmute negative energy into positive energy, how to transform negative situations into positive situations, and indeed how to transcend the problems in a reality where there seem to be no solutions. We are here to show you there is a new world and show you how to create it for yourself.

Thirdly, we are here because you are seeking answers spiritually that your traditional methods of spirituality no longer can supply. We are not putting those traditions down, clearly not, for they have their proper place. They have their proper perspective, and they provided answers for as long as they could.

However, now it is time to expand your awareness, to expand your consciousness, to expand the horizons of your understanding. To do that you seek spiritual answers, we seek a deeper sense of your own spirituality. We respond in order to offer that opportunity for you to complete your own growth.

WHY NOW?

Q: What prompted you to experience the Earth plane in this manner?

Lazaris: Many assume the answers, and assume that we are here, for example, to save the planet—which clearly we are not. Secondly, some assume that we are here, then, to save humanity—which clearly we are not. We are not here to save either the planet or humanity, because we have enough confidence and enough respect for the consciousness that is here to know that you can be responsible, and you can "save yourselves," if indeed you need saving at all. The planet can well take care of itself, if you and the planet will work together.

We know that there are many who claim to be coming for the purpose of "saving planetary systems" and "saving humanities." We would suggest here that as they grow, perhaps, in their own evolution, they will come to realize and understand that you as human beings are quite capable, quite evolved and quite beautifully evolving so as to be able to handle those concerns yourselves.

The purpose of our "visiting," the reason for our coming to this planetary system that you call Earth, comes down to four particular concerns:

The first of those components has to do with the fact that we are here to help you realize that you do create your own reality. Now that is a concept that has been presented throughout most of your metaphysical history.

Even in that which is called the "Old Age," in comparison with that which has been called the "New Age," it has been a philosophy, a point of view. And it has been aborted this way or that way, or adapted this way or that way, to serve particular and personal needs and purposes from time to time.

But the bottom-like truth is that you do create your own reality. There is no asterisk—there is no fine print. That's it. You do create your own reality. We are here not only to help you understand that intellectually, but also to help you begin experience it, and to help you begin working with it, and to help you begin functioning with the power of this truth. We are here to help you live your reality from the perspective of "I create it all—I create it all consciously."

The second thing that we have decided to do in coming and visiting is basically to offer to you and to remind you of—or to help you remember for the first time—the fact that there is choice. There is choice in this particular reality. You do not have to grow through pain. You do not have to grow through suffering, through the self-denial, and through the struggle which have so often been put forth in what is called the Old Age.

Now admittedly, the teachings of the ancients, and the teachings of the Eastern and the Western Mystery Schools have strongly advocated the necessity of "grand patience," the necessity of enduring great pain, the necessity of struggling, suffering, and going through the pain of self-sacrifice. Struggle has been nobilized. It has been elevated to a position and posture of grandeur.

We clearly suggest: We would not argue with such teachings as the method of the Old Age, the way things used to be done, but now (and everybody is talking of it) is a New Age—a New Age—which doesn't mean taking the old teachings and re-dressing them and putting new costumes on them and presenting the old ideas all over again.

New means new. New means something that hasn't been done before. New means something that has never been experienced, and, therefore, the New Age is perhaps newer than a lot of people want to believe, newer than a lot of people are willing to believe!

Therefore, there is a new way of growing that involves love, light, laughter, and the celebration of life rather than the pain, struggle and anxiety of life. What we are here for is not to force people, by any means, but clearly to offer you a choice: Look, if you want to grow by pain and by struggling, you can do so. We have great compassion for you. We will love you enough to let you do that as well.

But at least let us point out to you, at least let us offer you the choice, that there are other ways. If you'd like to grow through the laughter of life, the joy of life, the love and light of life, through the celebration of life, we want to offer you a way to do that—not only to tell you that it's available, but also to show you how to create that way.

Thirdly, we are here to remind you of, or to help you remember, your "future." Your world seems very frightening now. It seems so devastating out there. More than ever it feels like wherever you turn, to whomever you talk, you are receiving the message that the world is becoming more miserable and terrible—that it is hopeless. With broken hope and breached confidence, you concluded: "I must have done something horribly wrong."

We are here to remind you that you are loved. You are loved.

There is a God, whom we refer to as God/Goddess/All That Is, who does love you, who does care about you, who is concerned with you and your particular growth.

We are here to let you know that, to show you . . . not just: "Isn't that wonderful! Wouldn't that be grand! Oh, I wish that were true!" We are here to show you that it is true, and to show you the ways you can communicate with that God/Goddess/All That Is, the ways you can be touched such as to have your life so changed and so benefited by that love that you can say, "I know I'm loved because my life reflects it." That is the statement we want you to be able to make. We want you to know that you are loved.

We also want to help you realize that you do love "good enough." We want to help you begin the Journey Home by recognizing that you are loved and that you can love.

Finally, the fourth component of why we're here is to open you up to what we call The Dream, to remind you and to teach you that you must dream, that you need to be Dreamers. You need to stretch and reach in your imaginations. You need to have desire and not to put your desires aside for the betterment of others, but to hold on to your desires for that betterment. You need to have the sense of expectancy, to start really expecting things to work wonderfully with desire and imagination.

RAMTHA
AN INTRODUCTION
Edited by
STEVEN LEE WEINBERG, PH.D.

Creator, you have created your sorrow. You have created your depression and your anger. You have created your misery, hurt, and despair. And you have created your happiness and joy. You have created *every moment* of your life, and from each creation, you obtain feelings that allow you to better understand the fire that lives with you, called, if you will, God Almighty.

Now that all things have been created, what is the last frontier or creative value? *You*—the creator of this illusion. Now your drive is not to create; it is to understand the greatest mystery of all times—you!

Why are you the greatest mystery? Because your greatest desire is the desire to know and understand self—your worth, your power, why you do what you do, and how you relate to all other entities. And this life allows you to have emotional interactions with other entities through which you can gain that understanding. That is why you have chosen your family, friends, and labors. That is why you love, marry, and have your relationships. You are choosing to interact with certain entities in order to understand yourself, seen through their reflection; for whatever you perceive in another will represent you to yourself every moment. If you see another as horrible, ugly, despicable, it is only because you think that *you* are that. If you see beauty, kindness, compassion in another, it is only because *you* possess that. You never really understand yourself until you put mirrors in front of you who reflect all aspects of yourself—your ideals, your fears, your judgments of self, and how you are expressing in life.

Why is love so important to you? It is a wild, free-moving feeling that allows you to see who you are and to be profoundly moved by the *great* entity that you are. And whenever love is felt, it reminds you of the joy of being free and unlimited within your being.

Now, you never truly love another entity. You never can, because you can never *know* the other entity. You love the other only for what they express that you identify with. They mirror back to you "self," seen openly within them. When you see in another all the things you love in yourself, you become "in love."

Love is identity, love is feeling. Loving another allows you to experience myriad feelings, from jealousy, doubt, anger, and hurt, to passion, joy, and ecstasy. The interaction of self with self brings out the full spectrum of feelings that allows you to identify all the aspects of yourself, seen through an emotional understanding.

Love for another is the love of self. When lovers embrace they do not feel the other, they feel the self. When they are emotional with one another they are being emotional with self. God, in his wonderful love affair with self, is seen through the mirror of another. Deep and profound and magical love occurs when another blooms with the very essence you are within your being. That is why all love so intently.

Now, why have you returned to this plane? To complete your identity as God. That is simply the way it is. You did not come back here to be a great conqueror or healer. You did not return to be a minister or a politician (you have enough of them!). Your destiny was not ordained eons ago, for eons ago you had no conception of this moment. You came back to this level of life simply to fulfill emotional lackings within you. That is why you do everything you do—because you are *driven* to experience it for a feeling of knowingness within your soul. What does this add to the character called "you"? It means you need never experience that again, for wisdom now says "I have experienced myself in another reality of feelings. I now understand and I am complete with that emotion." And when your soul, the greatest scribe of all, closes its books—for no more emotional understanding can be obtained from *this* plane, and you know who and what you are—you go on to another adventure. And that adventure is *wherever* you wish to create it.

The reason for all creation has been feelings, emotion. Everything has been created for that sublime purpose. And the prize of all created values is called "completion."

To manifest *all* you desire in order to complete yourself in this life, speak forth your desires from the lord-god of your being. When you do, you are speaking from your lord-soul-god-light—the totality of your isness—as an aligned unit. When you speak from the lord-god of your being, *anything* you desire you will have.

The secret to manifesting your desires is: Whatever you want, become it *totally* in feelings. *Feel* your desire. *Become* the desire within your being. Become the feeling so that the emotion exalts the totality of your being—so that you utterly *are* the thing you have desired. Do not simply visualize the image of what you want. Whatever you want, *feel* what it would feel like if you had it. Then the Father, the platform of Life, will manifest into your life whatever object or situation that will bring to you the *same* feeling. That is how you become a magician. That is how you create your destiny. That is, indeed, how you complete whatever feeling is needed within your soul.

All of you are still beggars! You continuously fight the wills of others to have what you desire. You beg for the pence that buys your bread. You labor in the most pitiful ways to obtain food to feed the body so that it may continue to have the capacity to feel. Stop being beggars. Cease it! Speak from the lord-god of your being and *feel* what you want. Feel it, until you *become* what you wish within your being. The outward, material, lowest plane of all will manifest it to add to your material kingdom, so that the emotion gained from it will match the emotion of the "kingdom within," which will live on into eternity.

THE STARSEED TRANSMISSIONS

By

RAPHAEL (KEN CAREY)

As a child, your conceptual prison was not yet fully defined; you still retained the ability to enter the lands of eternal being. As an awakened child of God, you will again be able to speed up or slow down the passage of time, to stop raindrops on the window, or war in the Mid-East. With an awareness of the eternity in each moment, with your involuntary data analysis systems providing you with infallible reports many thousands of times per second, you will have plenty of time to correctly assess all the factors present in the moment of whatever circumstance presents itself to you.

You will determine the optimum course of action with the ease and grace of a dancer. You will always choose the path of optimum response, not because you lack free will, but because such a path represents for you both the path of least resistance and the path of greatest fulfillment. You will no longer use your free will to make unnecessary mistakes, but to find out what part you might most creatively play in the whole. In choosing to do God's will, you will discover the only true freedom. Your ability to function will reach the perfection of its potential, and you will have little difficulty correcting the disharmony of your historical situation.

Living in this state of grace, you will function much like a computer; monitoring the variables of any given situation, determining the optimum behavioral pattern, scanning, adjusting for new data, over and over, many times each second. All data pertinent to a given situation will automatically be processed on an unconscious level.

From *The Starseed Transmissions* by Raphael (Ken Carey), published by Uni-Sun Press.

Consciously, you will always be aware of a course of action that makes optimum use of the potential available to all factors in that situation. Your inner control mechanism, returned at last to the directive impulse of Life, will take care of this unconsciously. It will be as simple and as natural as breathing. Trusting in the design that God has already incorporated into your physical body is the key to this new type of function.

Can you imagine how awkward it would be if you were required to assume conscious responsibility for all the autonomic systems in your body? In a sense, this is what you are doing when you override your autonomic informational processing systems in deference to a rational thought process. Historically, your mind has been preoccupied with an overload of sensory input that was never designed to be processed consciously. Your conscious function is in another realm, a realm of spontaneous creation, dance, music and delight. For this is what you begin to do as your trust is restored once again in the Life impulse; you begin to dance—dance to the music of your soul.

There are seven primary vibrational channels maintained within the overall vibrational body of Planetary Being. Within each of these seven primary channels are seven subchannels. The conscious execution of your creative responsibilities in the overall design will occur on one or another of these primary channels. The discovery of which level within the Planetary Being you have been designed to function on will not come through conceptualization. It will come through inner sensitivity to feelings, vibrations, and planetary rhythms. Once you attune yourself to these rhythms, you will find that the functional duties you are called upon to perform are the very things that you most want to do. No longer bound by false responsibilities born of fear and addiction to past patterns, you will take up the tools of your trade and delight in the creative implementation of God's will.

As you work in this new way, each will hear the different notes of his or her own functional duty, and be dancing to the fulfillment of that particular obligation. On each of the primary channels, all melodies will have the same rhythm and base notes, and each channel will be in harmonic relationship with all the others. All around you all across the planet, joyful melodies will be sounding forth, all perfectly synchronized with each other, all playing together in an exquisitely balanced orchestration, a perfect symphony. This is the Creator's love song to the planet Earth.

In this state of grace, no longer will you be compelled by the narrow dictates of your rational interpretations. No longer will you be held prisoner within the structure of your conceptions. You will be free to flow in joyful, rhythmic oscillation between your reality as the unmanifest totality of God, and your reality as His specific functional projection in form. Tapping directly into the informational systems of eternal Being, your special species will usher the Earth into an age of unimaginable blessing and prosperity.

The blueprint for your true work here on Earth already exists within you. You do not have to be given instruction by anything outside yourself, not by this book, a book of old, not by any person, object or event. These things may be helpful at times, but your primary task is to awaken the living Christ in your heart. This is your true identity. Express God in all that you are, and throw away the crutches that have helped you stumble through history.

You are the means by which God loves Creation. You are the facilities for the emergence of the catalytic energies in the final stage of the creative process. You are high priests and priestesses, invested with the authority to perform the only real Mass, the Cosmic Mass of the World, in which Matter is lifted up lovingly into the presence of God, and instilled with the power and life of Spirit.

So be aware, child of light, of your own importance, not as an individual ego identity, but as a critical ingredient in the structure of all Creation. The things you do today, the things you do tomorrow, the things you do next week, have far greater significance than you suspect. Be conscious of what you do, for you are the seed, the origin of much that is to come. Through your actions today, vast worlds will be created and destroyed. Just as a telescope aimed at a distant star has only to move one tiny millimeter at the fulcrum in order to move many light years at the other end, so you too are at a place of beginning, with many effects on future worlds yet unborn.

OPENING TO CHANNEL

By

SANAYA ROMAN AND DUANE PACKER

What is channeling?

Orion and DaBen:

Welcome to channeling! Opening your channel to the higher realms will create an evolutionary leap for you, for channeling is a powerful means of spiritual unfoldment and conscious transformation. As you channel you build a bridge to the higher realms—a loving, caring, purposeful collective higher consciousness that has been called God, the All-That-Is, or the Universal Mind.

With channeling you can access all the ideas, knowledge, and wisdom that is and ever will be known.

When you "channel" you access these higher realms by connecting with a high-level guide or your source self, who steps down this higher vibration and makes it more readily available to you. Channeling involves consciously shifting your mind and mental space in order to achieve an expanded state of consciousness that is called a "trance." To achieve the channeling trance space you will need to learn to concentrate, get your own thoughts out of the way, become receptive to higher guidance, and request the connection to a guide. In this receptive state you become the vessel for bringing through higher energies which you can use for creating good.

You have an innate ability to reach these higher realms; you connect directly with these realms in moments of inspiration, inner guidance, and creativity. You might not be able to reach these realms as easily and as often as you would like. Guides assist you in developing your natural gift to connect to the higher realms. They do so by giving you a boost of energy, providing you with opportunities to grow in new directions, acting as teachers and interpreters, and showing you how to refine your abilities to navigate in the higher dimensions. Guides can help you reach upward in ways that are comfortable and aligned with your higher purpose.

Your guide is a friend who is always there to love, encourage, and support you.

Your guide will encourage and help you to discover your own inner knowingness. As you continue to connect with your guide, you build a stronger, more open and refined, constant connection to the higher realms. You will have more frequent and reliable intuitive insights and experiences of inner guidance or knowingness as the higher vibration flows directly into your mind.

Channeling is a doorway into more love; the higher realms are abundant with love. Channeling is a connection that will stimulate, encourage, and support you. Your guide's goal is to make you more powerful, independent, and confident. The qualities of a perfect relationship — constant love, perfect understanding, and unending compassion — are qualities you will find in your guide.

Channeling will give you the wise teacher you seek, one who comes from within rather than without.

Channeling can provide greater understanding, helping you find answers to such questions as "Why am I here?" and "What is the meaning of life?" Channeling is like climbing to the top of a mountain where the view is expanded. It is a way to discover more about the nature of reality, learn about yourself and others, and see your life from a more all-encompassing perspective, which will help you discover the greater meaning of the situations you are in. Your guide will assist you in finding answers to everything from mundane everyday issues to the most challenging spiritual questions. You can use channeling for healing, teaching, and expanding your creativity in all areas of your life. As you access the higher realms, you can bring through great knowledge, wisdom, inventions, works of art, philosophy, poetry, and discoveries of all kinds.

We, Orin and DaBen, are beings of light. We exist in the higher dimensions, and our goal is to assist you in opening your channel to these dimensions so that you may evolve more rapidly. We have great love for you and it is our concern that you grow and move upward as easily and joyfully as possible. We have put together this course for the purpose of connecting you with your own guide or higher self.

We want to help you understand what channeling is and how you can develop this natural ability. It is easier than you might think, and because it feels so natural, some people have difficulty believing that they have connected with a guide or their source self when they first begin.

SECTION EIGHT:

ORACLES AND DIVINATION TOOLS

The use of oracles, fortune telling devices, and various divination systems for interpreting the meaning of life is an ancient human obsession. Universal questions like "Who am I?" "What am I doing here?" and "What is the purpose of my life?" have driven humans to search the stars and the Earth to find answers, to gain power, and to connect with the Gods. Astrology, Tarot, geomancy, the *I Ching*, Viking runes, stone casting, and crystal balls are found in all historic cultures from Egypt to India, China to Africa.

Oracles and divination tools have found new life in the New Age movement because they are being reinterpreted to apply to contemporary society and the concerns of today. For example, astrology might be seen as a way to promote and assist a floundering relationship, or to direct and deepen connection with the spiritual self. There is an increased interest in the association of astrology with business and career choices. Crystals are being used by businessmen to focus energy and give insights to corporate questions. Even the Reagans had their own personal astrologers advising them while in the White House.

The *I Ching* and Tarot cards are used by most professional psychics and fortune tellers to assist them in gaining insights and in prophecy. Regular people use them too, because they are easy to use and fun. Often throwing the *I Ching* or picking a Tarot card will open up new options or bring a personal and surprising message. Let's say you are having a problem in your career with an employer. You throw the *I Ching* and the coins tell you to read the hexagram "Chin," which means "Progress." The hexagram says: "At a time when all elements are pressing for progress, we are still uncertain whether in the course of advance we may not meet with rebuff. Then the thing to do is simply continue in what is right, in the end this will bring good fortune. . . ." As you ponder the meaning of the hexagram, you receive interesting insight and some good advice. This information is processed by your brain and it opens your mind to a new interpretation of your problem. It causes you to think just a little differently.

The Tarot cards can be used in the same way. There is no need for an elaborate card layout pattern, simply form the question in your mind and draw a card. Let's say you drew the Two of Wands card from the Voyager Tarot deck. In the guidebook it says: "Purity. White candle light is symbolic of purity. Like the untainted white snow and impeccable white lotus, you are clean of character impurities. Purity, as the natural light of the candle, means being authentic and natural, true to yourself without the contamination of outside conditioning..." New information and another perspective is now available to you. These oracular devices will never "tell you what to do." Instead, they open up new ideas and choices, and approaches that might be available to you.

Some of the most famous and popular tools associated with the New Age are crystals. Beautiful, colorful rocks and minerals mined from all over the world have gained prominence and value over the past five to ten years because of their mystical and healing qualities. Many fascinating books have emerged hailing the magical, restorative abilities, soothing meditative assistance, and simple aesthetic beauty of all sizes and shapes of crystals.

From jewelry to paperweights, crystals have found their way into the lives of thousands. Why this fascination with rocks and minerals that were previously of interest to geologists and collectors alone?

In her books *Crystal Healing* and *Crystal Enlightenment,* Katrina Raphaell shares a bounty of information ranging from the historic and metaphysical origins of crystals to the healing uses of various specific types of stones. Like many crystal-lovers, she traces the first use of crystals to the inhabitants of the lost continent of Atlantis. In fact, the fall of the great magical civilizations of Atlantis and Mu are often attributed to the misuse of crystal energies and powers.

Most crystal healing involves meditation and relaxation while holding the crystals in each hand or placing crystals on the seven major chakras or energy centers of the body. Various colors are associated with these centers and careful placement of crystals and healing minerals is said to assist in the clearing of the energy in the centers.

The casting of crystals and colored stones is another version of ancient oracular pursuit. The Hawaiians cast many colored stones and told fortunes based on the placement of the stones. This activity was seen as divinely guided by the deep subconscious body-mind, which literally controlled the thrust of the cast and the tiny muscles of the hands to the point that there was no "accident" in the resulting casting arrangement.

In much the same way, the Vikings of Scandinavia cast rough-hewn stones with etched markings called "runes" to determine their course of action. It is said that these violent, rampaging navigators and invaders would not leave their ship upon landing in a new port until the runes had been cast and interpreted favorably by the runescaster, who was usually a woman. Ralph Blum has created a set of runes and a companion book appropriately called *The Book of Runes.* The runes are simple to use, yet profound in their beautifully written poetic messages. The book and stones are a wonderful tool that has gained much popularity in the New Age.

The Tarot cards have always held great power and insight for people who were not averse to the medieval artwork and slightly ominous feeling of the older Tarot decks. There are many different Tarot decks on the market (the Aquarian deck, the Rider deck, and the MotherPeace decks, for example, are very popular Tarot decks).

The Voyager Tarot deck and companion book are contemporary and fresh in their modern interpretation of ancient and powerful material. Created by master symbolist James Wanless and his partner Ken Knutson, this deck combines innovative collage artwork with psychological information in the divining of the pictured archetypes and symbols. Working with these contemporary oracles provides insight and education about one's inner world, exercises one's intuitive and instinctual impulses, and gives insight into one's life path and purpose.

The Illustrated I Ching by R. L. Wing is a simplified interpretation of the esoteric language of earlier *I Ching* translations. This version includes magnificent art and calligraphy along with a modernized text.

The point of using any type of power object or tool is to add to one's energy resources, not to give up personal power by becoming a slave of the tool. Power objects and oracles should be approached with respect, but it is not good to become over-dependent on portents and signs. They are extremely effective tools for connecting with one's intuition and psychic abilities. Oracles can give insight and guidance, but ought to be mixed with healthy doses of common sense.

THE I CHING
By
RICHARD WILHELM

55. *Feng / Abundance [Fullness]*
above-Chen: The Arousing, Thunder
below-Li: The Clinging, Flame

Chen is movement; Li is flame, whose attribute is clarity. Clarity within, movement without—this produces greatness and abundance. The hexagram pictures a period of advanced civilization. However, the fact that development has reached a peak suggests that this extraordinary condition of abundance cannot be maintained permanently.

THE JUDGMENT

Abundance has success.
The King attains abundance.
Be not sad.
Be like the sun at midday.

It is not given to every mortal to bring about a time of outstanding greatness and abundance. Only a born ruler of men is able to do it, because his will is directed to what is great. Such a time of abundance is usually brief. Therefore a sage might well feel sad in view of the decline that must follow. But such sadness does not befit him. Only a man who is inwardly free of sorrow and care can lead in a time of abundance. He must be like the sun at midday, illuminating and gladdening everything under heaven.

THE IMAGE

> Both thunder and lightning come:
> The image of *abundance*.
> Thus the superior man decides lawsuits
> And carries out punishments.

This hexagram has a certain connection with Shih Ho, *Biting Through* (21), in which thunder and lightning similarly appear together, but in the reverse order. In *Biting Through*, laws are laid down; here they are applied and enforced. Clarity [Li] within makes it possible to investigate the facts exactly, and shock [Chen] without ensures a strict and precise carrying out of punishments.

THE LINES

> Nine at the beginning means:
> When a man meets his destined ruler,
> They can be together ten days,
> And it is not a mistake.
> Going meets with recognition.

To bring about a time of abundance, a union of clarity with energetic movement is needed. Two individuals possessed of these two attributes are suited to each other, and even if they spend an entire cycle of time together during the period of abundance, it will not be too long, nor is it a mistake. Therefore one may go forth, in order to make one's influence felt; it will meet with recognition.

> Six in the second phase means:
> The curtain is of such fullness
> That the polestars can be seen at noon.
> Through going one meets with mistrust and hate.
> If one rouses him through truth,
> Good fortune comes.

It often happens that plots and party intrigues, which have the darkening effect of an eclipse of the sun, come between a ruler intent on great achievement and the man who could effect great undertakings. Then, instead of the sun, we see the northern stars in the sky. The ruler is overshadowed by a party that has usurped power. If a man at such a time were to try to take energetic measures, he would encounter only mistrust and envy, which would prohibit all movement. The essential thing then is to hold inwardly to the power of truth, which in the end is so strong that it exerts an invisible influence on the ruler, so that all goes well.

> Nine in the third place means:
> The underbrush is such abundance
> That the small stars can be seen at noon.
> He breaks his right arm. No blame.

The image is that of a progressive covering over of the sun. Here the eclipse reaches totality, therefore even the small stars can be seen at noon.

In the sphere of social relationships, this means that the prince is now so eclipsed that even the most insignificant persons can push themselves into the foreground. This makes it impossible for an able man, though he might be the right hand of the ruler, to undertake anything. It is as though his arm were broken, but he is not to blame for being thus hindered in action.

> Nine in the fourth place means:
> The curtain is of such fullness

That the polestars can be seen at noon.
He meets his ruler, who is of like kind.
Good fortune.

Here the darkness is already decreasing, therefore interrelated elements come together. Here too the complement must be found—the necessary wisdom to complement joy of action. Then everything will go well. The complementary factor postulated here is the reverse of the one in the first line. In the latter, wisdom is to be complemented by energy, while here energy is complemented by wisdom.

Six in the fifth place means:
Lines are coming,
Blessing and fame draw near.
Good fortune.

The ruler is modest and therefore open to the counsel of able men. Thus he is surrounded by men who suggest to him the lines of action. This brings blessing, fame, and good fortune to him and all the people.

Six at the top means:
His house is in a state of abundance.
He screens off his family.
He peers through the gate
And no longer perceives anyone.
For three years he sees nothing.
Misfortune.

This describes a man who because of his arrogance and obstinacy attains the opposite of what he strives for. He seeks abundance and splendor for his dwelling. He wishes at all odds to be master in his house, which so alienates his family that in the end he finds himself completely isolated.

THE ILLUSTRATED I
CHING

By
R. L. WING

ART AND THE I CHING

The *Book of Change* represents a profound effort on the part of its authors to observe the relationship between the behavior of humans and the constantly changing structure of the universe. The basic assumption put forth by the *I Ching* is that change (action) is not an isolated phenomenon but, in fact, affects every other facet of existence synchronistically. In much the same way that physicist Werner Heisenberg concluded that both the experiment and the experimenter are changed through the act of observation, an accomplished sage can intervene with destiny by selectively conforming and responding to environmental phenomena that he learns to perceive. The *I Ching* quite naturally becomes a powerful perceptual tool in the hands of such a person. This concept is called Taoism. To the uninitiated it seems like magic.

In early times, painting in China was regarded as magic, and certainly mystical, in its process of isolating the spirit of nature with a simple brush stroke—or capturing a mood with a nuance of color. In exploring the mysterious ways of nature, painting used much the same approach as was used in divination. In observing his environment, the seasons, and the weather, the painter learned to see the moods of nature. It is possible, too, that the painter may have been transformed while practicing his craft. The famous seventeenth-century book, *The Mustard Seed Garden Manual of Painting*, states: "He who is learning to paint must first learn to still his heart, thus to clarify his understanding and increase his wisdom."

In order to fully appreciate the position that painting has had in China's culture, it is important to keep in mind that painting was rarely a profession but instead an extension of life. It was an expression of thought and conduct and harmony that the painter experienced with the cosmos. Almost all of the master painters in China first distinguished themselves as scholars, astronomers, musicians, or officials who only took up the brush after reaching significant intellectual and spiritual maturity.

The esteemed painter Wang Wei, who was born in A.D. 415, wrote a discourse on painting in which he said: "Painting should correspond with the I Ching." He went on to explain that the painter must transcend the limitations of the eye and delve deeply into the spirit and interactions of nature; that paintings should express the ever-changing processes of nature just as the *I Ching* expresses the social patterns in those processes.

Painting in China made it possible to manipulate the veil of appearances so that it might be pulled away to reveal the hidden essentials of reality and lead the observer into an experience approaching "truth." Both art and the *I Ching* employ a triggering device that makes conscious that which has been buried in our unconscious. They both expose an intuitive, remarkably accurate awareness of the way things actually are at that moment—and the way things tend to change and transform themselves.

There is a peculiar faculty of the human mind that comes into play when viewing art. It is a form of universal consciousness where all of human experience is somehow touched by the edges of our awareness. This experience allows us to know more about the art we see than what is actually on the paper. Invariably, Chinese art incorporates the invisible seeds of future events while interpreting the lessons of nature. The artist attempts to draw the viewer into the painting and make him a part of the cosmic order.

This profound power of suggestion in Chinese painting is only recently being approached by the Western mind. In fact, until quite recently, all but the most decorative of Chinese paintings were too strange for even the most informed Western connoisseur to appreciate. Yet, the first real understanding that the Western mind achieved of Eastern philosophy came through art. Those paintings done during the philosophically evolved dynasties lucidly expressed Taoist concepts of change. A picture of bamboo growing on a steep hillside was not merely about bamboo growing on a hillside—it was about the struggle for survival, about adaptation and harmony, about slow change in the inanimate, and about the precarious existence of the animate.

If Western pictorial art is designed, generally speaking, to express the world around us as the artist perceives it with his physical senses, then Chinese painting could be called the painting of dreams. It only borrows elements from the world of appearances when necessary to convey an inner reality so profound that it cannot really be expressed by the artist, but only discovered by the viewer for himself.

LEFT BRAIN–RIGHT BRAIN PERCEPTIONS

The *Chuan Tzu,* an ancient philosophical treatise, states that: "Tao cannot be conveyed by either words or silence. In that state which is neither speech nor silence its transcendental nature may be apprehended." Perhaps painting best typifies that state which is neither speech nor silence, but manages to convey a unique mood that can transport us into a special awareness. Yet, if we, as Westerners, are to experience the tao in Chinese painting or in the *I Ching,* we must recognize and transcend certain limitations of mind.

The differences between Eastern and Western ways of knowing are just beginning to come to light as research continues on the characteristics of the left and right hemispheres of the brain. One critical difference begins in the written languages. As you read these words you are making sounds inside your head. These word sounds are then connected in the mind to their corresponding meanings. This is strictly a left-brain function (the hemisphere of the brain that functions in an analytical fashion). Occasionally we do "read" with the right brain when, for instance, we see a stop sign, act accordingly, and never hear the word "stop" inside our minds. The sign is recognized and its meaning understood in the visually oriented right hemisphere. More often than not, we do not think about our reflexive obedience to the sign.

On the other hand, the Chinese language is an imagistic language. It consists of ideograms that are actually pictures of the things and ideas that they represent. These complex picture packets are initially recognized by a function of the right hemisphere of the brain (that side of the brain that functions in an intuitive, holistic fashion). Reading Chinese is like looking at a film strip, watching a tiny movie unfold as the eye travels up and down the page.

This right-brain connection to the written language, one that is not highly functional in the Western mind, explains the serious attention to calligraphy in the East, and the calligraphy's extension into painting. A beautifully calligraphed ideogram for the word "waterfall" can be, to the Eastern eye, as expressive and alive as a painting of the same idea; while a small poem, expressively calligraphed, can be a major work of art in China.

So, while reading for the Westerner is generally a left-brain function, art reaches the Western mind through the right hemisphere. The artist's ideas are communicated to the mind in an intuitive, symbolic, imagistic fashion. In recognition of these perceptual differences, each of the sixty-four hexagrams appears in *The Illustrated I Ching* along with a painting that expresses the essential mood and experience suggested by that hexagram. The *Book of Change* is therefore presented here in a format that attempts to engage both hemispheres of the brain.

CRYSTAL ENLIGHTENMENT

By

KATRINA RAPHAELL

As the root civilizations rose and fell, the latent knowledge of the power and potential of crystal energy was hidden from those who were corrupt in their motives. Much of the information has been lost but some of the information has survived and sprouted in different cultures and civilizations throughout history.

It is recorded in Exodus in the Bible that a breast plate made of twelve precious jewels, combined specifically together in four rows and worn over the heart, would endow Aaron with the power of God. Although it is not known what specific stones were used in the construction of the breast plate, it is recorded as being divinely inspired and having incredible spiritual powers.

Kings in ancient India were advised to collect the very best gems to protect themselves from harm. Early works on astrology, written in Sanskrit and dating back as early as 400 B.C., make elaborate observations on the origin and power of the stones. In those days astrologers advised people stuck with misfortune to wear different kinds of stones to counteract the negative effects of the planets.

Medical practices of many ancient cultures included wearing talismans and amulets around the neck. Depending upon the ailment, specific stones were to bring about the desired effect. Old Rome believed that external objects, such as stones, had a direct and positive influence on the body. Early references in Greek and Roman writings indicate that stones were worn as talismans for health, protection, and to attract virtues.

Throughout history gems and stones have been associated with royal blood and were elegantly worn in crowns and jewelry, embedded in thrones, laid in swords, and used as decorations in other treasures. Many deceased royalty were laid to rest with elaborate collections of gems and stones. When the tomb of King Tut of Egypt was found, the array of riches astonished the world.

Mayan and American Indians have used crystals for diagnosis as well as for the treatment of disease. Large clear quartz crystals were used in ceremonies by the elders of the American Indian villages as "seeing crystals" in which images of future or distant events could be seen. Certain tribes of Mexican Indians believed that if you lived a good life, your soul went into a crystal when you died. If someone was fortunate enough to find that crystal, it would speak directly to their heart, heal, guide and make their dreams come true. . . .

. . . The power and potential of crystals cannot be overstated. It is one of the main contributors to the New Age and can and will be used in many forms for many purposes. The material contained in this book is part of a sacred knowledge of how to use crystals and stones for healing and advancement of consciousness. These teachings are for everyone and can be applied by anyone who is intuitively drawn or attracted to such information. Caution must be taken when using the power of crystals and stones in this way. This knowledge is only now, after thousands of years, again being made available to humankind. Intentions must be humanitarianly pure or the powers could be severely turned against the abuser. The information contained in this book (or any other book on crystal power) is to be used only in accordance with divine law and as a means to transform the human predicament and usher in the Golden Age of Aquarius.

. . . Crystals are there for anyone and everyone who chooses to work with them. They easily become teachers and friends as they share their knowledge and secrets and lend their light and radiance to our healing. All it takes is an openness and willingness to listen to their silent voice as it speaks directly to your inner knowing. Crystals are representatives of the light and if attuned to correctly can teach us how to gain access to and use more of our own light.

Have you ever listened to hear a special secret from a very important friend? That is how you open your mind and heart to communicate with crystals and healing stones. Drop any pre-conceived notion, expectations, or fears that it cannot be done, and allow the inner mind to receive the subtle impressions that the crystal will emanate. Open yourself to the possibility that the crystalline life forms want to share their secrets and wisdom with you. Accept without a doubt the spontaneous images that come into consciousness. As the mind is trained to listen and communicate in silence, responses will come quickly and clearly as the light and energy of the stones you are working with reflect your own wisdom back to you.

A method that has always worked for me is to practice yoga and meditation for at least an hour. Then I lie face up and place a crystal on my third eye point. As relaxation occurs and the mind becomes receptive, the subtle variations of the crystal can be felt. At this time you may want to ask the crystal if there is anything that could be shown to you to assist you in your understanding, or you may want to ask a personal question concerning some aspects of your life. Ask the crystal to reflect the answers from the truth within you into your conscious awareness. Then open your mind and receive the answers. It may come in symbols, images, visions, or direct knowing. However it comes, know it is a message from yourself to yourself amplified and relayed through the crystal with love. It is possible through this procedure to understand many things that you have not understood, come to know yourself on much deeper levels, and to have access to great sources of inner power and strength.

WINDOWS OF LIGHT

By

RANDALL AND VICKI BAER

Crystals are shamanic power objects par excellence. Shamans ascribe a singular importance to quartz above all other power objects, perceiving it to be a "live rock," a living being. As such, crystals are regarded as the most powerful of the shaman's "spirit helpers." To know the keys to activate and employ this solidified form of living Light is to become a man of power and the ways in which this power is used are manifold. Many of these supernormal abilities are associated with seeing, that is, amplified inner sight. Many shamans are able to "see right into things" in the manner of X-ray vision. In fact, quartz is the only power object that appears the same whether the shaman is in a normal waking state of consciousness or in an ecstatic trance state. Thus the crystal functions as a window that activates access to multidimensional octaves of Light and the resultant extrasensory and supernormal talents. Indeed, shamans are able to perceive past, present, and future events through powers of divination. They are also able to perceive disease conditions and the means to correct them.

. . . [C]enoi (spirit helpers) are believed to live in these magical stones and to be at the shaman's orders. The healer is said to see the sickness in the crystals; that is, the *cenoi* inside show him the cause of the sickness and the treatment for it. But in these crystals the *hala* (shaman) can also see a tiger approaching.

Northwest Coast shamans send crystal spirit helpers to fetch the image of a particular person. When the image has arrived, rattles with crystals inside are used to extract a harmful intrusion or disease condition from the image. In medicine bags, crystals are used as a center of power, emanating their Light- and Life-giving properties throughout the other diverse power objects, acting to energize them and to maintain their full potency. In ecstatic trance states, crystals are used as a catalyst and a rainbow bridge to project the soul to the Otherworlds. Once there, the shaman experiences these heavenly realms with full conscious awareness and is able to interact with various beings that are encountered. These and other applications of the crystal power object demonstrate the multidimensional Light inherent in quartz. It is certainly no mistake that shamans around the world collectively recognize the dynamic potentials of this "live rock."

The shaman's crystal is the primal forerunner of a diversity of subsequent applications. As many of the shaman-based hunting-and-gathering cultures transformed into agricultural societies, the spiritual and metaphysical fabric of mankind's culture changed greatly. With increasing degrees of organization and complexity, the unified role of the shaman as collective artist, healer, priest, mystic, and psychic protector divided into such specialized roles as alchemists, psychics, magicians, doctors, mystics, and priests. As this occurred, the ways that crystals were used diversified considerably according to intentionality, specialized knowledge, and the depth of spiritual understanding. In general, this whole time period reflects an instinctive attraction to the Light of quartz, though often knowledge was somewhat clouded by folklore, myth, and lack of in-depth insight. Save for a few adepts, mankind manifested but a hazy reflection of the highest applications. Nevertheless, the "sparks" of insight that do shine through demonstrate the ongoing conscious and subconscious recognition of the Light-properties of crystals.

Echoing the shaman's recognition of quartz as solidified Light, the root word of quartz crystal originated in the Greek word *krys-tallos,* "ice." For many centuries it was believed that crystals were actually ice frozen so hard that it could not melt. One common ancient legend held that crystals were originally holy water that God poured out of heaven. As it drifted toward Earth, it became frozen into ice in outer space. This holy ice was then petrified by various angels so that it would forever stay in solid form for the protection and blessing of humankind.

Throughout these centuries, quartz has been used in many ways, prized for its mystical, mythical properties. One of the earliest pieces of evidence for this is found on an inscription on a Babylonian cylinder seal of about 2000 B.C. It reads: "A seal of Du-shi-A (quartz crystal) will extend the possessions of a man and its name is auspicious." In ancient Tibet the eastern region of heaven was thought to be made of white crystals. In Japan quartz has been a symbol of the purity of the infinity of space and also of patience and perseverance. Crystal gazing, also known as crystal-lomancy, has been used by many seers, psychics, and political leaders for aeons. Divination of the past, present, and future has played a key role in the decisions of many of the most powerful leaders in history. The amethyst (violet quartz), too, was a highly prized and influential stone, valued for its abilities to endow the wearer with quickening of intelligence and invulnerability in battle. Its special virtue was the capacity to cure or prevent drunkenness, in the sense of being drunk with the illusions and passions of the world. Its violet coloration symbolizes royalty and was esteemed for its properties of aiding spiritual growth and its ability to impart spiritual power. A rare stone in earlier centuries, it is found in the crowns, rings, staffs, and jewelry of royalty and the higher levels of religious hierarchies. In the Catholic church, it is the stone of the priest and the bishop and is also found on the Pope's Fisherman's ring. The crozier of a Catholic bishop, his pectoral cross, the altar stones, the candlesticks, and certain crosses carry seven main stones, quartzes among them. These seven stones are diamond or clear quartz, sapphire, jasper, emerald, topaz, ruby, and amethyst. In the Episcopal cross the amethyst is placed in the middle with the sapphire under it, the diamond above it, and amethysts placed at the extremities. In the altar of the Free Catholic Church, six gemstones are placed around a central clear quartz crystal. It is often the case that either diamond or clear quartz was used in the central place of religious settings. This was done due to their transparency and clarity, which attracts pure White Light and helps to reinforce and centralize the more specific color emanations from the surrounding gemstones. The radiations from these groups of precious stones were thought to attract a complete spectrum of spiritual energies and to help activate them within a man's inner being.

On another level, there have been a relatively small number of alchemists, "wizards," and magicians through the centuries who have known and applied various "secrets" of the alchemical science of crystal energies. Through combining various gemstones and metals in conjunction with crystals in highly specific and complex ways, "power wands" were created that would serve as powerful amplifiers, modulators, and projectors of focused thought-forms and cosmic energies. Essentially these wands were highly tuned, very responsive scientific devices attuned to the individual-specific thought frequencies of the operator. In this way, these devices became an extension of the self, acting like a radio receiver, tuner, and transmitter of focused thought-energy. Fairy wands and wizards' staffs are mythical reflections of this reality. Similarly, the bejeweled crowns and staffs of kings and queens were no accident, being made by the more skilled craftsmen-alchemists as powerful energy generators.

The seeding of the Earth-plane from the stars and the celestial realms has taken place at numerous times in this planet's history. These "seeds of Light" were groups of souls who agreed to specific missions to uplift the less highly evolved souls within the Earth's karmic energy field on both spiritual and technological levels. These civilizations were intended within the patterns of the Divine plan to facilitate a collective quantum leap of consciousness for this jewel of the Heavens known as Earth. Many times the door was open for the fulfillment of the Earth's destiny as a Light-house literally in the Heavens, an emerald within the fourth-dimensional frequencies of Light. However, time and time again these peoples failed in the highest aspects of their mission due to a giving in to the lower frequencies of the Earth field. The desire for personal power, born of spiritual ego, created a number of situations in which their highly advanced technologies were used in spiritual ignorance as a means of control of others and self-aggrandizement. The crystal-based technologies were perverted by a relatively few, very powerful individuals. The time comes now again in the twentieth century to lift the Earth into higher octaves of Light, there to start anew as a shining crystal in the Father's Kingdom. Let us learn the lessons of history well.

THE BOOK OF RUNES

By
RALPH BLUM

It is difficult for us to imagine the immense powers bestowed on the few who became skilled in the use of symbolic markings or glyphs to convey thought. Those first glyphs were called *Runes,* from the Gothic *runa,* meaning "a secret thing, a mystery." The runic letter, or *runastaff,* became a repository for intuitions that were enriched according to the skill of the practitioner for *remel,* the art of Rune casting.

From the beginning, the Runes took on a ritual function, serving for the casting of lots, for divination and to evoke higher powers that could influence the lives and fortunes of the people. The craft of the runemal touched every aspect of life, from the most sacred to the most practical. There were Runes and spells to influence the weather, the tides, crops, love, healing; Runes of fertility, cursing and removing curses, birth and death. Runes were carved on amulets, drinking cups, battle spears, over the lintels of dwellings and onto the prows of Viking ships.

The Rune casters of the Teutons and Vikings wore startling garb that made them easily recognizable. Honored, welcomed, feared, these shamans were familiar figures in tribal circles. There is evidence that a fair number of runic practitioners were women. The anonymous author of the thirteenth-century *Saga of Erik the Red* provides a vivid description of a contemporary mistress of runecraft:

She wore a cloak set with stones along the hem. Around her neck and covering her head she wore a hood lined with white catskins. In one hand she carried a staff with a knob on the end and at her belt, holding together her long dress, hung a charm pouch.

To pre-Christian eyes, the earth and all created things were alive. Twigs and stones served for runic divination since, as natural objects, they embodied sacred powers. Runic symbols were carved into pieces of hardwood, incised on metal or cut into leather that was then stained with pigment into which human blood was sometimes mixed to enhance the potency of the spell. The most common Runes were smooth flat pebbles with symbols or glyphs painted on one side. The practitioners of runemal would shake their pouch and scatter the pebbles on the ground; those falling with glyphs upward were then interpreted.

Just as the Vikings used the information provided by the Rune Masters to navigate their ships under cloudy skies, so now you can use the Runes to modify your own life course. A shift of a few degrees at the beginning of any voyage will mean a vastly different position far out to sea.

Whatever the Runes may be—a bridge between the self and the Self, a link between the Self and the Divine, an ageless navigational aid—the energy that engages them is our own and, ultimately, the wisdom as well. Thus, as we start to make contact with our Knowing Selves, we will begin to hear messages of profound beauty and true usefulness. For like snowflakes and fingerprints, each of our oracular signatures is a one-of-a-kind aspect of Creation addressing its own.

Thurisaz
Gateway
Place of Non-action
The God Thor

With a gateway for its symbol, this Rune indicates that there is work to be done both inside and outside yourself. The gateway is a frontier between Heaven and the mundane. Arriving here is a recognition of your readiness to contact the numinous, the Divine, to illuminate your experience so that its meaning shines through its form.

Thurisaz is a Rune of non-action. Thus the gateway is not to be approached and passed through without contemplation. Here you are being confronted with a true reflection of what is hidden in yourself, what must be exposed and examined before successful action can be undertaken. This Rune strengthens your ability to wait. Now is not a time to make decisions. Deep transformational forces are at work in this next-to-last of the Cycle Runes.

Visualize yourself standing before a gateway on a hilltop. Your entire life lies out behind you and below. Before you step through, pause and review the past: the learning and the joys, the victories and the sorrows—everything it took to bring you here. Observe it all, bless it all, release it all. For in letting go of the past you reclaim your power.

Step through the gateway now.

THE VOYAGER TAROT

By
JAMES WANLESS
and KEN KNUTSON

Voyager Tarot is a vehicle for a journey into the inner universe of the self, a symbolic pathway to a full realization of your abilities. Through this symbolic voyage, you recognize that you are a universe and part of the larger universe we live in. That realization enables you to appreciate and utilize all your qualities and talents.

You are a voyager, a traveler through life, and like its namesake, the Voyager space probe, Voyager Tarot will take you on a journey of discovery. The Voyager Tarot reveals your inner universe through picture symbols.

The word "Tarot" is an anagram of tota, meaning "total," and rota, "the revolving wheel." Voyager Tarot reestablishes the original purpose of the tarot implicit in those words; the whole wheel of life in the outer world is re-elected in the whole wheel of life in the individual. Its symbol system portrays the human, animal, mineral, vegetable, elemental, artificial, and extraterrestrial worlds as well as the domains of mind, body, spirit, heart, and collective unconsciousness.

By internalizing symbols of the external world, we can realize the universe within. Voyager Tarot reasserts that primary function of tarot as a growth discipline, a yoga of the symbolic way. This guidebook is a dictionary of a universal language of symbols as well as a discussion of techniques for practicing self-discovery through tarot.

THE EVOLUTION OF TAROT

The three major lines of development of tarot merge in the Voyager deck to enrich its historical continuity with new understanding.

Tarot arose in the hieroglyphic texts of dynastic Egyptian mystery schools and in the ancient Hebrew Kabbalah. Tarot's "major arcana," or 22 principal cards, correspond to the 22 branches on the Kabbalah's Tree of Life. The Tree of Life served not only as a symbol of universal laws but as a psychological portrait of humankind and a philosophy of life, a symbol that could be studied and meditated upon for self-knowledge and personal growth.

In the Middle Ages, four suits of cards called the "minor arcana" were added to the original 22 to produce what we know today as the tarot. Those additions extended the psychological profile of the Tree of Life by providing symbols for mind, emotion, body, and spirit. The medieval deck was used as an entertaining and informative divinatory medium, an oracle for seeing into the future.

Tarot's third evolution, the New Age, has seen an abundance of symbolic designs that bring its core principles into specific cultural or philosophic expressions. The tarot has constellated with a wealth of symbols which speak to specific groups of people.

USES OF VOYAGER TAROT

Like its earliest analogs, the Voyager Tarot is a book of knowledge which reveals the laws of the universe. It is a holistic psychology that relates archetypal personalities with their mental, emotional, physical, and spiritual attributes. It is a multidimensional map of consciousness and a universalistic philosophy of life that counsels you to be like the universe—to be all. Its symbolic images are mandalas for personal contemplation.

As in the Medieval period, the Voyager Tarot may be used for defining the present and divining the future. Every reading of the tarot reveals where you are in the game of life, and this process of input and feedback can serve as a decision-making tool and game. In the game of worldly fortune, it will recommend moves that help you win; in the master-game of spiritual evolution, it will show you the way to progress.

As a product of the New Age, Voyager Tarot is also Aquarian, combining narrow world-views into a unified view of the future. This view is achieved through a visual medium that all can understand: symbolic art.

A prophecy of the Space Age, the Voyager embodies a new consciousness that embraces past and present, masculine and feminine, age and youth, East and West, black and white, nature and technology, science and mystery, primitive and sophisticated, earth and cosmos, individual and collective.

III EMPRESS

Standing before the Earth, the Empress is the Protectress. She symbolizes the law of preservation. As the Egyptian Goddess Selket, who watches over the spirit of Tutankahamun, she represents your responsibility to maintain and guard the seed-essence of life so that it can eternally flower. You are able to recreate, resurrect, and revive.

As Empress, you are the mother. Like mother-earth you preserve life by reproducing it. You are a creatress. You mother your creations into full bloom. You are a nurturer, a provider, and a giver.

You possess unconditional love for all of life's creations. Arms outstretched, you embrace life compassionately and non-judgmentally.

As the woman and mother, you are home and healer, center and synthesizer, abundant and earthy. You are fecund and sensual, magnetic and beautiful. You can turn these qualities, however, into those of a sedentary, homebound, possessive, smothering mother.

LINDA GOODMAN'S SUN SIGNS

By
LINDA GOODMAN

HOW TO RECOGNIZE SCORPIO

Scorpio is deeply interested in religion, curious about all phases of life and death, passionately concerned with sex, and violently drawn by a desire to reform. Yet he's also heroic, dedicated to ties of family and love, and gently protective of children and weaker souls. He can be a saint or a sinner. He can experiment with the darkest mysteries this side of Hades, or he can scathingly revile sin and decadence. Whether he emotes from the pulpit, a business meeting or from the stage, his hypnotic appeal pierces through his audience, literally transfixing or transfiguring them. It's really rather frightening. Even if the Scorpio has temporarily allowed bitterness, drink, or melancholy to drag him into the Bowery, you can bet your old copy of Dante's *Inferno* that the other bums will clear a path when they see him coming.

He's fiercely possessive of what he believes to be his, including success, but his ambition is never obvious. He quietly waits for the chance to move ahead all the while he serves, knowing he is qualified for the position above him. He takes control slowly but very surely. Scorpio can do just about anything he wants to do. If he really wants it, it's most definitely no longer a dream. The dark, magical and mysterious power of Pluto turns desire into reality with cool, confident, fixed intent.

Although a morbid desire to know the most sick and depraved humanity can create a grey lizard who dabbles in drugs and cruelty, he can reverse the path to a life of medicine, where drastic treatments with the same symbols have a deep fascination for him. Although many of the rumored sadistic surgeons are Scorpios, its equally true that many of the finest medical men in the entire world are inspired by Pluto to heal both the mind and the body, diagnosing and treating with strange, inscrutable knowledge. Scorpio was born knowing the secrets of life and death, and with the ability to conquer both if he chooses. But astrology constantly advises him that "he must know that he knows." The ancient mysteries fascinate his brilliant mind. Out of his powerful empathy with human nature grows the outstanding detective, the composer of great musical works, literature of depth and permanence, or the actor who projects with unusual dramatic intensity. Sometimes he lives alone, near the sea, as strong and as silent as the tides. Sometimes he faces the public, wearing a mask of calm reserve and control, to hide his intense desire to win. He can be a politician or a television star, an undertaker or a bartender, but he'll manage to top all his competitors. And he will do it so effortlessly it will seem like an act of fate rather than his own powerful will.

One of the strangest patterns in astrology is the death of a relative in the family within either a year before or a year after the birth of a Scorpio. And when a Scorpio dies there will be a birth in the family within the year before or the year after. It happens at least ninety-five percent of the time. Pluto's symbol is the triumphant Phoenix rising from its own smoldering ashes, and Scorpio personifies the resurrection from the grave. Both the grey lizards and the stinging scorpions can become proud eagles without ever revealing the secret of their sorcery. No use to ask — Scorpio will never tell. But he knows the eternal truth of the circle contained in the symbolic zero.

November's thistle is dangerous, yet it grows entwined with the heavy languid beauty of the Scorpio honeysuckle. Have you ever inhaled the sweet, overwhelming fragrance on a still midsummer's night? Then you will know why there are those who brave the thistles to seek the gentleness of Scorpio — exquisite gentleness. The explosive passion of Pluto has the rich, dark red wine color of the bloodstone. But Scorpio steel is tempered in a furnace of unbearable heat until it emerges cool and satiny smooth — and strong enough to hold the nine spiritual fires of Scorpio's wisdom.

THE TAURUS WOMAN

Taurus females are never sissies. They seldom whine or complain. This is a woman who will quietly take a job to support a husband in medical school or work at home if there is a temporary financial crisis in the family. She doesn't have a lazy bone in her body despite her often slow, deliberate movements and need for frequent rest periods. Taurus females are hard workers. She can climb a stepladder to paint or scrub the walls with the strength of a man but she needs that afternoon nap to keep her sturdy. She'll walk proudly beside her man and seldom try to pass him or stand in his shadow. Many a Taurean woman helps her man with his studies, if he's taking special courses in a professional career, or types up the business correspondence he brings home from the office. She's an excellent helpmate in these areas. Taureans never expect to be supported without doing their share, and they are miserable with a man who doesn't contribute his, though they will try to make the best of it. Taurus women dislike weakness in any form.

Her impassivity to pain and emotional stress is almost miraculous, often even surpassing that of the Scorpio female. I remember a scene I once watched in a hospital. A Taurus woman was going upstairs for serious surgery, so serious that her chances of surviving the operation were very small, and she knew it. It was a calculated risk. As her husband watched her being placed on the cart that would wheel her to the operating area, she noticed the tears in his eyes. But she never commented. She made jokes instead, until the nurses giggled and even the doctor smiled. The last thing her family heard her say as the orderlies were pushing and pulling, trying to get the cart into the elevator, was typically Taurean. Instead of glancing back at her loved ones with a tearful look of farewell, she raised up on one elbow and spoke to the young men firmly. "Before you put me back on this thing again, get some oil and grease those damned wheels." A Taurus woman never lets sentiment interfere with practicality.

A man who marries a female born in May won't marry a cry baby or a gold digger. She'll expect him to provide for her and manage the family finances sensibly. She'll also want the best quality when it comes to food and furnishings. But she'll always keep a sharp eye out for bargains, and be willing to wait for the luxuries that she craves.

Quick fortunes without a solid foundation don't appeal to her sense of stability. She'd rather see you build carefully for the future. Making a good impression is important to her, and lots of Taurean women encourage their husbands to aim for a secure future by inviting influential people to dinner. A Taurus wife is the soul of hospitality.

SECTION NINE:

NEAR DEATH AND REINCARNATION

The cycle of death and rebirth is called the "wheel of life" in the East. Hinduism and Buddhism have the concept of reincarnation and the transmutation of souls embedded in the very foundations of their religious and philosophical principles. The concept of Karma, a system of rewards and punishments meted out in response to the way an individual has led his life, is key to the understanding of Eastern morality.

In Western religious traditions, according to Joe Fisher in *The Case for Reincarnation*, the idea of reincarnation was "buried alive fourteen centuries ago" by the Catholic priests during their rewriting of the Bible. Many people feel that the earlier versions of the Bible contained a great deal of information about reincarnation as well as other metaphysical practices and beliefs.

Most advocates of the New Age feel that reincarnation is highly probable. People speak in casual conversation of knowing each other from a past life. Soulmates, discovering each other in their current incarnation, feel assured that they have lived and loved together before.

In *You Were Born Again to Be Together*, by Richard Sutphen, a prominent past life regressor who has worked with literally thousands of clients, tells how he uses past life therapy to heal current life challenges.

The classic reincarnation text, *Reincarnation, the Phoenix Fire Mystery* by Joseph Head and S. L. Cranston, chronicles many case histories and quotes such reincarnation advocates as Thomas Edison.

No survey of reincarnation would be complete without the inclusion of the works of Ruth Montgomery, a pioneer in the field of channeling through automatic writing. In *Here and Hereafter*, she tells the stories of many contemporary people and their experiences with past life recall.

In *Many Lives Many Masters*, psychiatrist Brian L. Weiss shares the true story of his relationship with a young patient and the past life therapy that changed both their lives.

Along with reincarnation, many New Agers also accept the idea of the alternative time/space reality that is said to exist "between lives." In many cases patients who were clinically dead and were brought back to life report that they went through a dark black tunnel, rushing at top speeds toward an image of light. Raymond A. Moody, Jr., M.D., shares many fascinating stories of near death experiences in his books *Life After Life* and *Reflecting on Life*

After Life. He reports on patients' descriptions of "cities of light," "bewildered spirits," and "supernatural rescues," among others.

The ideas of multiple lives and reincarnation open up many questions about life and death and the thin membrane that separates them. It also calls into question our concepts about time, space, and mass. Is this reality "real"? Are we just kidding ourselves here, lost in the amnesia that surrounds our true purpose? Are we living a movie of our own creation?

The Hindus consider this physical reality to be an illusion. The word "Maya" means "the veil of illusion," and the goal of spiritual evolution is to pierce and lift the veil that separates us from our true God-nature.

Ram Dass says that life on planet Earth is a "curriculum," that we all are here to learn and evolve at our own pace. Our educational curriculum may take one lifetime, or it may take several million. It may be taking place in parallel lives, all happening at the same time in different realities or dimensions. It is truly fascinating to observe these seemingly opposite ideas emerge in Eastern spirituality and in Western science. It is up to each reader and spiritual adventurer to make his or her own decisions about the truth or "reality" of the concepts shared here.

HERE AND HEREAFTER

By

RUTH MONTGOMERY

In our present state of development, it is no more possible to prove reincarnation than to prove the existence of God. But the doctrine of karma and rebirth is so logical that if two-thirds of the world's peoples did not already accept it, it would probably be hailed by Westerners today as a major philosophical breakthrough. The belief is older than recorded history, having been handed down by word of mouth until man learned to record his thoughts in hieroglyphics. It explains, better than does any one known creed, why some are born to affluence and others to abject poverty. Why one youngster is a genius and another a dullard. Why some are crippled or blind; others healthy and beautiful.

The Old Testament teaches "An eye for an eye, a tooth for a tooth," yet we need look no farther than our own neighborhood to observe that sin often goes unpunished here, while greed is seemingly rewarded. Only when one accepts the thesis that we have existed since the beginning of time, and that what a man sows in one lifetime will be reaped in subsequent ones does the Biblical injunction make sense. A major tenet of Brahmanism was stated long ago in the Bhagavad-Gita: "As a man, casting off worn-out garments, taketh new ones, so the dweller in the body, casting off worn-out bodies, entereth into others that are new. For sure is the death of him that is born, and sure the birth of him that is dead; therefore over the inevitable thou shouldst not grieve."

But if we lived before, why can we not remember it? Actually, many seemingly do. Who has not experienced the eerie feeling, on glimpsing a village street or foreign seaport, that he has been there before? Who has not found himself in a situation which seems startlingly familiar, although his reason tells him otherwise? Who has not met a stranger with whom he felt instant rapport, as if he had always known him; or taken a violent dislike to another before introductions were even completed? Could these inner stirrings perhaps be prompted by soul memories of past life encounters?

But does it matter whether we have lived before? Yes, because if this is not our first lifetime it will probably not be our last, and we consequently have it within our power to influence our future circumstances by present conduct. If all of us could accept the philosophy that life is a continuing force, and that what we do to others now will be done unto us in future incarnations, our behavior would dramatically improve. Who would want to cheat a business associate or steal another's spouse if he believed that by such conduct he would be damaging his own chances for happiness in a subsequent life on earth?

Is God so whimsical and unloving that He plays favorites with His children, granting radiant health to one and misery to another, or does the explanation for this seeming inequality lie within each of us? If we accept the philosophy of reincarnation and karma, we can see ourselves as in a mirror—knowing that we are what we have been, and that we will become what we are now, unless we drastically mend our ways. Such a tenet, firmly held, could revolutionize this strife-torn world.

YOU WERE BORN AGAIN TO BE TOGETHER

By

DICK SUTPHEN

When lecturing or performing group regressions, I always allow for a question-and-answer period. There are usually skeptics and non-believers present, and inevitably certain questions and challenges come up. The following are examples of the sort of questions most often asked. The answers are "my truths" based upon the regressions I've completed and nine years of intensive study and involvement with some of the country's leading psychics, mediums, astrologers, and metaphysical organizations.

Q. If we have lived before, why do we forget our past lives?

A. To handle the present and also remember all the past would be too overpowering for our present state of awareness to cope with. We ourselves have chosen this amnesia . . . we hope we have carried with us intuitive knowledge of what is right and wrong, so we do not make the same mistakes we have made in past lives. Everyone has strong feelings about certain things that cannot be traced back to any particular origin.

Q. How do you explain the population explosion?

A. There are simply more chances to be born now than at any other time in recorded history. There is no shortage of souls seeking the opportunity to advance themselves through earthly incarnations, only a shortage of bodies. The vibrational rate of today is higher than it has been within our "age," and thus it offers the chance for more rapid advancement than ever before.

Q. There are presently more people living on the earth than the sum total of all the people who have ever lived. Wouldn't this fact disprove reincarnation?

A. To begin, I don't know that this fact is true, in that general history would not include past civilizations of Lemuria and Atlantis, and perhaps many others. This is really unimportant for it can be easily explained. There are many souls experiencing life on the earth plane for the first time. They may not have lived a physical existence before, they may have lived within a different system (on another planet or within another dimension of time as we know it). Although I know of people within our country who are here for the first time, I personally believe that most first incarnations begin in more primitive or backward societies. Based upon the hypnotic regressions I have completed, at least ninety percent of those in the United States have had lifetimes in Atlantis, which was a highly evolved society. We are back again because we function well in this accelerated frequency or vibration which is similar to that of Atlantean times.

Another metaphysical theory, which is part of my own belief system, is the concept that an identity is capable of living several physical lives at the same time. In other words, one frequency of potential (soul) can occupy several bodies at once. Separate-selves seek to explore numerous potentials at the same time, during a period of accelerated vibrational opportunity. If this is the case, there are far fewer souls presently upon the earth than a census would confirm.

A good friend of mine feels she is also a nurse presently working in a hospital somewhere in this country. She has been drawn to and "merged" with a woman of totally different physical characteristics while experiencing an altered state of consciousness. My friend, Peggy, has attempted to communicate mentally to her separate-self (the nurse) that there are more ways of healing than those endorsed by the AMA.

Enough substantial evidence has been provided to me through psychic channels to conclude that I am presently experiencing many potentials of physical and nonphysical existence. Investigation of the examples provided from the other side, of parallel incarnations, proved to be almost more than I was capable of perceiving. They also provided many valid explanations for various influences in my life, for each portion of the potential exploration (individual identity) intuitively influences the others.

MANY LIVES MANY MASTERS

By

BRIAN L. WEISS, M.D.

"Do you know now what you needed to learn? It was another hard lifetime for you."

"I don't know. I'm just floating."

"Okay. Rest . . . rest." More minutes passed silently. Then she seemed to be listening to something. Abruptly she spoke. Her voice was loud and deep. This was not Catherine.

"There are seven planes in all, seven planes, each one consisting of many levels, one of them being the plane of recollection. On that plane you are allowed to collect your thoughts. You are allowed to see your life that has just passed. Those of the higher levels are allowed to see history. They can go back and teach us by learning about history. But we of the lower levels are only allowed to see our own life . . . that has just passed.

"We have debts that must be paid. If we have not paid out these debts, then we must take them into another life . . . in order that they may be worked through. You progress by paying your debts. Some would progress faster than others. When you're in physical form and you are working through, you're working through a life. . . . If something interrupts your ability . . . to pay that debt, you must return to the plane of recollection, and there you must wait until the soul you owe the debt to has come to see you. And when you both can be returned to physical form at the same time, then you are allowed to return. But you determine when you are going back. You determine what must be done to pay that debt. You will not remember your other lives . . . only the one you have just come from. Only those souls on the higher level—the sages—are allowed to call upon history and past events . . . to help us, to teach us what we must do.

"There are seven planes . . . seven through which we must pass before we are returned. One of them is the plane of transition. There you wait. In that plane it is determined what you will take back with you into the next life. We will all have a . . . dominant trait. This might be greed, or it might be lust, but whatever is determined, you need to fulfill your debts to those people. Then you must overcome this in that lifetime. You must learn to overcome greed. If you do not, when you return you will have to carry that trait, as well as another one, into your next life. The burdens will become greater. With each life that you go through and you did not fulfill these debts, the next one will be harder. If you fulfill them, you will be given an easy life. So you choose what life you will have. In the next phase, you are responsible for the life you have. You chose it." Catherine fell silent.

This was apparently not from a Master. He identified himself as "we of the lower levels," in comparison with those souls on the higher level—"the sages." But the knowledge transmitted was both clear and practical. I wondered about the five other planes and their qualities. Was the state of renewal one of those planes? And what about the learning stage and the stage of decisions? All of the wisdom revealed through these messages from souls in various dimensions of the spiritual state was consistent. The style of delivery differed, the phraseology and grammar differed, the sophistication of verse and vocabulary differed; but the content remained coherent. I was acquiring a systematic body of spiritual knowledge. This knowledge spoke of love and hope, faith and charity. It examined virtues and vices, debts owed to others and to one's self. It included past lifetimes and spiritual planes between lives. And it talked of the soul's progress through harmony and balance, love and wisdom, progress toward a mystical and ecstatic connection with God.

There was much practical advice along the way: the value of patience and of waiting; the wisdom of the balance of nature; the eradication of fears, especially the fear of death; the need for learning about trust and forgiveness; the importance of learning not to judge others, or to halt anyone's life; the accumulation and use of intuitive powers; and, perhaps most of all, the unshakable knowledge that we are immortal. We are beyond life and death, beyond space and beyond time. We are the gods, and they are us.

"I'm floating," Catherine was whispering softly.

"What state are you in?" I asked.

"Nothing . . . I'm floating."

LIFE AFTER LIFE
By
RAYMOND A. MOODY, JR., M.D.

THE BEING OF LIGHT

What is perhaps the most incredible common element in the accounts I have studied, and is certainly the element which has the most profound effect upon the individual, is the encounter with a very bright light. Typically, at its first appearance this light is dim, but it rapidly gets brighter until it reaches an unearthly brilliance. Yet, even though this light (usually said to be white or "clear") is of an indescribable brilliance, many make the specific point that it does not in any way hurt their eyes, or dazzle them, or keep them from seeing other things around them (perhaps because at this point they don't have physical "eyes" to be dazzled).

Despite the light's unusual manifestation, however, not one person has expressed any doubt whatsoever that it was a being, a being of light. Not only that, it is a personal being. It has a very definite personality. The love and warmth which emanate from this being to the dying person are utterly beyond words, and he feels completely surrounded by it and taken up in it, completely at ease and accepted in the presence of this being. He senses an irresistible magnetic attraction to this light. He is ineluctably drawn to it.

Interestingly, while the above description of the being of light is utterly invariable, the identification of the being varies from individual to individual and seems to be largely a function of the religious background, training, or beliefs of the person involved. Thus, most of those who are Christians in training or belief identify the light as Christ and sometimes draw Biblical parallels in support of their interpretation. A Jewish man and woman identified the light as an "angel." It was clear, though, in both cases, that the subjects did not mean to imply that the being had wings, played a harp, or even had a human shape or appearance. There was only the light. What each was trying to get across was that they took the being to be an emissary, or a guide. A man who had had no religious beliefs or training at all prior to his experience simply identified what he saw as a "being of light." The same label was used by one lady of the Christian faith, who apparently did not feel any compulsion at all to call the light "Christ."

Shortly after its appearance, the being begins to communicate with the person who is passing over. Notably, this communication is of the same direct kind which we encountered earlier in the description of how a person in the spiritual body may "pick up the thoughts" of those around him. For, here again, people claim that they did not hear any physical voice or sounds coming from the being, nor did they respond to the being through audible sounds. Rather, it is reported that direct, unimpeded transfer of thoughts takes place, and in such a clear way that there is no possibility whatsoever of either misunderstanding or of lying to the light.

Furthermore, this unimpeded exchange does not even take place in the native language of the person. Yet, he understands perfectly and is instantaneously aware. He cannot even translate the thoughts and exchanges which took place while he was near death into the human language which he must speak now, after his resuscitation.

The next step of the experience clearly illustrates the difficulty of translating from this unspoken language. The being almost immediately directs a certain thought to the person into whose presence it has come so dramatically. Usually the persons with whom I have talked try to formulate the thought into a question. Among the translations I have heard are: "Are you prepared to die?", "Are you ready to die?", "What have you done with your life to show me?", and "What have you done with your life that is sufficient?" The first two formulations which stress "preparation," might at first seem to have a different sense from the second pair, which emphasize "accomplishment." However, some support for my own feeling that everyone is trying to express the same thought comes from the narrative of one woman who put it this way:

The first thing he said to me was, that he kind of asked me if I was ready to die, or what I had done with my life that I wanted to show him.

SECTION TEN:

WOMEN'S AND
MEN'S ISSUES

The women's movement of the sixties and seventies began as a social and political upheaval that has had deep and enduring effects on the way women are perceived in contemporary American society. There can be no doubt that the work of the past decades, the heroic efforts by pioneers such as Gloria Steinem, Betty Freidan, and many others has created new roles and improved the quality of life for most American women.

In the eighties, much of the focus of the women's movement shifted toward women's spirituality. There is a tremendous interest in Jungian "Goddess archetypes" and the Gods and Goddesses of pantheistic world religions. Native traditions and rituals, all forms of earth worship, neopaganism and Goddess-based religions, wicca and white witchcraft are thriving all over the country. Most believe that the cycle is returning to a nature-based, "feminine" outlook on life after centuries of male domination. This leaning toward a more feminine and intuitive approach to life is being demonstrated in many areas of modern life, including advertising and sales. One need only look at the television commercials to see an overall softening taking place, and more soothing, peaceful, and powerful images from nature.

Women's spirituality has become one of the hottest topics in the New Age. A wonderful and surprising book, *The Mists of Avalon* by Marion Zimmer Bradley, was on the national best-seller list for three years. This highly recommended book explores the Arthurian legend from the point of view of all the women associated with Camelot.

Excellent books such as *Goddesses in Everywoman* by Jungian analyst and clinical psychiatry professor Jean Shinoda Bolen, M.D., are becoming national best sellers. *Goddesses in Everywoman* uses seven Greek Goddesses—Athena, Aphrodite, Artemis, Hera, Hestia, Demeter, Persephone—to categorize personality types and behavior in women. It is fascinating to read through the book and find yourself described to a T. By objectifying personality types and labeling them with a Goddess's name, the reader is able to gain perspective and understand her own behavior.

In *The Chalice and the Blade* by Riane Eisler, the discoveries of Goddess figurines at archaeological digs in Greece and other ancient burial sites have been reinterpreted by female anthropologists and scientists. This scientific re-evaluation of objects and sculptures previously thought to be minor fertility demi-Goddesses, or even forms of ancient promiscuity, has rippled through the anthropological, psychological, and women's communities. The examination of peaceful pre-Christian, prehistoric societies that worshiped the Goddess shows "a striking absence of images of male domination or warfare, [which] seems to have reflected a social order in which women, first as heads of clans and priestesses and later on in other important roles, played a central part, and in which both men and women worked together in equal partnership for the common good" (Riane Eisler, *The Chalice and the Blade*).

Historically, the emphasis in major world religions has been on the worship of a male God. Information about this God was gained by the study of the writings and teachings of male disciples and priests. After all, enlightened masters such as Buddha, Moses, Mohammed, and Jesus were male. Chauvinism runs rampant through the major world religions, in both subtle and obvious ways. Hinduism, for example, actually maintains that a spirit or being *must* incarnate into a male body in order to become enlightened.

These male-dominated religious views are unappealing to women, to say the least. The Goddess-based pre-Christian societies were more balanced and harmonious. There was true equality between men and women. The women ran the temples and held respected positions as oracles and priestesses. The invasions of violent marauding tribes during the Bronze Age wiped out these peaceful societies of the ancient world. Many feel that the ills of today's world can be blamed on the six-thousand-year reign of "masculine values" such as warfare, patriarchy, and competition.

Goddess-based spirituality, wicca, and neopagan feminism fulfill women's lives in many ways. Traditional religions have ignored women's need for spiritual authenticity, for acceptance of one's body and one's sexuality, and for empowerment of the divinity of the female incarnation. This warm acceptance of female sexuality clashes with the early Christian Church and its slaughtering of untold thousands of "witches" in Europe during the Inquisition when women were perceived as evil and sexuality was equated with sin.

There are many books on Goddesses and women's spirituality being published. Included in this section are those books and authors that emerged first. Starhawk is a high priestess of the Wicca religion who writes about the Goddess, empowering rituals, and ceremonies in her book *The Spiral Dance.*

Women's spirituality celebrates the ability to love, to develop self-esteem, confidence, and pride in being a woman, to give heartfelt thanks for the honor and joy of living in a beautiful, fertile, sexual female body, the temple of all human birth and creativity.

Statistically, there have been more women than men participating in New Age activities. Although many of the authors, psychologists, and workshop leaders are male, the movement's participants are predominantly female. Perhaps women are more open-minded when it comes to learning new forms of cultural and spiritual practice. Or maybe men are less willing to analyze their emotional, psychological, spiritual, "feminine" selves. Whatever the reasons have been in the past, happily they seem to be changing.

A powerful men's movement, born of group therapy and inspired by the various career and networking support groups of the seventies, is emerging. This movement is an encouraging sign that men are willing to share emotional depth with other men, to bond to heal themselves, and to redefine what it means to be a man in today's world.

Poet Robert Bly has been conducting yearly men's workshops at the Ojai Foundation in Ojai, California, for many years. At these weekend retreats, men explore issues of passion as they reclaim their masculinity, their inner warrior, and share deeply with one another in an environment of trust and safety.

Dr. Warren Farrell has been praised for his books and workshops in this area. *Why Men Are the Way They Are* is a powerful book that casts new light on the way little boys are raised in American society, along with the effects and inevitable results of damaging enculturation.

Dr. Ken Druck leads men's support groups and counsels couples along with his wife, Marjorie. In *Secrets Men Keep,* he shares the fascinating results of his years of research into men's realities. This information is essential for women who are trying to understand men, as well as for men beginning to understand themselves.

Joe Tanenbaum, author and popular seminar leader, conducts trainings on topics such as "Compassion Between the Sexes." In his book *Male and Female Realities,* he is insightful and often hilarious in his assessment of the differences and similarities between men and women. Joe writes: "What becomes apparent in virtually every setting is that men and women have difficulty truly appreciating each other. My women clients are certain that men are indulging in exasperating 'male behavior' while men are equally certain that women are indulging in exasperating 'female behavior.' Women think that men would be perfect if only they weren't 'broken' and need to be fixed; men feel exactly the same way about women." Ultimately each sex feels demeaned by this limiting and limited perception of each other.

Women's spirituality and the new men's movement point to new ways for men and women to understand themselves and each other. Forgiveness allows levels of compassion and understanding to increase and new bridges of love to form. It is time to heal old wounds and stop blaming the opposite sex for feelings of powerlessness and pain.

The New Age embraces a model of whole and balanced men and women who have access to both yin and yang (female and male) aspects of themselves. Out of this wholeness and healing comes true compassion and connection.

THE CHALICE AND THE BLADE

By

RIANE EISLER

For the androcratic Christians who were everywhere seizing power on the basis of rank, such practices were horrible abominations. [Editor's Note: "such practices" refers to the Gnostic Sects' practice of spiritual and sexual equality. The Gnostics honored women as prophets and disciples, and included them in their leadership.] For example, Tertullian, who wrote circa 190 C.E. for the "orthodox" position, was outraged that "they all have access equally, they listen equally, they pray equally—even pagans if they happen to come." He was similarly outraged that "they also share the kiss of peace with all who come."

But what outraged Tertullian most—as well it might, since it threatened the very foundation of the heirarchic infrastructure he and his fellow bishops were trying to impose in the church—was the equal position of women. "Tertullian protests especially the partici-pation of 'those women among the heretics' who shared with men positions of authority," notes Pagels. " 'They teach, they engage in discussion; they exorcise; they cure'—he suspects that they might even baptize, which meant that they also acted as bishops!"

To men like Tertullian only one "heresy" was even greater than the idea of men and women as spiritual equals. This was the idea that most fundamentally threatened the growing power of the men who were now setting themselves up as the new "princes of the church": the idea of the divine as a female. And this—as we can still read in

the Gnostic gospels and other sacred Christian documents not included in the official or New Testament scriptures—was precisely
what some of the early followers of Jesus preached.

Following the earlier, and apparently still remembered, tradition
in which the Goddess was seen as the Mother and Giver of All, the
followers of Valentinus and Marcus prayed to the Mother as the
"mystical and eternal Silence," as "Grace, She who is before all
things," and as "incorruptible Wisdom." In another text, the Tri-
morphic Protennoia (literally translated, the Triple-Formed Primal
Thought), we find a celebration of such powers as thought, intelligence, and foresight as feminine—again following the earlier tradition in which these powers were seen as attributes of the Goddess.
The text opens as a divine figure speaks: "I am Protennoia the
Thought that dwells in the Light . . . She who exists before the All
. . . I move in every creature. . .I am the Invisible One within the All
. . . I am perception and Knowledge, uttering a Voice by means of
Thought. I am the real Voice."

In another text, attributed to the Gnostic teacher Simon Magus,
paradise itself—the place where life began—is described as the
Mother's womb. And in teachings attributed to Marcus or The-
odotus (circa 160 C.E.), we read that "the male and female elements
together constitute the finest production of the Mother, Wisdom."

Whatever form these "heresies" took, they clearly derived from
the earlier religious tradition when the Goddess was worshipped and
priestesses were her earthly representatives. Accordingly, almost uni-
formly divine wisdom was personified as a female—as it still is in
such feminine words as the Hebrew *hokma* and the Greek *sophia*,
both meaning "wisdom" or "divine knowledge," as well as in other
ancient mystical traditions, both Eastern and Western.

Another form these heresies took was the "unorthodox" way they
depicted the holy family. "One group of gnostic sources claims to
have received a secret tradition from Jesus through James and
through Mary Magdalene," reports Pagels. "Members of this group
prayed to both the divine Father and Mother: 'From Thee, Father,
and through Thee, Mother, the two immortal names, Parents of the
divine being, and thou, dweller in the heaven, humanity, of the
mighty name.' "

Similarly, the teacher and poet Valentinus taught that although the deity is essentially indescribable, the divine can be imaged as a dyad consisting of both the female and the male principles. Others were more literal, insisting that the divine is to be considered androgynous. Or they described the holy spirit as feminine, so that in conventional Catholic Trinity terms, out of union of the Father with the Holy Spirit or Divine Mother, came their Son, the Messiah Christ.

THE GYLANIC HERESIES

These early Christians not only threatened the growing power of the "fathers of the church"; their ideas were also a direct challenge to the male-dominated family. Such views undermined the divinely ordained authority of male over female on which the patriarchal family is based.

Biblical scholars have frequently noted that early Christianity was perceived as a threat by both Hebrew and Roman authorities. This was not just because of the Christians' unwillingness to worship the emperor and give loyalty to the state. Professor S. Scott Bartchy, former director of the Institute for the Study of Christian Origins at Tubingen, West Germany, points out that an even more compelling reason the teachings of Jesus and his followers were perceived as dangerously radical was that they called into question existing family traditions. They considered women persons in their own right. Their fundamental threat, Bartchy concludes, was that the original Christians "disrespected" both the Roman and the Jewish family structures of their day, both of which subordinated women.

If we look at the family as a microcosm of the larger world—and as the only world a small and pliable child knows—this "disrespect" for the male-dominated family, in which father's word is law, can be seen as a major threat to a system based on force-backed ranking. It explains why those who in our time would force us back to the "good old days" when women and "lesser men" still knew their place make a return to the "traditional" family their top priority. It also sheds new light on the struggle that tore apart the world two thousand years ago when Jesus preached his gospel of compassion, nonviolence, and love.

There are many interesting similarities between our time and those turbulent years when the mighty Roman Empire—one of the most powerful dominator societies of all time—began to break down. Both are periods of what "chaos" theorists call states of increasing systems disequilibrium, times when unprecedented and unpredictable systems changes can come about. If we look at the years immediately before and after the death of Jesus from the perspective of an ongoing conflict between androcracy and gylany, we find that, like our own time, this was a period of strong gylanic resurgence. This is not a great surprise, for it is during such periods of great social disruption that, as the Nobel-Prize-winning thermodynamicist Ilya Prigogine writes, initially small "fluctuations" can lead to systems transformation.

If we look at early Christianity as an initially small fluctuation that first appeared on the fringes of the Roman Empire (in the little province of Judea), its potential for our cultural evolution acquires new meaning and its failure an even greater poignancy. Moreover, if we look at early Christianity within this larger framework, which views what happens in all systems as interconnected, we may also see there were other manifestations of gylanic resurgence, even within Rome itself.

GODDESSES IN
EVERYWOMAN

By

JEAN SHINODA BOLEN, M.D.

Everywoman has the leading role in her own unfolding life story. As a psychiatrist, I have heard hundreds of personal stories, and I realize that there are mythic dimensions in every one. Some women come to see a psychiatrist when they are demoralized or not functioning, others when they wisely perceive that they are caught in a situation they need to understand and change. In either case, it seems to me that women seek the help of a therapist in order to learn how to be better protagonists or heroines in their own life stories. To do so, women need to make conscious choices that will shape their lives. Just as women used to be unconscious of the powerful effects that cultural stereotypes had on them, they may also be unconscious of the powerful forces within them that influence what they do and how they feel. These forces I am introducing in this book in the guise of Greek goddesses.

These powerful inner patterns—or archetypes—are responsible for major differences among women. For example, some women need monogamy, marriage, or children to feel fulfilled, and they grieve and rage when the goal is beyond their reach. For them, traditional roles are personally meaningful. Such women differ markedly from another type of woman who most values her independence as she focuses on achieving goals that are important to her, or from still another type who seeks emotional intensity and new experiences and consequently moves from one relationship or one creative effort to the next. Yet another type of woman seeks solitude and finds that her spirituality means the most to her. What is fulfilling to one type of woman may be meaningless to another, depending on which "goddess" is active.

Moreover, there are many "goddesses" in an individual woman. The more complicated the woman, the more likely that many are active within her. And what is fulfilling to one part of her may be meaningless to another.

Knowledge of the "goddesses" provides women with a means of understanding themselves and their relationships with men and women, with their parents, lovers, and children. These goddess patterns also offer insights into what is motivating (even compelling), frustrating, or satisfying to some women and not to others.

Knowledge of the "goddesses" provides useful information for men, too. Men who want to understand women better can use goddess patterns to learn that there are different types of women and what to expect from them. They also help men understand women who are complex or who appear to be contradictory. . . .

I have divided these seven goddesses into three categories: the virgin goddesses, the vulnerable goddesses, and the alchemical (or the transformative) goddess. The virgin goddesses were classified together in ancient Greece. The other two categories are my designations. Modes of consciousness, favored roles, and motivating factors are distinguishing characteristics for each group. Attitudes toward others, the need for attachment, and the importance of relationships also are distinctly different in each category. Goddesses representing all three categories need expression somewhere in a woman's life—in order for her to love deeply, work meaningfully, and be sensual and creative.

The first group you will meet in these pages are the virgin goddesses: Artemis, Athena, and Hestia. Artemis (whom the Romans called Diana) was the Goddess of the Hunt and Moon. Her domain was the wilderness. She was the archer with unerring aim and the protector of the young of all living things. Athena (known as Minerva to the Romans) was the Goddess of Wisdom and Handicrafts; patron of her namesake city, Athens; and protector of numerous heroes. She was usually portrayed wearing armor and was known as the best strategist in battle. Hestia, the Goddess of the Hearth (the Roman Goddess Vesta) was the least known of all the Olympians. She was present in homes and temples as the fire at the center of the hearth.

The virgin goddesses represent the independent self-sufficient quality in women. Unlike the other Olympians, these three were not susceptible to falling in love. Emotional attachment did not divert them from what they considered important. They were not victimized and did not suffer. As archetypes, they express the need in women for autonomy, and the capacity women have to focus their consciousness on what is personally meaningful. Artemis and Athena represent goal-directedness and logical thinking, which make them the achievement oriented archetypes. Hestia is the archetype that focuses the attention inward, to the spiritual center of a woman's personality. These three goddesses are feminine archetypes that actively seek their own goals. They expand our notion of feminine attributes to include competency and self-sufficiency.

The second group—Hera, Demeter and Persephone—I call the vulnerable goddesses. Hera (known as Juno to the Romans) was the Goddess of Marriage. She was the wife of Zeus, chief god of the Olympians. Demeter (the Roman goddess Ceres) was the Goddess of Grain. In her most important myth, her role as mother was emphasized. Persephone (Proserpina in Latin) was Demeter's daughter. The Greeks also called her the Kore—"the maiden."

The three vulnerable goddesses represent the traditional roles of wife, mother and daughter. They are the relationship oriented goddess archetypes, whose identities and well-being depend on having a significant relationship. They express women's needs for affiliation and bonding. They are attuned to others and vulnerable. These three goddesses were raped, abducted, dominated or humiliated by male gods. Each suffered in her characteristic way when an attachment was broken or dishonored, and showed symptoms that resembled psychological illness. Each of them also evolved, and can provide women with an insight into the nature and pattern of their own reactions to loss, and the potential for growth through suffering that is inherent in each of these three goddess archetypes.

Aphrodite, the Goddess of Love and Beauty (best known by her

Roman name, Venus), is in a third category all her own as the alchemical goddess. She was the most beautiful and irresistible of all the goddesses. She had many affairs and many offspring from her numerous liaisons. She generated love and beauty, erotic attraction, sensuality, sexuality, and new life. She entered relationships of her own choosing and was never victimized. Thus she maintained her autonomy, like a virgin goddess, and was in relationships, like a vulnerable goddess. Her consciousness was both focused and receptive, allowing a two-way interchange through which both she and the other were affected. The Aphrodite archetype motivates women to seek intensity in relationships rather than permanence, to value creative process, and be open to change.

THE SPIRAL DANCE

By

STARHAWK

The primary symbol for "That-Which-Cannot-Be-Told" is the Goddess. The Goddess has infinite aspects and thousands of names — She is the reality behind many metaphors. She *is* reality, the manifest diety, omnipresent in all of life, in each of us. The Goddess is not separate from the world — She *is* the world, and all things in it: moon, sun, earth, star, stone, seed, flowing river, wind, wave, leaf and branch, bud and blossom, fang and claw, woman and man. In Witchcraft, flesh and spirit are one.

As we have seen, Goddess religion is unimaginably old, but contemporary Witchcraft could just as accurately be called the New Religion. The Craft, today, is undergoing more than a revival, it is experiencing a renaissance, a recreation. Women are spurring this renewal, and actively reawakening the Goddess, the image of "the legitimacy and beneficence of the female power."

Since the decline of the Goddess religions, women have lacked religious models and spiritual systems that speak to female needs and experience. Male images of divinity characterize both western and eastern Religions. Regardless of how abstract the underlying concept of God may be, the symbols, avatars, preachers, prophets, gurus, and Buddhas are overwhelmingly male. Women are not encouraged to explore their own strengths and realizations; they are taught to submit to male authority, to identify masculine perceptions as their spiritual ideals, to deny their bodies and sexuality, to fit their insights into a male mold.

Mary Daly, author of *Beyond God the Father*, points out that the model of the universe in which a male God rules the cosmos from outside serves to legitimize male control of social institutions. "The symbol of the Father God, spawned in the human imagination and sustained as plausible by patriarchy, has in turn rendered service to this type of society by making its mechanisms for the oppression of women appear right and fitting." The unconsciousness model continues to shape the perceptions even of those who have consciously rejected religious teachings. The details of one dogma are rejected, but the underlying structure of belief is imbibed at so deep a level it is rarely questioned. Instead, a new dogma, a parallel structure, replaces the old. For example, many people have rejected the "revealed truth" of Christianity without ever questioning the underlying concept that truth is a set of beliefs revealed through the agency of a "Great Man," possessed of powers or intelligence beyond the ordinary human scope. Christ, as the "Great Man," may be replaced by Buddha, Freud, Marx, Jung, Werner Erhard, or the Maharaj Ji in their theology, but truth is always seen as coming from someone else, as only knowable secondhand. As feminist scholar Carol Christ points out, "Symbol systems cannot simply be rejected, they must be replaced. Where there is no replacement, the mind will revert to familiar structures at times of crisis, bafflement, or defeat."

The symbolism of the Goddess is not a parallel structure to the symbolism of God the Father. The Goddess does not rule the world; She *is* the world. Manifest in each of us, She can be known internally by every individual, in all her magnificent diversity. She does not legitimize the rule of either sex by the other and lends no authority to rulers of temporal hierarchies. In Witchcraft, each of us must reveal our own truth. Deity is seen in our own forms, whether male or female, because the Goddess has her male aspect. Sexuality is a sacrament. Religion is a matter of relinking, with the divine within and with her outer manifestations in all of the human and natural world.

The symbol of the Goddess is *poemagogic*, a term coined by Anton Ehrenzweig to "describe its special function of inducing and symbolizing the ego's creativity." It has a dreamlike "slippery" quality. One aspect slips into another: She is constantly changing form and changing face. Her images do not define or pin down a set of attributes; they spark inspiration, creation, fertility of mind and spirit: "One thing becomes another,/In the Mother . . . In the Mother . . ." (ritual chant for the Winter Solstice).

The view of the All as an energy field polarized by two great forces, Female and Male, Goddess and God, which in their ultimate being are aspects of each other, is common to almost all traditions of the Craft. The Dianic tradition, however, while recognizing the Male Principle, accords it much less importance than the Female. Some modern, self-created traditions, especially those stemming from a feminist-separatist political orientation, do not recognize the Male at all. *If* they work with polarity, they visualize both forces as contained within the female. This is a line of experimentation that has great value for many women, particularly as an antidote to thousands of years of Western culture's exclusive concentration on the Male. However, it has never been the mainstream view of the Craft. I personally feel that, in the long run, a female-only model of the universe would prove to be as constricting and oppressive, to women as well as men, as the patriarchal model has been. One of the tasks of religion is to guide us in relationship to both that which is like ourselves, and that which is unlike ourselves. Sex is the most basic of differences; we cannot become whole by pretending difference does not exist, or by denying either male or female.

It is important, however, to separate the concept of polarity from our culturally conditioned images of male and female. The Male and Female forces represent difference, yet they are not different, in essence: They are the same force flowing in opposite, but not opposed, directions. The Chinese concept of Yin and Yang is somewhat similar, but in Witchcraft the description of the forces is very different. Neither is "active" or "passive," dark or light, dry or moist— instead, each partakes of all those qualities. The Female is seen as the life-giving force, the power of manifestation, of energy flowing into the world to become form. The Male is seen as the death force, in a positive, not negative sense: the force of limitation that is the necessary balance to unbridled creation, the force of dissolution, of return to formlessness. Each principle contains the other: Life breeds death, feeds on death; death sustains life, makes possible evolution and new creation. They are part of a cycle, each dependent on the other.

Existence is sustained by the on-off pulse, the alternating current of the two forces in perfect balance. Unchecked, the life force is cancer; unbridled, the death force is war and genocide. Together, they hold each other in the harmony that sustains life, in the perfect orbit that can be seen in the changing cycle of the seasons, in the ecological balance of the natural world, and in the progression of human life from birth through fulfillment to decline and death—and then to rebirth.

Death is not an end; it is a stage in the cycle that leads on to rebirth. After death, the human soul is said to rest in "Summerland," the Land of Eternal Youth, where it is refreshed, grows young, and is made ready to be born again. Rebirth is not considered to be condemnation to an endless, dreary round of suffering, as in Eastern religions. Instead, it is seen as the great gift of the Goddess, who is manifest in the physical world. Life and the world are not separate from Godhead; they are immanent divinity.

GENDER: THE ULTIMATE CULTURAL DIFFERENCE

By
DR. GEORGE F. SIMMONS

SCENE 1: A SHOPPING CENTER

Not having seen her friend since the birth of the twins three months ago, Jane is delighted to meet Doris who is pushing a carriage full of pink and blue. "Isn't he a kicker!" Jane smiles, pulls herself back, hands on her hips, shakes her head from side to side, and, imitating a male voice, growls, "Looks like he's going to be a tough guy—just like his Daddy." "And, what do we have here," Jane gushes, turning her attention to the pink bundle. Moving closer and bending over protectively, she touches the child. With a look akin to concern on her face she continues, "Isn't she the sweetest, the most delicate thing in the world!"

SCENE 2: A MORTUARY

Two bodies lie in state. Stanley Wojcik, retired mechanic, wears his best and only suit with a burgundy tie. His fingernails have never been so clean. Next door is Charlotte Bains, late vice-president of the Credit Bank. Charlotte, in a peach gown, is dressed for bed.

These scenes make us curious. Why do identical babies rate such different welcomes? In heaven (or some other after-life assignment) will Frank be promoted to a white-collar job while Charlotte is retired to the boudoir?

Unprecedented numbers of women have entered the workforce and hold managerial positions, the women's movement has been strong for decades and media attention has focused on women's (and now men's) concerns. However, men and women, in most situations, are talked to and talked about differently, touched and approached differently, dressed differently, and dealt with from the basis of divergent role assumptions and expectations.

Examine your own experience. This disparity of treatment goes on from the womb to the tomb. It is mostly habit, unconsciously learned and practiced, and is so deep that even insistent egalitarians, whose sons have dolls and whose daughters play tackle football, treat their boys and girls differently without even knowing it.

Women are paid less, promoted less frequently, allowed less "air time" at meetings, given less useful feedback on their performances, assigned domestic duties in the workplace, and on and on. But throwing laws and money at the public complaints and private distresses of women does not ameliorate them because they are symptoms of deeply entrenched cultural dynamics.

The separate treatment given to men and women throughout their lives irrevocably divides us into *two separate cultures with two distinctive languages*. These languages are always spoken in our minds and often with our tongues. The grammar and vocabulary of spoken and written English causes women to think differently from men and gives them lower levels of power and certainty.

You have probably, at least once, shuffled off after an encounter with the opposite sex shaking your head and muttering, "I don't think the two of us speak the same language." The statement is, of course, right. Even though you and the other person use English to communicate, what each of you mean by the words you use and the experiences that shape your vocabulary are not the same. What each of you pictures as you listen to and try to understand each other can send you down quite different tracks. What you say to yourself as you attempt to capture and send your own thoughts and feelings in the form of sentences to the other person can make you worlds apart.

We presume that our partners will understand and that they will behave according to our expectations. When they don't, we automatically tend to withdraw, blame, or punish them, either with a personal attack or in the broad strokes of traditional prejudice: "Just like a woman," or "Stupid, insensitive man!" Anger, frustration and resentment become the currency between women and men, instead of curiosity, creative exploration, fresh possibilities and workable commitments.

To benefit from our differences instead of condemning, denying, avoiding or trying to change each other, men and women must learn four precepts.

1. Be clear that our expectations about each other are only expectations, not commitments. An expectation is something we decide for ourselves about how another person should think, feel or act. "She should know not to disturb me with such a trivial question," or, "He should acknowledge my contribution to this relationship." Often we do not communicate this inner demand to that person, or, if we do, we fail to get them to agree to it. Yet behave toward them as if we had their agreement.

We need to spell out our expectations as partners and to negotiate agreements about what we will actually give to and receive from each other. This becomes possible only if we:

2. Ask questions which encourage our partners to paint a full picture of what they understand and mean to communicate to us. Here are examples of questions that ask for another's opinion without attacking the person:

What does my dressing up mean to you?

What do you say to yourself about how I dress now?

How would you imagine I might look dressed for the theater?

What do you see as the pros and cons of wearing dark colors?

Whether the other person asks us such questions or not, we can talk to them as if they had, if we:

3. Share fuller, more descriptive pictures of how we ourselves see, interpret and talk to ourselves about the issues at hand. We can preface our own opinions in such a way that the listener can recognize that we are stating our own experience and sharing our own way of seeing things rather than dictating our opinions to them as if these opinions were the whole and only truth. Here are some examples that can help us talk about ourselves and our opinions better: Here's how I see our managing the house together. . . Here's what

happened to me that leads me to think we should make some changes . . . I imagine that if I were to come home earlier on Friday we could . . . Some of my constraints are . . .

When we label our opinions this way, we invite others to accept the differences that separate us as men and women. We receive the information that enables us to bridge the cultural gap between us. We can then:

4. Make clear agreements and use this same four-step process to manage broken agreements when they occur. An agreement is made when one asks another to do something specific and measurable by a specific time, and that person says "Yes, I will," or "I promise."

We have an innate reluctance to ask for and promise things because we do not know the future nor do we know other people's moods or states of mind. Every commitment puts us at risk; we must fulfill the commitment or know what steps to take if this becomes difficult or impossible. Because we never understand each other perfectly, all commitments are in danger of breaking down at some point. Expect this, but instead of becoming upset when a breakdown occurs, simply go back to steps 1, 2, and 3 to deal with the other person. In so doing you own your feelings as well as making new commitments when needed.

Knowing how to obtain better information from each other, to use clear language to strike specific agreements and to apologize and start over when we fail reduces the risk and reluctance to commit.

Bundles of pink and blue can have a very exciting and satisfying future together if they regularly use these four steps.

WHY MEN ARE THE WAY THEY ARE

By

WARREN FARRELL, PH.D.

During the past two decades, women have been frustrated because the more they "find themselves," the more they seem to be placing their relationships with men in jeopardy. They have expressed frustration that they were the ones doing all the work in their relationships, and having to spoon-feed what they learned to men. Even the spoon-feeding created "feedback."

Over the years, I have seen women's body language alter as the frustration accumulated. They didn't like what they felt in themselves. I saw tears of hopelessness well in the eyes of more than a few women—women who were alternating between hopelessness toward men and a haunting fear that "Maybe it's me . . . maybe *I'm* doing something wrong."

Increasingly, women are finding men to be less and less lovable. Yet we say men have power. In this book I redefine power to include lovability. Which gives us a new look at male power.

When I wrote *The Liberated Man*, it was mostly women who responded positively. They felt understood. A woman would give it to a man with any excuse—Valentine's Day, Father's Day, birthdays, anniversaries—in the hope that he would understand her better. I think it is fair to say that the book accomplished that much. But I noticed that only a small number of men really changed. And those who changed the most changed defensively—because she wanted the man different. Over the years, though, I noticed women back off from these men. Their relationships became asexual. They were picking up on men's defensiveness. As one woman put it, "A man walking on eggshells doesn't have much sex appeal." Some men were even called wimps.

At first I didn't understand how a man who was more sensitive could ever be less appealing. But I came to understand the distinction between men who are *defensively sensitive* ("walking on eggshells") and men who are sensitive as a result of their own security. Only a secure man is appealing.

Women know how destructive it is when they change *for* men. Women changed so much for men that it shocks them now to learn that while they were adapting to men, men were adapting to women. Adapting in a manner that is so different from women's experience of adapting that at first it is barely recognizable as adaptation.

That's too bad—because women have done so much work on relationships. Yet the articles *on men* in women's magazines do not discuss life the way *men* experience life. So the questions they purport to answer, such as those in the opening questionnaire (about egos, listening, fear of successful women, and so on), are not answered in a way that rings true *for men*—only in a way that rings true *for women about men*. These perceptions cannot be applied to men without the men feeling uncomfortable, without knowing quite why. So it becomes easier for a man to escape via TV, sports, or behind a paper.

It has taken me much of the past seventeen years to understand that men do not become more lovable until they feel understood. Increasingly, I have altered my workshops to get both sexes to understand each other. But that understanding does not work if it is only on an intellectual level. So I started developing exercises to have each sex "walk a mile in the other sex's moccasins." That's when things started changing. I began listening more carefully to men. And as I listened, I observed some important paradoxes:

- I expected that the men who were asking—even demanding— that *their* stories be heard, would be chauvinists. In fact, chauvinists didn't think about their stories. I found that the men who understood their stories were those most in touch with their feelings. Their stories *were* their feelings.

· I noticed that men who were willing to read and discuss books on relationships were tuned into women. But if they were not also tuned into their own hurts, it was usually out of the fear of confronting women. Underneath they usually retained the attitude that women needed special protection. It was the first sign that the man was still not treating a woman as an equal. And a sign that the man was not secure enough to risk female rejection.

I found that those women who could hear men's stories — without seeing them as taking away from their own — were among the few whose independence seemed to come out of internal security, who were not turning life into a fight, and who had consistently good relationships with men. For some women, feminism had opened the whole vista of reexamining roles — including men's roles. For others, the deeper the feminism, the more closed the women were to men. Strict ideology is for women what macho is for men.

THE SECRETS MEN KEEP

By

DR. KEN DRUCK *and* JAMES C. SIMMONS

Men today are the guardians of some of the world's best-kept secrets. We lead secret emotional lives, often hiding our deepest fears and insecurities, as well as our most cherished dreams, even from those we love and trust. Perhaps we are hiding a fear we have carried around our entire life, perhaps a secret fantasy. Or we may be more sensitive and, as a consequence, more easily hurt than we care to admit.

We block off entire areas of ourselves, stamp them *"top secret,"* and file them away. And we keep their very existence a secret from wives, girlfriends, children and buddies. We see these parts of whom we are as a threat. Perhaps they embarrass us. Or maybe they fail to confirm a particular image we have set out to project for others.

We select any number of places in which to hide our secrets. We disguise them in roles like "Mr. Nice Guy" or "The Hard-driving Businessman." Our former jobs and failed marriages may have been burial grounds for secrets. Even our greatest successes can become hiding places for our deepest secrets.

But secrets have a way of making their presence felt. We may think that we are done with them, having filed them away and forgotten about them. But they are still there, often disguised in a stubborn feeling of unhappiness or uneasiness that refuses to go away. Perhaps they appear in a health crisis, such as an ulcer, high blood pressure, or a heart attack. Or they may come out in a sudden burst of temper, directed against our wives, kids, boss, or the world in general.

There is a distressing irony here. We live in the Age of Information, in which giant new computers process one billion bits of data almost instantaneously. We spend large amounts of time and energy assimilating new information. And yet at the same time we stubbornly avoid processing certain kinds of information about ourselves.

Many men end up prisoners in their jobs and relationships, held captive by their secrets. Stan, a client of mine, finally broke out of his secret hiding place and revitalized himself, as well as his marriage.

"My wife thought she knew everything there was to know about me. But there were a number of important things I had kept from her. Some of them I had trouble admitting to myself. Like how frustrated I felt about work. My father had been an unhappy man. I was becoming more like him every day. I can see now how my refusal to talk about these feelings with my wife affected our marriage. My secrets were like walls keeping us apart.

"After fourteen years on the same job, I hated what had become of my life. Like my father, I put in ten-hour workdays, six days a week. And like my father, I came home exhausted and kept to myself. I never felt I had the right to complain. My wife would ask if I was all right and I'd tell her, 'Leave me alone, I'm tired, that's all.' Inside, I was dying a little bit each day.

"Then my wife became ill. That changed everything. For the first time, I faced losing her. Both Lynn and I started opening up to one another. I told her how unhappy I'd been. I was surprised she had many of the same feelings. Listening to her, I felt relieved. We discussed ways that we could change our lives around. It was like lifting a tremendous burden off my shoulders. My unhappiness was no longer something I had to keep locked up inside.

"For the first time in years I did not feel alone. Lynn recovered and we were more like partners than ever before. I made some changes in my crazy work schedule. I'm a lot happier now. It took me a long time to accept how I really felt, and even longer to speak up. Saying what's really on my mind is still awkward, but that's all right. I'm doing a lot better."

Webster's Dictionary tells us that the word "secret" comes from the Latin *secretus*, meaning "to set apart." Forever hidden away, our secrets set us apart, keeping who we really are an enigma.

There is another irony here. Secrets are, by definition, meant to be kept. Yet it is their destiny to be told. Life itself is a secret unfolding. Nature (including human nature) provides endless mysteries, riddles, and camouflages, as well as endless discoveries. It is in the process of uncovering and telling our secrets that life takes on meaning. We learn to cultivate a relationship with the mysteries, as well as the realities, which confront us.

This book is an outgrowth of my work in the area of male psychology over the past twelve years. In addition to my general practice, I have worked extensively with men, particularly in the context of the Alive and Male seminars that I have conducted across the United States. College professors and plumbers, judges and retired Army officers, doctors and business executives have come together in these seminars to acknowledge and understand their individual and collective secrets. They have broken what I call "the silence barrier." In the seminars, we discuss our relationships with our fathers, mothers, life partners, buddies, jobs, and children. By the end of each seminar, these men discover that the inner life of a carpenter is not that much different from that of a surgeon. We all share pretty much the same fears and hopes. My work with these men, the participants in my men's groups, and the men and women I see in my private practice in San Diego form the basis for this book. From all of them, I have learned that beyond secrecy lies the "real" strength and sensitivity every man wants in himself—and what every woman wants in a man.

MALE AND FEMALE REALITIES: UNDERSTANDING THE OPPOSITE SEX

By

JOE TANENBAUM

WHAT MALES AND FEMALES WOULD "FIX" ABOUT THE OTHER

One of the questions I usually ask in my workshops is, "What would you fix or change about the opposite sex?" I have found that basically all women's responses are almost identical, regardless of the social, economic, religious, or cultural mix of the group (including teenagers to retirees); and the men's responses are also alike. My question deliberately emphasizes the awareness that men and women perceive our differences as negative rather than simply as "differences." Here are some of the responses.

MEN ON WOMEN

Male participant: "They're sissies. They're weak. If there is a jar to be opened, they come over: 'Can you open this?' and you know very well they can open it."

Male participant: "They are emotional. They're never logical. I hate that. They hate sports. Do you know a woman who will accept a man watching a basketball game? They cannot stand it."

Male participant: "When women grow older, they're just too serious, and they can't understand why guys just like to go out and have fun."

Male participant: "They have less sexual desire. They can't take a punch. Disorganized. Moody. Negative. Vengeful. And late."

Male participant: "They talk too much, and about the stupidest things. They change their minds constantly. They won't take control when you offer them control. They are vain. They nag. They pout."

Male participant: "They want to be mother forever. And that goes for mom, girlfriend, anything."

Male participant: "Too emotional, flippant, whimsical, capricious. They over-react. They have this typical knee-jerk reaction. They change their minds too quickly. Sometimes they are too sensitive—it's like you're walking on eggshells versus being able to 'roll with the punches.'"

Male participant: "They like you to read their minds."

Male participant: "They want everything. They're parasitic in nature, and overly possessive of children."

Male participant: "They use sex to control you."

Male participant: "They find the perfect man and then spend the rest of their life fixing him."

Male participant: "They want the flowers, but they're unwilling to shovel the manure. They can pick up an axe and kill an alligator if they have to, but in daily transactions they use this delicate business."

WOMEN ON MEN

Female participant: "They always feel like they do everything better. Even though I know what I'm talking about, they don't listen to me. They always expect me to be perfect, even though they're not. They are very demanding; they put their values on me."

Female participant: "Always looking for a way to get me in bed. Not really affectionate. Very self-absorbed."

Female participant: "I find men always calling for accountability from me. I find that I have a tendency to bring out hostility in men; I threaten them terribly, and I find them defensive with me. And because they are defensive, they then become antagonistic."

Female participant: "Not spontaneous. Sloppy. Unattentive. Not too creative. Judging. Evaluative. Take things for granted."

Female participant: "Expect me to put their needs and problems first. Always think that their job is more important than mine. Often tell me that I don't understand, don't know the facts, or am not acquainted with the reality of the situation. And they keep score— sometimes over years."

Female participant: "They are non-verbal. Often you want to have a conversation with them and you get grunts. They are often emotionally stunted. They lack intuition. They are too focused. If a guy is driving the car, it's like 'turn off the radio and shut up, I've got to make a left-hand turn.' They aren't able to do more than one thing at a time."

Female participant: "There's a strange way that they click in and out of crudity and insensitivity. And even though they allow themselves the expression and spontaneity, they don't want a woman to act the same way."

Female participant: "I usually take care of the really sticky problems on a one-to-one basis. He takes care of the finances. But if there is a human problem, I'm the one who has to do that."

Female participant: "Not intuitive. Uncompassionate. Don't like shopping."

Female participant: "Don't want to talk about their emotions."

Female participant: "Expect me to keep track of where he puts and loses things."

Female participant: "I would like men to share more in household chores, be a partner with me, and not make me feel like an employee."

It's easy to see from the Fix'em List how the summarized responses line up: literally men on one side and women on the other—in battle formation—with opposite "shoulds" for ammunition!

SECTION ELEVEN:

GLOBAL CHANGE AND SOCIAL TRANSFORMATION

In a gentle way, you can shake the world.
— MAHATMA GANDHI

As one practices spirituality in daily life, one begins to extend spirituality into one's relationships, then toward immediate community, regions and nations, and finally to the world. New Agers are very concerned about social and political issues such as world peace, nuclear disarmament, citizen diplomacy, and social transformation.

A basic premise in the healing process is to start from within. Heal yourself then heal the planet. Planetary disturbances are seen, by some people, as metaphors for individual, internal disturbances. What part of *me* is at war? How can I ask for peace in the Middle East when I haven't achieved inner peace? How am I polluting my inner environment?

The statistics for the world's resources indicate some very bad news. The world population is growing at staggering rates, we are destroying forests, plants, and animal species, we have serious climate changes and global warming, there is more waste and fewer means of disposal, and more and more toxic waste.

The United Nations environmental program has become increasingly active in this arena. Many famous celebrities and musical performers are using their star power to bring attention and publicity to the issues.

There is a very strong revolution taking place worldwide, a "Green Revolution." That is the phrase the press has used to describe the activities of the many groups trying to achieve global environmental clean-up and change.

As people become more environmentally aware, they look to change their own habits and behavior. They understand that in little ways we can change the world. Stopping consumption of certain fast foods by one's family and friends, for example, can be a step toward saving the Amazon rain forest. Recycling one's own garbage is a step toward cleaning up the oceans of the world. Hiring a homeless person is a way to help the widespread and heart-breaking problems of homelessness in this country. We have to start somewhere, and change begins at home.

Most of us worry about the situation of today's world. We are concerned that there may not be a future for our children to enjoy. In the wake of potential destruction and fear, we search for a sane interpretation of world events. Prophets of doom insist that the end is near. Revelations in the Bible, the amazing predictions of Nostradamus, the Mayan Calendar, and other sources predict major upheaval and change in our lifetime. A fundamental change in thought and behavior must be undergone for the world to survive. In the face of such a prospect, the spiritual approach seems to be the only way to effect conscious peaceful change.

The Chinese language has no character or word for "crisis." The closest translation means "possibility for change" or "opportunity for important decisions." That means that every time something looks like crisis and chaos, it is actually an opening to a new doorway of learning.

One person who is truly loving and peaceful can have a ripple effect on others, inspiring them to be more loving. This larger ripple becomes a wave, which becomes a movement that changes the course of history. One need only look at the life of Gandhi, or Martin Luther King, Jr., or Buddha, or, in fact, all the saints throughout history. "The pure unadulterated love of one person can nullify the hatred of millions," said Mahatma Gandhi.

Many futurists and inspirational world thinkers are writing in the area of global transformation. Willis Harman of the Noetic Institute states in his book *Global Mind Change:* "We are already well into the mind change. It is altering the way we interpret science. It is drastically modifying our concepts of health care, it is revolutionizing our concepts of education, it is causing major changes in the world of business and finance, it is in the process of delegitimating war and causing a total rethinking of the means of achieving national and global security."

What can the individual do when faced with the depressing statistics that are found in the daily news? How does one combat the overwhelming hopelessness of our world situation? For many people in the New Age movement, the change is taking place on an inner, spiritual level. Some see this change as inevitable. They welcome it as the dawning of a new age and are willing to suffer the painful transitions that await our world.

"Visualize World Peace" is a slogan and popular bumper sticker that sums up the approach many have taken. Affirm, visualize, meditate, and be peaceful in order to create an atmosphere of peace that will, one hopes, become contagious.

"All we are saying ... is give peace a chance" was the chant of war protesters of the sixties. The eighties and New Age approaches have changed that request to a personal invitation for a spiritual "act of power" in each heart. We feel the need to "take back the power and live in accordance with the laws of nature." Marilyn Ferguson's seminal New Age book, *The Aquarian Conspiracy*, has been used by churches, prisons, and government agencies worldwide, by many who harbor the dream of a better world. The book is considered a source of inspiration and encouragement for "continued striving for renewal of ourselves, our society and our planet (New Age Catalogue).

"Peace in the physical world can only be built on the cornerstone of peace in each of our hearts, and as we heal our sense of personal separation, peace on Earth is sure to follow," says Alan Cohen in *The Healing of the Planet Earth*. He goes on to say, "The most significant contribution you and I can make toward world peace is to be peaceful ourselves, to give peacefulness to those whose lives we touch daily, and to forgive ourselves for our errors, to the point at which we love ourselves no matter what we ever have done."

For many, the answer is in taking "right political action," creating Nuclear Free Zones in the communities, protesting and demonstrating at local nuclear sites, and communicating closely with government figures.

Citizen Diplomacy is a way that many Americans are reaching out to Russians. This exemplary program sends Americans to Russia and matches them up with their Russian "counterparts," Soviet citizens who are in the same or a similar line of work.

By linking and connecting people who have the same careers and interests, friendships are built that cross all political boundaries. This program has been very effective in opening up communication between normal Americans and normal Russians who find, upon encountering one another, that we all want basically the same thing—and that together we can learn to envision a positive future and work together to achieve it.

Prominent futurist and former vice-presidential candidate Barbara Marx Hubbard asks: "Is the threat of nuclear holocaust in fact one of nature's evolutionary drivers which is triggering a consciousness chain reaction, which in the twinkling of an eye, will bind the world together again in the white light of awareness that we are one with each other, with nature, with God, inheritors of the powers of co-creation in the universe of many dimensions, at the dawn of the universal age? Are we approaching a critical mass of consciousness which will trigger a sustained chain reaction of love that will never stop?" (quoted from her introduction to Alan Cohen's *The Healing of the Planet Earth*).

Transformation must begin on an individual level before it can affect the world. If each individual's consciousness is linked to every other individual, changes in awareness and behavior on smaller levels can create a critical mass change that affects larger groups. Within this model, it is possible for just one individual to act as a catalyst for powerful transformation. If we take responsibility for transforming ourselves and for living lives of peace and love, we can act as examples and mirrors to others. If we can heal violence and poverty in ourselves, we just might have a chance at healing violence and poverty in the world.

THE GLOBAL BRAIN

By
PETER RUSSELL

THE LIVING EARTH

The view of Earth from space brought with it yet another insight: the possibility that the planet as a whole could be a living being. We Earthlings might be likened to fleas who spend their whole lives on an elephant, unaware of what it really is. They chart its terrain—skin, hairs, and bumps—study its chemistry, plot its temperature changes, and classify the other animals that share its world, arriving at a reasonable perception of where they live. Then one day a few of the fellas take a huge leap and look at the elephant from a distance of a hundred feet. Suddenly it dawns: "The whole thing is alive!" This is the truly awesome realization brought about by the trip to the moon. The whole planet appears to be alive—not just teeming with life but an organism in its own right.

If the idea of Earth as a *living being* is initially difficult to accept, it may be due partly to our assumptions about what sort of things can and cannot be organisms. We accept a vast range of systems as living organisms, from bacteria to blue whales, but when it comes to the whole planet we might find this concept a bit difficult to grasp. Yet until the development of the microscope less than four hundred years ago, few people realized that there are living organisms within us and around us, so small that they cannot be seen with the naked eye. Today we are viewing life from the other direction, through the "macroscope" of the Earth view, and we are beginning to surmise that something as vast as our planet could also be a living organism.

This hypothesis is all the more difficult to accept because the living Earth is not an organism we can observe ordinarily outside ourselves; it is an organism of which we are an intimate part. Only when we step into space can we begin to see it as a separate being. Stuck like fleas on an elephant, we have not, until recently, had the chance to see the planet as a whole. Would a cell in our own bodies, seeing only its neighboring cells for a short period, ever guess that the whole body is a living being in its own right?

To better understand the planet as a living system, we need to go beyond the time scales of human life to the planet's own time scale, vastly greater than our own. Looked at in this way, the rhythm of day and night might be the pulse of the planet, one full cycle for every hundred thousand human heartbeats. Speeding up time appropriately, we would see the atmosphere and ocean currents swirling round the planet, circulating nutrients and carrying away waste products, much as the blood circulates nutrients and carries away waste in our own bodies.

Speeding it up a hundred million more times, we would see the vast continents sliding around, bumping into each other, pushing up great mountain chains where they collided. Fine, threadlike rivers would swing first one way then another, developing huge, meandering loops as they accommodated themselves to the changes in the land. Giant forests and grasslands would move across the continents, sometimes thrusting limbs into new fertile lands and at other times withdrawing as climate and soil changed.

If we could look inside, we would see an enormous churning current of liquid rock flowing back and forth between the center of the planet and the thin crust, sometimes oozing through volcanic pores to supply the minerals essential for life.

Had we senses able to detect charged particles, we would see the planet bathing not only in the light and heat of the sun but also in a solar wind of ions streaming from the sun. This wind, flowing round the Earth, would be shaped by her magnetic field into a huge, pulsating aura streaming off into space behind her for millions of miles. Changes in the Earth's fluctuating magnetic state would be visible as ripples and colors in this vast cometlike aura, and the Earth herself would be but a small blue-green sphere at the head of this vast energy field.

Thus if we look at the planet in terms of its own time scales, we seem to see a level of complex activity similar to that found in a living system. Such similarities, however, do not constitute any form of proof. The question we have to ask is whether scientists could accept the planet as a single organism in the same way they accept bacteria and whales. Could the Earth actually "be" a living organism?

This no longer seems so farfetched. On the contrary, an increasingly popular hypothesis suggests that the most satisfactory way of understanding the planet's chemistry, ecology, and biology is to view the planet as a single living system.

THE DIFFERENT DRUM

By

M. SCOTT PECK

. . . [T]here is a pattern of progression through identifiable stages in human spiritual life. I myself have passed through them in my own spiritual journey. But here I will talk about those stages only in general, for individuals are unique and do not always fit neatly into any psychological or spiritual pigeonhole.

With that caveat, let me list my own understanding of these stages and the names I have chosen to give them:

Stage I: Chaotic, antisocial
Stage II: Formal, institutional
Stage III: Skeptic, individual
Stage IV: Mystic, communal

Most all young children and perhaps one in five adults fall into Stage I. It is essentially a state of undeveloped spirituality. I call it antisocial because those adults who are in it (and those I have dared to call "People of the Lie" are at its bottom) seem generally incapable of loving others. Although they may pretend to be loving (and think of themselves that way), their relationships with their fellow human beings are all essentially manipulative and self-serving. They really don't give a hoot about anyone else. I call the stage chaotic because these people are basically unprincipled. Being unprincipled, there is nothing that governs them except their own will. And since the will from moment to moment can go this way or that, there is a lack of integrity to their being. They often end up, therefore, in jails or find themselves in another form of social difficulty. Some, however, may be quite disciplined in the service of expediency and their own ambition and may so rise to positions of considerable prestige and power, even to become presidents or influential preachers.

From time to time people in this stage get in touch with the chaos of their own being, and when they do, I think it is the most painful experience a human can have. Usually they just ride it out unchanged. A few, I suspect, may kill themselves, unable to envision change. And some, occasionally, convert to Stage II.

Such conversions are usually sudden and dramatic and, I believe, God-given. It is as if God had reached down and grabbed that soul and yanked it up a quantum leap. The process also seems to be an unconscious one. It just seems to happen. But if it could be made conscious, it might be as if the person said to himself, "Anything, anything is preferable to this chaos. I am willing to do anything to liberate myself from this chaos, even to submit myself to an institution for my governance."

For some the institution may be a prison. Most people who have worked in prisons know of a certain type of "model prisoner"— cooperative, obedient, well disciplined, favored by both the inmates and the administrative population. Because he is a model prisoner, he may soon be paroled, and three days later he has robbed seven banks and committed seventeen other felonies, so that he lands right back in jail and, with the walls of the institution to govern him, he once again becomes a "model prisoner."

For others the institution may be the military, where the chaos of their lives is regulated by the rather gentle paternalistic—even maternalistic—structure of military society. For still others it might be a corporation or some other tightly structured organization. But for most, the institution to which they submit themselves for governance is the Church.

There are several things that characterize the behavior of men and women in Stage II of their spiritual development, which is the stage of the majority of churchgoers and believers (as well as that of most emotionally healthy "latency"-period children). One is their attachment to the forms (as opposed to the essence) of their religion, which is why I call this stage "formal" as well as "institutional." They are in fact sometimes so attached to the canons and the liturgy that they become very upset if changes are made in the words or music or in the traditional order of things. It is for this reason that there has been so much turmoil concerning the adoption of the new Book of Common Prayer by the Episcopal Church or the changes brought about by Vatican II in the Catholic Church. Similar turmoil occurs for similar reasons in the other denominations and religions. Since it is precisely these forms that are responsible for their liberation from chaos, it is no wonder that people at this stage of their spiritual development become so threatened when someone seems to be playing footloose and fancy-free with the rules.

Another thing characterizing the religious behavior of Stage II people is that their vision of God is almost entirely that of an external, transcendent Being. They have very little understanding of the immanent, indwelling God—the God of the Holy Spirit, or what the Quakers call the Inner Light. And although they often consider Him loving, they also generally feel He possesses—and will use—punitive power. But once again, it is no accident that their vision of God is that of a giant benevolent Cop in the Sky, because that is precisely the kind of God they need—just as they need a legalistic religion for their governance.

Let us suppose now that two adults firmly rooted in Stage II marry and have children. They will likely raise their children in a stable home, because stability is a principal value for people in this stage. They will treat their children with dignity as important beings, because the Church tells them that children are important and should be treated with dignity. Although their love may be a bit legalistic and unimaginative at times, they will still generally treat them lovingly, because the Church tells them to be loving and teaches something about how to be loving. What happens to children raised in such a stable, loving home, treated with importance and dignity (and taken to Sunday school as well) is that they absorb the principles of Christianity as if with their mother's milk—or the principles of Buddhism if raised in a Buddhist home, or of Islam if raised in a Muslim home, and so on. The principles of their parents' religion are literally engraved on their hearts, or come to be what psychotherapists call "internalized."

But once these principles become internalized, such children, now usually late-adolescents, have become self-governing human beings. As such they are no longer dependent on an institution for their governance. Consequently they begin to say to themselves, "Who needs this fuddy-duddy old Church with its silly superstitions?" At this point they begin to convert to Stage III—skeptic, individual. And to their parents' great but unnecessary chagrin, they often become atheists or agnostics.

Although frequently "nonbelievers," people in Stage III are generally more spiritually developed than many content to remain in Stage II. Although individualistic, they are not the least bit antisocial. To the contrary, they are often deeply involved in and committed to social causes. They make up their own minds about things and are no more likely to believe everything they read in the papers than to believe it is necessary for someone to acknowledge Jesus as Lord and Savior (as opposed to Buddha or Mao or Socrates) in order to be saved. They make loving, intensely dedicated parents. As skeptics they are often scientists, and as such they are again highly submitted to principle. Indeed, what we call the scientific method is a collection of conventions and procedures that have been designed to combat our extraordinary capacity to deceive ourselves in the interest of submission to something higher than our own immediate emotional or intellectual comfort—namely, truth. Advanced Stage III men and women are active truth seekers.

"Seek and you shall find," it has been said. If people in Stage III seek truth deeply and widely enough, they find what they are looking for—enough pieces to begin to be able to fit them together but never enough to complete the whole puzzle. In fact, the more pieces they find, the larger and more magnificent the puzzle becomes. Yet they are able to get glimpses of the "big picture" and to see that it is very beautiful indeed—and that it strangely resembles those "primitive myths and superstitions" their Stage II parents or grandparents believe in. At that point they begin their conversion to Stage IV, which is the mystic communal stage of spiritual development.

"Mysticism," a much-maligned word, is not an easy one to define. It takes many forms. Yet through the ages, mystics of every shade of religious belief have spoken of unity, of an underlying connectedness between things: between men and women, between us and the other creatures and even inanimate matter as well, a fitting together according to an ordinarily invisible fabric underlying the cosmos. Remember the experience when, during community, I suddenly saw my previously hated neighbor as myself. Smelling his dead cigar butts and hearing his guttural snoring, I was filled with utter distaste for him until that strange mystical moment when I saw myself sitting in his chair and realized he was the sleeping part of me and I the waking part of him. We were suddenly connected. More than connected, we were integral parts of the same unity.

Mysticism also obviously has to do with *mystery*. Mystics acknowledge the enormity of the unknown, but rather than being frightened by it, they seek to penetrate even deeper into it that they may understand more—even with the realization that the more they understand, the greater the mystery will become. They love mystery, in dramatic contrast to those in Stage II, who need simple, clear-cut dogmatic structures and have little taste for the unknown and unknowable. While Stage IV men and women will enter religion in order to approach mystery, people in Stage II, to a considerable extent, enter religion in order to escape from it. Thus there is the confusion of people entering not only into religion but into the same religion—and sometimes the same denomination—not only for different motives but for totally the opposite motives. It makes no sense until we come to understand the roots of religious pluralism in terms of developmental stages.

Finally, mystics throughout the ages have not only spoken of emptiness but extolled its virtues. I have labeled Stage IV communal as well as mystical not because all mystics or even a majority of them live in communes but because among human beings they are the ones most aware that the whole world *is* a community and realize that what divides us into warring camps is precisely the *lack* of this awareness. Having become practiced at emptying themselves of preconceived notions and prejudices and able to perceive the invisible underlying fabric that connects everything, they do not think in terms of fractions or blocs or even national boundaries; they *know* this to be one world.

GLOBAL MIND CHANGE

By

WILLIS HARMAN, PH.D.

One of the critical arenas in which change is both imperative and ongoing is that of attitudes toward the planet Earth. Since it is obvious that modern man's abuse of the Earth is related to the prevailing image of our relationship to the planet, it is interesting to examine a recently announced scientific concept of the Earth as being in important respects alive. This is the "Gaia hypothesis" which, it must be admitted, has thus far created more impact on the conference circuit than in the halls of science.

James E. Lovelock, a British biologist and atmospheric chemist, is largely responsible for the modern form of the idea that we human beings are not just living motes on a vast mineral ball, but the *the Earth itself is a living organism*. The core notion is that the Earth regulates itself very much like the human body or other living organisms. Somehow, temperature, oxygen levels and other aspects of the composition of the atmosphere and the oceans, soil acidity, and other key environmental conditions are kept within the narrow tolerances necessary to sustain life. Those regulatory processes involve, in turn, the biota—the sum of all living things including plants, animals, and microorganisms. The Earth thus exhibits the behavior (except for a reproductive ability) of a single organism—of a living creature. Lovelock's name for that organism is Gaia, the name the ancient Greeks gave to their Earth goddess.

Could a planet, almost all of it rock and that mostly incandescent or molten, really be alive? Lovelock suggests comparison with a giant redwood tree: It is alive, yet 99 percent of it is dead wood. Like the Earth it has only a skin of living tissue spread thinly at the surface.

If the Earth is a living organism, does it also exhibit *consciousness?* That is a question not to be answered quickly, but, as implied above, not to be dismissed either.

Lovelock was hired as a consultant in the early 1960s by the National Aeronautics and Space Administration to help determine if there is life on Mars. While others were busy designing landing craft to go see, Lovelock took a different approach. He reasoned that in the absence of life, the gases in the atmosphere should react in such a way that the whole reaches a state of equilibrium. The presence of life on Earth disturbs this equilibrium, because the Earth's plants, animals, and bacteria are continually injecting gases and energy into the air. As is well known, for example, plants give off oxygen and use up carbon dioxide while animals do the reverse; thus the Earth's atmosphere contains far more oxygen and far less carbon dioxide than it would if the Earth were not covered with its particular life forms. (Mars, on the other hand, gives no such indication of life.)

The amount of oxygen in the atmosphere near the Earth's surface remains virtually constant at around 21 percent by volume, "just right" for the life forms that have evolved. The life forms themselves appear to regulate the amount of oxygen so that it stays "just right." If the proportion should drop even a few percent, many organisms would die; however, the excess of plant life that would result would tend to raise the oxygen content again. On the other hand, if somehow the oxygen content were to rise to 25 percent, fires would burn out of control. That would no doubt reduce the plant life and hence the rate of replenishment of oxygen, so the proportion would tend to go down.

The temperature, too, is apparently regulated by the biota to just what they need. The Earth's average surface temperature has remained between 10 degrees and 20 degrees Centigrade, even through the Ice Ages, and the biota seem to have had something to do with this. Lovelock explains how, using a computer-based model called "Daisyworld." Imagine, for simplicity, a world in which the only life forms are white daisies. Within the temperature range of 10 to 20 degrees, the higher the temperature, the more daisies. But since more daisies means more of the world's surface is covered with white flowers, the more sunlight is reflected, causing the temperature to lower. Thus an equilibrium temperature is approached. Adding other life forms into the model (such as rabbits to eat the daisies, and foxes to control the rabbit population) results in a similar phenomenon. Daisyworld exhibits a temperature-regulating behavior (homeostasis) similar to the temperature regulation of the human body.

As another example, the humid tropical forests of the Earth alter the climate in the immediate vicinity, both in terms of temperature and rainfall. Like Daisyworld, they create the local climate they require in order to flourish. But they also remove carbon dioxide from the atmosphere. As they are cut down, that contributes to the rising carbon dioxide level in the atmosphere (which is also increasing due to massive burning of fossil fuels). Through the "greenhouse effect," the blanket of carbon dioxide is causing worldwide temperatures to rise. Thus the fate of the tropical forests affects climate on a global basis.

The *connectedness* of our decisions and our actions to the whole Earth is one key message of the Gaia hypothesis. But another, equally important one is the role of cooperation of all organisms in the evolutionary process.

One's initial reaction to the idea of imagining a peaceful world is likely to be that it sounds like a simplistic version of "the power of positive thinking." It may seem difficult at first to convince oneself that by such an affirmation one is actually doing anything. True, it may be simplistic to believe that if we all just love one another and speak peace, peace will come into the world. It may be simplistic because powerful unconscious forces make our love ambivalent, and our peace tinged with hidden conflict.

Despite such justifiable caution, it remains the case that a collective belief in the achievability of global peace will contribute toward realizing that goal, just as the collective disbelief is now thwarting it. However, for affirmation to work well we need to be as specific as possible. The affirmation of sustainable peace will be most effective if it is not simply a general "pray for peace" outlook, but rather affirmation of a fairly specific plausible scenario based on an informed view of the factors and forces involved.

UNKNOWN MAN

By

YATRI

There seems to be a general agreement amongst modern evolution-aries that before any evolutionary initiative is provoked there is likely to be a crisis in the environment. It can be a dramatic change in the climate, a food crisis, a poisoning of the atmosphere with waste products or some other drastic upheaval in the planet's ecosystem.

We face just such a crisis now. Humankind consumes vast amounts of energy in the form of food and fossil fuels, chemicals and nuclear material, in such a way that widespread pollution and the wholesale destruction of our environment seem inevitable.

It appears that not only have our technological overspills created havoc within the environment, but our present cultural and techno-logical transformation has exploded so dramatically in the last four decades that it seems to far outstrip any previous evolutionary event of our species.

In biological terms such massive, simultaneous and, in our case, global fluctuations appear as a crisis in which organisms are forced to adapt to the changed conditions by jumping to higher levels of organization or to head off down some evolutionary cul-de-sac and ultimate destruction.

If an environmental crisis is the trigger needed to detonate an evolutionary time-bomb, then our generation certainly qualifies for a transformation of the species. It is said that trouble likes company. The company of crisis far exceeds the three categories of seven listed below but at least set the scene of our present situation and serve as indications of how many could collide at any moment.

Technological and Social Overspills
1. Population explosion and exploitation of the natural habitat
2. Pollution, the "Greenhouse Effect," acid rain and toxic, chemical soups
3. Severe damage to the ozone shield and dangerous levels of UV radiation
4. The dumping of hazardous wastes
5. Radiation leaks and hazards
6. Unthinkable wargames and nuclear terrorism
7. Stress and illness

Technological Innovations
1. Atomic Engineering
2. Instant Global Communications
3. Space Travel
4. Artificial Intelligence
5. Genetic Engineering
6. Solar Energy
7. Evolutionary Mindsets and New Paradigms

CRISIS IN NATURAL AND MYSTIC CYCLES

1. Possible planetary shift in axis
2. Planetary line-up and volcanic cycles
3. Psychic cycle of consciousness (532 years)
4. Astrological cycle
5. End of the century
6. End of the millennium
7. Turning of the "Great Wheel of Dharma"

There are seven major cycles which converge in the next decade. Some are natural and explicable and some are subtle and mystical.

There is, for instance, the obvious cycle of the ending of a century which may elicit a strong collective emotional response. On this occasion it is the end of the seventh millennium. The end of the last thousand year cycle on the 10th century saw Western Europe in turmoil. Hysteria gripped the Christians during that period, as it was believed that the year 1000 would bring the end of the worlds and that a new spiritual universe peopled by the heavenly host would take its place.

THE TAO OF POWER
By
R. L. WING

The *Tao Te Ching* explores a remarkable power that is latent in every individual. This power, which Lao Tzu calls *Te* emerges when one is aware of and aligned with the forces in nature (*Tao*). It is essential to Lao Tzu's system that we understand why and how reality functions, and that we come to realize that nature invariably takes its course. We already know that it is rarely worth the effort to swim upstream, but do we know which way the stream is flowing? We realize that it is difficult and unsatisfying to cut across the grain, but can we see which way the grain runs? Lao Tzu believed that a constant awareness of the patterns in nature will bring us insights into the parallel patterns in human behavior: Just as spring follows winter in nature, growth follows repression in society; just as too much gravity will collapse a star, too much possessiveness will collapse an idea.

Like all matter and energy in the universe, the emotional and intellectual structures that build are constantly transformed by outside forces. Much of our power is wasted in propping up our beliefs, defending them, and convincing others to believe in them so that they might become "permanent." Once we understand the folly in this, we gain power by using the evolution in nature to our advantage—accepting, incorporating, and supporting change when and where it wants to occur. Our cooperation with the forces in nature makes us a part of those forces. Our decisions become astute because they are based on a dynamic, evolving reality, not on fixed or wishful thinking. We are able to see things that others might not because the reach of our minds is extended throughout the contemplation of the universe. We develop vision and we help create the future with the power of our vision.

Lao Tzu believed that when people do not have a sense of power they become resentful and uncooperative. Individuals who do not feel personal power feel fear. They fear the unknown because they do not identify with the world outside of themselves; thus their psychic integration is severely damaged and they are a danger to their society. Tyrants do not feel power, they feel frustration and impotency. They wield force, but it is a form of aggression, not authority. On closer inspection, it becomes apparent that individuals who dominate others are, in fact, enslaved by insecurity and are slowly and mysteriously hurt by their own actions. Lao Tzu attributed most of the world's ills to the fact that people do not feel powerful and independent.

Powerful individuals never show their strength, yet others listen to them because they seem to *know*. They radiate knowledge, but it is an intuitive knowing that comes from a direct understanding and experience with the ways of nature. They are compassionate and generous because they instinctively realize that power continues to flow through them only when they pass it on. Like electricity, the more energy, inspiration, and information they conduct, the more they receive.

True power is the ability to influence and change the world while living a simple, intelligent, and experientially rich existence. Powerful individuals influence others with the force of example and attitude. Within groups, they have great presence—intellectual gravity—that influences the minds of those exposed to them. Intellectual gravity develops as a result of expanded identification—and identification that reaches far outside the self. Individuals who can identify with the evolution of reality develop significance and power because the force of their awareness is actively defining the universe around them.

There are two major changes that occur in the lives of individuals who achieve personal power: the rise of intellectual independence and the need for simplicity. Taoism, as a way of understanding the universe, is not based on faith; it is based on experience. The human mind is evolving, while all social systems are temporary experiments. Relying on systems of understanding created or interpreted by others will dull the instincts and prevent individuals from cultivating and expanding their own minds. Power will not develop in individuals who allow doctrine and dogma to stand between them and direct personal knowledge of the universe.

Simplicity in conduct, in beliefs, and in environment brings an individual very close to the truth of reality. Individuals who practice simplicity cannot be used because they already have everything they need; they cannot be lied to because a lie merely reveals to them another aspect of reality. An attraction to simplicity is essentially an attraction to freedom—the highest expression of personal power. We are taught to think of freedom as something one has, but is really the absence of things that brings freedom to the individual and meaning into life. To let go of things—unnecessary desires, superfluous possessions—is to have them. Lao Tzu believed that an individual life contains the whole universe, but when individuals develop fixations about certain parts of life they become narrow and shallow and uncentered. Fixations and desires create a crisis within the mind. As individuals let go of desires, feelings of freedom, security, independence, and power increase accordingly.

The *Tao Te Ching* has a self-selecting audience—it seems to attract individuals who are on the threshold of evolutionary intellectual growth. The philosophy presents an opportunity for psychological breakthrough—a breakthrough in attitude (because we must rethink our relationship with the universe) and a breakthrough in personal goals (because our desires become rooted in simplicity and we are freed of emotional delusion). Those who find a resonant voice in Lao Tzu are destined to transcend the commonplace and to use the power that comes from their personal freedom to shape the future.

The *Tao Te Ching* is written on many levels. There is a level waiting just below the one you currently understand. The deeper you penetrate, the more power you develop. The more potential you have for influence in the world, the stronger and more penetrating your insights become. The philosophy that Lao Tzu left behind is actually an experiment, one that individuals undertake when they are ready to enter the next phase of human evolution—that of fully conscious beings who are actively directing both their own destinies and the destiny of the world around them. In his ultimate vision, Lao Tzu believed that if each and every one of us could realize and gain control of our evolutionary power, it would visibly unite us and allow us to become a collective, compassionate, and fully aware social and universal organism.

CHOICES AND CONNECTIONS: BECOMING AN EFFECTIVE CHANGE AGENT

By
ROBERT THEOBALD,

Knowledge Systems, Inc.

Summary: We are ineffective as change agents because we misread the nature of the reality confronting us. Most of our efforts are spent attempting to convince people of the need for fundamental change. While this approach was necessary in the sixties and seventies, it is not only largely unneeded but actually counter-productive in the latter half of the eighties. Today people are frustrated, baffled and angry because they cannot make sense of the world; our responsibility is to empower them to find models and skills.

THE SIXTIES AND SEVENTIES

When industrial-era societies were first being challenged in the late fifties and early sixties, most people were apathetic. They thought the existing structures of the socio-economy were unchangeable. The optimist thought this was fine, and the pessimist believed this was the best that could be done. Both groups agreed that it was naive and irresponsible to try to build another system.

In the sixties, many people who contended that fundamental change was required compared society to a balky mule and justified their tactics with the image of hitting a mule on the head with a two-by-four to get its attention. It was argued, in many respects correctly, that people and systems would not look at alternative solutions until they had first been forced to look at the problems of the day.

We have largely forgotten how optimistic the early sixties were. President Kennedy created a period of hope and drive in which nothing seemed impossible. His assassination, the Vietnam War and accompanying socioeconomic disruptions soured this vision. By the end of the sixties, there was an increasing belief (and fear) that the problems that had been raised during the decade were real but probably unsolvable. Western cultures retreated into personal and social denial—unable to be effective, they preferred to look the other way.

The seventies, with their oil shocks, further diminished the willingness of people to face the need for profoundly new structures. The extraordinary rates of economic growth, which had provided greatly increased wealth to the rich countries, were coming to an end. People began to see that they would soon be faced with profound new challenges.

President Carter tried to force Americans to look at these issues. Unfortunately he made a critical misstep in his communication. Instead of showing the need for new "success" strategies to meet the changing needs of the times, he argued that it was necessary to learn to accept "failure." Such a strategy is fatal both for individuals and for systems—the acceptance of the inevitability of failure over a period of time necessarily leads to death.

The election of 1980 was, therefore, cast in terms of optimism versus pessimism. President Carter talked of limits; President Reagan talked about the ways in which America could once again be great. There was little doubt about which philosophy was more attractive.

THE EIGHTIES

The difficulty with the Reagan Administration is that it is largely unaware of the six primary revolutions that are altering the patterns by which we live. We must adopt these inherent pattern shifts if we hope to survive and flourish in the twenty-first century—only thirteen years away.

We need to come to grips with the *weaponry revolution*, which has made not only war but all violence infeasible as a method of settling disputes; the development of *computers and robots*, which will revolutionize production, the information industry and services; the *human rights drive*, which is leading individuals and groups to insist on equity and fairness throughout the world; *biological advances*, which will change not only production technology but also to the way we think of ourselves as human beings; *environmental limitations*, which are forcing us to reconsider maximum growth strategies; and finally, the *changes in our understanding of the world*, which require us to see that we all live in our own perceptual universe rather than within an objective set of realities.

Failing to come to grips with these six revolutions ensures that one's directions and policies are not only irrelevant but also destructive. This has been the cause of the breakdown of momentum in the Reagan Administration. The hopes and beliefs with which it operates, both domestically and internationally, are increasingly recognized as invalid. The very concept of national sovereignty, where a nation could defend its borders and order its commerce without taking the outside world into account, is no longer valid.

In many ways, we are being brought back to the agenda that President Carter tried to force upon us—the agenda we rejected because it was seen as failure. Those of us who want to be change agents need to develop profoundly new tactics to be effective in helping people look at what needs to be done.

ACTING IN THE PRESENT

Most change agents assume that the essential challenge of our time is convincing others of the need for shifting the ways we think and act. This strategy is unrealistic and counterproductive.

Across the country, most people are perfectly aware that present systems are not working. When I note this widespread awareness, I am often challenged on the grounds that the audiences to whom I talk are "special" and thus would be expected to be more aware of the realities of our time. But I speak to many audiences full of people who are dragged, kicking and screaming, to listen to me and are in no way committed to change.

To illustrate — I start my presentation with a quiz asking people to respond with a show of hands. One of the questions I ask is: "Do you believe that we are preparing children for the world in which they are going to live?" In the last five years, I have never encountered an audience where the number of hands raised exceeded five percent. Yet, most change agents *assume* that fifty percent or more of establishment audiences are still satisfied with our existing educational systems.

I need to be clear about the point I am, and am not, making. I am not suggesting that everybody agrees about the way education should change. I am stating that people are looking for ways to do things differently. Further information about the ineffectiveness of current systems is seen as frustrating because it adds to people's sense of powerlessness.

In another part of my quiz, I ask people how much change they expect before the end of this century. On a scale of zero to ten, most people respond in the six to eight range. Very few people fall below a five.

The implications are startling. A large percentage of people are *already* looking for alternatives to the industrial-era system. To a great extent, therefore, those of us who believe it is possible to build a more desirable and compassionate world are at fault. We have failed to deal with the real issues facing human beings. We have not looked at the growing gap between the rich and the poor, which not only marginalizes a large number of people but forces an intolerable choice on those going through the educational system.

PERCEIVING THE POTENTIAL

We are faced with the need for incredible changes in an impossibly short period of time. We can only confront our needs realistically if we realize that the task of convincing people about the need for a new culture is already largely complete. Now we need to find new images of success to encourage people to shift their living styles.

One of the most remarkable shifts is in the area of health. At the beginning of the seventies some friends and I developed a health network. This was widely seen as quixotic, on the grounds that Americans would never be interested in their health. Toward the end of the eighties, such a viewpoint seems incredible. We have not only seen dramatic shifts in attitudes toward diet, smoking and alcohol, but we are watching businesses discover that keeping people healthy is good for their bottom lines. Indeed, I use the example of health to show that profound short-run attitude shifts are indeed feasible.

Equally impressive is the shift toward an ecological perspective. Poll after poll shows that people see the preservation of the environment as a critical aspect of their lives. They are no longer only interested in a higher standard of living. They also want to develop a higher quality of life in a much broader sense than was desired in the industrial era. Similar shifts are now taking place in people's attitudes toward the revitalization of community, the development of better communications between different groups and the need for a redefinition of social justice.

What then should those of us who care about the future be doing today? The primary need is to provide individuals with the opportunity to talk about their concerns rather than giving them *more* information. Our meeting styles are obsolete because they are based on the belief that people are moved by information rather than by their sense of purpose and vision. We need to make it possible for people to face the new realities and find friends and colleagues who can work with them to create new directions.

Much of my work is devoted to developing new ways of providing "open space." Open space is a nonjudgmental opportunity for discussion and dialogue to discover what one really wants. It makes it possible to raise issues and questions which are "taboo" in normal institutional and community circles.

As an agent for change, we need to find out for ourselves how to be effective in the world. Many of our friends and colleagues may know profound change is needed, but they do not yet have the skills or, possibly, the courage to take the necessary first steps.

The key is to find some action which will test the waters without excessive risk. You should not take my word for the new realities. Look at them for yourselves. If you want to let me know what you find out by writing to me at Box 2240, Wickenburg, AZ 85358, I shall be interested in your discoveries.

CONCLUSION

If we go back to the principles of the New Age movement (generously shared by Jeremy P. Tarcher) that were stated in the beginning of this anthology, we remember that:

"1. The everyday world and our personal consciousness is a manifestation of a larger divine reality,
2. humans have a suppressed or hidden self that reflects or is connected to the divine element of the universe,
3. this Higher Self can be awakened and take a central part in the everyday life of the individual,
4. this awakening is the purpose or goal of human life."

These principles sum up the world view shared by many New Age thinkers and by most of the authors excerpted in this anthology. Obviously there are many other books that can provide a wealth of life-changing information.

I hope that the excerpts contained herein have been inspirational, and that you will continue to search for other books and material on these subjects.

The New Age movement is a blaze of light that is shooting through the consciousness of millions. Long after the concepts shared in this book are accepted by the mainstream, the New Age will continue to have a positive and powerful effect because these concepts and ideals will have become integrated into the culture. The New Age is much more than just a trend; it is a template for change, a model of transformation, a conspiracy of human spirit and beauty, a blueprint for planetary peace. By raising the awareness of each individual, the world is changed.

Thank you for sharing the journey.

SUGGESTED READING LIST

The following is a selection of excellent books that we highly recommend. They are divided and categorized in the same manner as the eleven anthology sections, with one extra section to cover esoteric spirituality, Eastern influences, and fiction.

SECTION ONE:
FOUNDATIONS OF THE NEW AGE

How to Have More in a Have-Not World by Terry Cole-Whittiker
Think and Grow Rich by Napoleon Hill
Man's Search For Meaning by Viktor E. Frankl
Your Erroneous Zones by Dr. Wayne Dyer
Time Is an Illusion by Chris Griscom
Healing the Planet by Alan Cohen
Creative Visualization by Shakti Gawain
Out on a Limb by Shirley MacLaine

SECTION TWO:
NEW PSYCHOLOGY, CONSCIOUSNESS, TRANSFORMATION

Archetypes and the Collective Unconscious by Carl G. Jung
The Magical Child Within You by Bruce Davis, Ph.D., and Genny Davis
Dare to Win by Mark Victor Hansen

Higher Creativity by Willis Harman, Ph.D., and Howard Rheingold
The Path of Least Resistance by Robert Fritz
The Power of Your Sub-Conscious Mind by Joseph Murphy
Center of the Cyclone by John C. Lilly, M.D.
Actualizations by Stewart Emery
EST by Werner Erhard
Lucid Dreaming by Stephen LeBerge
Mastery: A Technology for Personal Excellence and Evolution by Tim Piering
Das Energi by Paul Williams

SECTION THREE:

HEALING AND ALTERNATIVE MEDICINE

The Anatomy of an Illness by Norman Cousins
The Black Butterfly by Richard Moss
How Shall I Live? by Richard Moss
Everybody's Guide to Homeopathic Medicine by Dana Ullman MPH and Stephen
Cummings FNP
The New Holistic Health Handbook edited by Shepard Bliss
Minding the Body Mending the Mind by Joan Borysenko, Ph.D.
On Death and Dying by Elisabeth Kübler-Ross
Handbook of Bach Flower Remedies by Philip M. Chandellor

SECTION FOUR:

LOVING RELATIONSHIPS

Loving Relationships by Sondra Ray
Tantra for the West by Marcus Allen
Tantra: The Art of Loving by Charles and Caroline Muir
Sacred Dance by Maria-Gabriele Wosien
Sexual Secrets by Nik Douglas and Penny Slinger
The Dawn of Tantra by Herbert V. Guenther and Chogyam Trungpa

SECTION FIVE:

SCIENCE

Cosmos by Carl Sagan
God and the New Physics by Paul Davies
The Dancing Wu Li Masters by Gary Zukav

The Cosmic Blueprint by Paul Davies
A Brief History of Time by Stephen W. Hawking

SECTION SIX:
SHAMANISM AND NATIVE TRADITIONS

The Book of the Hopi by Frank Waters
Touch the Earth by T. C. Mcluhan
Journey to Ixtlan by Carlos Casteneda
Maps to Ecstasy by Gabrielle Roth
Kahuna Healing by Serge Kahili King
The Secret Science at Work by Max Freedom Long
Secrets of Shamanism by Jose Stevens, Ph.D., and Lena S.
Seven Arrows by Hemoyohsts Storm
Anasazi by Donald G. Pike and David Muench
Medicine Woman by Lynn Andrews
Daughters of Copperwoman by Anne Cameron
Second Ring of Power by Carlos Castaneda

SECTION SEVEN:
CHANNELS AND PSYCHICS

The Sleeping Prophet by Jess Stearn
I Come as a Brother by Bartholomew
The Sacred Journey; You and Your Higher Self by Lazaris
The Seth Material by Jane Roberts
Spirit Communication by Kevin Ryerson
The Course in Miracles
The Urantia Book
Opening to Your Psychic Self by Petey Stevens
Bridge of Light by Laura Huffines

SECTION EIGHT:
ORACLES AND DIVINATION TOOLS

Crystal Healing by Edmund Harold
First Steps in Ritual by Dolores Ashcroft-Nowicki
The Tarot Revealed by Eden Grey

The Complete Guide to the Tarot by Eden Gray
The Windows of Tarot by F. D. Graves
The Practical Pendulum Book by D. Jurriaanse
The Human Aura by Kuthumi and Djwal Kul
Mandala by Jose and Miriam Arguelles
What Color Is Your Aura? by Barbara Bowers
The Human Aura by Nicholas M. Regush
Human Aura by Walter J. Kilner
Hand in Hand by Elizabeth Brener
Meng Shu by Derek Walters
Feng Shui by Derek Walters
Tarot Made Easy by Nancy Garen

SECTION NINE:

NEAR DEATH AND REINCARNATION

Astrology and Your Past Lives, by Jeanne Avery
Reincarnation: The Phoenix Fire Mystery, by Joseph Head and
S. L. Cranston
The Psychic Explorer by Jonothan Gainer and Carl Rider
Intangible Evidence by Bernard Gittleson
Reincarnation and Immortality by Rudolf Steiner

SECTION TEN:

WOMEN'S AND MEN'S ISSUES

Truth or Dare by Starhawk
The New Our Bodies Ourselves by the Boston Women's Collective
The Mists of Avalon by Marion Zimmer Bradley
Drawing Down the Moon by Margot Adler
The Moon and the Virgin by Nor Hall
The Witches Goddess by Janet and Stewart Ferrar

SECTION ELEVEN:

GLOBAL CHANGE AND SOCIAL TRANSFORMATION

No additional suggestions

ESOTERIC SPIRITUALITY AND FICTION

The Occult by Colin Wilson
Applied Magic by Dion Fortune
The Secret Life of Plants by Peter Tompkins and Christopher Bird

The Findhorn Garden by the Findhorn Community
The Druids, Magicians of the West by Ward Rutherford
Agartha by Lady Meredith Young
Buffalo Girls and Other Animal Presences by Ursula K. LeGuin
The Kin of Ata Are Waiting for You by Dorothy Bryant
The Sea Priestess by Dion Fortune
The Little Prince by Antoine de Saint Exupéry